A
Harlequin
Romance

NURSE AT NOONGWALLA

by

ROUMELIA LANE

HARLEQUIN BOOKS   TORONTO
WINNIPEG

Original hard cover edition published in 1973
by Mills & Boon Limited.

© Roumelia Lane 1973

SBN 373-01745-6

Harlequin edition published January 1974

Printed in Canada

1745

CHAPTER ONE

THE train which had nosed its way across mile upon mile of desolate yellow land shunted to a stop beside a single spindly tree. One door was opened. A stout suitcase was set down beside a pair of sensibly clad feet. The door was slammed shut, the short burst of sound spinning away over the shimmering wastes, and with an impatient snort the train drew itself forward and rattled off, gathering speed to dissolve after a while into the yellow distance.

Alone in the crowding silences Alex picked up her suitcase. She turned to look about her. Beside the tree and herself in the endless rolling emptiness, one low flat-topped building stood on its own in the heat some yards away. Further down the line, two or three similar constructions were grouped around the curve of a dusty track. The only sign of life was a stooping grey-clad figure trudging the stretch between, pushing a trolley loaded with bulging sacks.

Stepping out over the rough earth Alex made her way towards him. As she grew near she thought he would stop, eaten up with curiosity to know what this other moving shape, beside his own, was doing out here in the wilds of nowhere. Instead he paid not the slightest attention to her. Even though she came up close alongside him he continued to trundle along, guiding his load with fixed, unblinking concentration.

She was obliged to walk with him until he reached his destination, an open doorway around which were stacked several more of the fat sacks. Awaiting her opportunity and finding there wasn't going to be one, she bent as the man bent to start unloading his trolley, and asked, 'Could you tell me how I get to Noongwalla from here?'

At first she got no response for her pains. Grizzle-chinned, his washed-out cotton drill suit flapping loosely on his tall thin frame, the weathered Australian went about dragging a sack into position with his long bony hands. Gathering it into his arms, he dropped it with a grunt against the wall. It wasn't until he had straightened himself unhurriedly and flexed his back ready to take the weight of another sack that he pushed some of his dogged concentration enough to one side to show that he had heard the question. It took about as long again for him to do anything about it.

Shifting his line of thought with an effort from his work, he took his flat blue gaze out over the sun-baked terrain as though to pinpoint the spot in his mind's eye. Then giving a knowing nod he came round to the subject at his own pace with, 'Got irrigation there a while back. Grow most things in the valley now, so they say. Apricots ... peaches ... pears.' He turned back to reach for the ears of another sack, still thinking about it. 'Noongwalla? Name covers a lot of territory. There's the settlement that sprung up on the northside.'

'Yes, that's it. How do I get there?' Alex asked patiently.

She had to wait until two more loads were thumped down before the reply came, 'Bus goes out every Tuesday.'

Alex thought about that. 'But this is Wednesday,' she said, smiling. 'That's a whole week away.'

It was some time before the rangy old man turned his voice up to her from where he was wrestling with a weight. 'People don't go in much for travelling in these parts,' he said abruptly. He came up to run a disapproving eye over her neatly fitting town suit and smart leather suitcase and added pointedly as he kicked a sack into place, 'Got too much to do, I'm a-thinking.'

Alex twinkled at his grumpiness and asked pleasantly, 'Could I get a taxi, do you think?' As soon as the words were out she knew it was an insane question. She waited and watched the spindly frame straighten itself in a pained show of disbelief. The faded blue stare came up to fasten on her with an accusing light as she was told, 'You can get them taxis in Adelaide.' In his slow Australian drawl he pronounced it 'Air-dal-ide.' 'Out here folks relies on their own transport.'

Not really surprised at this reply, Alex asked, feeling a

6

flicker of concern, 'How far is it, would you say?'

'To the settlement at Noongwalla?' The grey-clad figure swung back to work. 'At least forty mile, I reckon.' The reply was weighted with satisfaction.

Alex placed her suitcase down and looked along the railroad track the way she had come, considerably at a loss. The offices in Adelaide had been marvellous at supplying her with all the information she needed for travelling out here up to leaving the train at this spot, which was called – she couldn't imagine why, for there wasn't a drop of water to be seen – Denver's Creek. But they had omitted to tell her how she was to complete the last stage of her journey from Denver's Creek to Noongwalla.

She blinked against the sun around the vista of open plain, looking for a road, pondering over what she ought to do. Obviously she couldn't walk it, even if she did know the way. Yet how else was she going to get there? The only bus was a week away. There was nothing else on four wheels that she could see, not even anything on four legs! And from what she had gathered, the train along this line, back the way she had come, ran about as frequently as the bus.

She drew on her lower lip, a thoughtful frown forming above smooth dark eyebrows. There was no denying it. She had come up against her first problem – a giant-sized one.

Busy trying to work something out, she hadn't noticed that the grunting and snorting, and the scuffing of sacks beside her had come a stop. It was only when her glance travelled absently his way on its course around the landscape that she found the bony old Australian regarding her with sly interest.

With a shift of his frame, which gave away the fact that he had secretly enjoyed watching her stew for a while, he said with senile casualness, 'Could be it's Ben's afternoon for delivering the mail in them parts.'

Alex kept her gaze on him. The frown left her brow. Who Ben was, or how he got the mail to Noongwalla, she didn't much care. It was a ray of hope. She took a quick step forward and asked on a breath, 'Would he help me, do you think?'

7

For an answer the bewhiskered figure moved with a grim purposeful stride to the open doorway surrounded by the sacks and bawled with all the power of a ship's blast, 'Benj ... MIN!'

A faint reply came from the bowels of the low building, after which the ship's blast on the outside followed up with, 'You takin' the mail out Noongwalla s'arft ... NOON?'

Footsteps sounded within the gloom. As they grew louder another voice of similar rasping quality fired back testily, 'What if I am?' Carried forth on aggressive strides into the open, a grey-stubbled chin belonging to a face amazingly like the one on the outside of the doorway was thrust into view. Identical pale blue eyes blazed out at the world belligerently as the toothless mouth demanded sharply, 'Who's askin'?'

The only difference that Alex could see between this second gangling figure and the first was in his dress, which consisted of faded bib and brace dungarees, and cotton shirt open at the front to show a scrawny neck.

'Young woman 'ere wants to get to them parts,' she heard the cracked explanation beside her. Absolutely nothing happened! Not only did the toothless Ben look exactly like his brother, he also had the same clam-like attitude when it came to offering help. Shooting a baleful glare at Alex, he recited, when he was quite ready to, 'Don't take passengers.'

An uncompromising silence settled over them. Then after several seconds had drifted by, 'She's missed the bus. What else can she do?'

Alex felt heartened. The washed-out grey cotton, dead against her at first, was now squarely facing the blue-dungareed opposition on her behalf. 'You tend to what chores is your concern, Howell,' the stubble-chinned Ben said snappishly, 'and leave me to watch out for mine.'

Brother Howell didn't flinch a muscle. 'You could take her all right,' he glared.

'*I* run the mail department in these parts,' Ben glared back.

'You could take her,' Howell persisted doggedly.

Alex had no choice but to await the outcome. It was much as she had expected. The blustering over with, the brothers parted to go their separate ways. There was no sign of ill feeling between them. The work of transferring the sacks was resumed, the dust rising as, one by one, they were dumped down methodically beside the door. Ben had moved off round towards the corner of the building.

Before long Alex found him sneaking a look her way, and eyeing her with the same sly interest that his brother had shown earlier. True to the family nature, he unbent in his own good time to inquire, scratching his chin with bony fingers, 'Noongwalla, ye say?'

Alex decided it was time she spoke up for herself to the rustic head of the mail department. She picked up her suitcase and moved over to charm him with her brightest smile and warmest tones. 'I *would* be most grateful if you could give me a lift,' she glowed at him.

Ben swivelled his look away from her, scowling to hide the melting in him. 'Utility's not one of your fancy cars,' he snapped tetchily. 'Don't know if I can find a seat.' With that he clamped up his grizzled jaw again and munching on his toothless gums he made for the doorway. He reappeared a few seconds later carrying a green canvas bag and wearing a wide floppy-brimmed hat which made his nose and his chin stick out like rods from beneath it.

Not wanting to upset her chances at this stage Alex stood beside her suitcase watching him as he moved off, and displaying the right amount of anxiety. She was rewarded after a few moments by the sound of an engine of sorts chugging madly somewhere. Then clattering into view came a vintage vehicle with tall wheels and a green body open at the back to show a clutter of crates and ropes and ragged sacks.

Unassumingly she viewed the scenery until she was sure the utility was bumping in close to her. Inside the cab Ben was flinging things to right and left from the seat beside him. When he saw that Alex was watching him he shot back behind his shut down expression and clacked, 'Ye'll have to take what room there is and put up with it.'

Twinkling, Alex was aware that he had rapidly spun a

duster over the square of seat he had prepared for her, but she knew better than to let him see it. He came round to open the door for her and she turned a grateful look towards the other half of the rustic pair. The lanky Howell, however, was already striding off, doggedly pushing his trolley and apparently preferring not to be known that he had been rash enough to offer someone his assistance.

Alex climbed up into the cab and was met by a pungent odour of stale tobacco, dust and petrol fumes. Ben humped her case up and stuck it in the space in front of her feet. His eyes squinted closely at the travel labels spattered over it. With his usual deliberation he climbed in at his side and took the chugging vehicle out on to a dusty track which snaked away into the far distance, before he asked, 'You out from England?'

'That's right,' Alex smiled, casting her eyes over the view. She had been gazing at the land, burned brown and patchily bare, for some time when Ben got round to making a reply. 'Got a granddaughter living back there,' he said, shouting unnecessarily over the engine. 'Place called Hull. Married name's Graham, Betsy Graham. Ye know her?'

'Can't say I've heard the name,' Alex replied with a suitable degree of thoughtfulness, plus a certain inner amusement. Ben wasn't the first Australian she had met who regarded England as an outsize village where everybody knew everybody else.

Unperturbed, he went on, 'Met one of these English sailor boys down in Sydney, she did. Bin over there four years. Sez it's dinkum. Come back once for six weeks' 'oliday.'

Alex smiled her interest his way. His long bony knees high up under the wheel, his big knuckly hands gripping it, he clacked with a spark of reluctant humour, 'The ways of the world is odd. My kin came out here afore I was born. Now there's Betsy over there raisin' nippers. Deng if we ain't back where we started!'

'Perhaps her children will come to settle out here one day,' Alex offered tactfully.

Ben gave no sign of having heard. Following his own train of thought, he squinted through the windscreen at the road, nodding absently to himself, 'The ways of the world is odd all right.'

Alex kept her ear tuned as the vintage engine chugged out the miles. But that seemed to be the extent of the conversation.

Watching as a sea of stubbly yellowing grass dipped and rolled towards the horizon; as an occasional eucalyptus tree swung by, she found herself thinking about Betsy back in Hull.

How would she be living? In a spruce little terraced house perhaps, with the shops on the corner and a row of similar houses opposite. Alex had to smile to herself over Ben's words. It *was* odd, when she thought about it. When she thought about her aunt's house with its small neat rooms, two up and two down, the back kitchen leading out on to one in a line of walled paved yards not much bigger than a pocket handkerchief, the front door opening on to a pavement running past identical heavy panelled doors and lace-curtained windows as far as the eye could see.

At first Alex had found the compact living in the small north-country town less wearing than trying to cope with the sprawl of London. Recently qualified as a nurse at one of the city hospitals, and being the unattached niece without ties of any kind, it had been understood from the start that she should be the one to take care of her widowed invalid aunt. The married daughters expected it, and her aunt had come to rely on the idea. Though she was a niece only by marriage it had never occurred to Alex to refuse them.

She had travelled on the overnight train and settled in at number eleven Crabtree Terrace, quickly learning the art of manoeuvring a wheelchair about the tiny rooms, and attending to her aunt's endless requests.

The weeks of seeing nothing but the sombre wallpapered interior of the terraced house, or the square of bricked-in back yard, of going no further than the circle of formal gardens at the end of the street, had stretched into months, and the months into years.

Caught up in a life which she couldn't now out of duty's sake turn her back on, Alex had carved space. And then last

June her aunt had died. The married daughters had moved in to wind up her affairs and suddenly Alex found herself free. She wasn't needed any more. For the first time since her student nursing days her life was completely her own again.

Booking a passage to Australia had been something more than pure impulse. Her uncle, a printer by trade, had been an ardent reader of travel books, and in her bedroom which had once been his, she had passed the long evenings while her aunt slept, browsing through the works he had collected.

Australia had fascinated her from the start. The vast unbroken continent with its arid deserts, tropical rain forests, and tiny homesteads marooned in thousands of square miles of rolling bushland, had seemed the ultimate in contrasts to her congested world at Crabtree Terrace. She had read all about Alice Springs, the only town for hundreds of miles in any direction, gazed at pictures of giant blossoming trees, road trains taking cattle to market, and sheep grazing across sunburnt foothills.

It must have been some time then when she had made up her mind to see it all at first hand one day.

Paying the boat passage had presented no difficulties. There had been nothing mean about her aunt. She had paid her a good monthly salary. The only trouble was, she had never allowed her any time to spend it. Alex reckoned that with careful budgeting she had enough money to take an extended holiday Down Under of several weeks, plus her return fare, before she need think about finding a job.

She had chosen Adelaide for no other reason than the fact that one of her friends from her London nursing days had come from the state capital of South Australia. Alex had left the boat with the vague notion of looking her up. Only when she saw the milling city with its skyscraper buildings and sprawling suburbs did she realize with a wry smile that it would be like hunting for the proverbial needle in the haystack.

But there were friends enough in the elderly German couple who ran the small hostel where she had stayed, and

12

on the coach rides she had taken to various beauty spots inland and along the coast. Under blue skies sparkling with heat, amidst the laughter and life of a city surrounded by meadowland and mountains, Crabtree Terrace became just a dull memory; part of a world that she was rapidly deciding she was in no hurry to return to.

As the days flew by she began to consider the prospects of finding work in Australia. The flying doctor service intrigued her, and Karl and Helen Mueller at the hostel told her all they knew about the city hospitals. Alex had listened, too polite to douse their enthusiasm by telling them that after years of being hemmed in behind the closed doors of her aunt's house, she was looking for something far away from the confines of hospital buildings and walls.

Then as the result of a casual inquiry the job that might have been made for her had turned up. A nurse was required at a logging camp down in the south-east, near the borders of Victoria. The previous nurse had had to leave because of family commitments and a replacement was being urgently sought.

Within an hour of applying at the Trans-Asian Newsprint offices in downtown Adelaide, Alex had found herself in possession of a letter saying she had been given the job, plus her fare out to Noongwalla. She was to present the letter to a Mr. Grant Mitchell who apparently was the man in charge at the camp. She had left the bulk of her luggage with the Muellers and made her way across country, unable to believe her good fortune.

Still unable to believe it now, she gazed out of the cab windows at the endless rolling plains and uncluttered spaces, and without knowing it she breathed a deep sigh of appreciation. From beneath his floppy brim the weathered Australian looked slightly startled at her approval of the scenery. Scowling himself over the landscape, he chewed on his toothless gums to grumble, 'Droughtiest year for the past fifteen. Ought to be new fallow now, early spring. Grass looks as though it's bin afire.' His chin came up to touch his nose as he declared, squintingly, 'Thirsty land all right.'

Alex followed his gaze, experiencing none of his moroseness at the golden stretches, and later she was inclined to feel that there was little to complain about as the roadside began to show a sprinkling of pines, and the cool green floor beneath them was shadowed with the dapple of ferns and growing things.

They travelled onward until a curve in the road brought them out over a valley which stretched away into the distance on either side. The farm land in the valley was a neat patchwork of green and mottled strips and lost in the endless space, like matchbox houses on a vast, boundless ocean was the occasional sunbleached homestead.

The engine of the old utility wheezing as they climbed, Ben pointed to a cluster of corrugated rooftops showing above the curve of the hill ahead of them. 'That's Noongwalla,' he told Alex in his raised cracked tones.

A few minutes later they were chugging past rambling houses surrounded by work buildings, and huge store sheds probably used for fruit packing. The unpaved main street of Noongwalla was lined with low bungalows and timber-built constructions reminding Alex very much of movie pictures of the Old West of the United States. As Ben pulled up towards the far end of it, she looked out to where wooded hills swept down and along the mouth of the valley almost up to the main street, and asked, 'Is the logging camp far from here?'

'Few miles along the road,' Ben said from beneath his floppy brim. He fixed her with that suspicious, accusing glare of his to add, 'Ain't nothing there for a woman.'

'I'm going to work there,' Alex met his belligerent stare with a smile. 'I'm the new nurse.'

Ben exercised his stubbled jaws, scowling at her for a long moment until this news penetrated his slow-moving thoughts. Then he nodded as he reached for her suitcase. 'Aye, they did tell me that Mrs. MacTavish has had to leave. Couple of new grandchildren turned up unexpected. Daughter's not too good.'

He held out his knobbly hand as Alex stepped down beside him, then he took his gangling frame across the wide veranda where the utility had stopped, and disappeared into

14

a darkened doorway leaving her to follow.

In the interior gloom Alex made out a long room with a bar running the entire length of it, and crude tables and chairs scattered about the floor. On the other side of the doorway was a small wooden counter with a bell on it, and across from this a flight of wooden stairs curved away out of sight. This was the hotel, Alex presumed.

Ben clapped the bell and told her, 'Will Price runs it.' And when no Will Price appeared he shrugged his bony shoulders, listening to the hollow ring echoing around the whitewashed spaces, and muttered, 'Out at the back some-where.' He flicked the braces of his dungarees with calloused thumbs, and brought his chin up to touch his nose. When he had finished listening he strode round the counter, and taking one of the keys in his huge hand, he slapped it down in front of her with, 'Rooms is upstairs. Ye can see Will later.'

He dumped her suitcase at the foot of the stairs, and with a flick of his hat he took off with his long bent-kneed stride to the door. Alex smiled her thanks after him as he went. She knew better than to embarrass the irascible old Australian by putting her gratitude for his help into words.

When his shadow had disappeared beyond the doorway she looked at the number of the key he had given her and turned towards the flight of steps. At the top of them she found a landing with a line of doors. Hers was the second one along.

The room had a spartan-like air with bare floorboards and a tall window sprayed with dust, folds of heavy blanket-like material hanging drably at the sides. But there was a huge comfortable-looking bed, made up with clean linen, and reasonable washing facilities.

Travel-weary, Alex slipped out of her suit and shoes, and poured water into the bowl on the marble-topped stand. Later, dust-free and cool, she planned to sink thankfully on to the bed in her underslip. The thought that it might be better to shut out the sunshine first took her over to the tall window.

Peeping out, she looked along the dusty length of the main

15

street, unimpressed by its ghost town qualities. The only movement she could see was Ben lost under the floppy brim of his hat making his way out of the general store which was probably the post-office too, a little way along on the other side of the street.

Too tired at this time to react much one way or the other at her surroundings, she drifted over to the bed and sinking down, stretched out on it. The pillow was cool and sweet-smelling, the embroidered ridges of the heavy quilt not uncomfortable through the silk of her slip. Almost at once the bed seemed to float up and carry her away, as gradually, pleasurably, she began to lose her hold on her consciousness.

A thunderous hammering on the door awoke her. Jerking up with a start and watching the wood bend under the blows, Alex was sure the building was on fire, possibly the whole of the main street. Her nursing cool, however, allowed her to search calmly for her dressing gown in her case. Tying the belt around her waist, she opened the door and inquired in level tones, 'Yes. What is it?'

A man in his shirt sleeves, pale sandy hair bristling on his head and chin, confronted her with, 'You the noo nurse?' When Alex nodded he told her, 'Mitchell's downstairs waitin' ta see yer.'

Mitchell? Mitchell? Alex searched her sleep-clouded brain, trying to place the name. When at last it came to her than it must be Grant Mitchell, the logging camp boss, whom the man was talking about, she inclined her head and said quietly, 'Very well, I'll come down.'

Back inside her room she rinsed her face and dressed, an ironical light in her eyes as she smoothed back her hair. News certainly travelled fast in these parts. She hadn't been in Noongwalla more than a couple of hours. She had planned to go and search out the man who ran the logging camp as soon as she had rested. Now it looked as though he had saved her the trouble. White blouse buttoned, its plain front accentuating the neat cut of her brown suit, she stepped into her shoes, smoothed her slim skirt and went out. Had she stopped to glance in the mirror before doing so she might have noticed the slight pallor of her skin through want of a meal. She was unaware too that awakening abruptly from a deep sleep had given her a fragile look about the temples.

The change in the room downstairs was startling. Bare electric light bulbs combating the dark outside hung down at intervals amidst thick blue smoke. Picked out in the haze were the husky shapes of men. Roughly attired, they crowded along the length of the bar and swayed, beer glasses in hand, in groups around the tables. The noise was considerable, being mostly loud guffaws and ribald comments tossed back and forth above the general roar of conversation.

Nearby where she stood beside the counter with the bell on it, Alex felt a rush of air, and looking round, she was in time to see the figure of the be-aproned sandy-haired man, who was presumably Will Price the hotel proprietor, swoop into her as he swung past with a loaded tray to rasp, 'I'll tell Mitchell you're here.'

Alex watched with mild curiosity as he moved towards the wall of men at the bar. She saw him stop and say something to a big pale-shirted figure holding a briefcase but no drink. The head of dark hair close cut and waving almost to a curl down the sun-weathered neck nodded without turning.

Alex waited until Grant Mitchell's conversation with his companion, which was obviously of some importance, had finished. She had heard nothing about him except that he was a dedicated timber man, tough as they come, and used to having his orders obeyed. She could see much of this in the ruggedness of the muscular shoulders, in an imperceptible alertness about the heavy thickset frame. From what she could see of his face she would have said he was about thirty-seven years old.

He finished talking, lingering to share a joke with a group of strapping individuals, before turning away. As he moved across the room towards her she recognized that 'No time for women' look which men of his type wore when it became necessary. Arriving, he indicated a door off towards the side of the reception desk and waving her forward he clipped, 'In here.'

17

Passing him as he stood aside for her to enter, Alex got a vague impression of a face totally devoid of handsome lines, yet striking in a rough-hewn sort of way. Deep furrows were scored down the cheeks outlining the square jut of chin and the clamped mouth, which had the suggestion of a hard, humorous or – cynical – curl about it. Eyes flecked with hazel tints looked out from beneath an overhang of thick dark eyebrows. It was a face of firmness and inflexibility.

The small lit room they had stepped into was bare except for a table and two chairs and an ancient filing cabinet. Alex was nodded into one of the chairs as Grant Mitchell took the other one behind the table. His keen glance missing nothing of the figure before him, he noted the soft brown hair pinned in a no-nonsense coil at the nape of a slim neck, the dark-lashed grey eyes radiating an air of gentle calm. And seeing this he frowned as they were seated, to ascertain, 'Rumour has it that you've arrived to take over from Mrs. Mac?'

'Yes, I've brought a letter of introduction from the Adelaide offices,' Alex replied pleasantly. She searched in her handbag, unaware that he was watching the movements of her hands, milk-white and slender; flicking an impersonal glance over the slim legs and neat shoes. He took the letter she handed him. He read it rapidly, afterwards throwing it to one side as though he would have liked a waste bin handy. From this he brought his gaze up and clasping his hands in front of him he leaned back to ask vibrantly, 'Worked in a logging camp before, Miss Leighton?'

'No. I've only just recently arrived from England,' Alex replied steadily.

'So?' The big shoulders lifted with a trace of impatience. 'Logging camps are not peculiar to Australia. I worked in one just north of the Scottish border up to a year ago myself.'

Alex inclined her head in silence. She didn't know what she was supposed to reply to that.

He eyed her speculatively with that direct gaze of his and asked, 'What nursing experience have you had?'

'Enough to pass my finals at staff nurse level,' Alex found herself answering, with a certain coolness. It had been sufficient for the offices in Adelaide just to know that she was a qualified nurse. But obviously this man wasn't going to be satisfied with that.

'And since then?' he persisted in his clipped accent which was only just developing traces of the Australian drawl.

'I looked after my aunt,' Alex replied.

'Your aunt?' His voice grated harshly.

'She had an incurable illness,' Alex said quietly. 'I nursed her for four years until she died last June.'

The hazel-flecked gaze flicked over her. 'Does this mean you've lived alone with your aunt up to coming out here?' he asked.

'Yes,' Alex said.

Grant Mitchell breathed deeply, unclasped his hands and clapped them palms down to rest them on the table. 'How old are you, Miss Leighton?' he rasped at her without finesse.

'Twenty-five,' Alex told him, her grey gaze steady.

'Old enough to know,' his gaze swept over her again, 'that there's a great deal of difference between the world you've been used to and the one we've got out here.'

'Yes, I know that.' Alex met his gaze.

'Do you?' he glinted at her. 'Do you? I wonder?' He stood up and rapped the table, striding about as he spoke. 'The men here are a rough lot made up of characters from all corners of the globe. They're not too particular about their language or their habits.' His mouth twisted into a tight dry smile. 'You might call them a bunch of good-tempered apes.' He continued to walk in the small space. 'They get themselves into more scrapes with heavy machinery than a set of nine-year-olds would, making it rough on the person who has the job of patching them up afterwards. That's why I'm always badgering for male medical help here. Unfortunately as there's a doctor in the area we only rate the services of a nurse.'

He paused, and the loud guffaws could be heard clearly from the bar-room. As though to drive this point home he swung on her to state flatly, 'There's no padding around *this* job, Miss Leighton. Just dust and drought and a twenty-four-hour day in the forests and amongst the timber huts of the logging camp.'

Alex rose to face him unflinchingly. 'Your previous nurse seems to have managed all right,' she pointed out calmly.

Grant Mitchell heaved himself around and rapped impatiently, 'Mrs. Mac is a case-hardened old Scot. She knows how to throw her weight about amongst the men, and she knows how to keep the peace between them when it's necessary.' He aimed his sharp gaze Alex's way and snapped, 'You don't get that kind of experience nursing a sick aunt.'

'I'm willing to start collecting some now,' Alex said simply.

'Well, if I were you I'd forget it.' The logging boss thrust his hands into the pockets of his dust-pale slacks. His voice had a note of finality in it as he added, 'Not everybody fits in with the rougher Australian life.'

Alex looked at him. Not small herself, she was used to being on a level with most men. It was a new experience to have to lift her gaze a little. Unaffected by his tones, she remarked calmly, 'You seem to be doing all right.'

'*I* haven't been tucked away living a sheltered life with an aunt for the past four years,' Grant Mitchell retorted bitingly.

'In other words, you're not going to accept me for the job?' Alex faced him.

'No, I'm not,' he stated flatly. 'If I did I'd be looking for another nurse inside a week.' He turned and made his way towards the door, saying grimly as he went, 'You can go back to the Adelaide offices and tell them to send me another Mrs. Mac, or else. And while you're about it ask them why the delay in the equipment I ordered a couple of months back. If they were as quick to answer my requests for modern machinery as they are to send me a duff nurse, we might get some timber cut around here.' He turned in the doorway and inclining his head drawled dispassionately, 'Nice to have met you, Miss Leighton. Sorry we couldn't do business.'

Alex watched the door close, not moving from where she stood in the centre of the room. Well! She pulled in a deep breath, unsure of her emotions. Who would have suspected that the boss of the logging camp would wish to conduct his own private interview? She had felt from the start that she didn't come up to his requirements, but she had been ready to ignore this, assuming that the job was hers anyway. How wrong she had been!

Her smooth composed features creased wryly. The offices might have the say in Adelaide, but there was no doubt that Grant Mitchell was the boss around here. And having met the man and learning something of his exacting demands she thought she could see now why she had landed the job so easily.

Obviously finding his persistent requests tiresome, the offices were only too anxious to fob him off with whatever happened along at the time, in this case Alex, and then forget him — but they were probably learning that Grant Mitchell didn't operate that way.

Alex shrugged her neatly clad shoulders. Well, that was that! Whatever else now, she needed a meal. Tomorrow she would have to think about how she was going to get back to Denver's Creek to pick up the Adelaide train. As she moved to the door she thought of the rustic brothers Howell and Ben there with a certain ironic light in her eyes. Seeing the dour twosome again would be like meeting old friends compared to the glacial approach of Grant Mitchell.

Leaving the small room beside the reception desk, she discovered the sign DINING ROOM hung over a doorless aperture off to the side of the stairs. No more than a long shed built on to the back of the hotel structure, it was bare apart from a scattering of chipped tables and chairs which looked lost in the space. Alex chose a table near the side wall and waited. She had her doubts about being served as there was no one else in the room, but after perhaps ten minutes a plump teenage girl came scuffing up to the table in a pair of oversized mules.

Alex, seeing no menu, asked with her warm smile, 'What have you got to eat?'

The girl shrugged indifferently. 'Steak'n fried mince balls,' she recited in a thick Australian drawl.

Alex grimaced lightly. Her appetite was not at its best since her encounter with the logging camp boss, and she appealed humorously to the girl, 'Could I have an egg, do you think?'

'No eggs,' came the blunt reply. 'Steak'n fried mince balls.'

'Very well,' Alex twinkled resignedly, 'I'll have the steak.'

'Steak'n fried mince balls,' the girl nodded doggedly, and slopped off.

She returned some time later with a tray of outsize proportions and placed the whole contraption down on the table. Alex gazed down and tilted one dark eyebrow. Flopping over the edges of a plate half as big again as an ordinary sized dinner plate was an inch-thick steak, and sizzling across its middle were two perfectly shaped gold and white fried eggs. She looked up again at the server, the dark eyebrow slanting quizzically. 'I thought you said . . .?'

'Steak'n eggs,' the girl shrugged, offering no explanations as to the magical workings of her mind. Shirking the task of fathoming into it further, Alex smiled whimsically in reply and she was left alone with the giant-sized meal.

She savoured the coffee served in a thick mug, and ignored the wads of bread cut like bath sponges. She had intended to do the same with the steak, but one succulent mouthful told her it was going to take absolutely no effort to eat perhaps a quarter of it anyway.

The last of the thick sweet coffee downed at the end of the meal, she searched and finding no table napkin or anything remotely resembling a paper serviette, was obliged to dip into her handbag for lace handkerchief. Feeling outrageously satiated, she dabbed at her lips and fingertips and rising from the table left the room.

The noise from the bar dominated the night. As she walked through the pall of blue smoke to the outer door Alex kept her glance away from where the sound of heavy boots and shouts of laughter made the floor and walls shake.

There was a refreshing difference in the cool night air.

The thought of a brisk walk appealed to her, but silhouetted against the blood-red sky were the dark shapes of men leaning and smoking idly at intervals against wooden supports along the street. She decided to walk instead beneath the cover of the veranda which fronted the hotel and after a few minutes she retraced her steps inside and made for her room.

Thankfully the wild goings-on down stairs were reasonably muffled once she had closed the door of her own quarters. She spent a little while gazing down from her window along the faintly lit street, witnessing one or two reeling figures out in the open and others merging in with the shadows. Then she drew the heavy cumbersome drapes and prepared for bed.

Between the sheets, her thoughts, successfully held in tight control up to now, broke free from her tired hold on them. Against her will she found herself thinking of Grant Mitchell and her meeting with him tonight. Coolly philosophical, she guided her thoughts in another direction. Why dwell on the episode? In the man's opinion she wasn't suitable for the job. So that was it. There was nothing to be gained by bemoaning the fact that she had come all this way for nothing.

The darkness of the room closed in on her and she slept.

The air had a crisp sparkle about it when she rose the next morning. Drawing the drapes back as soon as she had knotted her dressing gown about her, Alex saw that the length of the deserted main street was bathed in spring sunshine. Shivering a little after the warmth of her bed, she moved about briskly, gathering up soap and towel. With toilet bag hung over her wrist she went out of her room to explore.

Towards the end of the corridor she found a bathroom of mammoth proportions with a cold water shower lost away in one corner. Her skin tingling after braving the icy jet, feet damp in leather mules, Alex returned to her room to dress. Her clothes were still packed for travelling, so she decided to keep to the plain brown suit and white blouse.

23

Perhaps someone had heard the mad gurgling of the shower water upstairs, for when she went down and into the dining room she found her lone table by the wall set out with breakfast. There was a loaf of bread with a knife and butter beside it, a thick slice of cold gammon, strawberry jam piled on an earthenware plate and a pot of hot black tea. Slicing her own bread, Alex ate a little of the strawberry jam and drank a thick mugful of tea.

She saw no one in the half hour that she lingered in the dining room. The bar, dusty and littered with cigarette ends, was equally deserted when she passed through on her way outdoors. There was, however, the distinct clump of someone working somewhere behind the scenes.

The outside air was invigorating. The sun lacked the warmth of the previous afternoon, but one had the feeling that the heat was on the way. Though it was only October, the start of the Australian summer, the temperatures were already reaching eighty on some days. Unsure of her plans, Alex decided to take a stroll to get her bearings.

Across the street she caught a glimpse of the general store standing back beneath its shadowed veranda and cluttered to the door with provisions, mopheads, lines of dresses and saucepans. Walking on the hotel side, she passed a barber's shop and several offices. A pleasant surprise towards the end of the street was a tiny courtyard with a grape arbour and a tall pitcher standing in the green shade.

There was more evidence of country living where the street ended. Along a track curving back from the road, crude fences guarded houses with corrugated iron roofs and gardens which revealed tender care for growing things. Last season's carrots were lined up with this season's turnips and radishes, and thriving beside hen-houses and woodsheds were patches of sage and thyme and other herbs.

Occasionally as Alex passed by, a figure stooping along a cinder path would raise itself and call to her in the Australian manner of greeting, 'Good day-ee!'

'Good day!' Alex would nod and incline her head in passing. More than once when she acknowledged a wave she caught the glimpse of a battered vehicle parked in

24

a driveway.

A natural reservation kept her from begging a lift back to Denver's Creek. There was bound to be a bus out from Noongwalla one day soon to correspond with the one that came in. It would be no great hardship to wait for it. Also there was the thought that the bus, when it did turn up, would most likely be timed to connect with the train to Adelaide, in which case if she tried to make it on her own before then she could find herself stranded at Denver's Creek.

Considering it wiser to wait, she walked back the way she had come. Seeing no sign of any local transport today at any rate, she entered the hotel for lunch with a view to taking a stroll in the afternoon where tall trees grew along the floor of the valley almost up to the end of the main street.

Much to her satisfaction her stay indoors was cut to the minimum. A fortunate meeting with Mavis, the plump girl of the dining room, who was helpfulness itself this morning as she swept out the bar, produced a picnic pack of bread, thickly sliced and buttered, a wedge of creamy Australian cheese and sundry wrappings of cold sausage, meat slices and thick savoury biscuits.

Where sunlight cast green-gold pathways beneath the trees Alex dined leisurely on a portion of the meal which would have fed an army, and drank a little of the soda water packed alongside it. Afterwards she hung the canvas picnic bag on the low branch of a tree and set off on her stroll.

To guard against losing her way she kept to the one area of forest that edged the settlement. The silence beneath the limpid crowns of greenery was the silence of a cathedral. As she walked she listened to the calls of birds unknown to her. A throaty chuckle here, a squawk there, a high-pitched trill from way up above somewhere.

When all was still at one point she could hear the muffled sounds of machinery in the far distance. The logging camp, presumably.

The afternoon slipped away almost unknown to her. The sun was a copper disc sliding down towards the wood-clad hills when she returned to the settlement. Night dropped early in Australia. Realizing that she couldn't afford to spend too many such lazy days, she decided to inquire about local transport as soon as she got back to the hotel.

In the bare expanse of the crudely-lit bar, Will Price was working in his shirt sleeves and apron in readiness for the evening rush. Alex walked across the empty space from the doorway and said in her calm pleasant tones, 'I have to get back to Denver's Creek. Will there be a bus fairly soon?'

'Yair.' The proprietor nodded his sandy head from behind the counter. 'The weekly one leaves at ten-thirty in the morning.' He shot her a look that held no curiosity and anticipated, 'You paying your bill now?'

'If you like.' Alex opened her handbag. After handing him the amount he arrived at after much scribbling on scraps of paper, she left the picnic bag with him and went upstairs to tidy up.

There was no avoiding the 'grilled steak'n fried mince balls' tonight. However, with appetite improved after a day spent out of doors Alex found one half of the contents of the plate a manageable meal.

The bar was alive with the sound of men's laughter and the shuffle of heavy boots when she made her way up to her room for the night. With the knowledge that her stay in Noongwalla wasn't going to be prolonged after all, she set about preparing for her journey back to the city. She changed into her dressing gown, brushed her suit and placed it on a hanger where it would be handy for morning. Her white blouse she washed and hung to drip and dry smooth overnight on a rail in the bathroom. With the polishing pack from her suitcase she rubbed the dust of the forest from her shoes and when they were gleaming again she set them down beside her suit.

When all the small tasks were finally taken care of she washed in cool water at the marble-topped washstand, using a crisp green fern soap, then discarding her dressing gown she climbed into bed. Resolutely closing her mind to the dull sounds of the bar downstairs, she slept.

The next morning she rose late and dressed leisurely. After breakfasting in the deserted dining room she left a tip for Mavis and returned upstairs to collect her things.

It occurred to her as she was coming down the stairs that she hadn't asked where the bus usually waited. However, a glance outside saved her the trouble of going in search of someone in the hotel to find out.

Where a line of gum trees provided a wind break in a clearing set back a little way along, across the street, a squat bulbous-looking vehicle with an ancient luggage rack on top was parked in the shade. Stepping out towards it, case in hand, Alex saw that several of the seats were already occupied. She wondered vaguely as she crossed the clearing, the sound of her firm footsteps echoing on the silence and heralding her approach, if everyone was going to cover the whole distance to Adelaide like her. More likely, she thought, noticing the luggage atop the bus, they were merely shoppers who would leave the train at some small township en route.

She climbed aboard and a dozen or more bland faces fixed themselves on her. It didn't come easy to Alex to smile at people she didn't know; a handicap the residents of Noongwalla seemed to share when not waving from the safe distance of their gardens. The result, as she moved into their midst, was an atmosphere of mutual aloofness tempered only by a sharp curiosity on their part. She found herself a seat and gazed ostensibly out of the window.

Towards ten-thirty the bus driver made an appearance. A stocky figure in rough trousers and shirt, only his peaked cap denoting his station, he came scuffing across the dusty clearing his mind apparently elsewhere. He tossed Alex's suitcase on to the low roof of the bus, grinning absently at people he knew, and with one or two joking comments around the bus as he came inside he dropped heavily into his seat. He started up almost at once and Alex gathered that he would be collecting the fares when they arrived at Denver's Creek.

There were no latecomers. Everyone aboard who had planned to be aboard, she watched as they pulled slowly away and out along the main street. A man was having his hair cut in the barber's shop. Fleetingly she caught sight of the little courtyard with its tall pitcher beneath the greenery, then they were chugging at speed past the sprinkling of trees and out on to the open road.

Alex didn't look back. She felt no pangs at leaving Noongwalla, and certainly no one at the settlement would miss her. Smooth-clad shoulders erect as the bus sped along the rough route, she trailed her gaze over the rugged landscape, reconsidering her position. Perhaps she wouldn't stay on in Australia after all. Perhaps Grant Mitchell had been right when he said she didn't fit in here.

The picture of the logging camp boss pacing around that small room at the hotel came back to her. Big and tough-minded, he had been aggressively confident of his own worth, coldly critical of hers. Well, who was she to argue with that kind of experience?

The bus, which was careering giddily down a slope, took a sharp curve. Alex was hanging on to her seat near the window when the man of her thoughts suddenly spun into view. He was sitting in a dusty shooting brake coming from the direction of the wide sweep of valley where the homesteads were dotted. She had just time to realize that he must have been trying to beat the bus to the road, and had had to shriek to a stop at the last second, when he had whirled from her view again.

There had been a moment in passing when his brown gaze had collided head-on with her grey one. She felt that it stayed on her sharply as, tight-lipped, he hung back to let the bus go by.

They continued to rumble rapidly on their way to Denver's Creek. Alex hadn't intended to give the man another thought, except perhaps to wonder idly why he wasn't at the logging camp. Then from her window she saw the dusty shooting brake streaking into view again. It came racing alongside the bus until the two vehicles were travelling nose level with nose. Even as she watched, the speeding car gave erratic nudges to the squat bumbling bus, eventually forcing it to a sickening stop at the side of the road.

The car lurched to a halt beside it. The bus door was flung open. The bus driver's heated exclamation, 'What the . . .?'

was cut off as Grant Mitchell strode stooping inside and snapped, 'Won't keep you a second, Dan.'

His face pale and working, he moved up to Alex and fired at her, 'Have you got a first aid kit with you?'

'I've got the pack that the company supplied me with,' Alex replied calmly, adding, 'It's in my suitcase up top.'

'Come on!' Grant Mitchell grabbed her arm.

Sensing the urgency in his touch, Alex rose quickly and preceded him out of the bus. From the step he swung her case down rapidly from the luggage rack and slamming the door he waved the vehicle on its way.

It rumbled off, leaving a stillness over the sunlit country-side as Alex waited beside the car. Above the clear sweet song of the birds Grant Mitchell told her grimly, dumping her case into the back, 'A fool lumberjack has got himself pinned by the arm under a tree. He's in bad shape. The doc was supposed to be out at the Peterson property, but I haven't been able to locate him. We'd better move.'

CHAPTER TWO

HE took her arm and led her to the front of the car where he helped her roughly into the seat. Slamming the door, he strode round to drop in behind the driving wheel and wasting no time he took the car sharply forward towards Noongwalla.

Alex sat straight-backed and composed as they sped along the road. Her gaze was directed ahead and she saw nothing of the blur of scenery whipping by. The car slowed down to take in the main street of the settlement, then they were streaking along a road that tunnelled beneath the greenery of towering pines.

After two or three miles they swung off abruptly on to a track which penetrated deep into the forest. The ground was crumbly and uneven and the car was soon forced to a stop.

'This way,' Grant Mitchell was out of the car and reaching impatiently for her arm again. Out of her seat in double-quick time herself, Alex went to the back to search out her first aid bag. Disregarding his scowl at the time she took, she moved in to accompany him.

The route amidst closely set, ruler-straight pines which shot clear up to the heavens was slightly uphill. The soft sandy-coloured earth was ridged and humped with tussocks of grass. Though Alex found it hard going in her light shoes she kept up a good pace.

The logging camp boss forged ahead rapidly in his stout working boots. When she lagged behind he would throw her an exasperated look. Occasionally he assisted her irritably with a hand under her elbow, when she got a little out of breath.

The trees began to thin out. Where several of them measured their lengths along the ground, in a clearing littered with various items of machinery a crowd of men were gathered at one spot. As the logging camp boss strode in, a thickset, check-shirted figure broke away from the group and hurried to meet him. The man's heavy-jowled, slightly puckish features were grey and serious now as he informed Grant Mitchell, 'We've cranked up the felled tree as much as we dare. Any more friction and the whole lot is liable to give way.'

Alex followed the glance he tossed back beyond the group of men. She could see what he meant. The tree in question had crashed to the ground at an obviously unexpected angle, slightly uphill, and was grazing a huge tractor-type vehicle loaded with giant-sized logs. The blow when the two met must have been considerable, for several of the logs were spilling over at a precarious angle like a heap of carelessly strewn matchsticks. The splaying branches of the felled tree wedged up against the pile was a comforting sight, but it needed little imagination to see that any rash disturbance would send the whole lot tumbling directly downhill where they stood.

The logging camp boss eyed the situation grimly. 'We can't risk using the cranes with Stronowsky in there,' he bit out, moving forward to disperse the men. They shuffled about, reluctant to move, and shouldering them aside he nodded for Alex to follow him through.

At the heart of the crowd she saw a man stretched out on the ground, his right arm lost from view under a massive trunk. A dark red stain mingled with the mud and dust on his shirt. His face, in the throes of semi-consciousness, was contorted with pain.

Grant Mitchell dropped down on one knee beside him and asked in cheerful tones which belied his searching gaze, 'How goes it, Mike?'

The man opened his eyes and shot the logging camp boss an imploring glare, at the same time struggling feebly and croaking, 'Get me out of here, you goddamned. . . .'

Ignoring his spate of highly coloured language, Alex took off her suit jacket, dropped it to the ground and knelt beside him.

Bending close to the log where his damp head rested, she could see, following the line of his shoulder, that his trapped arm was quite visible. However, the elbow joint appeared to

31

be still locked between the slightly raised tree and the ground. To work on pulling it out was unthinkable. Yet until it was free she couldn't help him.

Speedily she opened her medical bag and searched out syringe and a pain-killing drug. It was only a second's job to put this to use beneath the rolled-up sleeve of the other arm.

The syringe away again, she looked up to where the logging camp boss stood over her, and said quietly, 'The tree will have to be raised at least another two inches before I can be of any use here.'

Disregarding the alarmed looks of the men standing around and the glances they shot towards the dangerously suspended logs, she waited for Grant Mitchell's reply.

Grey-faced, he stood for a moment, then flicking a look towards the crowd of men he nodded, 'Two inches, boys.'

There was a shuffling of feet as several of the men scattered out of the way. A handful moved towards the centre of the felled tree where a small machine had the trunk in its jaws. Nervously they went to work.

Alex listened to the sounds of the delicate cranking-up operation. Her eyes were fixed on the injured man and she paid no attention to the poised overhang of logs at her back. When she was able to pass her hand between the crushed arm and the underside of the tree she called, 'That's fine.'

She could see now that perhaps because the tree hadn't crashed directly down but had come into contact with the loaded tractor first, the man's arm would possibly be saved. But the state of the ground and his colour told her that he had lost a lot of blood.

Turning her glance up to Grant Mitchell's again, she begged urgently, 'If someone could perhaps. . . .'

Anticipating her request, his eyes flicked round as before and several beefy figures rushed in to help move their comrade. Raising herself in their midst Alex spoke authoritatively, 'Gently now, and no more than the merest fraction if we're not to damage the arm further.'

The hefty-handed lumberjacks, checked in their rush, dissolved into a group of tender-hearted schoolboys and crept in as though to handle an injured bird. They kept their glances away from the pyramid of balancing logs, but one of two were hard put to it to hide their frustration at not being allowed to scuttle away with their pal to safer ground.

As the man was lifted out, Alex supported the crushed arm from the shoulder, gradually guiding her hold along and under the elbow as the arm came into view. When the limb was completely free she called briskly for a halt. The man with his big Slavic features had long since lapsed into unconsciousness. Kneeling beside him, Alex tossed a look upwards and stated, 'I shall need some splints . . . two . . . longish.'

The logging camp boss nodded and rapped out, 'Casey! See what you can find.' Someone sped away.

The tall trees grew thickly all around. The light of day was lost somewhere on the other side of the dense green roof. Below, no breezes stirred. In the cloying heat amidst the blood and dirt and the stench of sweat from men's bodies, Alex worked steadily. With small scissors she cut the shirt sleeve away. None of the men wore ties, so she made a tourniquet to stem the flow of blood, from a headscarf folded in her handbag. She had wrapped the arm with most of the small bandages she possessed and given the man an anti-tetanus injection, when the splints arrived.

It was a tricky job trying to support the arm and baste the splints into place. Watching her, Grant Mitchell lowered himself in on her struggles and held the splints so that she could bind them.

She worked quickly and knotting the bandages to finish the job she met the flecked brown gaze to stress urgently, 'He needs a hospital at once. He's lost a great deal of blood.'

Grant Mitchell nodded and raised himself beside her as she cleaned her hands with spirit. 'There's one at Oaktown. We'll take him in my car,' he said, rapping out more orders.

There was no shortage of help from the fidgeting lumber-jacks to lift the recumbent figure and transport it and them-selves rapidly out of the path of the precariously poised logs. Giving strict instructions to two of the men to give all their support to the injured arm, Alex followed on behind at her own pace.

Her white blouse had lost some of its crispness by this time amidst the mud and dust. Her hair was still in its neat coil at the nape of her neck, though a wisp or two had escaped around her temples. She carried her suit jacket, retrieved from the ground, and her first aid bag. The logging camp boss moved with his long stride beside her.

At the shooting brake with the injured man lying prone in the back and Alex perched on the seat beside him, Grant Mitchell tossed his glance back in the direction of the giant log spill and told the thickset man who had seldom left his side, 'Get the cranes and grappling hooks up there. And go easy, we don't want any more accidents.'

With this he slid into his seat, started the car and shot away. Leaving the uneven course of the forest track, they turned out on to the smoother road and sped on beneath the towering trees in the opposite direction to the settlement.

How long she sat in a twisted position, cradling Mike Stronowsky's crushed arm, Alex could only measure by the stiffness of her frame. When at last the first of Oaktown showed in a sprinkling of neat houses, she guessed that the distance they had come from Noongwalla was possibly thirty or forty miles – about the same distance that Denver's Creek was northwards from the settlement.

They raced through the centre of the country town, passing stores and shops, the post office, and the sandstone buildings of courthouse and council chambers. The hospital, surrounded by a narrow strip of green lawn, was down a side street. They swerved in through a gate and pulled up in front of a flight of steps leading to open double doors. Alex let herself out of the car at the side nearest the entrance. Briefly she explained to the two white-coated attendants hurrying down the steps what had happened. Inside at the desk she gave a detailed account of her actions after she had arrived at the scene of the accident, while Grant Mitchell supplied the patient's name and other information.

Mike Stronowsky was brought in on a stretcher. They watched him as he was trolleyed away for an immediate

34

blood transfusion and general doctoring up. As he disappeared through the swing doors across the open space of polished floor, Grant Mitchell's big frame seemed to slacken for the first time. Lighting the cigarette he had stuck between his lips, he rasped at Alex who stood beside him, 'Let's go and get some coffee. I could use one.' He led the way out of the door and round to the side of the block. Here a small open doorway showed a buxom white-coated woman working behind a long counter which was littered with trays of thick white cups, and two enormous brass urns.

He ordered two cups of sweetened coffee and stood drinking his beside the counter. Alex picked up her own cup and sipped facing the door. She wouldn't have said no to a seat, but as there were no chairs provided she stood uncomplainingly.

As she allowed the coffee to do its job in revitalizing her, and let her eyes wander absently over the outdoor scene of paved pathways and people in the distance, it was some time before she realized that Grant Mitchell was boring holes through her with his flecked brown gaze. Outwardly composed, she went on drinking, wishing he wouldn't eye her quite so keenly. She had left her suit jacket in the car and she felt incomplete without it.

His hooded look stayed with her. There was no doubt that now the harrowing sequence of the morning was behind them, his mind was rapidly going back over the events, to the moments when she had knelt in the mud amidst a crowd of cursing, sweating men and quietly attended to Mike Stronowsky's needs.

Carelessly she turned to place her cup down on the counter. Catching a glimpse of his face, she wondered at the curl of his mouth as he watched her. Was he disappointed because she hadn't folded up on him at the scene of the disaster as he had expected? She couldn't tell. Though later when they were driving back the way they had come, she thought she detected a spark of admiration in the glance he kept with the road as he almost sneered, 'You were pretty cool back there, with twenty odd tons of timber just waiting for an excuse to break loose.'

35

Alex lifted her neat-clad shoulders. 'We would none of us have loved ourselves if we'd left Mike to it,' she replied simply.

Her light dismissal of the affair seemed to irritate the logging camp boss further. Pressing down on the accelerator, he snapped, 'You're wrong if you think that all you need for this job is a dedication to duty.'

'I wouldn't presume to have a thought on the subject,' Alex answered with enigmatic calm.

'Oh no?' He gave a shrug of something like disbelief and continued with his half sneer, 'Well, what took you so long to start making tracks back to Adelaide?'

'There's only one bus a week to Denver's Creek,' Alex gave him a lightly iced smile. 'Or didn't you know?'

The tightness of his mouth twisted briefly into a grin as he reflected, 'That's right. I'd forgotten you were without transport.'

He drove on speedily. After a long stretch and a similar length of silence inside the car, they swung off on to a dirt road that curved in through giant trees and circled a clearing dotted with sprawling wooden huts and monster-like machinery. As they cruised along the circular road Alex realized that they were in the logging camp.

Eventually the car stopped. Grant Mitchell got out. Alex, not knowing what she was supposed to do, got out too. The strong smell of disturbed earth and new wood came to her on the breeze that played with the wisps of hair about her face. Her neat polished shoes settled into a ridge of crusted mud as she looked about her.

Grant Mitchell answered the question forming in her eyes by swinging her suitcase out and rapping with that odd twist to his mouth. 'You still reckon you can handle the job, so you might as well spend the week trying to prove it.' He added with biting cynicism, 'The bus will be waiting for you when you need it.'

Alex weighed up his words. Her grey gaze was steady. It was true she couldn't get to Denver's Creek by local transport now, but it would have hindered him little to drive her and dump her there himself. He hadn't offered to. He had brought her here instead. So she supposed she could take it that he intended to accept her services for the time being. Or to be more exact, he was throwing the job at her, convinced that she wouldn't be able to hold it.

Her expression unruffled, she stood by while he slammed home the catch on the rear opening of the car. As he moved off, her suitcase in his hand, she followed a step behind. She saw that the long low timber building they had pulled up beside stood back against a fringe of trees and faced into the logging camp complex.

It was a rough construction devoid of any soft lines or refinements. Its walls showed the bark and knots of thick crudely cut logs, its roof was of similar sloping lengths. Tall bare windows shone like sightless eyes along the front.

Grant Mitchell strode to the door towards one end of the building and turning a key inside the lock he pushed it open. Alex followed him inside. The interior, emanating a strong pinewood tang, was large and airy and glinted with the impedimenta of a modern clinic. Alex's eyes took in at a glance the trolley laid up with instruments, the glass-fronted cupboards, stocking bottles of lotion, cottonwool and bandages. Creating a partition just up the room from the door was a low metal drug cupboard and in the far corner beside the trolley was a hot water sterilizer.

In the centre of the room stood a big old-fashioned heavy wooden desk and under one window sprawled an equally ancient leather couch. The large expanse of floor was of smooth wood with a faint sheen on it. The walls were lined with board and painted white.

The logging camp boss gave her just time enough to view the scene, then he was moving over to a door across the room, opposite the entrance. This opened on to a dim corridor. Here he led the way past a collection of small disused offices and storerooms to an open doorway at the end of the passage. A step behind him, Alex looked inside when they arrived. She was struck forcefully by the contrast. The clinic might have its share of modern amenities, but obviously that was where it ended.

The small narrow room held a single bed with black-

37

painted iron framework. Screening the tall window from the darkness of the trees outside a strip of faded chintz hung limply from large wooden rings. The sole furnishings of the room, beside the bed, was a low cupboard in one corner, a packing case draped with a scrap of gaudy taffeta, which probably served as a table, and one straight-backed chair.

In the gloom Grant Mitchell tossed her suitcase on to the bed and as its springs complained noisily, he gave her a warped smile and bowed her in with, 'It's all yours. Our departed employee, the invincible Mrs. Mac's apartment.'

He turned to go, then turned back to say from his bulky height, 'The dining hut is number four. We eat at seven. If you want anything now,' he glanced at his watch and shot her a malicious smile, 'you'll have to try the cookhouse.' His wide shoulders brushing the sides of the passage, he disappeared.

From where she stood, adding a touch of grace to the shabby room, Alex listened and heard the outer door of the clinic being closed. She glanced at her own watch. It was almost three o'clock. She took off her suit jacket and hung it on the single wire coathanger hooked at the end of the bed. The very first thing she did after this was to push the strip of musty-smelling chintz curtain as far as possible to one side to let in the maximum light. Happily the tall gaunt window was constructed in two manageable halves. It was no trouble to take the lower sash and slide it up until it joined the half-way one.

Outside, the trees stood like grey-robed sentinels. Knee-deep in pungent-smelling earth, they stretched as far as was possible to see, row upon row of massive knotted trunks. The room was lit with their dappled green light; freshened by the pine-scented breeze.

Leaving the small space of it, Alex explored the disused offices and storerooms along the passageway. Next to the one that had been Mrs. MacTavish's room she discovered one tucked away in a dim corner which apparently served as a washroom. In it were the minimum of fitments plus a washbasin which had parted company from its metal ratchets and outlet pipe and stood propped up on its end against a wall, covered in a thick layer of dust.

From the mustiness of the washroom Alex returned to where the forest air had searched out every ounce of staleness in the sparsely furnished nurse's quarters. She wandered around, bent to look in the low cupboard in one corner. Her heart lifted at the sight of a small Primus stove and miniature kettle. And there were other unexpected delights. Half a packet of tea had been stuffed into a thick mug similar to the kind used at Will Price's hotel, and back in the shows beside a tin of Australian peaches and a smaller one of pineapple jam, she found a medicine bottle containing two or three teaspoonfuls of sugar. Down on the bottom shelf of the cupboard she discovered an enamelled washbowl and jug.

Taking the jug first, she made a trip to the washroom and brought back water drawn from the tap which was suspended drunkenly in the wall. Behind the curtain, pulled discreetly across the closed window, it felt good to strip and wash away the morning's dust.

Red dressing gown tied at the waist, she put the kettle on the stove on top of the cupboard, using the metal tray provided, and with the tin-opener hanging by a piece of string from a nail on the wall she opened the tin of peaches. She would have preferred milk rather than sugar with her tea, but on the whole the light snack proved quite substantial, and she was sure that Mrs. MacTavish would have wanted her to help herself. A rinse in the bowl and everything was soon tidied away again.

As yet she had found nowhere to hang her clothes, so from the contents of her suitcase which she had spread on the bed, she took one of the two tailored white overalls she had bought in Adelaide and buttoned it on over her slip. There was no mirror, so she couldn't see the effect, but she had satisfied herself when trying on the overalls in the store that they were a perfect fit and thoroughly suited to her occupation. The short sleeves were pleasantly cool and practical for working. She tidied her hair, using the mirror from her handbag, then made her way along the narrow corridor and into the clinic.

The afternoon sunshine, streaming in at the windows, slanted patterns of gold on the polished wood floor, giving the large airy interior an inviting look. Alex opened all the windows and swung the double doors back wide. Lighting the hot water sterilizer, she set herself the task of going over everything in the clinic with a clean damp cloth to eliminate the dust.

As she worked methodically through the remainder of the afternoon, life at the logging camp was much in evidence outside. There were men's shouts, the grind of machinery, the thud of falling timber somewhere. Occasionally a group of beefy lumberjacks would trudge by. Sometimes it was a tractor crawling noisily on its way.

The sun had long since left the room by the time she had finished her work. Tired, but not unpleasantly so, she put away her cloths and dusters and walked over to turn out the light on the hot water sterilizer. As she closed up the clinic for the night she could see men coming in from all roads into the camp. They were making for a long hut, set amidst a group of buildings across the open space.

Stifling a sudden awareness of nerves, Alex turned towards her room with a firm step. It was obvious that the lumberjacks were converging on the dining hut for supper, and according to Grant Mitchell, if she wanted any that was where she would have to go.

A cord from the ceiling of the nurse's quarters, when jerked, lit up an electric light bulb shrouded in a red beaded shade. In its dull glow she debated with herself. Like the men her work was finished for the day, so she saw no point in continuing to wear the white coat. She chose as an alternative a neat pearl grey blouse with self-coloured embroidery down the front, and a slim grey skirt. She re-combed her hair and pinned it into its coil, then turning out the light, she went out, handbag in hand, through the clinic.

It was now quite dark outside. Her only guide as she walked was the odd pinprick of light amidst the cluster of buildings in the distance. She traversed the open space towards them, treading carefully, avoiding where she could the ridges of ploughed up earth and stubs of old plant life.

As she approached she saw that there was no mistaking the dining hut, even if she hadn't watched everyone hurrying towards it earlier. Its number 4 was painted boldly on the door and on the roof in white, and shone out clearly in the darkness.

Slim shoulders straight, Alex aimed her steps resolutely towards the cracks of light showing around the door. She allowed herself no thoughts now on the matter in hand. Having decided on her course of action back at the clinic, all she knew was that physically she was in need of a meal, and that by making her way as quickly as she could towards the dining hut she was eliminating the time to when she would receive it.

In the darkness she felt her way gingerly with her feet over the last few inches of uneven ground. It was then that she heard another footstep coming up behind. Without consciously thinking about it, there was something she recognized in that brisk step; something vaguely familiar about the big dark bulk framed in the shadows.

She had been just on the point of stepping up to the door when her attention had been distracted. As though he suspected her of hesitating Grant Mitchell moved in behind her and swept her forward, saying deeply, with a malevolent gleam in his eye, 'This way, Miss Leighton. Right in here.' He flung the door open, then stood watching her ironically as she gazed on the scene.

The first blinding impression that Alex received was of a hut bursting at the seams with men; check-shirted, greasy-singleted, beefy-shouldered, hairy-armed, unkempt, unshaven men; all talking, rolling, lunging at the piled plates scattered on the three long tables running down the length of the hut and stuffing food into their mouths as though it was the last they would ever receive.

Admist the debris of strewn biscuits, brick-like chunks of bread, and slopped beer, piles of steaming vegetables were disappearing under dozens of grasping hands and vats of stew placed at intervals along the tables ran with rivulets of the thick brown contents and stood in spreading, congealed pools.

Eyeing her with a flinty gleam, the logging camp boss guided her inside and accompanied her towards the far lane over by the wall. Her shoulders straight, her glance level, Alex walked calmly alongside him past the lines of noisily feeding lumberjacks.

As they progressed down the aisle, she saw with an inward flutter of relief a slightly raised, railed-off platform at the far end of the hut, with two or three smaller tables set back from the main room. Her relief was short-lived, however, when, escorting her up the couple of steps to the platform, Grant Mitchell indicated a vacant chair at the head of a table seating eight or nine men and told her with his malicious smile, 'Mrs. Mac always used to sit with the boys.'

'The boys' were apparently the technicians on the camp. Alex recognized the thickset man seated at one side of the table as the one who had taken all the orders this morning at the scene of the accident, and one or two others she remembered as having handled the machinery around the felled tree. Unfortunately their raised status in the work field had done nothing to help their table manners and all of them were shovelling food into champing mouths at an alarming rate, though they did stop momentarily to look up and nod her a friendly welcome.

Aware that the logging camp boss was seating himself beside a small table against the wall a little way behind her, Alex sat down without a word in the place he had indicated as hers. There was no table napkin that she could see, and the veined plate staring up at her from the bare wood of the table had the size and depth of a large fruit bowl. She was just noticing thankfully that at least there was no congealing stew vat set amidst the wads of bread and biscuits on the table, when a bright-faced, bald-headed little man, a large apron tied around his baggy trousers and over-sized tee-shirt, came shuffling up the steps of the platform with a pail in his hand.

Before Alex had time to anticipate his actions, he had taken a huge ladleful of the brown mess with which she was becoming familiar by now, and slopped it on to her plate. Droplets of the goo landed beside her knife and fork and shreds of meat slid lethargically down the slope of the plate as the little man, happily absorbed in his task, grabbed scoops of vegetables from the container across the top of the pail and slapped them eagerly into the pool of stew.

Highly satisfied with himself, he shuffled hurriedly off again, and Alex's gaze was drawn down to the gruesome sight on her plate. The logging camp boss was sitting quietly enough behind her, but something told her that he was watching her with that satirical gleam of his. Stifling the flush of distaste stealing up her throat, she picked up her knife and fork and began to eat.

As she had partly expected, the food wasn't anywhere near as bad as it had been made to look. If her appetite hadn't been snatched away by seeing how it was served up she might even have found it delicious. As it was, by working hard at imagining that she was dining off a neat white tablecloth and using rather more delicately designed tableware, she managed to coax herself into wading around the edges of the meal.

The men at the table were already miles ahead of her. While she was still coming to terms with the mountain of creamed potatoes and diced carrots, they were bulldozing their way through chunks of baked jam roll swimming in bright yellow custard, the idea being, or so it seemed, to see who could cram the most into his mouth at one time.

Swilling it all down with beer, they left their seats one by one, shooting her a sheepish friendly nod as they clomped off the platform and away down the length of the hut. The three lanes of tables were almost empty by this time too. Outside there was the sound of lorries revving up, and the stragglers left behind stuffed a last morsel of food into their mouths or threw back a final gulp of beer, and hurried out to the transport that would take them to the settlement, Alex presumed. Mainly Will Price's hotel where she had seen them drinking and making merry during her nights there.

It was debatable whether the bar ought to be open at that time of night, but she had an idea that the drinking laws were stretched around here to accommodate the lumberjacks.

43

She now had the table to herself, and without the circle of furiously working jaws around her she was able to attempt the sweet, clapped in front of her some time ago, with a little more enthusiasm.

As though she was cutting herself a piece of cake, she sliced off a portion of the huge slab of jam roll and transferred it to one of the empty bread plates. This way she didn't feel quite so overwhelmed by the quantity, and eating it slowly it wasn't so much of a task. The pastry was well made, though after the sweetness of the custard she found herself longing for a cup of hot strong tea. Noticing that there were only empty beer tankards scattered around the table, she began to see now why Mrs. MacTavish had kept a kettle and stove in her room.

The meal finished, she sat back for a moment and listened to the quietness which had descended over the dining hut. She hadn't heard the boss of the logging camp leave. Judging by the occasional rattle behind her she gathered that he was engrossed in work papers of some kind.

When she was ready to go, she dabbed at her lips with the handkerchief she had tucked into the strap of her watch. Then rising from her chair she took the two steps down from the platform. The little man with the big apron, and one or two identical helpers, were emptying slops of food into their pails beside the tables. Carefully averting her gaze from the mess, Alex walked down the length of the hut and out of the door.

It took her quite a while to get used to the pitch black outside, and considerably longer to work out in which direction the clinic was situated. By this time Grant Mitchell must have finished his office work, for as she was about to start out to where she guessed her quarters must be, making a mental note to leave a light on over there in future, he came out of the hut into the darkness behind her.

There was pause after the door had closed in which she felt him sizing up her presence, then she heard his bitingly laconic tones drifting on the night to her as he asked, 'Enjoy your supper, Miss Leighton?'

'There's nothing wrong with the cooking.' Alex turned

44

away, leaving him to make what he could from her reply.

Whatever his reaction, she sensed him shrugging his shoulders with flinty amusement as he called after her, 'Sleep well, Miss Leighton, and pleasant dreams.'

His words prompted her to recall the oatmeal-covered mattress and rough blanket in her room, and she turned to call back in similar derogatory vein, 'Do I get sheets for my bed or not?'

A lighter flared in the darkness. In its glow Grant Mitchell's smile was twisted as though he hated having to tell her, 'We live rough, but not that rough.' He pulled deeply and leisurely on his cigarette, then informed her, 'The laundry will be shut now. You'll have to come with me and help yourself.'

Alex was just on the point of making her way back to him when the lighter was snapped off, plunging her into total darkness again. She heard the logging camp boss start out without a word, and she could just picture his uncharitable gleam. Struggling to distinguish his disappearing shape in the gloom, she caught up with him with some difficulty. She gave no signs of her breathlessness, but simply fell into step beside him.

He didn't take his time. Long legs moving over the ground, he stepped it out, maliciously sure of himself, smiling disdain of others who didn't know the layout of the camp as well as he did.

Back straight, Alex picked her way carefully alongside him. She wouldn't let herself falter, so it was perhaps just as well that her feet found level ground all the way. She arrived where the timber slats of a hut similar to all the others loomed up in front of them out of the darkness, only a step behind the logging camp boss. She heard the clink of keys and saw his big shoulders in front of the door. Then he was striding inside and flicking on a light. A room consisting of nothing but lines of racks from ceiling to floor, holding various piles of linen, sprang into view. He stood aside and waved her in with a dry, 'Help yourself.'

Alex stepped past him and went to examine the racks. She found one holding smooth white sheets and another containing neatly folded pillow-slips. She took two from each pile and returned to the door.

The light was switched off as she went out, and the door closed and locked again. She stood poised for a second, the clean linen across her arms, then she plunged off on her own into the darkness. A little while later when the big shape came heading alongside her, she told it aloofly, 'I know my way, thank you.' She wasn't at all sure that she did, but she had had enough of the superior Mr. Mitchell for one day.

In response to her remark he stopped and swayed lazily where he was, and convinced that he was watching her go with that cynical twist of his she stepped briskly away from him and into the gloom.

By fixing her sights on various pinpricks of light around the camp she did eventually find her way back to the clinic. Once inside, she switched on the light and closed the door, leaning to rest, perfectly composed, against it. Her grey eyes became lit with a certain humorous satisfaction when she considered that she had held her job down at the rip-roaring logging camp for the best part of one day at least.

But for all her bolstered confidence she was glad to discover two sturdy bolts on the door when she turned to lock it, and later, noticing two identical ones on the lower sash of the window in her room, she guessed that Mrs. MacTavish had insisted on having these fitted for her own peace of mind.

After a cup of tea, milkless, but nevertheless very welcome, Alex prepared for bed. Though the hour was early she considered it wise to fortify herself with plenty of rest for whatever lay in store for her the next day. She had cause to congratulate herself on this decision when some time later she was dragged out of the deep slumber by the sounds of great pandemonium going on outside.

At what she made out to be around one o'clock by her wrist watch, she was shook in her bed by the sound of lorries rattling and rumbling by, and above this din came the whoops and shouts of men obviously returning from the settlement. Away in the distance where they eventually disembarked, the night was split apart by bellowing guffaws

46

and piercing whistles as they kept up the bawdiness.

Tossing frustratedly at the disturbance, Alex turned her back on the noise, but it must have been half an hour or more before the last man finally retired to his bed for the night. It seemed to her that she had only just drifted off to sleep again when she was jerked awake by the sound of tractors grinding past the door, truck horns tooting, and voices carrying from right and left, as the logging camp came to life for the day.

The first light of dawn creeping in at her window, Alex buried her head irritably in the pillow. Did nobody need any sleep around here? Were they all supermen who could manage quite well without it?

She made herself doze for another half hour, then rising she washed and dressed. The early morning nip in the air prompted her to exchange her blouse for a smooth short-sleeved jumper. After re-pinning her hair and throwing back the bedding to air it before the open window, she went out of the clinic towards the dining hut.

There were no problems concerning direction this morning. The whole network of the logging camp, with its numbered huts touched faintly by the first golden rays of the sun, was spread before her, so that she couldn't have lost her way if she had tried. Bordering the camp on all sides, the towering pines brushed their green tips against a blue-washed sky.

Feeling unaccountably in tune with everything about this sparkling new world, she walked, slim and erect, across the open space towards hut number four. Only when she arrived at the door of the dining hall did her eyebrow tilt wryly. What was going on inside there this morning? she wondered.

She opened the door and stepped in, expecting the worst, and found the three long tables completely deserted. They looked little different from when she had left the elderly helpers clearing away last night, except that strewn down the length of them this morning were used coffee mugs, congealed porridge vats, remnants of bread rolls, and bacon rind curling on greasy well-cleaned plates.

47

The separate tables on the platform were also deserted. Walking down the length of the hut Alex ascended the two steps and took her seat at the head of the big table where her place was still set amongst the ruins of the technicians' breakfast leftovers.

She waited quietly, sitting straight in her chair and trailing her gaze absently over her surroundings. The only sounds of activity came from the cookhouse across from the open doorway at the side of the platform. After some time, when no one appeared she picked up her mug and plate and went down the steps again. At the end of each long table stood a huge coffee urn. She filled her mug from one of these, pleased to find the beverage still deliciously hot. Strolling on, she discovered over by the far wall a solid low cupboard-like affair set out with various additions in breakfast cereals, jam fillings and bread shapes. Here she helped herself to cornflakes, a scoop of honey from one of the big pots, and a long crisp roll. Nobody bothered her as she moved back to her place at the table.

While she was partaking of a leisurely breakfast, the sloppy be-aproned little man with the big toothless smile came in from the cookhouse. He took her presence as a matter of course and with a respectful, 'Mornin', miss,' he got on with his work of clearing away.

He was up at the far end of the dining hall by the time Alex had finished her coffee. Leaving the table and taking the steps down from the platform, she walked the length of the hut and nodded pleasantly to him as she went out.

The sun was already warming the world out of doors. Surrounded by cranes swinging clusters of logs through the air in the distance, loaded trucks rumbling back and forth, and monster-like machinery lurching over the uneven ground, she made her way back to the clinic.

It took little time to clean and tidy her room. Her bed made up again and after a cool rinse off with soap and water following her work, she changed from jumper and skirt to white overall, smoothed her hair and went to take up her duties as camp nurse in the clinic.

So far no one had come along to test her abilities in that

field. Nevertheless she had plenty to do investigating stocks and arranging things to her own way of working. She had checked off the instruments against the inventory, and was busy re-packing rolls of lint on a shelf, when the sound of a vehicle of sorts skidding and bouncing to a stop outside drew her attention to the open window. She was in time to see Grant Mitchell ease his frame out of a jeep and make his way over to the door of the clinic.

Alex continued with her work as he came in, re-stacking the blue packets of lint in the glass-fronted cupboard across the room. From this she went on to making a list of other medical stock.

No word of greeting passed between her and the logging camp boss. Big in pale dusty slacks and rough shirt, he stood inside the doorway for a moment. Then he began to saunter idly around the room, casting his glance over this and that. Alex ignored the derogatory curl of his smile. Cool and trim and perfectly assured in her own department, she wore an air of quiet authority as she went about her tasks.

He eyed her now and again with lazy arrogance when she moved past him, but something about her crisp white coat and straight slim shoulders seemed to deflate much of the mockery in him, leaving him with a slightly ill-at-ease grin.

When she had to stop close beside him to open the drawer of a metal cabinet, he dug a hand into his pocket and throwing something with a rattle on top, he drawled, 'I've brought you the keys to the drug cupboard.'

Her dark head bent while she checked over various rolls of surgical plaster, Alex replied carpingly, 'Thank you. It does help to be able to get in there.'

The antagonism crackled on the silence between them. It was the kind that said they knew just where they stood with each other. In the thick of it Grant Mitchell flexed his frame cynically and asked, 'Do you drive?'

'No.' Alex's reply needed no thought. In the years she had spent looking after her aunt she had rarely seen a car, apart from the doctor's, much less learned how they worked.

'It's just as well.' The logging camp boss shrugged,

49

eyeing her with a supercilious smile. 'I don' somehow see you behind the wheel of a jeep.' He strolled over to the field telephone on the wall, adding on a sour note as he went, 'That means working out a new scheme for getting you where you're needed.'

Alex watched him test the telephone, trying to visualize for herself what the previous routine had been. After some thought she asked, 'Did Mrs. MacTavish drive?'

The logging camp boss replaced the instrument and strolled back to look at her with that bent superior smile of his. He thrust his hands lazily into his pockets and told her, 'Mrs. Mac did everything. She could handle the jeep around the forests better than an Abo rides a horse.'

Alex closed the drawer she had been bent over, smoothly to hide her irritation. It seemed that the camp was not only full of supermen. It had recently employed a superwoman too!

She raised her head from her task. 'Well, if Mrs. Mac-Tavish drove a car—' She had been almost on the point of retaliating in annoyed tones, 'then *I* will too.' But remembering to keep a hold on her equanimity she finished mildly, 'Then I'd better, hadn't I?' Meeting the brown glance levelly, she asked, 'Does it take long to learn?'

'Depends on the pupil,' Grant Mitchell replied, looking her over in a way that displayed his own searing scepticism to the full.

Alex ignored it and looked out of the window. Indicating the jeep there, she asked, before moving purposefully towards the door, 'Is that what Mrs. MacTavish used to drive?'

Nodding, the logging camp boss fell into step beside her, taking his scepticism along with him in the form of a curling smile. He stood aside for her at the open doorway and as she preceded him out Alex asked, merely on the point of interest, 'By the way, what's an Abo?'

'Aborigine,' Grant Mitchell barked at her. 'Most of them work on the sheep stations in the outback nowadays. Any Australian knows that.'

He led the way to the jeep. Alex would have stepped in

behind the wheel, but she was guided round to the passenger seat to the sarcastic renderings of, 'Give the buildings around here a chance!'

She sat with a poker-straight back as the big frame slid in beside her. To disguise the discomfort she felt as the car shot forward and bounced out towards an open space alongside the trees, she asked on a higher pitched note, 'How is Mr. Stronowsky?'

'Still got both arms, so they tell me,' Grant Mitchell tossed at her above the breeze. And then as though to shock her he added, shooting her his flinty gleam, 'He'll survive to come back and turn the air blue again around here with that pretty mouth of his.'

Alex kept her gaze fixed in front of her. She struggled to keep a flush from creeping up into her cheeks. The contents of Mike Stronowsky's language, coming in for a gust of it as she had at the time of his accident, was something she would rather not recall.

On a strip of land away from the huts, the logging camp boss jerked to a stop and prising himself out of his seat came round to tell her unceremoniously, 'Move over.'

Alex took up her position behind the wheel, her glance travelling over the knobs and levers around the dashboard. She listened coolly to the crisp instructions she was given, trying her hand occasionally at the controls when she was allowed to.

Her first attempt at taking the car forward resulted in a series of leapfrog jerks which left her gripping the wheel with the slightly panic-stricken feeling that she had no idea how to stop the bucking monster.

Her second try wasn't much better. First the wheel was slack in her hands, then when she least expected it, it sprang into rigid life and started to drive itself. Snaking all over the open strip completely out of control was a trifle unnerving, to say the least. And her instructor didn't help, with his conflicting orders.

Trying to gain a firm hold on the wheel as they skidded around, she told him icily, 'If you would stop bellowing in my ear, I might get the hang of it.'

Grant Mitchell threw a frustrated glance to the sky, and guiding her over one obstacle after another, he cursed growlingly, 'I never thought I'd find myself playing nursemaid to a nurse.'

With unruffled tenacity Alex stuck at it until she was at least driving in a reasonably straight line. When she had done several comparatively smooth runs backwards and forwards along the strip, executing the turns gingerly at either end, the logging camp boss leaned back in his seat to drawl mockingly, 'Okay, you've proved you know the difference between the ground and the trunk of a tree.' In case there was any danger of her taking this as some form of praise, he tacked on laconically as he moved round to the driving seat, 'It might help if you could get the jeep to see it too.'

Alex, sitting rigidly erect in her seat, left him to his derisive mood. She was too acutely conscious by this time of certain bruised spots about her person, obtained by the bouncing action and hard seats of the jeep.

Bumping over the uneven ground back to the huts proved to be something of an ordeal, especially when she felt a certain whimsically taunting glint directed her way from time to time in between lurches.

Outside the clinic she dismounted stiffly, but not without dignity, and walked unwaveringly up to the door. Grant Mitchell was ahead of her with his easy strides. He stood aside to let her move past him, his big frame swaying with arrogant amusement. Alex would have been quite pleased to see the back of him there and then, but as though he was loath to terminate his enjoyment he strolled inside the doorway after her.

It must have been the rattle of food cans being loaded in the distance which prompted him to make another of his acrimonious remarks. As she stood examining her overall to see if she ought to change it for a clean one, he drawled with that warped smile of his, 'By the way, did I tell you? We have our meal transported out to us on the job during the day. That means the dining hut stays shut until the evening.'

Alex looked up at this. If there was no midday meal on

the camp, what was she expected to do?

Answering her unspoken question with undisguised pleasure, he flicked his glinting brown glance casually around the clinic to tell her, 'There's always the cookhouse, of course.'

Impassively Alex went back to scanning her overall. As he turned to leave she forestalled his parting shot by smiling tartly and crowing after him, 'I know! Don't tell me! Mrs. Mac *always* lunched in the cookhouse.'

His big shoulders framed in the doorway for a second before striding away, the logging camp boss twisted her a sardonic grin to reply, 'How did you guess?'

CHAPTER THREE

THAT was Alex's initiation into life in a South Australian logging camp with Grant Mitchell running things; a rough, tough existence far removed from anything she had imagined, but one she took on with a certain even-tempered cool.

During the first days she tackled the job of reorganizing her room, searching out oddments of wood and fittings from the disused offices next door, and experimenting with material derived from a pair of old but good quality curtains she had discovered tucked away on a shelf in the laundry hut.

After much careful measuring and sewing she was eventually able to walk into her room in her spare moments to see the rough wall shelves she had devised, neatly distinguished with pale-coloured cotton, and a matching piece gathered across the lower half of the window to give her complete privacy.

In the clinic she soon became used to attending to the various ills of the lumberjacks who passed through, cleaning cuts received through the clumsy handling of machinery, treating bruises and abrasions, and prescribing for torn muscles. Often too, she was asked in plaintive tones for something to cure a thick head; to settle a queasy stomach. More than once after a night of bawdy rowdyism on the camp, she was tempted to accompany the pills she handed out with the advice that a little less drinking and a little more sleep would work just as well. But guessing that her words would have little effect, she refrained.

Each lunchtime she learned to eat a lone meal amidst the steam and clatter of the cookhouse. Here she became acquainted with Pop Doolin, the little man dwarfed by his big apron and wide toothless smile. Running backwards and forwards to serve her with his enormous helpings of food, badgering the cooks for the best of what was going, on her behalf, he soon made it clear that he was prepared to go through fire and water for her.

In the dining hut in the evenings she gradually got to know the men at her table. There was Wes Brissac, the thickset, puckish-faced figure who was Grant Mitchell's right-hand man, Buff Riley of fire control, and Casey Hall on the engineering side, and his crew.

Naturally aloof after the years spent alone with her aunt, she was friendly with them in a distant way. They were respectful of this, greeting her and bidding her good-bye when they left, but otherwise keeping their raucous laughter and dubious conversation to themselves.

In time she became reasonably proficient at handling the jeep, but like the rest of her working routine there were no cushioned comforts provided. At least once a week, usually when he was teaching her the idiosyncrasies of the jeep, Grant Mitchell would remind her with his curled smile that the bus for Denver's Creek was waiting for her any time she wanted it.

On these occasions Alex found no difficulty in ignoring him. She was too intent on mastering the steering of this contraption she was going to have to drive.

In spite of its ruggedness the life suited her. In the mornings she would wake up to feel the sun putting a sparkle in the air. In the evenings she strolled in the mellowing light amongst the trees at the back of the clinic, gazing up at the roof of cool green, listening to the chuckle of the birds.

Despite her somewhat severe hair-style, there was a soft bloom on her cheeks, a calm good-humoured light in her eyes.

When she was sufficiently instructed in the ways of the jeep, though she was never at ease in the driving seat, she was able to take up full nursing duties. This entailed going out into the working areas in the forest when the occasion demanded it, to attend to minor injuries.

Here she got to know the lumberjacks at first hand; the married ones with wives and families in the cities, and the single ones, the drifters who moved around from camp to camp throughout Australia, working a summer here and a winter there, and enjoying their freedom to the full. Men with such names as Hunk Skopoploulous, Waldo Shannon, Shiner Davis, and others going by the outlandish nicknames of Mugsy, Cobby, Shank, Slim, to mention but a few. They were noisy, loud-mouthed, full of earthy humour, and it was inevitable that Alex would have to come in for their spate of catcalls, whistles and crude remarks, whenever she arrived on the scene. In their joking, teasing way they made no secret of the fact that they preferred the new nurse to the departed Mrs. MacTavish, a woman they referred to indecorously as Battling Bertha.

The air was so bawdy at times that Alex, though not unable to see the humour of it, was hard put to it to keep her dignity; to keep the blush from creeping into her cheeks.

An example of the men's ribald teasing was on an afternoon when she answered the ring of the field telephone on the clinic wall, to be told that Buzz Williams, working with the second thinning team on the north side of the camp, had jumped from scaling a tree and done something with his ankle. It was considered unwise for him to put his weight on it until it had been looked at.

Alex locked up the clinic and climbed in behind the wheel of the jeep. The air was hot with the beginnings of summer. She had just returned on duty after the midday break and to stave off the lethargy one always felt at this time of day, she had washed with fern-scented soap and re-combed her hair into its neat coil at the nape of her neck. These were the days when she congratulated herself on her choice of garment for the job. The white overalls she had purchased retained their crispness and tailored look in spite of constant washings, and they were always cool and comfortable to work in.

She drove following the directions she had been given, alighting only when the track she had been following petered out and the men could be seen working on a steep rise so thickly populated with the ruler-straight trunks of pines that it would have been impossible to drive any further even if the ground had been level.

Medical bag in her hand, she made her way up the slope, and soon spotted the injured man sitting leaning with his back against a tree and happily smoking a cigarette.

As she had come to expect now, the hoots and whistles and lewd remarks started the moment she appeared and followed her along the path, the lumberjacks working closest to the route standing to eye her in their openly impudent way.

Alex climbed, keeping her gaze trained steadily ahead. She knew their swaggering glances were raking every inch of her. She was careful to give no hint of this. The fact that Grant Mitchell, waiting to give her details of the accident, had moved out on to the path and was walking just a few feet ahead of her did nothing to lessen her ordeal.

At one section a curly-headed figure, stripped to the waist, gave an uncouth wolf-whistle as she passed by. His mate, eyeing her implacable slim frame cheekily, advised him in scoffing tones, 'She's ice, man.'

The curly-headed individual watched her remorselessly and growled back with a grin, 'But nice ice.'

Alex battled to keep an even colour and continued on her way. As it turned out, the injury she had been called out to attend was merely a sprained ankle, and she was able to leave as soon as she had strapped it up.

The hint of a humorous light would usually show in her calm grey eyes once she was well away from these boisterous work scenes. She knew the men's antics and taunts were a natural letting off of steam; a harmless fun which a crowd of men anywhere would indulge in, given the chance, and beneath her cool exterior she accepted this.

However, there was one of these workers, a lumberjack whom, much as she would have preferred to, she couldn't dismiss as lightly as the others. His name was Clem Atkins. He was big and brutish with small sharp eyes and a leer for a smile. He also had a habit of swaggering around and tugging his trousers up at the waist with his great hands, whenever she was near. Alex had disliked him on sight.

Though he was as open and as loud-mouthed as the others with his ribald comments, his eyes, when they followed her, held something which belied his harmless apeish pose. She had always made a point of looking through him with an arctic stare whenever they met, in the hope of withering him on the spot. So far she hadn't succeeded.

Luckily her duties didn't bring her much into contact with him, and when they didn't, she forgot him.

She put no special significance on his appearance one day in the clinic. He had sustained a cut on his finger which admittedly was only small, but because of the high rate of infection caused by a substance in the soil, the practice was to take every precaution.

She cleaned the finger with antiseptic lotion, checked for any foreign bodies around the cut, then applied a suitable plaster to finish the job. She hadn't expected to see the man again, but the next day he came in to say that the finger was giving him pain.

Alex examined his hand carefully. In her professional capacity she asked him how he had received the cut and listened to his leering explanation with clinical reserve. She cleaned and treated the small wound again, which looked to be healing perfectly well to her, and applied another strong plaster.

The following afternoon she was occupied with matters concerning the business side of the clinic. The logging camp boss was supervising the unloading of supplies to the camp and she had just received a new consignment of medical stock. Going through the items, she was anxious to reassure herself that she had ordered wisely, otherwise she might have been more on her guard when Clem Atkins made yet another appearance.

Seeing him lumber in through the open doorway, she left the carton of supplies and stepped towards him to listen to his renewed complaints that his hand was still troubling him. Suspicion began to form at the back of her mind only when she had once again removed the plaster from the grubby finger. The cut was healing perfectly.

The big lumberjack was brushing close to her. Her nerves tensed a little at the hot breath she felt on her cheek. Still looking at his hand, she summoned up her iciest tones to tell him, 'Mr. Atkins, there's nothing at all the matter with this finger. You're wasting both your time and mine. Please leave the clinic at once.'

Clem Atkins' reply was to bring his bulk up close to her. His big mouth flopped into a sheepish smile as he murmured hoarsely, 'Aw, c'mon now, nursie. You know why I'm here.'

In the quietness of the hut, with no sound outside except the occasional stirring of the breeze at the open windows, Alex was suddenly riveted with fear. Masking it as well as she could with a formidable expression, she forced a withering note into her voice to inform him, 'Mr. Atkins, kindly take your games somewhere else. I at least have work to do.'

The small flame-lit eyes remained to hover above her. 'Nursie, I told you!' Clem Atkins whined, his slack mouth glistening, 'I'm here on business. Important business.' These last two words delivered with a menacing smile, his great arms came out and fastened themselves around her. At first Alex was too suffocated to do anything in the beefy embrace, until she saw that leering mouth straining to reach hers. Then she struggled with everything she possessed to avoid it. For a few brief seconds she managed to keep it at bay, but she might have been pitting her strength against an eight-foot bear.

Holding her with little cost to his hulking frame, Clem Atkins smiled over her thickly, 'Stop making out I'm not good enough for you, nursie. You don't know me yet.'

Locked as though her whole body was encased in granite, Alex thought her senses would explode as the big moon-like unshaven features and the fleshy lips came down to black everything out. She heard no sound except the rush of blood pounding in her ears, the hammer of a pulse somewhere in her head.

The voice that cracked out from the doorway was but a faint noise in the background of her struggles, until the hairy face unfastened itself from hers and she heard the voice rip out again, 'Atkins!'

The octopus-like arms dropped quickly away from her. Through a red mist she saw Grant Mitchell standing just inside the doorway. On the tail of his sharp call he fired another order at the man up the room, 'Get back to work!'

'Yes, boss.' With a slack grin the swaying lumbering frame stumbled towards the door. As he passed by, Grant Mitchell eyed him to clip, 'If I find you hanging around the clinic again, I'll break your skull.'

'Aw, boss!' The ape-like features took on an injured look. 'Just for trying to get a bit of . . .?'

'You heard me,' Grant Mitchell nodded him out briskly. 'Now move!'

Big feet shuffled reluctantly out of the door. When the sound of them faded in the distance the logging camp boss sent his gaze up the room. His voice travelling along the silent length of it towards Alex, he asked, 'Are you all right?'

Alex closed her eyes over her revulsion, clutching at the desk for support. 'Of course I'm all right,' she snapped quiveringly.

Oh, he didn't have to tell her! She knew what he was thinking. She had been warned of the hazards of working amongst a crowd of lusty lumberjacks. It was no one's fault but her own if she couldn't look after herself.

She waited, listening to the wild thud of her heart. It was several minutes before she felt strong enough to stand without support. She turned then, expecting to find herself alone in the clinic, and was mildly surprised to see the logging camp boss still standing there.

She smoothed her hair about her drained features and he moved in at last. He flicked the paper he had been holding in his hand to tell her, 'I've brought you the invoice. I thought you might want to check off your stock.'

'Thank you,' Alex nodded, not looking at him. 'Please put it on the desk.'

She heard the slip of paper being placed down, then after a few moments the footsteps turned towards the door. She reached for the invoice in time to see Grant Mitchell striding away.

On the Friday at the end of the month there was an undercurrent of excitement about the camp. At the table in the dining hut that evening, Wes Brissac explained to Alex that the following morning was the day when everyone went to Oaktown to cash their monthly pay cheques. He offered to give her a lift.

If she had known that the conveyance he had referred to was a lorry and that they would be sharing the cab with two other men from their table she doubted whether she would have accepted so readily. As it was there was little she could do about it when she hurried to the arranged departure spot in the mid-morning sunshine to find the vehicle loaded with high-spirited lumberjacks, all stamping their feet with gleeful anticipation and impatience, and Wes with his rubber-like, good-humoured features, waving her into the seat next to him.

As silk stockings, slim grey skirt and neat white blouse was not exactly the attire to go climbing up into lorry cabs with, it took some time to negotiate the difficulties. But taking it carefully she made it at last. With much cat-calling and whistles from the back and considerable noise from the cab, the door was shut and the lorry rumbled off.

On this second trip to Oaktown Alex was able to see much more of the countryside than she had had time to notice when she had been crouching supporting Mike Stronowsky's injured arm. Above the occasional bursts of singing and raucous laughter behind them, Wes talked to her about his family in Melbourne. He told her proudly about his two oldest sons, each one managing a sheep station in Queensland, and of his two grandchildren by one of them, whom he hoped to see in the autumn.

Coming into Oaktown, Alex saw the timber mills on the outskirts, clusters of low buildings surrounded by piles of logs many of which had probably been cut at the Noongwalla logging camp.

The town itself when they drove into it was lively with Saturday shoppers, the wide verandas fronting the buildings thronging with gay-clad figures. Wes showed her the procedure for cashing her pay cheque at the bank, then went his own way.

After the bank Alex looked for a café. She planned to do some shopping, but as it was nearing lunchtime she decided it would be better to eat first. Along the main street she found a quiet corner in a small wood-panelled interior set out with check-clothed tables and knobbly wooden chairs. The men at the tables wore brilliant white shirts and neat striped ties. The women were less formal in sleeveless cotton dresses or bright blouses and skirts. Alex felt at home in the friendly Australian atmosphere.

Relaxed and refreshed after a leisurely meal, she started out to investigate the shops. There was one item she had set her mind on from the moment she knew she was coming into town. The tall bare windows in the clinic were crying out for something to soften their gauntness. What each one needed was a length of gossamer drape, something that would waft gently in the breeze, giving a soothing restful effect to the room. If she could find a suitable fabric she could charge it to the company later.

It took her most of the afternoon hunting through the rolls of cloth stacked in the small shops. Then when she was on the point of giving up, having seen everything but what she had in mind, she spotted the very thing in a store she had passed earlier that morning close to the bank.

The curtain fabric trickling through her fingers was smooth and creamy and had a faint check design in the open weave. Measuring the windows in her mind's eye, she bought generously, allowing for wide hems.

The rest of her shopping was negligible. She bought half a dozen tablets of good quality lavender-perfumed soap, and a box of tea-bags, Mrs. MacTavish's half packet of tea long since being exhausted. She was tempted to go back to the same café along the main street for an evening meal, but bearing in mind that Wes Brissac had told her they wouldn't be returning to the camp until late, she decided to spend the time walking out of town a little way.

She dined eventually in a leafy walled-off area, where flowering gum trees cast dappled shadows on the table, and the menus were painted on the end of sawn-off barrels hung around the walls. She lingered until the sun went down leaving the sky a molten gold.

Lights were twinkling in the centre of the town when she

walked back. Whereas in the daytime the shops were the only thing one noticed, now everything was shuttered and the bars had come into their own. Amply lit and crowded with men, there was one every hundred yards or so along the main thoroughfare.

Making her way towards the civic buildings, Alex found a library. She sat in the peace and musty-smelling cool, browsing through a book on the plant life of Australia, but at nine o'clock a smiling attendant told her that it was time to close, so once again she was out in the night.

Nearby were the usual civic gardens of a small country town, stretches of green lawn bordered by formal flower beds and lit discreetly by playing fountains. She walked here for a while, then turned her steps purposefully to where the lorries would be parked. She didn't know what the men's idea of a late hour was, but hers was any time from now.

On the way out from town towards Noongwalla, she found the vehicles waiting in the spot which Wes Brissac had pointed out to her that morning, a dusty open space surrounded by a few stunted trees and various trading establishments. The only building showing any sign of life at the moment was a long low structure down one side which was fronted by a corrugated iron-roofed veranda and a row of brilliantly lit open windows and doors. The din of loud voices, hearty laughter and clinking glasses spilled out on the night.

With a wry smile Alex made her way along to the first of the lorries. Trust the men to park within stumbling distance of a bar!

With difficulty she made her way up into her seat, then dropped her parcels thankfully beside her. At least she could wait here in reasonable comfort apart from the fumes of petrol and oil under her nose.

It was dark inside the cab. After a while her gaze was drawn towards the main entrance to the bar, a distance from where she was sitting of no more than a few yards. Amidst the noise and commotion there, she could see in the bright glow masculine shapes propping up the pillars of the veranda, glass tankards in their hands. And as one would expect

in a community the size of Oaktown, there were girls too —
young, and not so young. Attractive, smooth, they hung
about the entrance, swishing their hair provocatively, sending their laughter in through the doorway towards the groups
of unheeding men. At least the men appeared to be unheeding until around ten o'clock when one after the other
they stumbled out, slow grins forming on their faces as they
reached for a feminine shoulder for support.

Alex, sitting quietly waiting to be driven back to the
camp, stirred herself at what looked to be signs of an exodus
at last, although she could see Wes Brissac and most of the
other family men lingering over their beers and their conversation at the bar.

It was while she was watching and wondering a little impatiently why they too didn't get themselves out to the
lorries that she saw Grant Mitchell move out towards the
doorway.

Clad in a pale summer suit, he strolled out with the same
firm step he used around the logging camp. Hardly had he
got two strides out of the doorway than the flurry of girls
fluttered towards him. He came through the group with one
in each arm, holding them close to him on either side and
smiling down at them with his white even smile.

Alex found she couldn't remove her eyes from that smile;
nor from the silken tresses spilling on to his shoulders, and
the smooth feminine glances turned up to his. Oblivious to
the fact that the lorry she was seated in was parked almost
opposite the doorway, and that in her neat white blouse she
was perfectly visible, her gaze remained glued on the big
figure. So much so that when inevitably Grant Mitchell's
own glance lifted from his sophisticated companions and
came straight up in a path to collide with hers, she was
powerless to do anything about it.

She noticed that nothing faded from his smile as he saw
her. In fact it was harder and whiter than ever. And what
was more disconcerting, he seemed in no hurry to take his
openly taunting glint elsewhere.

Alex turned her head abruptly the other way, and
began to study the faint lettering on the signs around the

shadowy square.

From there she must have dozed, for it was after twelve when the door of the cab finally opened and Wes Brissac and his companions climbed inside. As they made their way back to the logging camp, she sat watching the darkened countryside flash by. The tuneless singing and riotous laughter coming from the back of the lorry defied any further attempts on her part to rest until she reached the peace of her bed.

She was laying up the trolley with clean white covers fresh from the laundry on Monday morning when Grant Mitchell came into the clinic. Apart from being aware of him when he had been sat at his table in the dining hut the previous evening, she hadn't seen him since his darkly smiling glance had lifted from his feminine companions and collided head on with hers, outside the Oaktown bar on Saturday night.

If she was thinking of that moment now, it was obvious, as he strolled around with a hard gleam in his eyes, making no move to explain the reason for his visit, that he was too.

He flicked a cursory look over the papers on the desk, then turning to watch her as she continued with her work, he asked with that warped smile he reserved for her, 'Enjoy your day out in Oaktown?'

'Very much, thank you,' Alex replied starchily. She picked up the sponge-holding forceps to polish them and added caustically, 'No need to ask if everyone else did.'

Though they both knew specifically who she was talking about, the logging camp boss, deliberately choosing to misinterpret her implication, gave her his brown glint and drawled, 'The men, you mean? They always do.'

Alex found herself polishing a little more vigorously. Adopting his tactics, but unable to keep her tones quite steady, she stated acidly, 'It's obvious they don't make the trip just to cash their pay cheques.'

'Be pretty dull for the town if they did,' came the ironic reply.

Alex didn't share his obscure amusement at the way they

were juggling with the subject. In fact she was surprised to find her mood distinctly waspish as she reiterated on a carping note, 'You *did* say for the town?'

'That's right,' the logging camp boss countered, watching her cold disapproval with a slant to his smile. 'Let a crowd of men loose in one and they're liable to want to paint it up a bit.'

Alex felt slightly suffocated under his meaningful, whimsical look. Floundering, she clutched at the memory of Wes Brissac and all the other family men who had stayed with their tankards of beer at the bar, and whisking a scalpel handle back into place, she remarked stiffly, 'The married ones have more sense, of course.'

His big shoulders hunched, Grant Mitchell kept his brown glint on her long enough before he replied with a lazy smile, 'Depends how you look at it.'

Fighting the rising colour at her throat, Alex busied herself unfolding fresh covers and flapping them out noisily. She wished he wouldn't be so smug about his female acquaintances. She was sure *she* didn't care what he did with his free time in Oaktown.

It must have been a full five minutes later when, stirring himself to stroll about again, the logging camp boss said offhandedly, 'I went to see Stronowsky while I was in town.'

Partly in relief at the change of topic, but mostly with genuine concern for the man who had almost been crushed by a tree, Alex turned to inquire, 'How is he?'

'Making a rapid recovery,' Grant Mitchell replied dryly. He looked at her to add, 'In spite of the tussle he's been having with the doctors lately.' At Alex's questioning glance he moved in to rock back on his heels beside her as she worked and went on, 'He was all set to go down to the coast for convalescence, but he's got this fool notion he wants to meet the nurse who saved his arm.'

Alex lowered her gaze over a new rush of embarrassment. Her hands moving rapidly around the trolley again, she said in brisk tones, 'I only did what any trained person would have done in the circumstances.'

'That's what I tried to tell him,' Grant Mitchell drawled with his curled smile and his big shrug, 'but Mike's always been a stubborn cuss. The only way I could get him to go was to tell him I'd bring you down to Port Brennan as soon as he's settled in.'

Alex gave him her clear straightforward look and said civilly, 'Naturally I want to do all I can to speed his recovery.'

Having disclosed the purpose of his visit, the logging camp boss moved towards the door. 'I'll pick you up after work on Saturday,' he said unceremoniously. 'Port Brennan's about eighty miles south, just beyond Mount Gambier. We should do it in an afternoon.'

Alex, busy dusting over the glass front of the liniment cupboard, nodded coolly in agreement as he went out.

CHAPTER FOUR

SHE had plenty to keep her busy during the following week. When she wasn't working in the clinic, she spent all her free time measuring up and tacking the lengths of curtain material in preparation for stitching. Saturday came round almost before she knew it.

After lunch over at the cookhouse she made her way through to her room, discarding her white overalls as soon as she was in the privacy of the dim corridor leading to it. In silk underslip she washed liberally with cool water and lavender-scented soap.

Normally it wouldn't have taken her more than a few minutes to decide what to wear, but today for some reason she found herself being over-critical. Plain white blouse and straight slim skirt somehow didn't seem satisfactory. Nor did any of the other garments that hung on hangers from a rope she had suspended across one corner of the room.

The nearest thing she could find to appease the critical light in her eyes was a dove grey suit in tailored linen, with self-coloured embroidered cuffs on the short sleeves, and matching collar. Her hair was no trouble, of course. Waving away from her face and caught back in its usual coil, it would stay unmolested like that, as it did every day, until she unpinned it for bed at night.

She had picked up a brown leather handbag containing oddments she might need during the course of the afternoon, when the sound of a car came from out front. She made her way through and out to the door of the clinic, the heels of her shoes tapping evenly over the polished wood floor.

With the keys in her hand she stepped out to lock the door, allowing herself only the merest glimpse of the big figure waiting beside the shooting brake, casually attired in lightweight suit and pastel-coloured shirt. Grant Mitchell's glance, in turn, seemed to be more with the secured premises of the clinic than it was with her as she stepped towards the car. The only indication he gave that he knew she was wearing something other than her work uniform was in the moment she was about to move past him and into the car. As he held the door open for her, he said curtly, 'Hold it!'

Taking a cloth to the seldom used passenger seat, he rubbed off the dust of the forest and the stray twigs, then nodded her in. Alex stepped inside and with her handbag settled neatly in her lap she said in her naturally unfussy tones, 'Thank you.'

Within a few minutes they were out of the logging camp and speeding along the road towards Oaktown. From there, leaving the usual Saturday afternoon shoppers crowding the pavements in the centre of the town, they took the route south.

With only the hum of the tyres on the road to break the silence, Alex kept her gaze on the scenery, her back and shoulders straight. She made no attempt at conversation with the man seated beside her. What was there to say? She was nurse at the logging camp, running the clinic as she saw fit. He was the camp boss. A man whose sole occupation was in seeing to it that enough trees were cut down, trimmed and shipped to the timber mills, and who spent his free time when it pleased him, relaxing in a town where there was no shortage of women.

Oh yes! Much as it irritated her, she hadn't been able to banish from her mind the picture of those smooth-haired enigmatically smiling females, gazing up into his eyes and leaning close against him.

For his part, Grant Mitchell made a few taciturn comments during the journey. They had left the forest lands behind, and Alex was noticing the parched look of the countryside, when he told her, 'It doesn't normally get so arid this far south. We've had an unusually low rainfall this year.'

The road was good and they speeded on to where groups of sheep were grazing on the dry yellowing stubble as contentedly as if they had been in an English meadow. Then the proximity of the coast, with its humidity, began making itself evident in the bursts of clover and clumps of foliage. The pastures became progressively greener and low-spreading trees were dotted across the landscape, their stark branches a riotous tangle of blossom. In a humorous moment Alex thought of them as so many old ladies all desperately in need of new hair-do's.

They bypassed the city of Mount Gambier with its signs urging one to try its motels, to see its volcanic lakes, or to swim in its olympic pool. The coast, with its pale dappled sky and line of blue sea, came into view after several miles of dune ranges and sandy plain. Despite her rigid posture, Alex breathed deeply, enjoying to the full the fresh salty tang of the sea air.

Port Brennan was little more than a fishing village, with a horse trough in its centre, and a stone soldier blowing his bugle amidst a circle of trees. Out on the sea front the road ran alongside a white beach littered with seaweed and small boats. On the land side cottages climbed up a green incline. A long low building, spanking new and blending in perfectly with the greenery around the curve of the cove, turned out to be the convalescent home they were looking for.

Grant Mitchell parked the car beside a small jetty, and they walked through lawned gardens to the entrance. Carved in stone along one wall of the reception lounge was a series of hefty workmanlike figures wielding tools of some kind. Alex viewed the work while the logging camp boss inquired at the desk for the whereabouts of the man they had come to see.

When he had obtained the information he nodded towards one of the ground-floor corridors for Alex's benefit. He accompanied her down the length of it, his shoes tapping over the polished tiles at longer intervals, alongside her short brisk step.

A long line of doors behind them, they came to the correct number at last, almost at the end of the corridor. Grant Mitchell knocked briefly, then stepped in to hold the door for Alex.

As she followed him inside she didn't try to mask her delight at what she saw – a window almost the entire length of the opposite wall looked out on to a view of blue sea, green tropical foliage, and curving craggy headland.

The room she was in, sunnily lit by the wide expanse of sky, was small but beautifully furnished, with armchairs, coffee table, television and bookshelf. An open doorway to the left showed a similarly tiny furnished bedroom, with bed neatly made up. Another open doorway beside the long picture window led on to a small balcony holding basketwork chairs and glass-topped table.

Because of the compact size of the apartment, all this Alex was able to take in at little more than a glance. Which was just as well, for in one of the armchairs, obviously poised waiting for this moment, his face shining and splitting into two parts by a smile that was forming there, his deep-set eyes glazing over with pleasure, sat Mike Stronowsky.

He threw out a big hand as the logging camp boss approached. 'Grant! You old son of a b. . . .' and stopped himself short by clamping his jaw up to his grin and sliding a sheepish squint over towards Alex.

Grant Mitchell shook the hand warmly, his own white smile much in evidence. 'Quite a pad you've got here, Mike,' he drawled, looking about him. Then lifting an arm towards Alex he made the introduction, flicking his glint between them, 'This is Miss Leighton, whom I believe you wanted to meet.'

The huge frame rose momentarily from the chair. Alex stepped up and took the big hand. 'It's nice to see you looking so well, Mr. Stronowsky,' she said pleasantly.

'Aw, call me Mike.' His mountainous bulk went slack with embarrassment, while his grip was wringing her hand off.

He dropped back into his seat and waved her clumsily into one of the two places across from him, stating with the pride of a small boy, 'I got you a chair all ready, see.' And sidling a twinkling squint at the logging camp boss from beneath his shaggy overhanging eyebrows, ' 'Cos like Grant said, he vos bringing you down today, and like I told him, if he didn't I'd br . . .' His ugly battered countenance collapsed, all sheepishness again, after which an unsuppressed eagerness drove him to inquire avidly for news of the logging camp from his boss.

As he slapped his knee and threw in his own comments on the tales he heard of his workmates, Alex was able to observe him at her leisure.

He had a big square head covered with mottled stubble and long flat ears. At the moment the pallor of his skin and slackness of his body was that of a man who had recently been through a great deal. His injured arm was lost in the roomy sleeve of his clean striped hospital shirt, topping old slacks, but she had an idea that there would be quite a few scars to show.

There was nothing at all the matter with his voice. Loud and rumbling, it leapt to all corners of the room and beyond, each time he opened his rather cavernous mouth. His Slavic accent was enhanced by a thick meaty Australian drawl that thundered up from deep inside him and came chuckling out with all the ebullience of his nature. If he had a serious side to him it didn't show.

Watching him bulldoze his way in after the preliminary chat to monopolize the conversation, Alex was already finding herself fascinated by his pungent wit and mischievous turn of phrase. Within half an hour of taking her seat she was completely engulfed by the sheer clumsy force of Mike Stronowsky's personality, and liking it.

Relaxing with his visitors in the bright cheerful room, his great uncouth shape clashing with the dainty decor, he went on from discussing the idiosyncrasies of his work pals and how he had been the only lumberjack too slow to sidestep half a ton of timber that day, to relating earlier forestry scrapes he had been in.

With his big weather-bashed features doing all sorts of things and his deep-set squinting eyes darting back and forth, he was pure entertainment to listen to. He had a way of describing a situation which made one rock in one's chair. It occurred to Alex while she was watching him describe to her his dilemma one day when coming face to face with a six-foot kangaroo on a narrow ravine path that she hadn't laughed like this in years.

At one time during the afternoon, when her eyes were damp with amusement, they accidentally met Grant Mitchell's across the room. She had no idea what his thoughts were in that moment when his gaze rested on her. For her part she remembered thinking fleetingly that he didn't look at all like the logging camp boss she knew today, in his well-cut grey suit, its paleness accentuating his dark hair and his relaxed white smile.

The conversation came to a sudden halt when Mike, all remorse, remembered he had offered no refreshments to his guests. It was obvious he had gone to great pains to lay on everything he considered necessary for the afternoon, in the way he reached out with a lumbering flourish and drew forward a well-stocked trolley, his big ugly face beaming with pride.

Alex looked uncertainly at the array of bottles which were displayed for her benefit. In the silence that had descended Grant Mitchell drawled, 'Women don't usually go in for hard liquor, Mike.'

'Uh?' The big man's smile dropped lopsided. 'They don't?' He looked amazed and then askance. Coming to his rescue, Alex said, eyeing the small kitchenette in one corner of the room, 'I've got an awful weakness for tea.'

'*Tea?*' Mike's horrified stare swung from her to a patterned tin standing all on its own on a shelf in the corner. 'That is vot they ask me to drink here all the time!' He slumped. 'However, if . . .' As he made to rise, heavily intent on doing his best, Alex rose quickly, putting a hand on his arm. 'No, please! Let me,' she said with a smile.

After her rough home-made shelves plus one thick beaker and a well worn teapot, it was a delight to work in the super-de-luxe little kitchenette. She liked the idea of the convalescing patients being given the independence of preparing their own snacks as well as being supplied with the main meal of the day.

In gay tins she found sweet biscuits and plain ones and cellophane-wrapped crackers containing dainty portions of cheese. Reaching for cups and saucers, she asked who wanted what, over the men's conversation. The logging camp boss said lazily he would have tea. Mike gave a grimace, but with a suffering air said he would have tea too. Twinkling, Alex turned and put three good spoons in the pot.

To make a change of scenery she set the afternoon tea out on the glass-topped table out on the balcony and sat on a small stool, letting the men have the chairs. It was funny watching the ham-fisted Mike holding a dainty cup and saucer, something he obviously didn't make a practice of. But wanting to please and having resigned himself to the torture, he made valiant efforts to fit in with the scene.

Afterwards, Alex washed and replaced everything in what she was now convinced was, as far as this room patient was concerned, a seldom used kitchenette – the more so when she returned to her armchair and Mike got his own back on her by craftily insisting that she drink his health.

After all he had been through she couldn't think of refusing, as well he knew, though she drew the line at half an inch of the strong-smelling liquid in the bottom of her glass. As she sipped it and shuddering inwardly at the vile taste, she couldn't think what Mike saw in it to toss it back and smack his lips on. The logging camp boss drank no more than Alex.

The strip of sky across the window was deepening into the pink glow of dusk when they rose to go. Standing at the open door which Grant Mitchell held for her, Alex said her good-byes to the big good-natured lumberjack. Lacking the polish to express himself, he hadn't said thanks to her in so many words for what she had done for him, but she knew by his strong grip and his big smile that his gratitude went deep.

Grant Mitchell slapped him on the shoulder and told him to get the best out of his convalescence, while Mike in turn disclosed to him with a wicked grin details of the card game he was hoping to organize in his room that night. Then with a final wave from along the corridor, Alex and Grant Mitchell left.

Outside as they walked out of the gardens and towards the car Alex breathed in the sea breezes and watched the

74

waves lapping not far from her feet over the seaweed-strewn sand. Fascinated by the clear water and thinking of the lengthy drive back, she said with a longing look at the small jetty, 'Do you mind if I stroll a little?'

The logging camp boss stood shielding the cigarette he was lighting. 'Go ahead,' he said, keeping his eyes down over the flame. 'I'll wait by the car.'

Alex picked her way along the strewn concrete projection which was no more than a few yards long. At the end it fell abruptly away to reveal clusters of limpets and whirlpools of waves rapidly fading under a darkening sky.

Her head and body erect, she listened to the sighs and swishing sounds while welcoming the breeze on her face. There was something about standing out here suspended between sea and sky. All this space! The deep breath she inhaled escaped as a grateful sigh from her lips. Space! How she loved it! The forests, the fields, the sea! So different from the cloistered life she had led at Crabtree Terrace.

A silhouette against the gathering night, the breezes plucked at the hem of her skirt, rustling the wisps of hair about her face. She knew the logging camp boss was watching her from where he stood waiting beside the jetty, but strangely enough she didn't care. Only when her few minutes were up and she realized they must be on their way did she turn and walk briskly back to the car.

The door was opened promptly for her when she arrived. As she brushed past the big frame to step inside, she felt the brown eyes flicked over her, taking in her subdued sparkle. Dropping her own gaze to the ground, she took her seat and settled down for the journey back.

The lights of the little port were soon left behind, as they speeded towards Mount Gambier. After the blurred illuminations of the city had receded there was nothing but the grey ribbon of road unwinding itself in front of the headlights.

Alex found the silence restful, the hum of the tyres soothing. She had no idea where they were, and she made no effort to pinpoint their whereabouts by looking for signs along the road. Just now the shadowy interior of the car was

75

enough for her. The only thing the darkness tended to do was make her slightly more aware of the grey-suited figure seated behind the wheel. But that was inevitable, wasn't it? in such a small space.

She supposed the hands of her watch must have moved considerably by the time the lights of Oaktown began to show in the distance. Coming into the outskirts, Grant Mitchell spoke for the first time. 'All the cookhouse staff will be at the Noongwalla bar tonight,' he said crisply. 'We'd better get a meal in town.'

Alex watched, wondering what place he would make for. She was glad when he turned away from the main street with its groups of men and Saturday night ribaldry. An even more pleasant surprise was the fact that he knew of the leafy courtyard affair that she had more or less come upon by accident the previous Saturday on her walk out of town. There had been a leisurely air about it then, with its afternoon tea customers and sun-dappled shadows. Now it was clothed in evening elegance, its tables draped with rich damask cloths and silverware glinting in the soft lights, and yet the same tranquillity remained.

Alex waited at the entrance while Grant Mitchell parked the car, after which he guided her to a wallside table. Scanning the menu briefly, he didn't ask her what she preferred. Luckily everything he ordered was to her taste. He made no mention of it, but at the end of the meal he saw that she was served with a pot of tea for one.

It was while she was sipping this and Grant Mitchell was sat pulling leisurely on a cigarette that a sizeable group from a corner table rose and began to make their way out. Passing not far from where they were sitting, one woman, smooth, curvaceous, with cascading golden hair and a brilliant sparkle in her wide dark-fringed eyes glanced over, looked again, and detaching herself from the group, she swayed up, her arms wide, to exclaim, 'Grant darling! I didn't know this was your Saturday for town.'

Small white teeth showed in a parted vivacious smile, she bent as the logging camp boss half rose, so that for a moment broad shoulders and dark head were lost amidst a cloud of trailing golden strands and exotic perfume.

The fair head lifted briefly while Alex was looked over as though she was part of the tableware, then vivid pink finger-nails curling around the grey-suited sleeve, the low laughing voice was suggesting coaxingly, 'We're all going over to Bart's place. Come and join us, Grant, the gang will be tickled pink.'

With a crooked grin the logging camp boss straightened his rumpled tie and resuming his seat he drawled, 'Sorry, Martha, I've had a long day. Some other time.'

As though she knew better than to pursue the matter, the woman pouted attractively, shrugged her shapely shoulders and swayed resignedly on her way.

Hating herself for the tartness she couldn't conceal in her voice, Alex said, sending a satirical smile across the table, 'Don't let me keep you from anything.'

Grant Mitchell tugged deeply on his cigarette and leaned in towards the ashtray. He stubbed out the red ash lengthily, then rising, he replied casually, 'Like I said, it's been a long day. Let's go.'

Alex picked up her bag and was escorted out to the car.

The journey back to the logging camp between giant pines falling away into the darkness at the side of the road was completed in silence. At the door of the clinic Grant Mitchell took the keys from her and went in first to switch on the light. He flicked a look around, then gave her back the keys and made for the door. In the entrance he stopped and turned for a second while Alex was smoothing her hair and still blinking in the light. His glance hooded, he bade her a brief good night and went out to his car.

Alex locked up after him listening to his swift departure for his own quarters in a quick burst of life from the shoot-ing brake and an almost instantaneous fading of sound. As he had pointed out, he had had a long day.

With a heaviness she put down to tiredness she pushed the bolts home and turned towards her room. Of course it must have been trying for him driving her all the way down to the coast and back. After all, they weren't exactly good friends.

CHAPTER FIVE

WARM Saturday sunshine flooded in at the open door and windows of the clinic. Flexing her aching muscles, Alex soaked up the peace of the afternoon as she worked. It had been an irksome week.

On Monday morning, one of the big crane lorries which did most of the work with the heavy timber overturned. Thankfully no one had been hurt, but all the available help had been needed at the scene of the disaster to sort out the mess, including Alex who had been kept busy dabbing small cuts and removing splinters from hands.

Chaos had ruled for a couple of days with uprooted trees balancing on end, and the men grumbling at not being able to get on with their usual jobs. And to make matters worse, as the sprawling crane was the only up-to-date piece of equipment on the camp, Grant Mitchell's mood hadn't been very sweet.

Slowly order had been restored, then just when they had everything under control again, fire broke out. No one knew who had tossed the lighted cigarette down, but with every twig being tinder-dry, the tongues of yellow flame had leapt up from the bushes like an attacking animal and spread at an alarming rate.

Because they knew the source, the men trained in fire control were able to isolate the damage to one small section of the forest. Just the same, fighting the flames had meant a sleepless night for everyone, and constant vigil after that in case a stray spark had gained a hold elsewhere.

Alex, doing what she could for men choking with smoke, had hardly known at times how to stand herself, with her chest bursting and eyes smarting. It seemed that as fast as she got one firefighter back on the job, another came stumbling up, looking for some kind of relief. When at last the fire was out and only a desolate steaming area remained, she had driven back to the clinic and slept the clock round.

That had been a couple of days ago. Apart from a stiffness now she felt no worse for her adventures, all of which she came to accept as part of her job. Still, it was good to be free of nursing duties for the week-end.

She busied herself, listening to the drone of insects beyond the windows, musing generally over the past days. Only when a dusty twig-littered shooting brake pulled up outside did she remove her attention from her task long enough to tilt an eyebrow at the big figure emerging.

Having worked alongside him all week, the last person she expected to see out of company hours was the logging camp boss; though with the week's work-sheets in his hand, which he was possibly only just finding the time to attend to, he was quick to make it clear he had good reason for the visit.

His voice holding its usual crispness, he strode in with, 'Perhaps you would be good enough to explain this?' He rapped a hand at one of the entries on her work sheet and read out, 'Drapery for windows. Forty dollars.'

'Drapery means curtains,' Alex's voice floated down coolly from somewhere up the room. 'The place looks like a church hall without them. And psychologically they produce a restful effect for the patients.'

Grant Mitchell's reply was to finger the cascading lengths scattered around, stating sarcastically while he did so, 'This is a medical hut for lumberjacks, not a Harley Street waiting-room.'

'The soothing influence applies just the same,' Alex replied levelly, standing firm on the issue.

Over by the drug cupboard the logging camp boss put a tick on the work-sheet he was looking at and growled under his breath, 'Keep up with the interior decorating and the company's liable to go broke.'

He put his pencil away and tossing the clipped board down as though he was tired of holding it, he thrust his hands into his pockets and turned. It was then that he saw Alex for the first time since entering, and how she was positioned at the far window up the room.

The curtains were finished and ready to hand, and she

79

had wondered at first how she was going to manage to get up almost to the roof without steps or ladder, until it had occurred to her that the desk was heavy and solid and of a reasonable height. It had taken her some time to push it over to the wall, but standing on tip-toe in stockinged feet she found she could just about make the top ledge of the window.

As she strained now to find an anchor for the cord, Grant Mitchell fired up at her, moving in to eye her sharply from below, 'What the hell are you going up there?'

'Your language is not much better than your men's,' Alex replied haughtily from up on high. 'I'm fixing the curtains, as you can see.'

'Fixing to be the next patient around here, more like,' he barked. 'You'll break a leg leaning out like that. Get down!'

'I will, just as soon as I've finished,' Alex answered coldly. The man was never happy unless he was giving orders to someone.

Her fingers trembled slightly from the effort of stretching. Left on her own she knew she wouldn't have taken the same chances, but something about the figure standing below made her unsteady and reckless. She had a stubborn desire to reach the corner just to show him that she was quite capable of the job.

In his way he was stubborn too. Watching her balancing above him, calmly ignoring his order, he shot out a hand and gripping one teetering ankle he told her menacingly, 'You heard what I said. Get down. Now!'

Hardly had he uttered the last word than Alex was obliging him quicker than either of them had expected. Whether she had overreached in a blind bid to prove her superiority, or whether his powerful grip on her ankle had unsteadied her, there was no saying. All she knew was that suddenly the desk had ceased to support her and, her finger clutching at air, the cord, the curtains finding their own way down, the polished floor was racing up to meet her at an alarming rate.

Almost in the same moment the big frame whipped in to

80

block it out. Arms feeling like steel chains caught her, practically snapping her in two, while the weight of her body in turn shook the muscular rock-like one it fell against, nearly keeling the two of them over.

It was a full minute before the earth came to rights again. And even then Grant Mitchell's frame was still blocking out most of the scenery.

Alex came to life against him. Winded and angry at her helplessness in his arms, she struggled to find her feet quivering snappishly, 'If you hadn't come along interfering, I could have done the job easily.'

'Sure you could,' Grant Mitchell said sarcastically. The old antagonism glinted in his eyes as he looked at her, but he seemed to have forgotten that his arms were still gripping her. Alex went rigid and broke loose, embarrassed almost to the point of colouring up at his nearness.

She picked up the length of old cord and tossed it down again, saying to herself in exasperated tones, 'It's no good. I can't work without the proper fittings. It's useless trying to hang curtains without rings or hooks.'

'Wouldn't it have been an idea to buy them when you bought the stuff?' Grant Mitchell said irritatingly, bending to retrieve the cloud of material.

'It so happens, I didn't think of it at the time,' Alex replied acidly. 'And the shops don't exactly abound around here.'

He fingered the rusty nail dangling at the end of the cord, which annoyed her even more, and pointed out, 'The Noongwalla store's pretty good for odds and ends.'

'I've thought of that,' Alex snapped impatiently, 'but how do I get there? I can't take the jeep on the road.'

'And even if you could,' he lifted his head to slant her his deprecating glint, 'they'd have to clear the area first. Cars that move are slightly different from trees, which you only just manage to miss.'

'I get by.' Alex smote him with an icy look. She turned a pensive gaze to the windows and added, 'And that's a thought, isn't it? I could go through the forest. There must be a route that way. It goes right up the edge of the settlement.'

The logging camp boss heaved himself up to his big height and thrust his hands into his pockets. 'There's a way through all right,' he said with his curled smile, 'but with your sense of direction you'd probably end up back at the laundry hut.'

Her mind already having seized on the idea, Alex straightened herself purposefully. Turning, she threw him a demolishing look and cooed, 'Well, if you've finished with the encouragements I'll lock up. And I *will try* to avoid the laundry hut.'

Ignoring the work-sheets on the desk, Grant Mitchell accompanied her outside. As she locked the door and dropped the keys into her handbag he said in his laconic drawl, 'For the firm's sake, I'd better come along with you and watch out for company property.'

At the jeep he blocked the way to the driving seat and told her forcefully, 'I'll do the driving on the first run. It will save a lot of time.'

Alex opened the other door and took her seat beside him, haughtily ignoring his lazy gleam as he started up and zoomed off. She knew she looked out of place in the vehicle in her smooth white blouse with its ruffled frill edging the front and circling her throat, but she couldn't help that. She sat rigid, taking the bounces with apparent nonchalance until it occurred to her that she had better be watching the route in case she wanted to use it again.

Out of the camp and amidst the thick butts of the trees, they followed an old logging trail which was no more than a sprinkling of pine needles ground to dust by the wheels of forest machinery. At times it disappeared completely, but in spite of steep slopes and rocky valleys there was always a trace of it turning up somewhere.

When they came at last to within sounds of the settlement, with its barking dogs and chidren's shouts, Alex was confident that she could find her way easy enough, should she want to come this way again.

Grant Mitchell parked the jeep in a shaded clearing a few yards from the road into Noongwalla. They walked in the warm sunshine, past the scattering of houses and on into the main street.

The general store was just as Alex remembered it from her brief stay at the hotel opposite. It looked especially gay today with cotton dresses and patterned pinafores waving in the sunshine amongst the piles of other goods. The inside, as she soon discovered, was even more cluttered than outside, but there was a delightful treasure chest atmosphere in the garment-draped beams, and barrels spilling over with this and that. Shelves from ceiling to floor on three sides of the walls were packed with goods of every description. There were dress rails too, and bolts of material and kitchen ware, and running the length of the store a wooden counter was littered with everything imaginable from vegetables and bunches of flowers to bottles of wine and ballpoint pens.

Where a jolly-faced woman in a red blouse stood behind weighing scales and cash book, half a dozen people were waiting to be served. With pleasurable anticipation Alex prepared herself for a lengthy browse. It was ages since she had enjoyed a little nonsense shopping.

While she fingered lacy traycloths and flowered toilet bags, the logging camp boss waited in relaxed pose beside the counter. It must have been a good twenty minutes later when she eventually came upon boxes of various sized curtain hooks and sundry other fittings, which would be useful if she was to do a good job of hanging the curtains.

Her shopping completed, she made her way, hands full, to the counter, trailing a satisfied gaze over her buys; amongst other things, a crisp new tea towel, a neat table runner for the top of her walled shelves and a sachet of hair shampoos. As Grant Mitchell moved up alongside her she ignored the satirical glance he slid over the delicately flowered teacup and saucer she had carefully placed down. Just because the men on the camp were content to drink out of mugs as thick as soup bowls, it didn't mean that she couldn't indulge in a little civilized living when she was on her own.

The woman in the red blouse looked up after serving the customer in front and exclaimed, her plump cheeks wobbling witht good humour, 'Grant Mitchell! I haven't seen you in weeks.' Her grey eyebrows lowered in mock accusation as she taxed him with, 'Where are you buying your cigarettes these days?'

The logging camp boss gave her a lazy grin. 'Hello, Alma,' and to her question, 'I usually send Pop Doolin to pick them up.'

'I know.' She nodded, giving him a teasing look as she reached for a plastic shopping bag. 'While you're otherwise occupied across in the bar.' She moved her penetrating gaze on to Alex to comment cheerfully, 'And this must be the new nurse we heard about but nobody's seen sight nor sign of since she left the hotel that day.' Blatantly ignoring the logging camp boss, she twinkled at Alex while she wrapped her purchases, 'Don't they ever let you out up there, love?'

'I've been very busy,' Alex smiled.

'I know.' The store proprietress rolled her eyes understandingly, prattling as she worked, 'The doctor's the same. Run off his feet half the time tending to the families in the valley . . . and him not very strong himself. . . . It's too much for one, that's what I say.' She snapped the plastic handles of the shopping bag shut and handed it to Alex, taking the Australian dollar notes and counting out the change.

As they turned to go she said cheerily, 'If ever you want a bit of female company, I'm always here. Come and look round the shop any time.'

'Thank you, I will,' Alex smiled from the doorway, liking the friendly face.

Grant Mitchell stood aside for her to precede him out into the sunshine, and accompanied her with his leisurely strides to the end of the main street and out on to the smooth road. At the jeep he took the shopping bag from her and said with his superior smile, 'Okay, now let's see if you know the way back.'

Allowing him to give her a hand into the driving seat, Alex said, coolly succinct, 'The laundry hut, isn't it?'

'If we're lucky,' he shot back at her, equally succinct, as he lowered himself into the other seat.

Sitting erect behind the wheel, Alex watched as he placed her shopping in a leather compartment between the seats. She was glad to see it would be safe from any jolts there. It was also a consolation to know that the cup and saucer she had purchased had been swathed in several sheets of tissue paper inside its cardboard box.

She started up, not as smoothly as she would have wished, and took them forward on to the rough semblance of track fading away through the trees She drove as she always drove, disliking the job intensely, but putting up with it as long as she had to. Perhaps in an ordinary car she might change her mind about driving, but she doubted it. There was something unfeeling and ungiving about these cold mechanical machines. It was as though they knew that they were boss, but they suffered your handling of them, mainly for their own amusement.

Her slim white hands held the wheel firmly. She kept her gaze fixed coolly ahead. She had no doubt of the way whatsoever. Though the ground was dry it was still possible to see the faint signs of tyre marks they had made coming into the settlement. Even over the rocky areas there were snatches of trail to point the way ahead. Skimming copses and circling tree butts, she drove steadily but with prim assurance. Know the way indeed! Was it only men who could follow a simple route through the forest?

Though she had no doubt of her abilities, her concentration was taxed a little when she came to a shadowy slope pitted with hollows and the sawn-off stubs of trees. Climbing it wasn't too easy, and the swords of sunlight striking down through the gloom at her eyes confused her aim so that, for a moment, she realized she had lost the path. However, not to worry, there it was just ahead, winding away beneath the green roof of trees.

She swung confidently towards it, unaware of a deep hollow filled with powdery leaf mould directly ahead of her wheels. With a sickening lurch the jeep nose-dived into the pool of black soil as though it had an urge to disappear completely.

Keeping her composure, Alex put into reverse, unfortunately forgetting to look where she was reversing to, so that the jeep came up to catch its rump squarely on the first of two sawn-off tree stumps. She tried to look unconcerned and battled to free herself, without success.

After her third attempt, the logging camp boss came in with his irritating smile to grip the wheel with her, so sure that he was going to get her out of trouble. But despite his efforts to swing them out, this way and that, the jeep swayed, locked in its cradle of soil, front wheels bogged down in the feathery fineness, tail end up and wedged securely on the tree stump.

After revving the engine for the tenth time he shut it off and sat back to throw his glance up to the roof of green above, cursing beneath his breath, 'Trust a woman to do the impossible.' And with a thin smile at her, 'The jeep has a reputation for never getting stuck, but you made it all right.'

Sitting straight-backed and refusing to look contrite, Alex snapped, her gaze fixed rigidly ahead, 'Well, it's a ridiculous route to have to follow, anyway.'

'They were built for ridiculous routes,' he sneered, 'with the right driver.'

'It's a pity *you* didn't decide to take the wheel then,' she aimed back at him.

He lumped up her shopping and said testily, 'It won't do any good having a post-mortem on it. We've got a two-mile walk ahead of us.'

Taking up her handbag, Alex made her own way down out of her seat, saying with frigid assurance, 'A little walking never hurt anyone.'

She started out at once, disguising her uncertainty about which was the best way back to the track, by stepping briskly but covering very little ground, until the logging camp boss came up alongside and led the way ahead through the trees.

The route winding slightly uphill, it wasn't long before he was several yards ahead of her, crunching on his way through the green twilight. Alex stumbled along eyeing the big receding figure crossly. It was all right for *him*. He was still in his logging clothes; his tough boots, rough shirt and slacks. *She* was in a straight, restricting skirt and cumbersome frilly blouse, and her shoes were not the stout leather ones she wore during the week.

86

And in any case – she looked around at the leafy world stretching out on all sides of her – if she was going to walk, she was going to do it pleasurably. Two miles wasn't all that far, and she would be back in time for supper, even if she strolled.

Ignoring the rapidly diminishing shape, she slowed down, then stopped to examine a bush of small white flowers. Intrigued, she was reminded of English jasmine, but disappointingly the flowers had no perfume. She stood for a moment. When one came to look around, the whole forest floor was dotted with colour; tiny stars of yellow hiding under thick fleshy leaves, a blur of lilac entangled in a thicket, spots of palest orange trailing amongst a hedge of ferns.

Strolling again, she began to look with a critical eye at the trees. She had never given it much thought before, but she noticed now that occasionally one was different from the straight spiky pines she had long since come to accept as the tree that made up the logging forests. This provided an interest, watching for the odd ones out amongst the pines.

As she came round a bend in the trail her eyes picked out a perfect column of blue-grey. Fascinated by its size, she moved up, ignoring the fact that Grant Mitchell was leaning negligently against it, pulling on a cigarette. As she turned her gaze up, and up, he pushed himself away from it to inform her lazily, 'Karri tree.'

'It's tremendous,' Alex said, her neck breaking from the effort of trying to see to the top.

'Nothing like the real thing in Western Australia,' he remarked dryly. 'With girths of up to seventy feet, they've been known to reach close on three hundred feet high.'

'Don't they make good timber?' Alex asked, bringing her gaze down from the topmost branches.

'They did while they lasted, for the early settlers,' Grant Mitchell pulled a disapproving grin and started to walk again. 'There's not many left.' He slapped a slim knotted trunk as he passed. 'Nowadays we concentrate on radiata pine.'

'Sounds terribly scientific,' Alex mused, falling into step

beside him.

'You've got to be scientific to grow trees in Australia,' he told her with a grim smile.

They followed the trail back, in the shadowy green silence, their footsteps muffled in the soft peaty soil. Somewhere a bird gave a loud chuckle.

'Kookaburras.' The logging camp boss nodded his glance to where a group of trees had taken up the chuckle. And later, listening to a clear ringing tone, he said, 'That's a bellbird.'

Alex walked on, grateful in an aloof way at being given this information. It was useful to be able to label the birds she had listened to on her lone evening strolls behind the clinic.

The blue sky was purpling into dusk when they came out at last into the logging camp clearing. His face set in its familiar cynical lines now that they were back on work territory, the logging camp boss led the way to the clinic. Her own features retaining their chilly reserve, Alex made her way there as though he didn't exist.

He waited beside her as she took the keys from her handbag at the door and lazily followed her inside. She let him see by her glance as she placed her handbag down and smoothed her hair that he wasn't welcome.

Perhaps to return the compliment he gave her his bent smile and moving in to drop her bag of shopping down beside her, he drawled with a provoking gleam, 'I overestimated your capabilities behind a wheel. You didn't even make the laundry hut.'

Alex held on to her temper, but only just. No more than a foot away from him, she quivered acidly, 'Are you always so insufferable?'

He leaned in towards her tauntingly and murmured, bringing his dry smile close to her, 'Always.' Then reaching in to retrieve his clip board and work-sheets from behind her, he turned and strolled out.

Alex swung her back on the sound of him revving up his precious shooting brake, and made her way through to her room.

Half an hour later she was washed and tidied up and seated at her place in the dining hut, her poker-straight back set squarely against Grant Mitchell's broad-shouldered figure as he sat at his table behind her.

A lot of the family men went home when they could at the week-end, so that the number of lumberjacks at the tables tonight was cut by more than half. But with everyone's thoughts centred on Saturday night, and the Noongwalla bar, there was still enough noise and clatter and general jollity around for her to lose herself in while she ate a sedate meal and ignored the man behind her.

Wes Brissac's place was empty, otherwise she might have used the opportunity to chat with him on some subject or other. However, Ted Reed, one of the engineering crew who was sitting three empty seats away from her, was fortunate enough to have a sister married to an orchard farmer in the valley, and now and again they exchanged remarks on his afternoon visit there.

None of the men lingered over their meal on a Saturday night. By the time Alex had got through her sweet the whole of the dining hut was practically cleared. She drank a little water, and dabbing her mouth with her handkerchief she rose, averting her gaze from the bulk at the table behind her, and left.

She was glad of the usual bawdy comments aimed at her good-naturedly by the remaining lumberjacks as she walked down the length of the hut. They gave her something to think about.

Outside she felt considerably more relaxed. With the buildings of the camp rising up here and there out of the darkness she made her way back to the clinic. Inside with the light on, the lengths of curtain material were draped around just as she had left them in the afternoon. There was nothing she could do now until morning, so she spent some time folding the pieces neatly to avoid crushing, and tidying the room generally.

Later, in her own quarters, she indulged in the small pleasures her purchases gave her, arranging the creamy embroidered table runner along the length of curtained wall shelves, and hanging the gay checked tea towel on a hook beside gleaming kettle and tray. The pretty flowered cup and saucer took pride of place on the tea chest table beside two colourful-jacketed books she had borrowed from the camp library.

Standing in the doorway, she eyed the room with a certain satisfaction. Though far from looking elegant in any way, it did have a kind of homely simplicity and neatness which it had lacked before. The main eyesore in her opinion was the corner where her clothes were hung from the rope she had suspended. Unfortunately there was nothing she could do about that at the moment.

The light bulb, brighter now beneath its shiny plastic shade which she had fashioned from surgical wrapping, she drew the curtain at the window and picking up one of the books she sat on the chair beside the table with it.

For some weeks now she had been battling with that type of masculine literature which graced the shelves of the library hut. Passing over covers depicting skeletons hanging out of car doors, and tortured-looking individuals carrying all kinds of blood-dripping wounds, she had taken a chance with the older unjacketed books only to find herself knee-deep in some terribly complicated spy plot, or following the grisly account of someone's fate at the mercy of a jungle tiger.

After that she had gone back to the gory covers again. With practice she learned to pick what was for her the occasional readable story. At the moment she was lucky. She had found a tale to do with the early settlers in New Zealand. Providing she overlooked the gruesome details of some of the suppers of the early Maori savages, it was really quite an interesting story.

She read for half an hour or so, then lifting her head she listened, as she did every night about this time. There wasn't a sound to be heard outside. Satisfied that the entire camp would have departed for the Noongwalla bar by now, she stirred.

Quietly she placed her book face down and rose to move about the room, unfastening the buttons of her blouse. Ten minutes later she was knotting the belt of her red dressing-gown securely about her waist. Picking up toilet bag and fleecy towel, she switched off the light and went out.

There was no light along the narrow passageway. This always made it a tricky business fumbling her way along until she came to the dim interior of the clinic. From here she crossed the stretch of faintly gleaming floor, then opening the door she closed it softly after her as she went out.

When there was no moon on her trips, as was the case tonight, it was even more tedious finding her way towards the blacked out buildings which clustered together across the open space from her. Her leather mules whispering over the hard ground, she guided herself more by memory than by sight. Ahead in the distance would be the building housing the machinery and offices. To the left of this were the library and the laundry huts, to the right, beyond the cook-house and the dining hut, were the men's quarters.

Carefully Alex made her way in the direction of the latter. The absolute stillness gave her heart. Taking her time, she breathed in the wood-scented air. It was a beautiful night. Above her the sky was awash with stars. All around her the forests were astir with night life; birds whooping, insects tapping and chirping.

She skirted the first of the huts sampling the breeze, laced with that first balmy warmth of summer, on her cheek. There wasn't a sound except for her own scuffling mules. Everything was shuttered and dark. She could see the men's quarters up ahead.

Feeling perfectly confident that she had the whole place to herself as usual, she was aiming her steps blithely towards the line of box-like compartments off to the side, when something loomed up out of the darkness to cut straight across her path.

Alex, though not of a nervous disposition, was startled into rigidity by the sudden overwhelming nearness of a big black shape. Searching rapidly in the gloom, her eyes made out the familiar bulk of the logging camp boss. Under his arm he was carrying the company ledgers she had seen him working on earlier in the evening. He was coming from the direction of the dining hut, and in her assumption, before she had started out, that everyone would have left for the bar in the settlement, she had forgotten that after a hectic working week he was behind with his paper work. Obviously he had stayed on at his table in the dining hall to catch up with it.

During the half dozen seconds that her mind was registering these facts, Grant Mitchell had uttered his own growling exclamation, 'What the . . .?' at the sudden collision. Then his eyes like hers were swiftly searching the gloom. Slowly, as he came to recognize her shape, his frame slackened. Immediately the sarcasm was there in the hunch of his shoulders. The tones of his voice very pointedly harking back to their escapade of the afternoon, he blocked her path with, 'Well, fancy meeting you. Don't tell me you're out for another stroll?'

'Do you mind? This is not the time for jokes,' Alex said frostily. 'Kindly let me pass.'

'Pass? Where to?' he asked lazily.

'To take a shower, of course,' she replied shortly.

His gleam trailed over her, then he turned it in the direction of the clinic and drawled, 'You're a little off route, aren't you?'

'I don't think so,' Alex returned crisply. And then with impatience as he made no move to step aside, 'Having no bathing facilities of my own, I have been in the habit of using the men's showers for some time. I come down here most evenings when it's quiet.'

'You *what*!' The gleam in the brown eyes hardened suddenly into a blaze of steel. And in tones surprisingly like anger he rasped, 'You realize you could run into some drunk around here?'

'That's a chance I have to take, isn't it?' she said coolly. She stepped around him, eyeing him with a calm 'Excuse me,' and continued on her way.

The shower block was just ahead. Brushing the encounter to one side, in her mind, and leaving the dark shape to carry on to wherever he was going, probably his own quarters,

Alex chose a cubicle at random. Inside, and locking the door after her, she switched on the light and disrobed.

There was no suggestion of luxury about the metalled walls and floor, but the jet of heated water, combined with fragrant lavender soap, made up for her rough surroundings.

After a leisurely scrub she dried off and reached for her coffee-coloured slip and underwear. Later, red dressing-gown tied at the waist again, she unpinned her hair before the small mirror on one wall. It was amazing how it had grown since her arrival in Australia. It seemed to take her longer each evening to brush out the burnished brown waves which fell on to her shoulders. Still, she was pleased with its silkiness. Something about the local water obviously suited it. She smoothed it back from her face and left it to swing loose. It was always more relaxing to wear it for a little while without clips or fastenings of any kind.

Feeling superbly fresh and highly satisfied with her venture, she gathered together her toilet articles and towel, and after a last look round to make sure she had forgotten nothing, she switched off the light and went out.

The inky blackness, in contrast to the vividly bright cubicles, took a little getting used to. She felt her way blindly with her feet, wondering irritably why the logging camp boss didn't cater for more lighting on the camp. Perhaps, unlike her, he didn't think it was necessary.

She had hardly taken half a dozen steps along the path when the subject of her thoughts reared up in her vision, making her start almost as violently as she had done earlier. There was no mistaking him this time, for the red glow of his cigarette lit up his craggy features as he pushed himself away from some leaning post to meet her. Judging by the company ledgers still under his arm, he must have been waiting there since she had passed him by, some time ago.

He picked up the towel she had dropped to the ground in her fright, and draping it over his shoulder, he asked, 'Enjoy your shower?'

'Very much, thank you,' Alex replied, trying to give the

picture of possessing a steady nerve.

'Water all right? he asked smoothly.

'Quite all right, thank you.' Rapidly regaining her composure she tacked on, adopting his smooth manner, 'Not too hot and not too cold.'

As she faced up to him, she became uncomfortably aware that his gaze was tracing the line of her unpinned hair. Colouring ridiculously, she turned and struck off into the darkness, only to be chivvied by a broad shoulder as Grant Mitchell told her aggravatingly, falling into step beside her, 'You're going the wrong way again.'

Voicing her earlier complaints, she took a stab at his superiority as she fumbled blindly with, 'If there were more lamps lit around here, I would be able to see what I was doing.'

'There are lights for those who know where the switches are,' he said, channelling her with his bulk in the right direction.

'Well, that's a help, I'm sure,' Alex scoffed with a haughty laugh.

'The idea is,' Grant Mitchell reverted to his derisive tones, 'to discourage pointless wanderings at night. This is a logging camp, not a city square.'

Unable to think of a rejoinder to this, Alex set her mouth and ignored him. Or at least that was what she had intended to do.

Now that her eyes were becoming accustomed to the gloom, she could make out the silhouette of his dark head and shoulders against the starlit sky, the muscular swing of his pale-clad frame close alongside her dark-robed shape.

She began to feel acutely conscious of the sound of their footsteps mingling together and echoing away into the darkness, as they crossed the open stretch of ground. Yet she dispensed with the idea of searching around for something else to say. That would only draw attention to this ridiculous self-consciousness which had come over her, and she had no intention of doing that.

She had thought that he planned merely to accompany her as far as the clinic door. She opened it expecting to see

94

him disappear into the night. Instead he drifted lazily inside, behind her.

Loath to switch on the light in his company, she moved towards her room. She said across the shadows, trying to sound offhand, yet injecting a note of dismissal into her voice, 'You can drop the towel anywhere.'

'I'll do better than that,' he said, the faint gleam of a dry smile matching the fleecy white length over his shoulder, 'I'll bring it through myself.'

Alex turned, refusing to get flustered. He had a perfect right, she knew, to inspect her quarters, so what was the point of arguing?

She groped her way along the narrow corridor, sensing his big shape close behind her. In her room she reached reluctantly for the light switch, wishing for once that the bulb's brilliance was still as unrevealing as it had been under Mrs. MacTavish's red-fringed shade.

As the four walls sprang into life, tinted brightly by the pink surgical plastic, Grant Mitchell moved in and made a pretence of tossing the towel down. His glance toured the room, resting pointedly on her little additions and touches. Fingering the curtains of her walled shelves, he drawled with a cynical smile, 'The female mind works the same, from mice to bush rabbits. Give 'em a hole and they immediately start to make a home out of it.'

Alex, standing near the doorway, eyed him and his cynically trailing gaze unflinchingly. Placing her toilet bag down, she replied in her own deft way, 'You don't have much use for anything you can't put a tree saw through, do you?'

His warped grin in evidence, he faced her, thrusting his hands into his pockets. 'That's my business, shipping timber,' he said easily. Though he seemed to want to look anywhere but at her, his gaze kept flicking in to cruise over her unpinned hair.

Acutely aware of its tumbling state, and of her red dressing-gown, Alex said stiffly, 'Mine, at the moment, is getting to bed. Do you mind?'

He rode her abrupt request to be rid of him with lazy

95

arrogance, nodding to the cup and saucer on the table to chafe, 'Aren't you going to christen the new chinaware?'

'If I make tea,' she said, ignoring his sardonic gleam, 'it will be exactly when I feel like it.' She tacked on, giving him her own cool smile, 'Another irritating female habit.'

He shrugged, hunching his big shoulders close to her. After a while, he moved himself to say with a casual grin, 'Women are all right. In small doses.'

Alex watched him make his way leisurely to the door. Unable to restrain herself, she tossed after him, 'And when they're conveniently situated in Oaktown, of course.'

The logging camp boss stopped and turned to give her a fathomless smile. 'Where else?' he drawled, relaxing his frame before her glintingly. He made no further attempt to move. Alex wished now that she had kept the remark to herself. Though she had never intended it to, she found her gaze becoming locked with his. For no reason that she could think of, her breath started to come in snatches in her throat.

With an effort she dragged her glance away and busied herself fiddling with the runner on top of the wall shelves. She had vowed she wouldn't get flustered, yet here she was fighting off a burning in her cheeks, her hands fluttering about as though they didn't belong to her.

It seemed an age to her, before the man across the room said laconically, 'It's time I was getting on my way.' His ledgers under his arm, Alex watched him move into the doorway. 'Good night, Miss Leighton,' he nodded from there.

'Good night, Mr. Mitchell,' she said briskly, stepping about as though she had a hundred and one jobs to do.

As an afterthought, the logging camp boss said over his shoulder, 'You'd better come through and lock up after me.'

Alex moved up to follow him out, saying crisply, 'I had no intention of doing otherwise.'

Though there was enough light from the room to start with, it soon petered out, leaving her groping her way along behind big shoulders, but not, heaven forbid, touching them.

Out in the clinic there was more room, and more air. Oddly enough, she was a little breathless again.

At the outside door she held it as it was opened, accidentally brushing her hand against the tough brown one that had swung it inwards. At pains to pretend she hadn't noticed, she waited, her slim robed figure erect.

One arm still brushing across her where he held the door, Grant Mitchell seemed to pause. For a moment a peculiar light battled with the familiar glint he trailed over her, then he was turning abruptly and making his way outside. From there he strode away, his big frame rapidly disappearing into the darkness.

Alex locked up after him, listening to the queer haphazard beating of her heart. Feeling curiously weak, she turned back towards her room. Perhaps now would be an ideal time to make that cup of tea.

CHAPTER SIX

THE first thing after breakfast the next morning, Alex applied herself once again to the task of hanging the curtains. The sun was slanting past the tall windows as she busied herself searching out the newly purchased hooks and fittings. She had just tugged and pushed the desk over to the wall again when there was the sound or struggling at the door.

She looked round to see Pop Doolin wrestling with a pair of wooden steps in the entrance. He came gasping in, rested his load up against the inside wall and paused to mop his brow. He shot a disapproving look at Alex and the desk she had been wrestling with, then looking around the roof, he clacked, 'Now these y'ere curtains you're wanting fixing. Jist let me know where they go an' I'll stick 'em up.' Possessively he handled the steps he had brought, positioning them at the first window to reprove her with a look of squinting severity, 'T'ain't right for a lady to be climbing about.'

'Well, thank you, Pop!' Alex smiled pleasantly, and with a drape in her hand. 'Could we see if they're the right length first? I've never really checked.'

As the frail frame mounted the rickety wooden pyramid Alex held on to it wondering worriedly if perhaps it wouldn't have been better if she had gone up herself. Pop was not much more than half her height and he had to stand on the very top step to reach the ceiling ledge. However, once up there, he worked a lot steadier than she would have done.

Watching him fixing the screws and fittings, once they had ascertained that the curtains were the right length, she marvelled at this little man, who along with one or two other elderly assistants, coped with the cooking and the laundry and everything else that needed to be done on the camp.

Throughout the morning she measured and stitched on

hooks and rings and when each curtain was completed it was taken from her and hung with the utmost if a little knobbly-handed concern.

Towards lunchtime the steps and Pop had disappeared, the desk was back in its place, and Alex was strolling, arms folded, a light of critical satisfaction in her eyes as she gazed at four smoothly draped windows, the gossamer lengths floating up gently with the breeze.

Altogether that week was a notable one. On Monday evening it rained, the first that Alex had seen since her arrival at the camp. It started as a steady drizzle, later reaching hail-stone force as the clouds swirled and darkened above the pines.

After supper, when the trees were dripping and the bracken crackled with life, Alex donned her light mac and stout shoes and hazarded a stroll. It was a new world to her, the forest behind the clinic; a lively smiling world with crickets chirruping ecstatically and damp-winged butterflies chasing one another through the gloom. All kinds of insect life that she never knew existed here were scuttling busily across the streaming paths. The trees creaked and crackled with grubs happily at work, yellowing ferns uncurled themselves voluptuously upwards to drink in the life-giving moisture.

It came to Alex in an odd moment as she walked that she was like the land in a way; parched and dried up inside, after the years spent nursing her aunt; waiting for something, she didn't know what. Something to come along that would penetrate the surface of her unawakened senses and stir her, like the rain had stirred the forest, into animated, smiling life.

On Wednesday afternoon the sun was brilliant again, and she was called out to a lumberjack who had collapsed in the northern logging area. When she arrived it was to find that the man, Shank Brophy, was suffering from nothing worse than too much to drink the night before. This didn't stop him from being very ill, of course, and looking it.

After giving him a pill and getting him into a sitting

position, she promptly advised his removal to bed. Casey Hall, in charge of the crew in that part of the forest, said he couldn't spare a man to go with her, but he assisted her in walking the invalid to the jeep – none the worse after its sojourn in the hole over the week-end – and gave her the man's hut number.

Alex drove off with the lumberjack slumped in his seat, his head rolling loosely. She had no trouble finding his sleeping quarters. The problem, once she arrived, was how to get him inside the hut.

From the doorway she looked around. There wasn't a figure to be seen on the camp. The interior of the hut, with its line of beds along either side of the walls, was completely empty. With a sigh she resigned herself to the fact that she would have to manage.

Walking around the jeep, she said briskly, opening the door, 'Now, Mr. Brophy, if you can help yourself to step down, I'll give you my arm.'

'Sure, nurse.' A smile dawned on his flabby, pallid features. Brophy leaned out and turned his great arm around Alex's neck. The way he put his whole weight against her as he climbed out, she soon knew she had another Clem Atkins on her hands.

Though she still had trouble with the big hulking lumberjack who had made himself unpleasant in the clinic, having to suffer such boasting remarks voiced for the benefit of his friends as, 'Are you coming to the bar with me tonight, nursie? I'll buy yer a drink that'll melt the ice in yer,' he never attempted anything beyond teasing her crudely, and she knew how to cope with him.

In fact, she told herself now, setting her shoulders woodenly as a dusty balding head came brushing against her cheek, she was fast learning how to handle all men of his type.

She struggled clumsily with the top half of Brophy's weight draped around her, saying in a stern shaking voice as they went through the door, 'Can't you support yourself a little more?'

'I'm trying, nursie, I'm trying.' Brophy hugged her and

gave her a smile.

'Which one is your bed?' she asked with a businesslike look up the room, ignoring his leer.

'Right over here, nurse. Fourth one up.' He guided her over, leaning heavily on her.

Alex extricated herself firmly at the side of his bed and gave him a gentle push. His physical state was such that he had no resistance to sprawling flat out on it. She untied his boots with the spikes in the soles and placed them under a locker at the foot of the bed. His hands were covered with oil or grease of some kind, his face streaked with mud. She could see nothing for it but to clean him up a little, otherwise he would have the mess all over the pillows. She went off to look for water and came back with a small bowl, and soap and towel.

He fixed her with a wicked light as she worked, content to let her have her way with the soap and water. It was when she had finished drying his hands that he shot one out and grabbed her wrist. 'Give us a kiss, nurse,' he pleaded playfully.

Alex remained cool. She had given him a sedative and she knew he was in no condition to throw his weight about. All the same his grip on her wrist was like a steel clamp.

'Mr. Brophy,' she said in her most arctic clinical tones, 'I haven't time to stand here, playing games.'

'Who's to know?' He pulled her towards him with a flame-lit leer. 'We've got the place to ourselves.'

'*You* have,' she smiled succinctly, freeing herself with some difficulty.

Well clear of his grasp, she gathering up the washing articles and nodding towards the small envelope she had placed on the locker, she sailed away, advising him, 'Take the other pill about ten o'clock tonight and you'll feel fine.'

Back at the jeep she brushed herself off with a humorous light. If it went on like this, she'd be qualifying for the title of *Battling Bertha* the second!

The sun was lowering in the sky when she drove along the circular road leading to the clinic. A feeling of weariness crept over her. She had been out all afternoon on various errands around the camp, taking the call about Brophy from Wes Brissac in the works office, so that by now she was ready to call it a day.

The light over the forest had a softness about it, as it always did at this hour, making the circle of pines look like dark cardboard cut-outs against the creamy-gold backcloth of sky.

Coming into sight of the clinic she thought she saw a movement at the door, amongst the lengthening shadows. As she neared it she discovered that it hadn't been her imagination. A man had come out and was making his way towards a van parked at the front. As he climbed into the driving seat, another man appeared from inside the clinic, and turned and paused to do something. It looked as though he was locking the door. Alex noticed that both men wore dungarees.

She arrived at the spot where she always parked, in time to see that the van was from Oaktown, and then it was pulling away in the opposite direction.

Strange! Alex stepped down and watched it disappear. Reaching for her own keys, she gathered that there must be a duplicate set in the office. Even so, it didn't explain. . . .

Her glance fell to her feet where a dusty powdery path led up to the door. Inside, the same gritty mess and grey footprints continued in a trail across the gleaming floor towards the other door. Alex followed it with increasing curiosity. It went along the passageway and turned, as far as she could make out in the dimness there, into the disused section which housed the washroom.

Proceeding with it, she came upon wood chippings, old screws and washers, and finally, in the washroom itself, she saw that the washbasin had been re-fitted to the wall, its taps once again in position.

But this wasn't the reason for her captivated look. Alongside the washbasin towards the end section of the room, the walls had been cased in aluminium, so had the floor, and a trough that surrounded it, and behind a screen of rigid opaque plastic was fixed a brand new set of shower fittings.

Alex examined everything in wonder. It was a spartan construction, no more luxurious than the men had in their quarters, but it was a shower and – she turned the tap a little way – it worked. She tilted an eyebrow over it pensively, moving away. It was certainly a useful addition to the wash-room.

Retracing her steps back into the passageway, she turned without thinking into her own room. She saw at once that someone had been in here. Covers were askew, and the items of furniture had been disarranged. Worst of all, her clothes were draped in a heap on her bed. Then she saw why.

Over in the corner was a wardrobe of sorts. Of utility make and scratched with wear, it had obviously been brought over from one of the other huts. Nevertheless, Alex inspected its clean roomy interior; noted the long mirror inside the door, with pleasure. There was ample space here for everything she possessed, and a little polish in the right places would banish that knocked-about look.

Well! She busied herself putting the room to rights. It had been quite a day on the whole. Her clothes hung neatly in their new home, she went back to gaze again on the shower.

It would have been too much to expect hot water, of course, but later when she had cleaned and swept up the mess that the workmen had made, and locked the clinic doors for the day, she doused away her work-weariness under the streaming jet, and had no complaints.

The unexpected luxury made her a little late in the dining hall. There was the usual guffawing din coming from the three lanes of tables as she went in. Passing down the hut, she saw that besides all the technicians being in their places at her table, Grant Mitchell had also arrived and was seated at his. She wondered perfunctorily if she ought to thank him for the changes that had occurred in the nurse's quarters. On second thoughts she decided against mentioning what was probably to him just a matter of bringing the clinic up to camp standards.

As she came up the steps on to the raised platform she saw him flick his gaze in her direction, but there was nothing new in his expression as far as she could see. She didn't meet the brown glance on her, of course, but carried on feeling a little conspicuous in the pale lilac blouse she had chosen and slim charcoal skirt.

As she was about to take her chair, Buff Riley, an irrepressible type who was never too particular about his choice of words, was entertaining the other men at the table with his earthy humour, a common practice. Tonight, however, the logging camp boss shot a look across and rapped with a tight-lipped humour of his own, 'Watch your language, Riley, or I'll put you down with the money.'

The uncouth, crew-cut engineer grinned sheepishly and continued his tale in less colourful tones.

At the end of the week, a new camp member on the technical side arrived. After much badgering with head office, it seemed, Grant Mitchell had secured himself a fully trained crane engineer, a position that had previously been shared by anyone who felt capable of handling the big spidery machine.

Alex caught glimpses of the new man throughout the day, a husky bearded individual who was instantly at home in the company of the other joking lumberjacks. She had no idea then that his coming would mean yet another change in camp routine for herself – a change that happened more or less by accident.

Walking over to the dining hut that night, she became caught up with most of the technicians going in, in a bunch. Grant Mitchell was there. So was the new man. She was introduced and had her hand crushed as they all filed in.

She didn't see the bearded figure again until they were at the tables. Being one of the last ones on the platform with the logging camp boss coming up at the rear, she watched as the new crane engineer, chatting away to the others, inadvertently took her chair and settled himself expansively.

For a moment Alex stood nonplussed, then seeing that it would be petty to point out that he was sitting in her seat, she started to move to where another single table had a chair beside it.

Grant Mitchell, who had been hovering, watching to make sure that the new man was made to feel at home, saw what had happened. Standing beside his own table, he blocked Alex's way as she was about to brush past him, and pulling out a chair he said casually, 'You'd better sit here. No sense in giving Pop extra work to do.'

Alex brought her glance back from the other table, realizing he had a point, and acquiesced politely.

Dining in the evenings after that was a totally new experience. To help oneself to vegetables served up in separate tureens, instead of having them slapped at you in a mountainous mush, was sheer heaven. It was also a relief not to have to breathe in the fumes of the beer mugs or listen to that kind of inane masculine chat that grated on one's nerves. Seated near the wall, she could let all that float over her head. Grant Mitchell sat with his back to it beside her, which was an added protection. He usually dined with company papers somewhere around him, and nothing stronger than coffee in his mug. She ignored him, of course.

CHAPTER SEVEN

On the Saturday when the pay cheques were issued, Alex turned down the offer of a lift into town in Wes Brissac's lorry. There was nothing she needed, and she had spent little of last month's money. Besides, she had no wish to go into Oaktown.

Dusting briskly around the clinic, she listened to the revving up of the lorries, and the men's high-spirited whoops and whistles at the thought of spending a whole day and the best part of the night in town. The hand holding the duster moved with increasing rapidity at what sounded to her like a shooting brake pulling away. As her mind went off with it to Oaktown, she tried to ignore the empty feeling which had settled where her heart usually lay.

At lunchtime she ate a solitary meal in a lifeless cookhouse, and walked back to the clinic with an aimless step. Nothing she attempted in the afternoon went right. At last, fighting this unaccountable gloom which assailed her, she washed and changed into a neat linen suit, took up her handbag and went out and locked the door.

She would take the jeep and drive through the forest to the settlement. It would be much better than mooning around an empty camp. She could browse round the store, and perhaps chat with the jolly-faced woman there.

Behind the wheel of the jeep she made her way steadily to where the old logging trail wound its way off through the trees. Bracing herself, Alex followed it slowly, taking care this time to be on the look-out for unseen obstacles. She needn't have worried. The ride was without incident apart from her handbag bouncing out on a tricky slope, and a minor skid on a greasy stretch, probably with the recent rains.

Otherwise unscathed, she trundled out into the open, and parked the jeep in the same shaded clearing that Grant Mitchell had chosen when he had shown her the way through the forest.

She walked, handbag in hand, up to the road. The sun was shining as brilliant as ever as she made her way into the settlement. Yet somehow the afternoon lacked the sparkle of that previous excursion. Even the store with its gaily cluttered front looked commonplace today. Inside, she found that her dull mood persisted. The Aladdin's cave atmosphere of last time had disappeared. Now, as she looked about her, she saw it as just a thriving village shop, full of customers waiting to be served. Which, incidentally, put paid to any ideas of social visiting on her part.

Never mind! She straightened herself philosophically. She had the whole store to go at to while away the afternoon, and at least it was better than the empty camp.

At pains to amuse herself, she strolled around the shelves, picking up intriguing boxes, studying brightly illustrated packets in a desultory way. Then her eye caught a row of cotton dresses on a rail. Now *there* was an idea, the weather was becoming hotter by the day. She had often thought that blouses and skirts were not perhaps the ideal off-duty wear for forestry life.

Her interest perked up a little as she fingered through the gay prints. A pretty pattern, of bunches of forget-me-nots on a slightly paler blue background, took her eye. She unhooked the hanger from the rail to view the style. Still not certain whether she liked it or not, she held the dress up against herself, before the long mirror provided.

It came as a shock at first to see herself amidst so much colour, after knowing only the paleness of her blouses and white overall. But perhaps, when one got used to it . . .?

She was tilting her head critically, liking it, not liking it, when a voice drifted over to her from somewhere nearby to say, 'Buy it. It suits you.'

Alex turned with a mixture of curiosity and surprise. She had thought she was alone in this remote corner of the store.

A little way from her she saw a scholarly-looking man of about middle age eyeing her playfully from beside a loaded vegetable rack. It was impossible to feel annoyed by his remark, or even embarrassed. He stood there leisurely packing his pipe, his blue eyes twinkling with nothing but kindness.

Alex smiled and slotting the dress back on to the rail she said lightly, 'I might.'

She turned with a view to browsing again. As she did so, the man, who was lighting his pipe now and pulling on it to make the match flare, came in to scrutinize her with his inoffensive twinkle. 'Yours is a face,' he said good-naturedly, between puffs, 'I haven't seen before in these parts. Don't tell me someone's got relatives visiting that I don't know about?'

Closer to him, Alex saw that he was perhaps no more than forty, but with his prematurely greying hair, and a slight, not too strong build, he looked older.

Her own clear grey gaze meeting his friendly blue one, she satisfied his curiosity smilingly with, 'I'm the new nurse at the logging camp.'

'What!' The pipe was whipped from between firm lips. 'Mrs. MacTavish's successor? I don't believe it!' Renewed pleasure crinkled his gentle, rather nice features beneath the raised eyebrows. Then he was offering her his hand in a comradely fashion. 'I'm Lloyd Downing – Doctor Downing. Rather belatedly, I'm afraid,' he smiled apologetically, 'welcome to Noongwalla.' Her hand in his firm grip, he mused reflectively, 'It means something in the Aborigine language, but I've never had the time to find out what.'

Alex introduced herself by name and stood beside him to point out conversationally, 'The storewoman was telling me how busy you are.'

He sloped a grin that took years off his face. 'I caught a little trouble in a war, which makes me unsuitable for the rigours of the flying doctor service. So they put me out here, which is twice as backbreaking.'

'Couldn't you get some help?' Alex asked sympathetically.

The doctor shrugged uncomplainingly. 'When I first came to Noongwalla there were no more than a dozen families in the valley. The powers that be are inclined to forget their multiplication tables.' The twinkle was in evidence again as he lifted his wrist to take in the time. 'Mrs. Strasser is about to call me to deliver her fourth at any minute.'

As though reminded of the pressures of work, he turned and picked up a wire basket near the grocery section. Taking a second one, he handed it to Alex, saying helpfully, 'If you're shopping, you'll need one of these.'

'I'm really only browsing,' Alex smiled, taking the basket. But the doctor wasn't listening. Busy rifling the shelves now, he chatted on, 'Now these soups are very good. I often make a scratch meal with one when I've been out on a night call.'

'Perhaps I'll take some tea,' Alex said after a while, reaching towards a box.

Doctor Downing's voice came from another shelf. 'Cocoa's a satisfying drink for us medics, you know. This is a new brand they've got in. . . . Gives you a bit of a head, though, if you don't watch it.'

His warm companionable humour acting like a tonic on her jaded spirits, Alex found herself drifting along beside him, lightly discussing the merits of this and that, and dropping the odd useful item into her basket, which she would have had little interest in debating over earlier.

Emerging eventually from between the piled-up barrels and racks, they approached the counter together and joined the group of people waiting to be served. The doctor spoke with amiable charm to an elderly woman who had stopped him nearby. Alex had a moment to notice the well-worn but tailored look of his cotton jacket and dusty slacks. He was pure Australian, there was no doubt about that. But his drawl had a cultured ring about it, and he held himself in a different way from the men of the land who trudged along the main street.

Slowly they moved along the counter. The storewoman beamed when she saw the doctor, taking her smile on to Alex and dropping a few cheerful remarks as she cashed up their purchases. But there were customers to the right and left of her, handing up the odd item, and soon her attention was distracted elsewhere.

Alex took the plastic shopping bag the doctor handed her. Walking out alongside him, she was preparing to say her good-byes at the door, when he turned to her and suggested cordially, 'Look here, my veranda's just at the end of the street. I can boil the billy in five minutes. If you've got nothing else to do, we can sit and drink tea and swop medical yarns.'

Feeling comparatively lifted by his company, Alex laughed, 'All right.' As they started out she added, 'But I'd better warn you, my nursing experiences are few. For the past four years I've been taking care of a sick aunt.'

'What was the trouble?' Doctor Downing asked, guiding her round a group of children who were crouched over a game. Alex told him and he nodded his head to say sympathetically, 'Unpleasant.'

From the main street they turned off into an open space circled by gum trees. Here a white-painted picket fence guarded a small weatherboard cottage. Its broad veranda held oddments of peeling furniture, and the fairly extensive garden was a tangle of vegetables run to seed, and overgrown shrubbery.

One thing which Alex noticed, though, as she walked in through the gate, was the vast creeper bearing brilliant red flowers which climbed at one side of the veranda. Its presence offset the run-down look of the house and gave it instead something of an exotic appearance.

The doctor led the way up the front steps and opened one of the double glass doors, enjoying her obvious interest. 'Don't look at the dust,' he said humorously, as they walked inside. 'I'm the type who likes to leave everything to take root in it, so that I know where it is.'

Alex looked around a room devoted to comfort rather than elegance. Cushions were scattered around on upholstered chairs, and across the faded divan under the window. An open desk in one corner overflowed with letters, syringe boxes and scraps of paper. The rest of the pieces of furniture were lost amidst a hundred and one household oddments.

From this room Alex was conducted to the kitchen-living-room beyond, where the doctor filled the kettle from the bench tap and lit the stove. 'Now we'll boil the billy,' he said jovially, taking the teapot to the back door and tossing the tea leaves out. He returned to ask her, 'How do you like your tea? Weak, or very healthy?'

'Fairly strong,' Alex smiled, feeling at liberty to wander out on to the back veranda and in again. Watching him ignore the sink full of crockery and reach for clean cups and saucers from a wall cupboard, she asked, 'Are there no cleaning women in Noongwalla?'

'I've tried it,' the doctor laughed, 'but with me it doesn't work. When I'm in, I like the house to myself. When I'm out, it's nice to know that some well-meaning old lady isn't turning the place upside down.'

Alex nodded understandingly and strolled to a mantelpiece opposite the windows.

'Family photographs,' Doctor Downing said easily of the framed pictures strewn along its front. 'That's my nephew at the end. He's studying law at Sydney University. His sister, my niece ... the teenage girl in the white dress ... she's married to an opal miner in Andamooka.'

Alex's gaze was caught by the picture of an attractive woman of about thirty-five. Something about the carefree pose prompted her to ask, 'Is this your wife?'

'Yes. She's dead.' Doctor Downing finished arranging biscuits on a plate.

'I'm sorry.' Alex looked at him.

'Don't be,' he said kindly. 'What happened seven years ago is no reason for you to lose your smile.' He added reassuringly, 'I got mine back some time ago.'

He screwed the lid back on the biscuit tin and replaced it in the cupboard. Then turning to gaze at his handiwork he said cheerfully, 'Now, the tray's all ready. The kettle will take a little time. Where shall we sit?'

'Could I go on wandering for a little while, do you think?' Alex begged shyly, sending a questing look along the veranda. 'I have to admit I'm fascinated. This is the first time I've been in an Australian house.'

'Please do.' The doctor waved his arm with an amused

look and escorted her through the door. He opened another door along the veranda and showed her rooms in the other half of the house. Outside, at the back again, he took her down the steps and led her to other lean-to sections. 'This is the meat house,' he said goodhumouredly. 'That's the laundry shed. The henhouse at the end I use as a woodshed.'

Under his blue gaze, Alex popped her head into everything. He had struck her at first as being older than his years. Now he was almost boyish as he teased her. She was tempted to ask him what a meat house was used for, but seeing the mischief in his eyes, she thought she'd better not. After he had failed to come up with the name of a resplendent tree which dominated the back half of the garden, they returned laughingly to the kitchen.

The kettle was almost boiling. Waiting for the final rush of steam, the doctor was telling her of a botanist friend of his, who had been fascinated by the tree, when commotion at the front of the house, plus a succession of children's cries, cut across his conversation. 'Doctor! Doctor, come quick! It's Shelley, she's burned!'

Doctor Downing cocked his head at the scrabbling footsteps coming up the path. 'Sounds like trouble.' He went immediately through the house to the front.

Alex listened, but she could make out nothing except the high-pitched gabble of small voices. Almost at once the doctor returned. 'It's the Carmichael toddler,' he explained. 'Got herself scalded, by the sound of it. I'll have to go.'

Alex took the kettle off the stove. 'Can I be of any help?' she asked as he reached to where his bag rested on a chair.

The doctor smiled. 'Take my advice, nurse,' he said checking over his instruments, 'never give up your free time unless you have to.'

'I don't mind, really!' Alex assured him. 'I haven't a thing to do until Monday morning.'

Doctor Downing rested his blue gaze on her. Then snapping his bag shut he gave a worn grin to tell her, 'Nurse Leighton, you've let yourself in for it. Close the back door. We'll go out the front.'

Beyond the picket fence, he led the way to the dusty little

car parked in the space. Standing beside it were three small boys. The oldest was about seven. The youngest, his face stained with tears, must have been no more than four. In grubby dungarees and play-shirts, their eyes turned upwards apprehensively, they looked a sorry little bunch, shuffling against each other.

'Inside, boys,' the doctor said briskly, opening the rear door. 'We've got to get to that sister of yours.'

'The Carmichaels are from Port Lincoln on the other side of Adelaide,' Doctor Downing explained to Alex when they were moving. 'Donna Carmichael has relatives living on the south side of the valley. Her husband Tony is going to work for them.' He swung the car on to a dirt road just to the side of the cottage and nodded ahead. 'They've just moved into a disused property near the old timber mill. I expect they're still trying to get straight.'

A few seconds later the car drew up around the curve of the road, and it looked as though the doctor was right. A dusty open space was littered with kitchen equipment, prams, saucepans and all manner of household goods. In the centre of the space a small flat-topped house sprawled haphazardly, its open window frames hanging askew, a flowering potted plant placed strategically beside the leaning doorway. Overriding the melancholy scene were the wailing screams coming from within.

The doctor opened the rear door of the car and the boys tumbled out. Alex accompanied him behind their scattering shapes up to the house.

Directly inside, in an almost empty room, the distraught parents were helplessly trying to do what they could to soothe the screaming child, hugging her and walking with her between them.

The mother turned at the footsteps, relief flooding her strained features. 'Oh, doctor, am I glad to see you!' Sending a distracted gaze towards the portable stove on the floor, she gave a disjointed account of what had happened. 'Normally I wouldn't have dreamed of using it there, but Shelley was outside playing with the boys, and we desperately needed a meal . . . it seemed perfectly all right . . . and then I turned and there she was prancing about near the boiling kettle. . . .'

The doctor nodded understandingly and put his arms up. 'Come along, young Shelley,' he said cheerfully, 'let's see what you've done to yourself.'

His smile had a calming effect on all concerned. The flaxen-haired tot brought her wails down to a series of coughing sobs as she went to him. The mother's tremulous features took on a trusting look. The father moved back a little from his anxious hovering and explained, 'I came in just before you, Doc. Found her bawling the place down. We didn't know what to do.'

'She looks as though she's escaped most of it,' the doctor said encouragingly, supporting the child on the rough wooden table and going over her limbs. At the wet patch on her dress, he murmured, looking for the fastenings, 'We'll have this off, I think.'

'Here, let me.' Alex stepped forward to cope with the tiny buttons.

'This is Nurse Leighton. She works at the logging camp,' the doctor mentioned pleasantly as they stripped the child.

The mother gave Alex a pale smile, but her eyes were all for her daughter.

The clothing removed, one angry red patch showed up on the tiny tummy. Doctor Downing reached for his case. 'Not as bad as you thought, eh, Mrs. Carmichael?' He gave the mother his encouraging look. 'We'll soon have her getting into mischief again.'

After rinsing his hands in the bowl of water she brought for him, he broke open a special medical pack and took out the yellow gauze pad and brown bandage. Placing the pad on the scalded area, he started to turn the roll, but Alex found she had more of a knack at bandaging than he had. Gradually she took over from him. When she had fastened the length securely and not too tightly around the small tummy, the doctor asked, 'Has she a nightgown? It will be more comfortable. And a blanket.'

Everyone went scurrying around, even the three small

boys who had been standing by watching everything hypnotized. The mother came up with a clean fleecy nightgown. The father willingly produced the blanket. The youngest of the boys brought a mangled object in his hand which he thrust with brotherly affection towards the table shouting, 'Here, Shelley, I brought your doll, Shelley!'

Angelic in flowery nightgown, the blanket wrapped about her, Shelley sat in the doctor's arms clutching a chocolate biscuit he had found for her from a box on the table. Two big tears glistened on her cheeks, her lower lip pouted uncertainly at all the fuss that was being made over her.

Doctor Downing handed her back to her mother, advising, 'Keep her warm, and don't let her climb about too much for a day or two.' He added reassuringly, 'She'll have a scar on her tummy no bigger than a dollar piece.' He fastened up his bag and turned with Alex to the door. 'I'll drop by in a couple of days to check the dressing,' and as a twinkling afterthought, 'And no more stoves on the floor, eh?'

'Oh no, doctor!' Mrs. Carmichael agreed feelingly beside her smiling husband.

They gave their thanks profusely all the way to the door, including Alex in their tumbling words of gratitude.

'I'm glad I was able to help,' Alex smiled, and went with the doctor to his car.

'It could have been nasty,' he sighed, as he drove back along the dirt road. Then, regaining some of his old humour, 'Happily young Shelley's one of those volatile little imps who doesn't hang about once she sees what mischief she's done. She must have got clear of that boiling water pretty smartly.'

As the house disappeared from view he shelved any more comments on the subject and suggested, swinging the wheel buoyantly, his attention on the road, 'Now how about those refreshments, nurse?'

'Fine, doctor.' Alex gleamed her approval.

He turned to give her his blue gaze. 'Let's forget the professional titles, shall we?' he said with his easy manner. 'My name's Lloyd.'

'All right,' Alex agreed, feeling that there was no unbending to be done. She might have only met the doctor at the start of the afternoon, but to her it seemed as though they had been friends for a lifetime. She had never known a man with whom she could feel so content and relaxed.

Back at the cottage, the water in the kettle had retained much of its heat. They had been away less than half an hour, so it wouldn't be long before it was singing again.

Quite naturally Alex placed it back on the stove and busied herself checking over the tray, while the doctor washed his hands. Walking around with the towel, he cast his glance towards the plate of biscuits as though he was having second thoughts about them. 'Our afternoon's work calls for a little more sustenance, I think, don't you?' he said after a while. 'There's some sweet scones in the cupboard. I like mine with butter. How about you?'

'Plain, I think,' Alex said, reaching up to the shelf and bringing out a dish of golden brown cakes. 'They're home-made!' she exclaimed delightedly, cutting a couple and buttering them.

'Everything like that is around here,' the doctor grinned, rolling down the sleeves of his jacket. 'We haven't quite got to the supermarket stage in Noongwalla yet, you know.'

'I was forgetting,' Alex laughed. 'It's just the change, I suppose, from cookhouse fare.'

'Do you miss England?' Lloyd asked, throwing a white cloth over the small circular table.

'Not terribly,' Alex replied as she juggled with the boiling kettle. 'There was only my aunt. When she died, I had no particular ties.'

'What made you choose Australia?' he pursued humorously, seating himself beside the table.

'Who wouldn't?' she shrugged lightly, bringing over the tea pot and then the tray. 'It's a wide and wonderful country.'

'You don't look the type to me, to go out in search of adventure.' He watched her as she poured his tea.

'Don't I?' She smiled down at him, her skin taking on the faintest tinge of pink under his strolling gaze. 'Well, that just goes to show how deceiving appearances can be, doesn't it?'

She poured her own cup and brought her chair round so that they were both facing on to the garden. In companionable mood they ate and chatted about life generally in England. The clock ticked away merrily on the mantelpiece, the birds swooped amongst the shrubbery. Alex had risen amidst the conversation and was just about to refill the doctor's cup when she felt rather than saw that a shadow had fallen across the doorway.

The teapot poised in her hand, her face animated at the discussion in progress, she turned to see the logging camp boss on the veranda.

It was strange – she had thought the afternoon needed nothing to make it brighter. And yet now the room seemed suddenly flooded with sunshine, as he stood there draped in the doorway, big in fawn shirt and slacks.

'Hello there, Grant!' the doctor greeted him with boyish exuberance. 'Come in and join us, won't you? We're taking English tea.'

'Hello, Lloyd,' Grant said easily. His eyes went straight to Alex. 'I saw your jeep on the way in from camp. Alma at the store told me you'd left with the doc.'

'Your charming nurse agreed to pander to the old doctor's wishes, to boil the billy with him,' Lloyd said, in a playful mood. 'And very efficient she is too.' He drew up an extra chair, his blue gaze on Alex, who was trying to appear at ease as she wielded the teapot. 'We've already been out on a case together.' He proceeded to give an account of what had happened at the Carmichaels.

Grant seated, listened in silence, reaching in occasionally for his cup. From the scalding incident, the conversation moved on to other things. Alex, back in her chair, gathered that Lloyd spent his evenings in the bar when he wasn't working, mainly for companionship.

The two men were apparently good friends. They talked leisurely about their mutual acquaintances there, and how each other's work was going. Eventually Lloyd brought up the question which Alex had been longing to ask.

Looking at the date on his watch, he exclaimed, 'Come to

think of it, what are you doing in Noongwalla today? Isn't this your Oaktown Saturday?'

'I was there earlier,' Grant explained casually, lighting up a cigarette.

Alex rose to clear the table and left the men to their chat. She was folding the tablecloth when the sound of a vehicle squealing to a halt outside made everyone look up.

'The Stassers' utility, I bet,' Lloyd said, rising heavily and making his way through to the front door. Before Alex had time to do anything about the weight of the atmosphere in the kitchen, he returned, striving to hold on to his jocular mood as he told them, 'Tea party's over, I'm afraid. That was Joe Law who works for the Strassers. I'll have to drive out to their property right away.'

He began collecting his things, commenting with a worn smile as he worked, 'I'm not looking forward to this one. Mrs. Strasser has a history of difficult births.' He sighed. 'But some mothers get this phobia for hospitals.'

Alex watched him as he struggled into a sports coat. Something vulnerable about his pale features, the way his smile did its best to hide the weariness in him, touched her heart.

'Let me come along with you. I'm sure I could help in some way,' she said impulsively.

Lloyd fastened up his jacket with a rueful grin. 'I'm selfish enough to take you up on your offer on this one, Alex,' he turned to pick up his bag, 'but I might have to stay out there all night. I wouldn't be able to drive you back, I'm afraid.'

'That doesn't matter,' Alex persisted, shrugging lightly. 'It's Sunday tomorrow. And I can sleep on the floor out there if necessary.'

She would have found it no hardship and she was taking a step forward to prove it, when Grant rose to his big height and said lazily, 'I've got my car. I'll bring her out there, Lloyd, and drive her back to the camp later.'

'That's good of you, Grant,' Lloyd beamed his appreciation. He made his way through towards the front, saying as he went, 'We take the south track and turn off at the

Hanlons' place. If you stay behind me you won't miss it. Close the back door, will you, Alex,' he called.

Alex did as he had asked, aware of Grant waiting for her to precede him out to the front. As she brushed by him, her shopping and handbag in her hand, she asked him, with a pointed look, 'Haven't you got other things to do?'

'Nothing that won't keep,' he glinted back, lifting an arm to guide her out to his car.

The doctor drove out of the settlement towards Denver's Creek, turning off on the track that led into the valley. Alex, seated beside Grant, in the shooting brake following behind, knew herself to be absurdly conscious of the logging camp boss; of his big shoulders, his rugged unhandsome looks and dark hair. She tried not to show it by giving her attention to the view.

The road coursed through a dusty emptiness at first, later coming down on to stretches of patchwork fields, each planted with ruler-straight lines of shrubs and fruit trees. The distance between each homestead was considerable, the cultivated areas sometimes going on for dozens of miles at a time. Occasionally the cars would hit a barren sandy stretch, then the orchards would start picking up again.

They passed the Hanlons' property, a picturesque group of buildings set amongst leaning trees and green stretches, afterwards taking the track that curved away towards more barren country.

Alex saw all this clearly enough, but it registered little on her unstable emotions. She wished she could have made light conversation, but everything seemed against it. And she had never been any good at that kind of thing anyway. Certainly Grant seemed in no mood for a chat, being frowningly preoccupied as he swung the wheel behind the doctor's car.

After several miles' more driving, they came at last to the Strasser homestead, a neat house in an open space surrounded by worksheds and outbuildings. There was a garden showing splashes of colour. Kookaburras chortled at the commotion of crunching tyres, and a magpie swooped over the hens making them cluck around indignantly.

A tall blond-haired man stepped out on to the veranda as the cars drew up. His face was a study in paternal anxiety at the coming birth. He made a valiant effort to conceal his agitation with a smile, as Lloyd introduced Alex and Grant to him, then taking the doctor's arm he urged, 'Right in here.'

Grant settled himself in a chair on the veranda. Alex went with the doctor inside. In a large bright room, gay with curtains and solid furniture, three children with buttercup-yellow hair stood and turned china blue eyes upwards at the visitors. Their father scooped them towards the door, ordering sternly, 'Outside, you littlies. Off to play with you now.'

He opened a door towards the back of the house. Following the two men inside, Alex saw a youngish woman, half propped up in a huge double bed, wringing the edge of the sheet in her hands.

Her strained features showed a glimmering of relief at the entry and she exclaimed, 'I'm glad you've come, doctor. I thought you weren't going to get here in time.'

'Relax, Ilka,' the doctor commanded gently, placing his bag down. And to her husband, ushering him out kindly, 'Off you go, Paul, and romp with the three you've got outside. We'll see to the one in here.'

Closing the door on the reluctantly departing figure, he turned to take off his coat, saying cheerfully to the forlorn figure in the bed, 'This is Nurse Leighton. She's come to give both you and me a hand.'

'Hello.' Alex bent to smooth the pillows, and smiling down apologetically at her linen suit she asked, 'Have you got an apron or something I could wear? I came out just as I was.'

'Oh yes!' Mrs. Strasser sat up helpfully and pointed to a heavy chest of drawers. 'Second one down. I think you'll find something there.'

While Alex sorted out a suitable pinafore in a cheerful pink check, the doctor washed his hands and made his examination.

'Oceans of time yet, Ilka,' he told her as he replaced his

stethoscope. 'The nurse and I would have had time to go to Oaktown to see a movie and back.'

Mrs. Strasser looked at him disbelieving. 'Doesn't feel like that to me,' she said distrustfully. 'I feel as though everything's going to happen at any minute.'

'You've had three,' the doctor admonished jokingly. 'You ought to be learning the ropes by now.' He set his things out on a scrubbed table, while Alex busied herself at the wood stove set in the fireplace at the other side of the bed.

There were saucepans of water, and a kettle, and logs for the stove. Everything had been placed in readiness. It was just a matter of arranging the layout to suit her own way of working.

His own preparations made, Lloyd came round and stood about uncertainly. 'Go and sit with the men,' Alex said with a practical smile. 'I'll let you know when something happens.'

He gave her a grateful look and moved away, saying reassuringly towards the bed, 'All right, Ilka?'

Ilka sighed frustratedly, then nodded, smiling. 'Yes, all right, doctor.' She watched him go out and close the door.

Alex draped clean white covers over the utensils, and checked that the few embers in the stove weren't getting too low. With nothing else to be done for the time being she placed a chair at the side of the bed. She had only the sketchiest knowledge of midwifery, of course, but it seemed to her that what Mrs. Strasser needed at the moment was a bit of feminine chat, to take her mind off her aches and pains.

She settled herself on the straight-backed chair, and started in lightly with, 'What would you like the baby to be, a boy or a girl?'

Ilka, as fair as her husband, with girlish features though she must have been approaching thirty, responded with a friendly if half-hearted shrug from the pillows. 'Be nice to have a boy, I suppose,' she admitted, 'then we'd have two boys and two girls. On the other hand,' she shrugged again, smiling this time, 'three girls and a boy would be just as nice.'

'What are the ages of your other children?" Alex pursued pleasantly.

'Helmut is the oldest, he's seven. Kaaren is five, and Annina is almost three.' Ilka stirred. 'When Paul and I got married we planned to have seven.' She grimaced good-humouredly, shaking her head at her present plight. 'But oh, I don't know. . . .'

'You'll feel different when the baby's tucked up in its cot and you're up and about again,' Alex said cheerily.

'I expect you're right,' Ilka nodded resignedly. She gazed at Alex, her interest growing as she asked, 'Are you from England?'

'Yes,' Alex smiled. 'I came out in September.' She returned the open friendly gaze and asked, 'Are you a new Australian?'

'Me? No!' Ilka laughed. 'I was born here. At Northam just outside Perth, if you've ever heard of it.' Clearly amused at Alex's question, she was soon giving the run-down on the family history.

Her grandparents had migrated from Frankfurt, Paul's from Stuttgart. The two of them had had a home in the deep south-west of Australia, perched above the rugged coastline. But Paul had always been interested in fruit farming. He had read of the Noongwalla property for sale a year ago. His father had helped him with the money. It was hard work, but they expected to be clear of the debt within three years.

Ilka talked in between bouts of apprehensive fidgeting. Alex listened, lighting the lamps when it grew dark, and re-kindling the stove now and again. In turn, she spoke of her own life in England, concentrating on her student nursing days rather than the depressing talk of when she was nursing her aunt.

The doctor looked in for a moment after dark. Paul appeared with a tray he had prepared himself, trying to look nonchalant, but showing his nerves in the way the teacups rattled at his handling.

At eight o'clock Ilka began to show signs of extreme discomfort, but it was after eleven before the sounds of a healthy squalling wail broke the silence of the night around the house.

Alex was on hand to clean up the baby and don the hand-me-down fleecy underwear and nightgown. Later, wrapping the well-washed shawl around it, she went into the living-room to show off her prize.

Paul started to breathe again. Young Helmut, who had managed to stay awake, went into the bedroom holding his father's hand.

Alex looked out to where the big dark shape was lounging on the veranda. 'Would you like to see the newest entry into the world?' she invited. 'Young man by the name of Paul junior.'

What she had hoped to achieve by getting Grant to come to her at this moment, to wave a new-born baby under his nose, she didn't know, but if it was a desire to shock him, or embarrass him in some way, she failed.

With the gauze strip she had given him to hold across his mouth, he gazed on the bundle in his lazy way and took a tiny hand in his firm one, as though he had been greeting new-born babies all his life. 'Ugly little feller, isn't he?' he drawled.

'He'll be beautiful in a week,' Alex found herself adding with a hint of briskness, feeling the most embarrassed of the three of them as Grant's dark head came in close to hers above the downy blond one; as his shoulder brushed hers. She lingered only as long as she had to, then she hurried back to the bedroom.

After a meal prepared by the hired hand, who proved himself a useful man in the kitchen, Alex, with Lloyd and Grant, retired to the veranda, leaving the family to themselves for a while. The night was warm, and the armchairs were comfortable. The mood was one of complete relaxation after the rigours of the evening.

Grant sat pulling lazily on a cigarette in the darkness. The doctor, puffing on his pipe, remarked above his lethargy, after a while, 'Things went better than I expected. Thanks to your help, Alex.'

Alex, from deep within her chair, said seriously, 'I wish

there was more I could do to take the weight off your shoulders.'

'My dear!' Lloyd said deeply, but with humorous undertones. 'You mustn't spoil me with your concern.'

'Why not?' Alex stirred uneasily in her chair. 'I hate to think of me lazing every evening and week-end away at the camp, while you're run off your feet in the settlement. I'm sure there must be something I can do for you in my spare time, if it's only the paperwork at your desk.'

'You're more likely to crack up than I am, trying to do two jobs,' he said gently.

'Nonsense,' Alex tossed at him lightly, 'I'm as strong as an ox.'

She sensed the glimmer of his twinkle roaming over her in the darkness as he mused softly, 'That's not the way I would have put it.'

'Don't change the subject,' she admonished, turning to smile at him, and with determination, 'I shall come down at least twice a week, to see that you're not too bogged down with work.'

'That's very sweet of you,' Lloyd dropped a hand over hers, 'and I do appreciate your thoughtfulness.'

Grant rose and tossed his half-smoked cigarette down. Grinding it under his heel, he said with a harsh note underlying the easiness in his tones, 'If you don't need Alex any more, Lloyd, we'll be getting along.'

'Of course,' Lloyd pushed himself to his feet and tapped his pipe out over the side. 'And I must be getting back to my patient. With a little luck I should be away myself by morning.'

He waved them off into the darkness, then went inside and closed the door. Alex had left her shopping and handbag in the car, so there was no need to disturb the Strassers further. There was only one dim light on in the bedroom at the back, which made it difficult to see one's way over strange ground. Grant took her arm while she was faltering and guided her along beside him. She couldn't help noticing the piercing grip of his fingers on her skin; his grim look as they seated themselves in the car.

Pulling away and following the beam of headlights along the road through the valley, he said after a while, sloping a drawn smile, 'You and the doc seem to make quite a team.'

'He ought to have more help,' Alex said, sighing.

Grant took a bend over-fast and asked, 'How do you intend to administer these spare time services of yours? The camp is three miles from the settlement.'

'I take it I will be allowed to use the jeep in off-duty hours,' Alex said a little coldly, sensing his hostility to the idea. No doubt he was thinking her work on the camp would suffer in some way.

Grant didn't refuse his permission, but his tones were sarcastic as he swung the wheel. 'You won't be much use to Lloyd wrapped round a tree, or knocked out in a ditch. You're not a driver, and never will be.'

'Maybe not,' Alex agreed smoothly, 'but I think I can manage the disused logging track all right.'

The subject closed, they sat side by side watching the road. Alex was glad of the silence. She had to admit she was completely exhausted after the night's work. At the moment she would have given anything for her bed.

She sat as straight as she could, but the soothing motion of the car was at times too much. Her head would keep on rolling to one side of its own accord. She had to keep jerking it back into position hazily.

Grant took his eyes off the road for a moment to look at her. 'Relax,' he said raspingly. And with a sour smile, 'Nurses sleep, don't they?'

They do, Alex thought, but not draped against their boss's shoulder. To guard against this she let her head rest back against the seat. The padding across the top cushioned the back of her neck nicely. She would just close her eyes for a moment. . . . Well, a few minutes, perhaps. . . . She knew it was far longer, much longer, but drifting off on the recurring waves of sleep, she was too drugged to care.

Only when her subconscious sensed the swishing sounds of the forest pines passing by overhead did she open her eyes to listen.

Grant turned his brown gaze on her. 'Better?' he asked, glinting in a peculiar way before he swung his glance back to the road.

'A little.' Alex raised her head and stretched stiffly, looking out of the windows. 'Are we almost at the camp?'

'Five minutes,' Grant nodded.

She peered at her watch. 'It's after two.'

'Quite a night,' he said vibrantly. She caught the gleam of his tight white smile in the glow from the headlights.

Coming up ahead she recognized one of the turn-offs into the camp. Grant took a short cut across rough open ground which brought them on to the circular road leading to the clinic.

Passing the storehouses and portable machinery sheds, they were almost there when the car had to slow down to a crawl to cope with a scattering of rowdy lumberjacks who were rolling about the road singing thickly to themselves, obviously the worse for drink.

Alex, seeing more ahead, some of them guffawing weakly amongst themselves as they stumbled along, wondered what had gone wrong. It wasn't the normal practice on an Oaktown Saturday, or any other night for that matter, to let the men go wandering all over the camp in their inebriated state. The unwritten rule had always been to dump them at their own sleeping huts. She blinked at the noise around the clinic. Where were the lorries that usually brought them in?

Grant, grim-faced, was obviously wondering the same thing. Finding it impossible to go forward or back for fear of brushing one of the careless figures, he swung off to the side into a screen of rough bracken and rapped at Alex, 'Stay in the car. I'm going up to the road, to see what's happened.'

Alex sat, refreshed after her sleep, watching from the open window, the dim curve of the road into the camp. From what she could see, the area was clearing now. One or two stragglers were offering raucous renderings to the stars, after which an argumentative group rolled by. Alex recognized Clem Atkins and one or two others more by their lusty voices and wild boasts, rather than their appearance.

These men were in no hurry and kept standing swaying in one spot to drive a point home. Shouts of scoffing laughter mingled with slurred curses as they made their way slowly along the road.

Gradually silence settled around the car. As the minutes ticked by, Alex listened to the voices fading slowly away into the darkness. She was relaxing at the thoughts of a peaceful night after all, and musing idly on the Strassers' baby, when nearby sounds came hammering into her thoughts again.

The voices she had expected to hear no more of rang back forcefully on the breeze from only yards away up the road. Raised and aggressive now, they seemed to be at the centre of a new commotion. Alex gathered that the final group of men had met up with others up ahead and some new differences of opinion had sprung up. She smiled to herself. One could only hope that the rumpus would die down.

This didn't turn out to be the case, however. If anything the noise grew louder. Alex turned her head and listened as thuds and bangs and wild shouts of beery laughter drifted along the road. On a sudden silence a crash rent the night air. That was glass, wasn't it . . .? The clinic windows!

Immediately she was up from her seat and groping for the door handle. The men could lark about as much as they liked, but when it came to camp property . . . and a hut that was her responsibility into the bargain. . . .

In warlike mood, she found a path through the bracken and quickly made her way up the road. As soon as she arrived at the clinic, she saw with relief that the windows were all intact. All that had happened was that some high-spirited individual had tossed a bottle against the water hydrant. She could see the pieces glittering in the starlight.

The swaying lumberjacks were scuffling amongst themselves, some banging on the sides of the hut as a form of encouragement to those who were getting the worst of a hefty shoe, but the mood was a playful one, rather than one of hurt feelings.

Discovering this, Alex felt somewhat superfluous moving in. In her hurry to get up here she hadn't thought to pick up her handbag with the keys in it. She debated with herself whether to carry on. Already the men were becoming aware of her. First one and then another ceased his antics and swaggered up to her.

Intent only on finding out what was going on, she hadn't stopped to consider either what effect her slim pale-suited figure would have on a crowd of irresponsible, drink-happy lumberjacks.

However, now that she was here she decided with sudden determination to assert her authority as nurse on the camp, and act as Mrs. MacTavish would have done.

Pulling herself up straight and putting on her most clinical air, she spoke around the group. 'Isn't it time you men stopped behaving like small boys and got back to your own huts?'

Terry Dale, a young thickset man with a mop of fair hair, lurched to brush close to her and smiled thickly, 'What's the hurry? The night's just getting interesting.'

'Yair,' Clem Atkins breathed his foul breath on her, 'we didn't expect to find Nursie waiting at home for us.'

She felt a rough grip on her arm as Shank Brophy shrugged the others off with a surly look. 'Stow it, Clem,' he growled, then leering at Alex, 'Me and Sister Kenny here got some unfinished business to 'tend to. Ain't that right, nurse?'

Alex, determined to bluff it out, said coldly, ignoring an apprehensiveness inside, 'I shall expect to see all of you gone from here in one minute. I'm going indoors now. Good night to all of you.'

She moved a little way, but Clem Atkins, bigger than any of the others, manoeuvred himself to pin her against the wood beside the door. 'Aw, you don't mean that, nursie,' he slurred with his cavernous smile. 'I ain't a bit tired.'

Amidst the swaying, jostling shapes Shank Brophy was there again. 'Back off, Clem,' he croaked in nasty mood. 'I tol' you, she's with me.'

Her back against the wall, Alex battled to keep her nerve as the air around her became less breatheable. She was reaching a hand out towards the door with a calm air, as

128

though she fully expected to open it and disappear inside, when the sound of a car skidding wildly to a halt on the road in front made her hand stay where it was.

Hard on the heels of the screaming brakes a voice came to slice like a whiplash across the group of men. 'Brophy! Atkins! Get to your bunks!'

The lumberjacks' minds, dulled with drink, were slow to register. They shuffled around, rumbling and grumbling to themselves, and emitting hoarse laughter under their breath. Taking their time amidst a lot of earthy abuse, aimed at no one in particular, they lurched in ones and twos back to the road and eventually reeled away into the darkness.

Alex stayed where she was, leaning a little against the hut as she listened to the gradually disappearing sounds. All had been completely still for some time before the footsteps came in from the car.

Feeling now that her actions had been just a little fool-hardy, she lowered her arm slowly from the door, as Grant moved in. What he had thought when he had come back and found the car door wide open in the bracken and her seat empty, she couldn't have said, but his face was pale as he looked at her.

Striving to bring normality to the scene, she asked, unable to disguise the shaking in her tones, 'What was the trouble with the transport? Did you find out?'

Grant nodded, tight-lipped. 'The second lorry broke down in Oaktown, there was no one capable of driving the third, so Wes has had to run a shuttle service getting the men back and dropping them off at the top of the road. He's gone to pick up the last load now. There'll be no more trouble tonight.'

The silence dropped heavily after his words. With his eyes still on her Alex found herself explaining with a lame smile, 'I heard a commotion from the car . . . it sounded like windows breaking, but when I got here it was just a broken bottle.' She added weakly, 'I forgot to bring the keys with me.'

A muscle was flexing in his jaw. She realized that he too had given no thought to the keys. As he made his way back to the car she stumbled along beside him, and from her seat gathered up her handbag and shopping.

She found the keys with some difficulty. Grant took them from her trembling fingers and scooped her along within the curve of his arm to the door.

Inside he slammed it behind them, went to switch on the light, then swinging on her, he blazed, 'What the hell do you mean by laying yourself open to a situation like that?'

Alex, stunned at his anger, swayed for a moment. Though her legs were shaking, she lifted her chin to him to say quiveringly, 'I could have handled it.'

Grant threw an exasperated hand up through his hair and paced to thunder, 'You're not here to win medals for coping with a pack of drink-crazed men!'

'Aren't I?' Quite ready to admit now that her nerves were torn to shreds, Alex stormed back, 'I thought you gave me to understand that you wanted a nurse who could do just that,' she gulped, '. . . yet when I try to act as Mrs. MacTavish would have done . . .' Hating herself for the emotion she was displaying; for the tears she knew were shining in her eyes, she faced him to trail off chokingly, 'I find it difficult to know what you *do* want!'

Grant, towering over her, said nothing. His face was battling with his own emotions. Slowly he slackened his frame. The anger died down in his eyes as he said gratingly, swinging away, 'Just bolt those doors after me, and get some sleep.'

Eyes glistening, Alex wasted no time in locking him out. She turned her back to the door, as he drove off, blinking away the dazzle.

She knew the cause of his foul mood, of course. He had made no secret of the fact that he didn't approve of her working for the doctor in her spare time.

CHAPTER EIGHT

GOING down to Lloyd twice a week and most weekends opened up a new dimension in Alex's hitherto narrow world. But mostly she found it a relief to get away from camp life, and Grant, when she could.

She worked alongside him amongst the men, when she had to, and discussed with him in the office the needs of the clinic. Every evening she sat at his table in the dining hut. Their conversation, which was sparse, was usually to do with camp routine. Occasionally in workaday tones he would ask her if she was going into the settlement and offer to drive her in, saying casually that it was on his way to the bar.

In workaday tones, Alex would decline his offer, telling him that she could manage.

Spending much of her free time in Noongwalla enabled her to become better acquainted with the small community there. In helping the doctor out, she got to know Mrs. Calhern with a bungalow on the main street, who had a 'heart', old Walter Kingsford, Mrs. Price's father at the hotel, who had brought his gout with him from England. She got used to popping in to see young Rosemary Schallert who was an asthmatic, and of course there were the toddlers and babies of the families in the valley who developed the usual childish complaints and needed watching.

After the first two or three visits to Lloyd's house, when she would sometimes find him in and sometimes out, they came to an arrangement where he would leave particulars of any routine calls that needed to be made on a pad in the kitchen.

Occasionally, when she opened the door with the key he had given her and walked through, she would find the pad empty. If this were the case she would use the time while he was away on a call, sorting out the chaos at his desk, attending to the standard government forms, and eliminating the

131

mass of hospital literature and medical circulars.

Often, though, there was a lull in the demands on the doctor's time. Then they would sit on the front veranda and drift with the afternoon, or the evening, a long cool drink each on the table between them.

Sometimes Alex had an urge to do something about the garden, and Lloyd would sit pulling leisurely on his pipe while she trimmed a bush or experimented with a splash of flowers in a pot at some focal point.

To Alex the times were satisfying in the sense that she knew she was being of some use to Lloyd; it cheered her to see the lines of strain fading from his face. And yet she had this persistent ache inside which said that life wasn't as satisfying as it could be.

Throughout December the main talking point in Noongwalla was the Christmas festivities. It seemed strange to Alex to be making plans to eat turkey and Christmas pudding when the sun was blazing down from a cloudless sky, and the heat was inclined to be oppressive. As the time grew near, excitement mounted for the annual dance which would be held in the big hall, only just recently completed for the occasion.

Along with the doctor, Alex found herself roped in to help with the decorations. This was an occupation she enjoyed, delving into the streamer-trailing hampers to see what glittering tinselled object she could discover, and later debating on where each item would be displayed to its best advantage.

The hall was sandwiched between the barber's shop and a storing shed, and still smelled strongly of new wood. Its walls lined with a row of chairs, it boasted cloakroom facilities at the far end, and a bar just in from the entrance. As it stretched twice as far back from the main street as the other buildings there was a considerable area inside to be strung with garlands. Alex and Lloyd took their turn along with half a dozen others to work there, everyone dropping in whenever they had the time to spare.

Towards the end, when the hall was looking quite a picture, Alex went over with Lloyd to put the final touches to the tree, a beautiful Monterey pine delivered specially for the occasion from the timber camp. They had decorated most of it together, but now they couldn't agree on what should be its final crowning glory.

The last rays of the sun were slanting through the open doorway, the hot evening air was misty with dust from the main street. Alex held up a resplendent fairy complete with wand and spangled dress and argued good-humouredly, 'I still say this young lady deserves the place of honour, if it's only for her beauty.'

'But look at my star,' Lloyd said with a plaintive twinkle, holding up the glittering shape. 'What could be more inspiring at Christmas time than the star of Bethlehem?'

'Fairies are Christmassy,' Alex said practically. 'The children will like it.'

'Everyone will like my star,' Lloyd opined, admiring it ostentatiously.

Fighting playfully, they each made their way to the steps. Close together at the foot, Lloyd looked at her to concede with a grin, 'Let's toss for it.' At Alex's disapproving twinkle he shook his head. 'No, that wouldn't be right, would it?'

In the deadlock Alex espied, amongst the straw in the hamper a tall spired bauble in twinkling silver and gold. 'That looks as though it was meant for the top of the tree,' she said thoughtfully.

'Give it to me quick,' Lloyd laughed, 'before we have another change of mind!'

She held the steps as he climbed to slot the spire on the top of the upright branch, staying where she was until he was safely down again. They stood back together to nod happily over the effect, then each raced to hang their pet item in another obvious position.

The fun of the last few moments between them, they were handling the garlands of tinsel amidst a warm laughing intimacy, when a footstep sounded in the doorway and Grant strode in.

He spent the time it took him to move from the door to

the tree, absorbing the scene. When he arrived he gave Lloyd a smile which seemed to hide a certain testiness and drawled, 'You took some finding. I went over to your house, and to the bar.' He took a fold of paper from his shirt pocket and explained, 'I've got a form here for Mike Stronowsky. It needs the area doctor's signature.'

'Oh yes,' Lloyd turned to him good-naturedly, 'the man who had his arm crushed some weeks back. Is he fit now?'

'Well enough to take on a light job at the timber mill in Mount Gambier,' Grant nodded at the form.

'Yes, I see.' Lloyd flicked his glance over the paper and taking out his pen, moved off with a smiling, 'Excuse me a moment.'

While he was resting on a chair across the room, scrawling his signature, Alex continued to work silently at the tree beside Grant. She wished she could have acted gay and natural with him as she could with Lloyd, inviting him to drape a garland or two while he was here, laughingly urging him to try his hand with the baubles. But instead something about his nearness made her move woodenly; made her fingers unsure of themselves as she worked.

It was with relief that she saw Lloyd bringing the form back. Giving her the impression that he was similarly tightened up inside, Grant saluted mildly and made his way out.

Alex watched him go, her heart spiralling down from its strung up height to a dull uncertain feeling, as her hands worked at weaving a length of tinsel round the tree. She had no idea what his own plans were for the festivities. He might even be leaving the camp for the two-day holiday.

With the heat increasing by the day it became evident to Alex that a blouse and skirt or linen suit would be totally unsuitable for the Noongwalla dance. In a mad moment she bought three cotton dresses. They were of excellent quality and style, and Mrs. Truslow, Alma at the store, let her go through to the back to try them on. Satisfied that each was a good fit, she took them back to the clinic and hung them carefully in the wardrobe, planning to wait until the last moment before she made a final choice.

Work finished early at the camp on Christmas Eve. After a traditionally festive meal laid on by the cookhouse in the dining hut, and partaken of rowdily by all concerned, the lumberjacks departed to go their different ways.

Taking the whistles and good wishes from the men in his smiling way, Grant guided Alex along with him through the high-spirited crush around the tables. Once they were outside she went off to prepare for her evening in Noongwalla.

She showered leisurely, loving the fragrance of sweet-scented lavender on her skin, and afterwards choosing the coolest in underwear. She had laid out the three dresses on the bed. The forget-me-not clustered design had been amongst her buys, but she passed this over now in favour of one with multi-coloured flowers on a pale peach background. Sleeveless, with scooped neckline, and gathered skirt, it was a simple dress, yet in it she felt almost carefree.

Her hair, recently washed, shone as she brushed it. It took her some considerable time to take it back into its neat coil, because it had grown madly in the last few weeks. Once it was set, however, it seemed to look fuller and smoother somehow.

She had never been one to think much about make-up, but tonight she experimented with a touch of lipstick. The warm peach colour lifting out the pale glow of her skin, the effect didn't seem too bad. In a pair of low-heeled sandals, and with a small white handbag in her hand, she viewed the finishing touches before the long mirror. All it needed now, after all her efforts – she smiled wryly – was for Lloyd to get called out on a case, leaving her to cope at the dance on her own.

Still before the mirror she asked herself, ponderingly, would she mind terribly, if he had to go? A pent-up sigh escaped her lips. She turned away. It was time she was starting out for Noongwalla.

Outside, the camp was like a ghost town. There was sight of neither man nor machine. Only the huts stood, dark silent shapes in the sun-washed evening light. All unsuspecting Alex turned and walked round to the side of the clinic to find the space where she always parked the jeep empty. Now who would . . .? She stood looking about her wonderingly. So busy in her own rooms, she had heard nobody come up and take the jeep away. Yet very obviously someone had.

After some moments she walked across the open space towards the main buildings, staring round at the emptiness . . . and whoever had removed it had tucked it away most thoroughly along with everything else, so it seemed.

She was about centrally placed in the open area of the camp, making her way towards the machine sheds, when a car, the only living thing in a dead world, curved out from the men's quarters and came slowly towards her.

As she recognized Grant's shooting brake, Alex's spirits soared only to drop quickly again. Was he just starting out to spend Christmas away from the camp like everyone else? He pulled up beside her, his hooded brown gaze through the open window darker in some way as he flicked it over her summer look.

Feeling suddenly very conscious of her bare arms and throat, Alex chased up a smile and asked lightly, 'I've been looking for the jeep. It's been spirited away. Have you seen it?'

Grant nodded, looking devastatingly striking in silk coffee-coloured shirt, dark brown tie and matching slacks. 'Company rules,' he said drily. 'All camp equipment has to be locked away for security reasons, during holiday periods.'

Alex looked blank at his words. While she was wondering how she was going to get to the settlement, he leaned to open the door for her and drawled, 'I'm going your way.'

Alex bent and climbed into the seat. She sat straight, feeling her insides behaving peculiarly as Grant brushed close to fasten the door across her. She watched as they moved out on to the main road, a sweet singing note at the back of her mind. There was no luggage in the car, and Grant was dressed only casually as though . . .

Not wishing to get carried away, she gave herself up to the pleasure of the summer night. Above, the branches of the majestic pines merged to make an emerald green lacework against the steadily fading blue sky. Colourful birds darted amongst the lengthening shadows at the side of the road. On the warm breeze wafting in at the windows came all the mingling scents of the countryside.

Alex wanted to close her eyes over an overwhelming surge of tear-jerking happiness that seized her. She wished that the car and she and the evening and Grant could go steadily on for ever.

All too soon the houses of the settlement showed up. As they cruised along into the main street, she could see the lights streaming out into the dusk from the gaily decked out hall. Already people were surging about around the entrance. Battered utilities belonging to the outlying homesteads were parked in the space alongside.

Alex kept her gaze eagerly pinned on the building, only to find Grant pulling up outside the hotel bar. She stepped out as though she had never assumed for one moment that he was going anywhere else, and summoning a smile of thanks for the lift she left him to close the door of the car after her. As she walked on past the hall, she had a feeling that he stood to watch her cross over to Lloyd's house.

The doctor, looking relaxed and happy in well pressed trousers and tailored shirt, was waiting on the veranda. As she went in at the gate and up the steps, he trailed his blue glance over her and smiled in his kindly way, 'We certainly can't have anyone coming up with an appendicitis tonight. It would ruin everything.' One arm out, he drew her towards a chair.

After a leisurely drink, over which they talked generally on the day's happenings, they started out to join in the evening's festivities.

The hall was reverberating with the sound of children and adults when they arrived. Immediately swept into the midst of the warmhearted crowd, along with the doctor, Alex was soon lost in the whirl of the evening.

There were games to be played with balloons popping and streamers flying, and drinks to be served to relieve the overworked ladies at the bar. Old Walter Kingsford, who made a very impressive Father Christmas, needed a hand to distribute the presents to the children, and the older members of the community, sitting watching from their chairs at the side, needed to be made to feel that they were included in the celebrations.

Cool in her summer dress, a friendly smile on her face, Alex went from one crowded moment to the next, in her natural serene way.

After the children had wandered off sleepily to the sides to play with their presents, there was dancing for the parents and younger people. Taped music filled the hall and more and more people drifted in, to crowd in groups at the door, and around the floor.

Not all of them were from Noongwalla, of course. Many, Alex knew, were relatives of the residents, visiting for Christmas. She recognized also some of the younger lumberjacks at the camp, who had romantic attachments with teenage girls in the settlement. Wherever they came from, they crowded the floor of the hall in couples, making the most of its smooth shiny dancing surface.

Apart from a few turns with the male members of the families she had come to know on her nursing calls, Alex danced most of the evening with Lloyd. Wherever she was, chatting professionally with a group of mothers, or caught up with acquaintances who had just arrived, he would come and pluck her away and guide her smilingly on to the floor.

She felt comfortable in his arms. He was her own height, and he moved in a relaxed way so that she hardly knew they were dancing at all. At odd moments they would chat amidst the din, discussing couples with young families, who hadn't made it to the dance, possibly because of the remoteness of their homestead; the Strassers in particular.

He held her gently, his blue gaze and smile for her most of the time, and Alex was ashamed of herself at having to hide a flatness inside. Frequently without appearing to, she would cast a quick searching glance around the room. What she was hoping for was ridiculous, of course, but she couldn't stop herself, for all that.

As the evening wore on she tried to accept the futility of

hoping. And then, on one of those fleeting searching glances amongst the laughing groups, her heart gave a jolt at the sight of Grant a little way down from the bar.

Moving in Lloyd's arms, she lost the view of him for a while. When she saw him again he was dancing with the schoolteacher who managed the infants in the settlement. She was an attractive woman. Alex's throat constricted painfully at the way she reacted to Grant's lazy white smile and the nearness of his powerful frame.

When the doctor had to go off to pay his respects to an old farming couple who had made a considerable journey for the event, Alex found the scenery less trying behind the bar. Most people were talking now, not drinking, so she had little to occupy her nervous fingers. When she looked up she saw familiar wide shoulders not far away.

While she was pretending not to notice them, Jeff Crisp, who was the manager of a timber mill in Oaktown, and who had relatives in the settlement, came up to slap him on the back, exclaiming matily, 'Grant, you old son of a gun! What are you doing at a hop like this?'

Alex turned briskly away to answer a request for lemonade. After this she spent her time folding a tea towel neatly, listening to the men's voices floating nearer. She could hear Lloyd's there now, and one or two other settlement dwellers. They were in fine festive mood all of them. She didn't know about Grant because she wouldn't let herself look his way. She didn't even realize he was close beside her at the end of the bar, until he took her arm and led her forward to drawl glintingly, amidst the gaiety of the group, 'It wouldn't be Christmas without a dance with the camp nurse.'

Alex moved with him to the edge of the dance floor. An odd pain shot through as he drew her close. His big frame in comparison to Lloyd's seemed to overwhelm her, and yet, though his steps were forceful and demanding as opposed to the doctor's leisurely ones, he moved in an incredibly relaxed way.

Alex couldn't remember dancing seriously since her student nursing days. With Grant the steps came as naturally as though it had been only yesterday. She followed him with her eyes about level with his big shoulders. She couldn't smile radiantly up at him, as the schoolteacher had done. She couldn't do anything except feel that she had been moulded to fit into the curve of his arm, to move with the muscular line of his body.

When the music stopped and she had to turn away she felt as though the light had suddenly been switched out on life.

Grant didn't take his arm away immediately. He guided her through the groups, many of which were dispersing now as the evening came to a close.

Most of the children were fast asleep on the chairs around the side, or were being taken out to the cars. Beside the bar, the group was pretty much the same as when she and Grant had left it. Jeff Crisp was still there talking shop to Lloyd and one or two of the other men. He wasted no time in roping Grant, a fellow logging man, into the friendly argument which was in progress.

Alex went to collect her bag from behind the bar, and came back to chat with the womenfolk of the group who were gathering. The men's jocular argument eventually came to an end and the conversation became general as the wives mingled in to take part.

With the hall fast becoming empty Alex found herself a smiling member of the group. She knew that Grant, talking lazily to Jeff, was only a little way behind her. Deep inside, away from her calm smile, she nursed a tiny hope again. She had no jeep tonight, and Grant had driven her into Noongwalla. . . .

Couples were drifting towards the door. Her own party was preparing to break up. Alex talked on lightly along with the others. The spark of hope inside her grew into an all-consuming longing, only to die as Lloyd, beside her, turned an arm about her shoulders, and said easily, though he knew nothing of her being without transport, 'If you're ready, my dear, I'll drive you back to the camp.'

Alex kept her smile carefully for Lloyd. She moved to the door with him and left Grant where he had been standing close to her.

Outside, the night air was warm and scented with flowers from the nearby gardens. She walked with Lloyd to his car which was parked in the open space under the trees fronting his house. When they were seated in the car he lingered for a moment before turning the ignition key. His mood, normally one of warm geniality, seemed mellow now after their night of gaiety. His sincere blue gaze fixed on Alex, he said, smiling, 'You look as fresh now as you did five hours ago.'

'Thank you, Lloyd,' Alex smiled back, trying not to notice a certain depth in his blue gaze. 'It's been a lovely evening.'

Over the flatness inside, she sat and watched him start the engine and turn out into the main street. They drove back along the road to the logging camp in silence, Lloyd outwardly content with his own thoughts, Alex striving not to let her own show too much. Soon the turn off to the camp loomed up. The car swung in, its headlights illuminating the clumps of bracken and tree butts.

The doctor knew his way along the circular road. He drew up in front of the dark shape of the clinic. Stepping out of the car, Alex was uncertain what to do next. She moved to turn the key in the lock. Lloyd opened the door and went inside to switch on the light.

He strolled around, his twinkling blue gaze everywhere at once. 'You've made quite a few changes, I see.' He paused to observe the draped windows, the rearranged medical equipment. 'There's hardly a sign of our "battling MacTavish" here.'

Alex followed his gaze and said simply, 'Everyone has their own ways of working, I suppose.'

They stood in mutual agreement, then Lloyd suddenly turned to take both her hands in his to face her. 'It's Christmas Day tomorrow.' He reached down to her heart with his eyes. 'Are we going to spend it together?'

Alex strove to appear natural. 'It's been rather hectic these past few weeks,' she said lightly. 'I think I'd like to spend the two days quietly, catching up with little jobs of my own.'

'I understand,' Lloyd nodded with his warm smile, and

141

squeezing her hands. 'Don't let it be too long before you come to Noongwalla.'

'I won't.' While she faced him, her hands clasped in his, Alex heard the hum of a car engine outside. Without looking she knew that Grant had just passed the clinic, and as the windows were tall and brightly lit, he couldn't have failed to see her there with Lloyd.

A few seconds later she was walking with the doctor to the door. She watched him stoop into his car in the shaft of light. He reversed and waved as he left. All was still and silent on the camp when she closed and bolted the door.

The hundred and one little tasks she had looked forward to pottering with around her room during the two-day holiday Alex found merely burdensome. Working without zest, she washed the covers and ironed them, using Mrs. MacTavish's flat-iron on the stove, then she polished the oddments of furniture and the floor, turned out her wardrobe, and washed and ironed various blouses and skirts and oddments.

When she felt in need of a meal she walked across the open space to the cookhouse and opened the door with the key which Pop Doolin had given her before he left to spend Christmas with his daughter in Adelaide. The long empty hut with its cold stoves and lack of clatter and bustle might have been cheerless but for the hot summer sunshine slanting through the windows and lighting the vast stew-pans and gleaming ladles. Using a small electric stove powered by the camp generator, she came in at odd moments through the day and cooked whatever food she required. She wondered, as she watched an egg frying, or the contents of a saucepan bubbling, if Grant was doing likewise.

She could see his car parked in the same spot over by the men's quarters each time she walked across from the clinic.

She spent the evenings strolling amongst the trees at the back of the clinic, gazing at the brilliant birds with an unseeing eye. When dark had dropped, she sat in her room and persevered with the current library book. Sometimes when sitting became too much, she would drift through into the clinic, switch on the lights and find some small job to do. Later in the darkness again she would return back towards her room and her book, after gazing through the windows cross the open space into the distance.

In the whole blacked-out area of the logging camp there were just two tiny pools of light. One casting a blur from her own back window, the other spilling out faintly from Grant's hut over in the men's section.

CHAPTER NINE

WITH January came the real heat. Each morning the sun rose in fiery splendour and climbed to blaze down from a sky untrammelled by cloud or wind. In the forests the temperature was often as high as ninety degrees in the shade. Amidst the drone of the bulldozer and clank of the cranes, the lumberjacks worked stripped to the waist, their bodies dripping with sweat.

Alex was glad now that she hadn't bought nylon overalls for working in. Her present cotton ones, though they needed rather more care if one were to maintain their snowy whiteness and pressed look, were at least passably cool, and she was able to wear the minimum of underwear underneath.

In the clinic, with the windows opened their widest to catch the merest flicker of a breeze, she worked in comparative comfort. If she had to go out, she took care to move at an unflustered pace. She was lucky in the respect that no outstanding accidents occurred in the forests demanding on-the-spot attention. The usual sprains, barked shins, and trapped fingers, the men brought to her to clean up and dress in the clinic. She was doubly inclined to appreciate this last fact when she learned that the tree-felling crews were now operating up in the southern section of the woods, an area stretching through wild and difficult terrain.

In the all-embracing heat with nothing to do except attend the odd minor casualty, the days passed, taking little toll on Alex's energy. They might have continued to do so but for an unforgivable oversight on her part.

One stifling afternoon, she was checking over her medical stock to see if there was any item she needed to put in with the weekly order list for supplies to the camp. The shelves, and drawers held their usual complement of lints and bandages and cottonwool. The drum of disinfectant was still fairly full. There seemed to be no shortage of anything as far as she could see. Then opening the drug cupboard, she discovered with a rush of colour, while checking over the analgesics, that she had allowed her supply of the main pain-killing drug to run pitifully low.

If it hadn't been for that rather hectic week just before Christmas she would never have overlooked so important a detail. But that was no excuse. If a serious accident happened on the camp right now, she could find herself without the means to give the right kind of help.

Immediately she sat down and filled out the necessary chit. Then locking up the clinic she took the jeep and drove over to the offices. Her heart sank to find the main section deserted, apart from Casey Hall, who had the field telephone apart in pieces on the desk. For such an important drug she had to have Grant's signature on the chit, and if she didn't get it this afternoon to include in the camp's supply order it would have to wait a whole week.

She thanked Casey for his help in pointing out to her on the forest map the logging crew's whereabouts, and went outside into the baking heat. Seated behind the wheel of the jeep she set off with an ironic light in her eyes. This was one afternoon when she wasn't going to be able to get out of sampling an Australian summer!

If there had been any remnants of humour in her mind at the outset, they soon disappeared after ten minutes on the route. The track wound uphill over ground that seemed to have every obstacle planted in it that had ever been thought up. She jolted sickeningly over pyramids of rock, bounced over tree stumps, and gritted her teeth over the narrow space between crowding gum trees. It was a miracle in her eyes how the bulldozers and machinery had got up this way. But they were there all right, she could hear them clattering and whining in the distance.

Her passage disturbed a small flight of white cockatoos from the trees, but she was too occupied to take much heed of the sight. When she reached the uppermost ridge, she found to her dismay that the men were working in the lowest regions of the valley below her. Climbing uphill in the jeep wasn't exactly her strong point. Going down with practically everything that could offer itself in her path was going to be even less of one.

Thankfully she was screened completely from the sun by the forest foliage. But the strain of following in the tracks of the heavy machinery, watching out for possible looming objects, and holding her speed, soon had her arms trembling from the effort of gripping the wheel, her head spinning with concentration.

If it had been cooler it might have helped. Alex doubted it. She had possibly been driving for no more than half an hour. When she arrived at the work scene she felt as though it had been all day.

Her legs unsteady, she went to look for Grant. She found him in the heart of the clatter, supervising a grappling machine which handled huge logs as though they were wisps of straw. When he turned and saw her almost at his side, he put an arm out and led her away from the swinging logs.

Alex walked with him to a small glade away from the noise. Ever since their dance together on Christmas Eve, she had found it a battle to contain certain feelings. Whenever they met she tried to appear unaffected by his presence. If she succeeded it was because she made a superhuman effort to look solely concerned with her nursing duties.

Assuming a clinical air now, she withdrew the chit from her overall pocket and asked him for his signature. He took the slip of paper, flicked his glance over it, then swung his penetrating gaze back to her. She knew he was taking in her jaded look. Unfortunately there was nothing she could do about that, though she strove to keep her shoulders straight, her head up, as he looked at her.

'You drove down here just for this?' he snapped.

'It's very necessary,' Alex replied truthfully. 'I have only a little of the drug left. It would be unwise to wait another week before ordering.'

'Casey Hall's in the camp somewhere,' Grant barked. 'Couldn't you have asked him to drive you over?'

'Mr. Hall is busy with his own duties,' Alex replied coolly, and in businesslike tones, but with a hint of shakiness, she told him, 'And I'm simply fulfilling mine.' He had never considered her capable of handling the jeep. She hated to be proving him right.

Grant took his eyes back to the chit. He felt for a pen to sign it, and growled at her testily, 'Sit down. You don't have to prove you're made of cast iron twenty-four hours a day.'

Alex sank down on a huge log behind her, hardly caring that he watched her. It was a relief to take the weight off her legs, to let her body sag. He went off then. She thought it was for the purpose of putting his signature on the slip of paper.

She sat for some considerable time. Gradually the strength returned to her limbs. The blur of strain disappeared from her vision. Relaxed, she was able to appreciate, for the first time, the green cool of the glade she was sitting in.

Grant came back just as she was turning to look for him. He gave no explanation for staying away so long. Nor did he give her the chit he was holding in his hand. After waving it before her, he folded it and put in in his shirt pocket, asking, as he threw his glance around, 'Where did you leave the jeep?'

'Just before the entrance to the clearing.' She rose and pointed. Refreshed, she led the way, picking a route through felled logs and discarded branches, while Grant took his time behind her.

Arriving at the vehicle, she waited before climbing into the driving seat, thinking he would give her the paper she had brought for his signature. Instead he moved in behind the wheel himself. Alex viewed his action with set lips. 'I brought the jeep down here,' she pointed out thornily. 'I certainly think I'm capable of taking it back.'

'So do I,' he said drily. 'But driving on your nerves is a hell of a sight more uncomfortable than driving on four wheels. Get in.'

Alex had no choice but to do what he said, though she did it under sufferance. As soon as she was seated he started up, and swung round in the direction of the camp. He sped up the track, miraculously missing everything she would have hit, swinging the wheel effortlessly as though they were careering along a country road.

Alex sat, barely disturbed in her seat, coolly watching their progress. Being a nurse she knew all too well what Grant meant, of course, when he had talked about driving on one's nerves. Anyone could handle one of these things, even Grandmother MacTavish, if they were sufficiently relaxed at the wheel. The jeep was designed to take anything in its stride. Unfortunately Alex wasn't. Though she battled to give full measure as regards efficiency, she couldn't apply herself to driving the jeep without tensing over it. And it was the tensing up that had worn her out on the run down just now.

She knew all this, but it didn't make her feel any less of a disappointment to herself.

With Grant at the wheel, experiencing hardly a bounce, her own tortuous ride seemed ridiculous by comparison. They were approaching the camp in half the time it had taken her to do the trip.

Arriving at the clinic eventually, Grant climbed out and came round while she was still struggling to find her feet. He gave her a hand down, sensing, she thought, the tiredness which engulfed her. While she was smoothing her hair and trying to give the impression of being totally unaffected by the trip he rapped at her, 'Stay away from the southern sector in future. It's tough enough on the men.'

Was he making excuses for her? Alex gave him a straight look. 'What happens if I'm called out to that area?' she asked.

'We'll meet that if and when the occasion arrives.' He patted the drug chit in his pocket and left her with, 'I'll put this through in the office.'

Alex might have known, of course, that because she had been forbidden to go to that particular part of the forest, her troubles would start. Life was like that. In the same week a mishap occurred there which could have happened to any one of the lumberjacks. Young Terry Dale was loading tree trunks one morning on to a trailer truck. The chain broke and the trunk rolled back, whipping his crowbar back and trapping his hand on the next trunk down.

148

Wes Brissac told her all about it on the field telephone. He said there was no sense in bringing Terry all the way down to the clinic. If there was anything broken it would be quicker to go on to the Oaktown hospital from where they were working.

While Alex was preparing in her mind to disobey the orders she had been given, Wes told her to wait at the clinic. She hung up after he had rung off, puzzling over this last strange request. He had gone to the trouble to call her and give her full details of the accident, and then he had told her to stay where she was.

She soon learned why. Less than a quarter of an hour later, she heard Grant drive up in his dusty shooting brake. As she stood at the door, he changed over to the jeep and asked, 'Have you got your medical gear?'

She went in to collect her case and walked out to the jeep. Without a word he assisted her in. Within minutes they were on the track bearing south through the forest.

Arriving at the tree-felling scene, Alex found Terry Dale sitting nursing his hand on a sawn log. With Grant looking on, she arranged a clean towel and examined the fingers of his hand gently. Every one was in working order. He was pleased to hear that. She cleaned and disinfected the grazes, and bandaged the whole of his hand with care. He was told he could take the day off, but, pulling his working glove on, he showed no particular inclination to leave. He was young, with a healthy appetite, in spite of his argument with the log, and his eyes were fixed on the cookhouse food cans being unloaded ready for the midday meal.

Alex replaced her medical tackle and closing her case, turned to go. Grant escorted her back to the jeep and took the wheel. When they were cruising back along the rough track, the midday sun casting shafts of gold down through the trees, she said as gracefully as she could manage, 'I appreciate your assistance with the driving in this country, of course, but we both know you haven't the time to be neglecting your own work for mine.'

The reply came from behind the wheel as they skirted a leafy copse. 'We'll keep this routine until we can think of something else,' and drily, 'Maybe we'll get you a horse.'

Alex kept her gaze ahead. She couldn't joke with Grant. She was too conscious of him as a man; too aware of his big check-shirted shoulders, his sunburnt arms and craggy features.

Though she didn't look at his face now, she knew that, conversely, he wasn't in the habit of smiling when he was with her. His mouth these days was usually set at a disagreeable slant, his brown gaze when he flicked it over her glinted moodily.

Throughout those January days, Alex learned to expect nothing else from him. On another of the occasions when she had been obliged to let him drive her up into the rough working section of the forest she was left with some considerable time on her hands. She had finished her first aid work on a man with a cut eye. Grant, however, had got caught up in a problem to do with the bulldozer and a difficult stretch of land. She could of course override his authority and drive herself back to the clinic. But she was a coward in this area, and she knew it.

There seemed nothing for it but to take it easy for a while. Going back to the jeep she saw now that the shade in which she had parked it had moved on, for as the men gradually eliminated the trees, they and the forest floor came in for the direct rays of the sun.

Alex had never tried her hand at sunbathing. It hadn't occurred to her to indulge in the pastime when she was younger, and there had never been time living with her aunt. To be truthful, she didn't see herself with a tan, but as everyone seemed to look that way in Australia she supposed she ought to acquire one.

With the sun streaming down on the jeep now and the men working some distance away, it seemed the ideal time to start. Sitting in her seat, she soon found she couldn't stand the heat on her head and face, but finding a position where her arms below the sleeves of her overall were exposed, she relaxed back and waited for results. She was favoured with a light breeze which flapped around her, belying the heat of the sun.

It was pleasant sitting. And sleep-inducing too. With an effort she kept her thoughts marshalled. It wouldn't do for the camp nurse to sleep on duty. Eyes closed, she passed the time listening to the clatter of machinery. She knew the noise of the bulldozer well enough; a roaring acceleration of the motor followed by a few seconds of steady running, then a period of idling. There was a few seconds more of light running as the thing reversed, then the rhythm began again.

She followed the cycle over and over again, hearing it roar and recede, roar and recede, in the drowsy confines of her mind.

It was a noise near at hand, cutting across the rhythm of the bulldozer, which made her open her eyes as she sat. Grant was beside her, his face taut with anger. He was doing something with the fittings of the jeep. She didn't know what until he flung the rain roof into position over her head. His eyes blazed as they raked the lobster pink patches on her arms. His gaze working up over the paleness of her throat, he rasped at her, 'Your skin wasn't meant for the sun. Isn't it enough that all the men are burnt black around here?'

Alex watched him take the wheel and slam on the starter, riveted by his violent mood. On the drive back she could find no words to meet it. There was something in his anger that seemed to add to the air of strain between them. She could do nothing to overcome it, as he drove grimly into camp. She sat white-faced beside him, her insides tightened up over emotions that were new to her. He left her outside the clinic and thundered away in the jeep.

Though he had taken complete control of the vehicle since her rough ride that day to get the drug chit signed, she noticed it was always there, parked at the side of the clinic, in the evenings and at the week-ends.

Of course, she took advantage of it to escape to Noongwalla whenever it was possible. There was a restfulness at the doctor's house that didn't exist at the camp. She found it a relief not to have to be on her guard in case her thoughts or her feelings showed. With Lloyd she had no fears of displaying her emotions. He was a man with whom she could relax completely. Also she had the consolation of knowing that she was helping him. He tired easily, and with her on hand to take some of the work off his shoulders, he had a much smoother existence.

He never failed to thank her for this at least once during each of her visits, when, after their round of medical activities, they would sit drowsing the summer evenings away together on the veranda, or strolling side by side in the garden.

Their work had created a bond between them. Since Christmas and the night of the dance, it seemed strengthened by Lloyd's gentle attentiveness towards her.

After the rigours of the day, working at the camp knowing that Grant was somewhere around, making stilted conversation with him at his table in the dining hut, Alex found the doctor's company quietly soothing. And she didn't always have to go to the settlement to find it.

Often nowadays, having more time on his hands, Lloyd would take a run out to the clinic. As he was the area supervisor for all medical activities, the logging camp came under his jurisdiction, so his car cruising along the circular road was a normal sight.

On those sunny afternoons he would relax, half-sitting on the desk watching Alex work. Sometimes she would make tea for them both, and they would sip it gazing out across the logging camp through the curtained windows. With things running smoothly in the settlement they were leisurely times for the doctor.

It was in February when the 'flu bug struck.

A virulent summer virus, confined mainly to the cities, it was inevitably finding its way into the sparsely populated areas. Luckily most people seemed to be able to combat it. The ones that didn't, however, were hard hit for a while.

Will Price at the hotel was the first one to go down with it in Noongwalla. He was very ill, and his wife and daughters had to do the best they could coping with the bar. There wasn't a lot one could do for the illness, except prescribe the usual tablets, and let the germ run its course, taking care to keep a special watch on the very young and the aged.

Coming to Lloyd's rescue in the sudden rush of work,

Alex soon became adept at following his instructions regarding the prescribing of the necessary pills and tablets, and using her own judgment when she called in on a case on her own. She couldn't go out into the valley, of course, because she had no authority to drive, outside the camp. But while Lloyd was obliged to make long trips attending to elderly members of fruit-farming families, she was able to make herself useful around the settlement.

There was probably no more than half a dozen people down with the malady at one time in the whole of the compact community, yet she found herself working every moment of her off duty periods away from the camp, at some task or other.

Always in these cases it was the ones who had to shoulder the heaviest responsibilities who went down with the bug — namely, the young mothers. They would drag themselves around before they were sufficiently recovered, trying to run the home and manage a family in the usual way. Alex helped with the children in these cases where she could. She drove through the forest in the evenings and leaving the jeep in its usual spot in the clearing went off to bathe babies, and feed toddlers, and perhaps rub through a few smalls here and there.

Mrs. Carmichael was one of the mothers hit by the 'flu. She lay in bed, a white ghost of herself, trying to take care of her young family from there, while her husband went out to work. Though it was quite a walk from the settlement for Alex, down past the old timber mill overlooking the valley, she tried as often as she could to fit the Carmichaels in with the rest of her calls.

She hadn't seen little Shelley since the day she had got herself scalded. She was now a pint-sized packet of trouble, climbing everything in sight and getting into worse scrapes than her three brothers. It was a half-hour's task scrubbing the grime off her sturdy little limbs in the evening. The hullabaloo coming from the bedroom where all four slept was enough to split their mother's aching head in two.

One night when the children were particularly boisterous, Alex, folding tiny garments and clearing away toys, wondered if she would survive the racket herself. She put her throbbing ear-drums and jagged nerves down to over-tiredness, and left at last when all was peaceful to make her way back to the logging camp.

It seemed an endless trek, following the winding track faintly lit by the stars, until she eventually arrived at the doctor's darkened house in the tree-lined open space. From there she walked the length of the dimly lit main street out to the shadowed clearing.

When she arrived at the jeep she was more than ready to sink back thankfully into the seat. She drove slowly along the disused logging route, watching the headlights pick out the looming shapes of the trees, and tangled undergrowth, through a blinding headache.

Though it was only a little after nine when she arrived back at the clinic, she decided to call it a day. Quite simply, she was worn out, she told herself, smoothing her hair back from shadowed eyes before the mirror in her room. What she needed was a warm relaxing shower and an early night to put her on her feet again.

Exchanging her summer dress for a cotton dressing gown, her light shoes for her mules, she wasted no time in getting between the sheets.

Everything was fine when she awoke to the sunlight slanting through the trees. The headache had gone, and she felt the old energy surging through her limbs. She ate a reasonable breakfast and came back from the dining hut to set about the chores in the clinic. Though they were only light tasks, she was amazed how quickly she tired. Her body, which had seemed so fresh on rising, soon began to feel like a lead weight. By mid-morning she had to admit to being plagued by the most appalling head pains.

After lunch she took two aspirins and worked to ignore her aches and discomfort throughout the afternoon. Thankfully no one came into the clinic, so she could drop down on to the chair by the desk after each bout of polishing or scrubbing, without being seen.

She washed and tidied herself up before going over to the dining hut for the evening meal. A careful look in the mirror showed her a slight flush on her cheeks. Fortunately it could have been a look of the outdoors, the glow of the sun. Crisp in a fresh white overall, she could almost fool herself into believing that that was all it was.

The sight of food nauseated her. She sat at the table beside Grant, making an effort not to let it show. Fortunately he was absorbed with company papers most of the time. His face was paler beneath his tan and tensed in some way, and he had taken to saying little on these occasions, apparently preferring to sit and work. Alex congratulated herself on eating a passably normal meal. Rising to bid him a polite good night, she took her leave of him as soon as the other men had gone.

As she walked back to the clinic she knew she would have to give the settlement a miss tonight. Prescribing two tablets from the drug cupboard for herself, she undressed and showered, then sank into bed.

She passed a restless night finding that she needed constant drinks of water to ease a violently sore throat. In the morning she shirked the walk over the empty dining hut for breakfast and settled for a cup of her own hot strong tea.

How she got through her work up to lunch time she couldn't have said. Perhaps it was the thought that today was Thursday which spurred her on. If she could get through tomorrow, she would be able to rest up the entire weekend.

She skipped lunch for another cup of tea. She would have liked to forget the evening meal, but the men would be in the hut tonight, and Grant would be at his table. Lethargically she prepared, unable to react much to her washed-out features and heavily shadowed eyes.

With any luck, Grant would be working over his papers. As soon as she had put in an appearance and made a show of eating something, she could leave.

In the dining hut while the other men on the platform were scraping into their seats, she took her place beside him, relieved to see a sheaf of office papers near his plate. He flicked a look up as he always did when she joined him. Tonight she felt the brown glance stay with her a moment.

She tried to carry on as normal.

She would have liked to appear more interested in the food. If only the very smell of it didn't make her want to close her eyes over her revulsion. Once or twice while pushing it around her plate, she felt Grant's penetrating gaze on her. On these occasions she took a forkful of something, not knowing how she was going to get it down.

It seemed a lifetime to her before the meal ended. She sat, not knowing how she held up, while the technicians drifted leisurely away from their seats and wandered out into the night alongside the lumberjacks. When she was sure she wouldn't get caught up with them, she prepared to leave her own chair.

Whether she rose too quickly, or whether her eyes hadn't focused properly after following the men down the length of the hut, she couldn't have said. The only sensation she recollected was a sudden spinning of the room when she stood up, and a desire to hold on to something.

In the space of that second Grant, who had seemed to be absorbed in his work, jumped up and grabbed her. Steadying her with both hands, he asked gruffly, his gaze raking her, 'Are you all right?'

'I'm fine.' Alex gave him a wan smile, then turning from his searching look she added, 'Just a little tired, that's all.'

Grant escorted her to the steps of the platform and said gratingly, 'When you try to run two jobs at once, something's got to give.'

Alex let the comment go. She couldn't very well tell him that he was the cause of her wanting to lose herself in work at the settlement. She made an all-out effort to walk erect and steady along to the door of the dining hut, knowing that his eyes were watching her all the way.

CHAPTER TEN

BACK at the clinic she stripped off in her room, rinsed hazily under the shower, donned a nightdress and dropped into bed. Her only consolation when she awoke the next morning was that it was Friday. Her throat was thick and dry, her head a mass of pain. She felt a little better after washing and drinking a cup of tea. In her overall, her hair fastened up, her drained features would not be easily detectable from a distance. To anyone passing and glancing in at the opened curtained windows of the clinic, she was working as usual.

She got through until lunch time mainly by sitting at the desk, making a pretext of filling out various forms. During her mealtime break she dozed fitfully on the bed, rising with tremendous effort at the appointed time to wash and tidy her hair for the afternoon period. If her luck held and she had no emergency calls, she would be free in four hours.

Every second of the brilliantly sunny afternoon seemed like a year. Sometimes she would be chilled to the bone by the breeze wafting in through the open window. At others she was so hot she could feel her overall burning up.

Around three o'clock, Lloyd's car drew up outside. Alex stood up. She hadn't been near the settlement since Tuesday night. She had guessed he might be wondering what had become of her. He came in, looking brown and relaxed, his greying hair contrasting in such a way as to add to his air of warmth and maturity.

His smile went straight to Alex as he complained banteringly, 'My nurse hasn't been down to boil the billy with me lately.'

Alex smiled and tried to look busy. 'I've been taking a few early nights,' she made an attempt at lightness.

'Wise girl,' Lloyd strolled in. 'The worst of the trouble is over now anyway.' His glance suddenly catching her as she turned from the window, he added on a medical note, 'You should rest more.'

Alex nodded and made an effort to keep moving. She thought she had passed the moment off, until she found Lloyd approaching slowly and eyeing her keenly. She moved away to another job, but though she tried to give an air of brisk activity she found it impossible to escape his professional scrutiny.

Stopping her from swaying around to take her wrist, he said, his blue eyes clouded with concern, 'Let me look at you. Are you sure it's only over-tiredness?'

'Now, Lloyd,' struggling for a humorous note, Alex took her wrist away, 'stop looking for work! Of course I'm all right.'

She didn't know whether to be glad or sorry when at that moment Wes Brissac stepped into the clinic. His appearance put paid to Lloyd's probing for the time being, but if he had come to inform her of work to be done, she had no idea how she was going to contend with it.

She soon learned that his visit was to do with himself. His puckish features lost in a grizzled beard, he lifted a hand, and told her with a grin, nodding through the window, 'Got me a splinter working over at the loading bay just now. I was all for letting it go, but Grant sent me over. Said I ought to have it looked at.'

'It's the wisest course, Wes,' Lloyd nodded. 'A neglected hand could give you a lot of trouble.'

Alex, wondering how she was going to stay on her feet, called from beside the instrument trolley, 'Come over here, Mr. Brissac. Let me have a look at it.'

She saw through swimming senses that the sliver of wood was about an inch long, though not too deeply implanted. Thankful for that at least, she washed his hand and disinfected the punctured area, then set to work.

It should have taken no more than a few minutes to remove the splinter. Her temples prickling with heat, her body a mass of shooting pains, Alex laboured considerably longer. Her fingers trembled to grasp the last small piece. It was stubborn. She couldn't get a hold on it. A mistiness started to creep in at the edges of her sight. She saw the final piece of splinter between the tweezers, a second before the roaring sound in her ears brought a sudden rushing black-ness.

In the dim swirling darkness of semi-consciousness, she knew vaguely that Lloyd was beside her, holding her. That with Wes Brissac's help, amidst a spate of sharp staccato comments, she was being supported along the narrow corridor to her room. She felt the pillow under her head, and decided there and then to give up the fight. Almost grate-fully, she allowed the black abyss to claim her, and she knew no more.

After travelling wearily in a world where everything was crazily distorted and nothing made sense, she floated back into the dim greyness of her room, aware of great changes. The tightness of her overall belt had gone. Her arms lying on the sheet were bare and cool, with no encumbrance now except the straps of her underslip.

The noises which had brought her back from far away, she realized after some moments, were voices, coming from two blurred shapes in the doorway. Struggling to bring her-self out of the mist, she recalled that Wes Brissac had been there when she had collapsed, but he would have gone back to his work. Now the voices were different. She could hear Lloyd's, and she could hear Grant's.

There seemed to be anger on both sides. To some dark biting comment from the big shape as he looked at the bed, she heard Lloyd's expostulation, 'Good God, Grant! I *am* a doctor!'

There were further exchanges amidst which Grant rasped, 'There isn't room for a cat to breathe in here.' Hear-ing movement, she opened her eyes to find him approaching the bed. Seeing his face, white and working as he bent over her, she was reminded of a day when she had thought to sunbathe and merely incurred his wrath for the pink rash she had got on her skin. She closed her eyes again because for some reason they became damp. A moment after this she felt the sheets and blanket being thrown round her and she was up into a pair of powerful arms.

Through the returning grey mist, she was aware of the

narrow confines of the corridor, a waft of cool air on her cheek, then the pine dust and leather interior of Grant's car. After that, half-lying on the back seat, seeing the familiar dark head and big shoulders over the wheel, she gave herself up contentedly to oblivion.

She would have liked to stay like that for the next two or three days, but having settled on her as its victim, the 'flu germ was determined that she should know all about it. For the first day she lay, her head and body a mass of shooting pains. For the second, she knew the miseries of not being able to swallow, and the third, only a gradual easing off of the two.

When she wasn't fully engrossed with the business of suffering she turned a lack-lustre gaze over her surroundings. The bedroom she was in was made completely of wood. Of the garments hung in the slightly open wardrobe and hung over chairs, she recognized Grant's light grey summer suit and Grant's blue and white checked shirt. Through the open doorway she could see another spacious room, with armchairs and a fly-screened door opening on to a small veranda.

All this she took note of in an abstract way while the little men with hammers kept busy inside her head.

Lloyd came frequently to give her tablets and scold her gently for not having capitulated earlier. She smiled wanly at his tender bedside manner.

For the most part of the day all she wanted to do was sleep. She would float off at the oddest moments and dream the strangest dreams, waking up to become hazily aware of the sunshine streaming into the rooms; of the sounds of the logging camp drifting in through the open door on the veranda.

Sometimes when she came out of these drugged slumbers it would be to find Grant in the room, reaching for something in the wardrobe or from the back of a chair. As her eyes opened to watch him, he would turn his dark head her way and say with a tight smile, 'How's the patient?'

Alex, finding it difficult to appear cool and clinical with her head on a pillow and the lacework of a nightdress taking the place of her crisp overall, would strive to give the impression nevertheless, with the bland reply 'Recovering!'

By the end of a week with Lloyd's constant calls and attention she was doing just that. And yet, drifting around the rooms in cotton dressing gown, after he had left, she couldn't be glad about it. Though she was finished with bed and the sun was shining from a pure blue sky, there wasn't one thing she could think of to smile about. On the contrary, she found herself wanting to weep at the slightest provocation.

One afternoon Pop Doolin brought her a bunch of greenery picked specially for her by the lumberjacks. It was about the ugliest bouquet ever presented to a woman, yet when Alex received it her eyes filled with tears. Pop left in a hurry, taking his embarrassment with him.

Her hair was another problem. Because of her days in bed, it had missed its periodic brushing. Consequently when, one morning, she taxed what little strength she had in trying to attend to it, its tangled state brought her down to her lowest ebb.

Some nurse she was, she told herself through blinding tears. She was completely hopeless at everything. She couldn't drive the jeep properly. She had caught the first germ that had come along. And now the comb wouldn't go through her hair.

White-faced and spent, she was sat battling in an armchair when Grant came in. She heard the footsteps and flung a glance up, hardly caring who or what was approaching in her irritation. She hadn't meant Grant to see the tears, but the brown gaze seemed to know they were there even though she quickly lowered her head again.

He said, after some time watching her trembling fingers at work, 'You ought to be out on the veranda getting some fresh air.'

'How can I go anywhere with my hair like this?' she flared at him.

'Take your time,' he said easily. 'You'll soon get it straightened out.'

'I'm sick of it,' she snapped, resisting a desire to fling the comb across the room, when it snagged painfully for the hundredth time. 'Lloyd suggested having it cut, and I think I'd like nothing better.'

'By that I take it you mean have it trimmed?' Grant looked at her with that tightness of expression which had a habit of springing up from nowhere.

'No. I mean the whole lot off . . . some shorter hair-style.' She tugged a knot out angrily. 'It's more trouble than what it's worth.'

'Or worth more than the little trouble it will take to put it right,' Grant twisted her words enigmatically. He drew up a wooden chair and sat down beside her, taking the comb our of her shaking hand.

'What are you going to do?' She turned on him.

'Sit still,' he said gently but firmly. On the arm of the chair Alex had laid her open toilet bag. From it he took a small pair of scissors and began to snip. He cut about two inches off the end of her hair all round. After this the comb was a lot more amenable to the idea of sliding through the lengthy strands. Where it got caught up, Grant took his time in working out the trouble. From the comb he switched to the brush. Feeling the silken smoothness returning, from her temples down to the slightly waving clouds on her shoulders, Alex climbed up a little from her black hole of despair.

When every strand was free, Grant brushed her shoulders impersonally and rising drew her to her feet. He glanced at the dark remnants scattered around and then at her to say drily, 'In my opinion the hair looks better on you than it does on the floor.' He seemed about to make some other joking comment when his gaze came to meet hers.

Fleetingly she wondered what kind of a disreputable picture she made, white-faced and smudged-eyed, her hair tumbling about her instead of being pinned up in its usual neat way. And because she wished she could have looked more presentable, her eyes became ridiculously damp again and she had to turn away. Reaching shakily for a mirror and hair-grips, she heard herself saying pedantically, 'For a man who fells trees you show a remarkable aptitude for scissors and comb.'

Fixing the mirror on a nearby bookshelf, she rapidly set about arranging her hair, while Grant watched her. When it was pinned up in its usual style, he asked, his eyes still on her, 'Feeling better?'

Alex said over a sigh, turning to toss her things down, 'Quite a bit, I suppose.' Though she felt she ought to show some gratitude to Grant she couldn't find it within her to produce much of a smile. As she drifted around, and then towards the door, he nodded to a shady chair on the veranda to say with half a grin, 'That's a good spot. I usually sit there myself.'

Alex was glad she had the grace to say then, 'It can't be very convenient for you, me staying here like this. I ought to be getting back to the clinic.'

'You've got more privacy here,' Grant nodded to the secluded area beyond the veranda, and added, 'Wes's bungalow has two beds in it. We're doing okay.'

Hardly listening now, Alex drifted lethargically outdoors and dropped into the chair he had suggested. She closed her eyes because she had no particular desire to look at anything.

She heard Grant moving about in the bungalow, collecting the things he had called in for. When he came out he went off without saying anything, probably assuming she was dozing. Finding it too much of an effort to even open her eyes, she heard him start his car from somewhere around the side, and drive off.

On her first days down with the 'flu she had bothered with no food at all, simply bowing to pressure from Lloyd now and again to take some of the fruit he brought for her, or to down some of his tonic. But since about the middle of the week one of the men from the cookhouse had been bringing a tray over for her. Today she was no more enamoured of the steaming contents of the dishes which were placed before her than she had been yesterday. Having the sense to realize, however, that she needed food to regain her strength, she made herself eat a fair proportion of all that had been sent over.

Later, she also made herself rinse off the dishes and the

mug in the bathroom, then dry them with a cloth so that they were clean and shining when they went back to the cookhouse. After that, she was fit for nothing again. Her suitcase in the bedroom, which Lloyd had filled with things she might need and brought across, was in a complete mess. And it could stay that way. Dully she wandered about in her cotton dressing gown. She picked up a book and put it down again; flicked through forestry magazines disinterestedly and finally ended up back in the chair on the veranda.

About the middle of the afternoon she was sat staring out, looking at nothing in particular, when Grant drove round and into her view in his dusty shooting brake. She followed his movements with a lack-lustre gaze as he opened the door and turned, straightening just a fraction, when she saw a tiny movement on the back seat.

Her eyes opened with the mildest flicker of interest as she watched Grant pick up a furry little creature and carry it up to the veranda. They hadn't quite arrived when Alex got to her feet, her gaze searching out the cone-shaped nose and wide slanting eyes of a tubby little brown animal. 'What is it, Grant?' she asked a little uncertainly at first, and then in slow disbelieving pleasure, 'It's . . . not – a koala bear?'

'That's right,' Grant gave a grin, climbing the steps.

Alex put a hand out tentatively to stroke the mottled fur, exclaiming, 'I haven't seen one in all the time I've worked here in the forest.'

'There aren't enough variety of gum trees around here to feed them,' Grant explained. 'I found this young fellow up on the north shoulder.'

'Can I hold him?' she asked, liking the feel of the furry warm body.

'He's all yours.' Grant handed the bear over, adding drily, 'He's not very old, so he's probably missing a soft spot.'

Obviously he was, for as Alex held him he rested his chest and head against her in an almost affectionate way. 'He's rather like a teddy bear, isn't he?' she smiled at the sleepy slant-eyed expression.

'All except for his claws,' Grant said. 'A scratch from one of those,' he nodded to five splayed-out toes resting on

Alex's white skin, 'could cause trouble.' Gently lifting the claws from her arm, he took the animal under his armpits and set him down.

'Won't he run away?' Alex asked anxiously.

'I doubt it,' Grant stretched up to his big height and grinned. 'He might go for a stroll.'

They watched as the koala bear stood and looked about him, then ambling down the steps, he walked across the narrow stretch of clearing towards the trees.

'We ought to go after him,' Alex looked at Grant worriedly. 'He might get lost in there with no food.'

'We can stroll and keep an eye on him,' Grant suggested easily.

Alex nodded. She had moved a few steps with him before it hit her that she was wearing her dressing gown. 'I'll have to go and put a dress on,' she laughed, turning inside.

Moving quicker than she had done for a week, she slipped into cotton dress and light shoes, behind the closed door of the bedroom, and smoothing her hair from her face, returned to the veranda. Her eyes went straight to the koala bear who was disappearing along a green aisle of the forest. Grant's lazy brown gleam, she knew, was on her. Curiously it didn't bother her. Without giving it a thought she took the hand he offered down the steps, glad of its steadying influence across the clearing, when she found that her legs were not as strong as they used to be.

In the cool green beneath the trees they walked, watching the slow progress of the koala bear. He couldn't make up his mind about the pines. He would clamber leisurely a few feet up one, then turn and drop to the ground again, afterwards strolling a few yards before giving it another try.

Occasionally Alex would take her gaze from him to turn it around the shadowy green stretches bathed in the veiled glow of afternoon light. She had forgotten how beautiful the world could be. Her heart lifted at the sight of a clump of yellow flowers waving in a grassy hollow; at a group of tall ferns unfurling majestically beside an ageing tree.

When they had been walking for about twenty minutes, Grant grabbed the koala bear as he was making one of his half-hearted attempts to settle for a pine instead of a eucalyptus. 'Okay, young feller. Maybe it's time to take you back to the family fold,' he said, turning.

Alex was torn between an urge to keep walking and a desire to sink down somewhere. When they arrived back at the veranda and Grant handed her into the chair, she decided that he had timed it just right. She couldn't have walked another step.

She gave the small furry creature a final stroke before it was taken back to the car. Her gaze was more with Grant's big heavily built frame in dusty logging clothes, as he moved away from her. It didn't seem possible that a man like him could sit and run a comb through a mass of tangled hair with such incredible gentleness. And the koala bear? He must have brought it all the way down from the tree-felling area, just for her to see.

It was ridiculous to feel a dampness in her eyes. Especially when he had lifted her completely out of her doldrums. That was why she stood up and turned as though going inside, when she might have waved to him.

CHAPTER ELEVEN

THE following day was Saturday. Alex rose with rather more zest than she had known of late, and soon had all the jobs that yesterday had seemed mountainous smoothly behind her. It was true she felt like a limp rag when she had finished, but the feeling of satisfaction was there. Also, having a clear conscience, she felt entitled to relax for the afternoon with a library book she had found in her suit-case.

After lunch, all sounds of activity on the logging camp ceased. With the men's departure for their various week-end pastimes, only the birds were left chuckling and calling to each other in the forest, and the breeze dancing with gay abandon around the deserted huts.

Fresh in the forget-me-not sprigged summer dress after her work, Alex sat, her eyes partly with the book she was reading, and partly with the sunlit scene beyond the ver-anda.

A little after two, Grant strolled round from the direction of Wes Brissac's bungalow. Though she had learned to school herself into showing nothing in her gaze, Alex couldn't stop her heart lurching at the sight of him.

He had changed from his dusty logging clothes, and wore now fawn slacks and casual cream-knitted sports shirt. His lined sunburnt features and dark hair contrasted in such a way as to make her feel slightly breathless.

At first, she thought he had called to pick up something he needed. However, as he reached for the latest issue of the forestry magazine and lit up a cigarette, she realized he had come to relax, which he had a perfect right to do, in his own quarters. Ostensibly reading her book, she knew also by his movements that he was preparing to pour himself a drink. All the furniture in the bungalow was of a plain utility type, built to stand up to the rough life of a logging camp. Amongst the items Alex had noticed the drinking cabinet.

From beside it now she heard the clink of drinking glasses.

Grant came out carrying two drinks. She saw that his was a long summer cooler, the same as her own. She thanked him and pretended interest in her book as he took the chair at the other side of the table.

A long time afterwards she lowered her book to take a sip at her drink. She was able to see then that Grant was sitting turned slightly away from the table, the ankle of one immaculately trousered leg resting on the knee of the other. His gaze, half with the magazine he held, and half with the smoke drifting from his cigarette, he appeared to have about as much interest in reading as she had.

In fact, the printed word was dead for her now that she found she could let her gaze roam over him unheeded. Slowly, in the lazy warmth of the afternoon, the fragrance of pine heavy on the air, she traced the curve of his jaw with her eyes; followed the line of his hair where it curled in a close-knit way down the back of his neck. Unable to help herself, she lowered her glance to take in the sun-tanned muscular arms, then lifted it again to the lined craggy features. Her pulses gathered momentum as she let it linger on his mouth, set in its usual firm line. Those lips, well-shaped, but knowing how to be cynical, almost ruthless ... what would they be like ...?

Afraid of herself and her feelings, she rose abruptly, dropping her book on the table with a small thump. Searching desperately for an escape from his nearness, she paced the veranda and asked in odd high-pitched tones, 'Is the jeep around?' and with a rush, 'I thought I'd take a little run through the forest, or something.'

'I think not,' Grant said curtly. 'You're in no condition to drive yourself.'

'I'm perfectly well. And I *must* get away from here.' She swung about, later disguising her desperation with, 'I need a change of scenery.'

'Where do you want to go?' Grant placed his magazine down. 'I'll bring my car round.'

'I thought I'd take a run down to see Lloyd,' Alex said, clutching at straws. As her doctor, he had found it necessary to terminate his calls on her towards the back end of the week, in order to catch up with other work. But she knew he wouldn't be working today unless he was compelled to.

At the mention of Lloyd's name, Grant looked as though he had expected nothing else. He rose and, head bent, stubbed out his cigarette, his brow knitting together heavily, perhaps over the smoke that smarted his eyes.

As he strode off round the side of the bungalow, Alex went indoors to pick up her handbag and a light cardigan. The car was crunching to a stop out front when she got back to the veranda. Grant held her hand down the steps as though he knew better than she that her legs were still unsteady.

He helped her into her seat, and went round to take his own place, his brown gaze lowering immediately to the ignition key and the wheel as he moved in.

They made the trip to Noongwalla in silence. Alex nursed a heaviness of her own at the weighty atmosphere inside the car. She and Grant had never been ones to chat happily away to one another.

Lloyd's veranda was empty when they arrived outside his cottage. For one awful moment Alex thought he was out on a call, then she saw that only the fly-screen panel was in place at the front door, and there was movement inside the room beyond.

Grant opened the gate for her, and almost at once Lloyd was there, welcoming her with his smile, his pleased blue gaze searching every inch of her pallid features with a professional eye. 'Alex, my dear! Are you sure you're well enough to be out?' He put an arm about her and led her inside as though she were made of glass.

'I'm almost as good as new,' Alex made an attempt to joke, knowing that Grant's big frame was coming up behind.

Lloyd waved his arm expansively towards the kitchen-living room where the back door was wide open to show a picture of greenery and flowers beyond the veranda. 'I was just about to put the kettle on,' he said in his hospitable way, urging them along. 'We can sit and enjoy the view back here.'

As he began to busy himself around the kitchen area, lighting the stove and setting out crockery, Grant said levelly, 'Count me out, Lloyd,' and to where Alex had sunk down in an armchair, 'I'll be over at the hotel if you want me.'

Lloyd slanted a look after him as he strode away along the back veranda, and spooning the tea into the pot, he said, twinkling, 'Show a timber man a domesticated scene and watch him run for the nearest bar.'

'Some of them marry,' Alex said lightly. 'Wes Brissac's a grandfather, don't forget.'

'True,' Lloyd opened the cupboard for milk and sugar. 'But Grant would never fall for that. He belongs to that special breed of forestry man who prefer the impermanency of their working life to any other.'

'Is it impermanent?' Alex tried to put a laugh into her voice.

'Of course,' Lloyd reached out scones and butter, and searched for the right knives, chatting absently. 'Logging camps are transient affairs, to be moved on to some other district as soon as all the ripe timber has been cut.' He shook a biscuit tin close to his ear to see if there was any significant rattle and continued, 'They usually have a life of about two years. After that, the average logging man is more than ready to pull up stakes.' Lloyd gave his boyish grin as he sliced fresh scones. 'A new stretch of forest to work means a new town to be discovered somewhere . . . new bars . . .'

And new women friends, Alex said to herself despondently. In other words, for Grant, just another Oaktown. She fought to keep the smile on her face, while they lightly discussed him. What was the use of letting such talk drain her of every spark of life? Wasn't it what she had always known about him?

The kettle boiled, and the subject was changed to Lloyd's work in the settlement over the past few days. Facing the veranda, the scents from the garden drifting in through the open door, they sat and talked through the afternoon and into the early evening.

The sun was gilding the leaves of the trees with burnished copper when Grant came back along the veranda. As Lloyd had promised to make a call on Mrs. Calhern some time during the evening he gladly handed Alex into Grant's safe keeping for the drive back to camp.

'And straight to bed, young lady,' he said with mock-sternness as he walked out with them to the car. 'Those cheeks are far too pale for my liking.'

Alex gave him her smile, and took her seat. Only she knew that her drained look had nothing to do with convalescing from 'flu.

Grant drove her back to the logging camp without a word. He dropped her outside his own bungalow, and after they had exchanged brief goodnights he swung off in the direction of Wes Brissac's quarters.

Lloyd wouldn't let Alex start work until the Monday of the following week. After a fortnight of being away from the clinic, she returned to find it slightly chaotic, where the men had been in to help themselves to plasters and liniment, and other aids, leaving drawers open and boxes strewn around.

She worked a full week getting everything back to normal and gradually drifting into her nursing duties. Still Grant wouldn't allow her to take the jeep, though he offered to drive her anywhere she wished to go.

She chose to stay around her own room, ostensibly taking Lloyd's advice in getting plenty of sleep. After a meal in the dining hut, sitting beside Grant, when often no word was spoken on either side, she would return to take a walk before dark in her own private stretch of forest behind the clinic.

With February there had been a slackening of the heat. It was necessary to put on a light cardigan when the sun had gone down. One evening after a drizzly day, she was reduced to raincoat and stout shoes.

Though there had been the odd shower on and off through the previous weeks, she was reminded now, as she tramped through the dripping forest, of that first day she had seen rain here after the drought. How the ground had gobbled it up then! And how the trees and greenery had laughed and crackled in elation. Hollow-eyed, she remembered that she had likened herself to the parched land then; lifeless and dried-up after the years spent nursing her aunt, waiting for that elusive something to come along, like the rain, and stir her in the same laughing, animated way.

Well, it had come. But she wasn't laughing, not even smiling like the forest. She felt like death.

And if she didn't want to catch pneumonia, she told herself with a wry ache, she had better get back to her room and into some dry clothes.

On the Saturday afternoon Grant asked her if she would like him to drive her anywhere. She chose to go to Lloyd's because she had to get away from the camp, and she could think of nowhere else. Also she had to admit that Lloyd's welcoming smile and kindly attentiveness towards her was like balm to her jaded spirits.

Grant, devastating in pale shirt and slacks and soft suede shoes, drove her right up to the cottage gate, then parking his car in the tree-shaded space, he swung off on his own without coming into the house.

Now that she was fit again Alex wasted no time in taking up where she had left off, in helping Lloyd with whatever work he had on hand. She spent the afternoon sorting out his correspondence and tidying up his desk, afterwards putting the kettle on and setting the table, while Lloyd did his weekly check through his medical bag, sterilizing his instruments and making an inventory of his drug stock. He preferred to be ready for the odd call which could come along at any time.

Later they sat out in the early evening warmth and talked lazily, watching the colourful birds swoop over the garden. There were no chairs on the back veranda. Just a padded bench outside the kitchen door. Lloyd had taken to guiding her out to this quite often. Alex realized that it was rather more intimate than sitting in armchairs with a table between them. Somehow she didn't mind.

Lloyd was in an amiable mood this Saturday night. Not that he was ever anything else except pleasant-tempered, but tonight there was a mischievous spark in his blue eyes, together with a happiness – a contentment, she might say, as he looked at her. He had the gift of humour, and though deep in her heart she knew an aching emptiness, she could laugh with him, simply because he was a sincere kind-hearted person with no wish but to make life pleasant for others.

She sat amused with his casual conversation, until dusk began to edge down the sky. It was in an animated moment while her gaze was touring the garden that she noticed the unusually long silence which had settled between them. Turning, she was in time to catch Lloyd's eyes resting on her. At her questioning light he smiled and explained with his usual gift for words and totally without embarrassment, so that she felt none either, 'I've been sitting here trying to decide what it is about your face that suggests such avail-ability and warmth. At first I thought it was your eyes, because they brighten easily and laughter comes into them. . . . They're the attractive eyes of a gay and eager woman, not the clinical self-possessed ones you like to think they are,' he teased, and as her lips curved, 'Then all at once I made up my mind. It's your mouth. The smile, the spell-bound expectancy, then the sudden laughter. It's all there in that full, generous mouth.'

Alex didn't know what she would have said to all this, if in that same moment she hadn't been aware of a big shape just about to turn the corner on to the back veranda. In the gathering dusk only she caught a glimpse of Grant, because she was sitting with her head turned that way beside the door. It was no more than a glimpse. For one fleeting moment one soft shoe was there bringing him round, then in the same fraction of time he changed his mind and disappeared.

She was smiling and talking easily over the moment when the sound of his car horn came sharp and staccato from out at the front. She rose as though it was the first she knew of his presence and commented lightly, 'That's Grant's car. He must be ready to drive back to camp.'

Lloyd didn't come out with her to the car, because it was

almost dark now. In his comfortable way he was wearing only carpet slippers, relaxing to the hilt until someone came and ruined his peace with a call, so she waved to him from the gate, as he stood at the front door, and watched him scuff off happily inside.

She worried a little about Grant's speed on the way back. She knew he had been over in the bar, but she doubted whether he ever drank more than one glass of anything. She knew he was in complete control of the car, yet they had never before raced quite so madly along the road beneath the trees. They were back at the clinic while she was still trying to gather her thoughts.

Grant waited long enough for her to turn the key in the door, then he thundered away to his own quarters.

After that she noticed the jeep parked in its usual place at the side of the clinic at the end of each working day. It was a relief not to have to ask Grant to drive her around any more. As soon as she could get away in the evenings she took her own private route through the forest. It was no use pretending she didn't know what the position was approaching between her and Lloyd. She wasn't blind to the way he looked at her these days, and she had noticed the lingering touch of his hand when they said good-bye.

The only reason she left things to drift this way was because she saw it as some far-off and distant thing; something she would be able to handle when the time arrived. She wasn't to know then that certain factors were at work which would precipitate matters.

On the Wednesday evening of that following week, when she least expected it, Lloyd proposed.

She had arrived at the cottage about dusk, and they had spent the time clearing up the loose ends of his day's work. Apart from his usual warmth and amiability, he had shown no sign of what was on his mind. Around nine o'clock they drifted out towards the padded bench on the back veranda.

Seated in the glow from the doorway, listening to the sounds of the night birds, it was something she felt in Loyd's manner then which told her what to expect.

He had been letting his eyes rest on her for some time, after which he took her hand and held it in both of his. When she brought her glance round as she knew she must, he said gravely, 'Alex, my dear, you must know how I've come to feel about you these past few weeks . . . how I've come to depend on you,' he smiled. 'I can't imagine now how I ever managed without you around the cottage,' and clasping her hand, 'If you can see your way to making it a permanent arrangement I'd like you to be my wife.'

Alex was completely bowled over by this sudden development. Falling back on her only excuse, she stared at him and laughed, 'But, Lloyd, I can't leave my job at the logging camp, just like that!'

Lloyd kept his smile and his hold on her hand as he faced her to say, 'Haven't you heard? Mrs. MacTavish is coming back.'

'Mrs. MacTavish?' Alex echoed the name, hearing her voice come in from a long way off.

'Yes, her family are on their feet again. She wants her old job back. So that lets you out.' Lloyd looked pleased at being able to give her the news. He chatted on beside her as they sat in the glow from the kitchen. 'We could be married in a week. There's a little church in Oaktown you'll like,' and with his old humour, 'I don't think anyone would fall sick on us on our wedding day.'

Trying to gather her scattered thoughts, Alex put a hand over his and said with feeling, 'Let me think about it, Lloyd. . . .' And searching for a smile, 'It's all . . . just a little sudden. . . .'

'Of course.' Lloyd squeezed her fingers with an understanding nod and reached for his pipe.

They talked on about other things for a while, then Alex rose to go. She gathered up her cardigan and handbag and walked through the front room with its shaded lights to the outside door. Seeing her off at the gate, Lloyd took her hands in his, beneath the black star-strewn sky, and said simply, 'Come to me when you're ready.'

Driving through the forest in the silence, watching the

headlights pick out the track, Alex tried to gain a hold on her whirling thoughts. Mrs. MacTavish was coming back. She wanted her old job back, Lloyd had said, which meant she hadn't applied to head office. She was coming back in the hope that Grant would re-engage her.

Alex swung the wheel, narrowly missing trees. And there was no doubt at all what Grant's reaction would be to *that* proposition.

CHAPTER TWELVE

THROUGHOUT Thursday and Friday she continued with her duties at the clinic as normal. No mention was made of Mrs. MacTavish, but something about Grant's face at their table in the dining hut told her he knew as much as she did about the woman's imminent return.

Alex had already made up her mind what she was going to do. Rather than give him the satisfaction of telling her that her services would no longer be required, she rose on Saturday morning and started to pack.

To make sure of a lightweight suitcase, her three summer dresses were the only additional things she decided to include. The oddments she had bought for the room, she left in the hope that Mrs. MacTavish would be able to make use of them, as she had found the other woman's kettle and tea-pot useful.

Around mid-morning she was busy folding the clothes she had piled on her bed when she heard someone come into the clinic. Grant should normally have been working at the tree-felling area in the forest at this hour, yet somehow she knew that those footsteps pacing the floor were his. Whether he had got some idea what she was up to, she didn't know. She certainly had no intention of going out there to confront him.

As she might have expected when she didn't put in an appearance his booted footsteps sounded loud and clear along the corridor leading to her room. She raised her head from placing a garment in her case as he stood framed in the doorway. For a moment she hardly recognized him. It might have been the shadowy interior, but his face looked grey and deeply etched, despite the fact that a drawn smile distorted his mouth.

His eyes flicking pointedly over the suitcase, he taunted raspingly, 'Getting out?'

Alex replied just as pointedly, carrying on with her work,

'The room is hardly big enough for *two* nurses.'

He curled his smile at her piled clothing and sneered, 'You're not wasting much time in running to Lloyd.'

So he had guessed about that too. Hanging on to the last vestige of hope, she found the words to say quiveringly, 'We both know that in your opinion I don't come up to Mrs. MacTavish's standards as nurse around here.'

'I'm not fooling myself that you're as well suited to the job as she is,' he stated harshly.

Alex swallowed on the ache in her throat. That was it. That was all she wanted to hear. Folding a dress to hide her unsteadiness, she said in strained tones, 'I'll take the jeep and leave it in the clearing, if that's all right.'

'It will be picked up,' Grant rapped, nodding. He let his gaze rest on her for a second, then without another word he turned and strode off.

White-faced, Alex carried on, though her hands were shaking. Towards noon she had confined all her belongings to her case and cleaned the room from top to bottom. After that she went through into the clinic to make sure that everything was in order for Mrs. MacTavish to take over. She finally put away her polishing cloths and dusters when she was satisfied that all had been done.

The camp wore the deserted air of a Saturday afternoon when she went across to the cookhouse to make herself a meal. If she could have kept going she would have done, but she had eaten nothing all morning, and she would achieve nothing, she knew, by allowing herself to reach the point of collapse.

She cooked herself a substantial meal and forced herself to eat, though the food held no interest for her. Walking back to the clinic, she listened to the breeze, which caught the wisps of hair at her temples, blowing on its lonely way across the open space, where nothing moved.

In her room she had laid out the lilac linen suit with self-embroidered front, and a pair of pale matching shoes. After taking a shower, she dressed carefully and re-set her hair. When she was all ready she packed the last of her belongings in her case, locked it and picked up her handbag. In the doorway she turned and looked back with a gloomy smile. It was odd, but in a way she had grown attached to this dark ugly room.

Out of doors, though the sun shone brilliantly, the air was sufficiently cool for her to feel comfortable in her choice of dress. With a last look round she locked up the clinic, and taking her suitcase to the jeep she put the keys on the seat beside her. She drove steadily across the open space towards the men's quarters and pulled up outside Grant's bungalow. Picking the keys up from the seat, she added the drug cupboard set from her handbag and stepping down, walked into the bungalow.

The veranda door was wide open, but the living-room was empty. She would have called, had she been able to bring herself to say Grant's name. When she had hung about for a few moments she caught sight of him moving about just beyond the open door of the bedroom. Approaching she could see that he had washed and shaved and was wearing his light grey summer suit.

Her throat constricting at the sight of him, she stopped herself in the doorway and as he turned she explained her presence with, 'I thought you would prefer me to leave the keys of the clinic with you.'

She held them up for him to see, struck again by his lined look, but if he made any comment she didn't hear it. Her gaze was fixed on the small week-end travelling bag lying open on the bed. It was empty all except a few oddments, but obviously it had been placed there for a reason.

Watching Grant move about before the open drawers, she heard herself carping on a tremblingly high-pitched note, 'I wondered what you did when you got bored with the life around here. I was forgetting. There's always Oaktown.'

Grant tossed a shirt into the bag, and gave her his peculiar drawn smile to grate, 'There's always Oaktown.'

Fighting over the pain in her throat, Alex waited for him to take the keys from her. She thought he might have shaken her hand or made some similar offer of farewell. Instead he went on moving around, and when she didn't stir, the keys clinking between her fingers, he threw over his shoulder harshly, 'Put them on the table.'

Alex turned then and without looking back she did as he asked, then walked out.

The world had an eye-smarting brilliance about it when she walked down the steps from the veranda. Through the wet dazzle around her lashes she made her way, head erect, to the jeep, and fumbled in behind the wheel.

The sound of the engine, when she started up, split the oppressive silence that lay over the bungalow. Her hands cold as she steered, she took the jeep slowly forward, and steeling herself not to look back, she turned away and in the direction of the old logging track.

The same oppressive silence seemed to hang over the forest as she drove along. The breeze had died, and the trees, and leaves, and greenery stood in a petrified stillness, as though listening and waiting for something. Occasionally a bird's call would go echoing through the green tunnels, like someone's demented laughter.

Moving steadily forward, Alex saw everything through a glazed unhappiness. Even the clusters of wild flowers which turned up every so often along the way, like someone's smile, failed to stir her.

Instead, they reminded her bleakly of the stroll taken with the koala through here, that day. She could see its little padding gait as it investigated the trees. But clearer still she could see Grant walking beside her, rough in his logging clothes, but not too busy to take time off to show her the furry animal.

With an effort she shook off the picture and the pain it brought with it. What was the use of lingering over thoughts of Grant? The track through the forest lay ahead of her, and she had to get to Lloyd's.

Shadowed grey eyes fixed forward, she drove, listening dully to the wheeze and strain of the jeep engine, as she haphazardly negotiated one desolate stretch after another.

At last the clearing edging the settlement showed up, a splash of sunlit ground through the trees. Alex parked the jeep in a spot where it would easily be located, and swinging her suitcase down and looping her handbag over her arm, she started out for the road.

Noongwalla had that sleepy air of a Saturday afternoon, when everyone was either enjoying the leisure in their own homes, or they had gone further afield to do some town shopping. Alex walked the length of the main street without encountering a soul. She circled the tree-shaded space where a familiar small car was parked, and approached the white picket-fenced gate. She passed it for a moment to leave her suitcase a little distance away between two leaning trees. She didn't want to take it inside with her, otherwise Lloyd would feel obliged to help her.

The gate gave its usual little creak when she opened it. The fact that Lloyd didn't appear told her that he would be out at the back somewhere. She walked through the front room noticing the clutter that had built up on his desk.

When she stepped through into the kitchen-living-room he jumped up from the armchair he had been sitting in, his blue eyes leaping at the sight of her. Her heart contracted at the scene of the table laid neatly for two, with her favourite cup and saucer in place, the plate of home-made scones, sliced and buttered ready.

Lloyd took her hands and breathed softly as he drew her towards him, 'Alex!'

She tried to give him a smile, but it went hopelessly trembly as she told him, 'I'm sorry, Lloyd, I'm not staying.'

Somehow they got out to the padded bench on the veranda, and holding his hands, as he had held hers only a little while before, she broke it to him gently. 'I couldn't marry you, Lloyd. You deserve someone much better than me for a wife.'

His face, grown suddenly older, had a greyness about it, which reminded her fleetingly of Grant's. She went on because she had to, 'I just came to say good-bye.'

'Good-bye?' Lloyd found his voice, cracked though it was, at last.

'Yes. Mrs. MacTavish will be starting at the camp again soon, so I've decided to leave Noongwalla.' She stood up in an effort to break off the conversation. Lloyd, wearing an uncomprehending look, rose too. As they moved inside, she quavered, 'I hope everything goes well for you, Lloyd, and that you ... don't get more work than you can manage.' Briefly she brushed a kiss along his cheek and gave him a last smile. 'Good-bye.'

She left him sitting in the chair, his greying head bent. Her eyes were brimming with tears as she fled out the front. She opened and closed the gate, then hurried blindly towards her suitcase, wondering why life had to be like this. Why couldn't she have loved Lloyd, who needed her?

She walked up to the road and out of the settlement, knowing with an aching heart that she had no alternative but to keep moving. Lloyd was one of those people in the world who didn't deserve to get hurt, but probably always would.

In the afternoon stillness her footsteps sounded hollowly along the road. She moved out to where the valley sloped away from the winding highway, its undulating stretches a pattern of purple and gold where the light and shade touched them.

During her stay at the camp she had learned that there was a Saturday train to Adelaide, which passed through Denver's Creek at four o'clock. With a little luck – she listened for anything that might be coming along the road behind her – she should make it.

She could have asked anyone in Noongwalla to take her, of course, but they would have wanted to know why she was leaving and she didn't feel like explaining just now. Though she had no doubt that what little help she had been able to give in the settlement was much appreciated, she had always felt that everyone looked on Mrs. MacTavish as more or less a permanent fixture at the camp, so she guessed that her leaving would really have little effect on their lives.

As she walked she thought, with a painful ache in her throat, of Grant preparing for a week-end in Oaktown over forty miles away. With Denver's Creek about the same distance in the opposite direction, that would put almost a hundred miles between them. By the time he returned to the camp, late Sunday night or early Monday morning, she would be on a boat to somewhere – anywhere, she didn't much care.

The sun shone brilliantly as though to make a mockery of her pent-up misery. After twenty minutes on the road, she had to keep stopping for a rest. Her suitcase was becoming something of a burden. She was beginning to give up hope of seeing anything, when an old fruit-laden truck came rattling up on its way out from the settlement. The pleasant-faced young man at the wheel, one brown arm in old cotton shirt resting on the open window, stopped to give her an inquiring quirk.

'I want to get to Denver's Creek to catch the Adelaide train,' she told him. 'Are you going anywhere near there?'

The young man opened the door and jumped down. His long legs in washed-out jeans, he bent and swung her case up in amongst the fruit crates, crooking his grin with, 'You're lucky. Most of my boss's produce goes to Mount Gambier, but this load's for the Adelaide train.'

With a relieved smile Alex went round to the other side and accepting a polite hoist up into the cab, she sat down carefully amidst stray crates and the pungent odours of fresh fruit. When they were chugging on their way again the youthful driver gave her an understanding smile and commented, 'Bit inconvenient, only one bus a week from Noongwalla.'

'Yes, it is,' Alex smiled briefly.

Seeing that she didn't want to talk, he settled down to the business of steering the truck, obviously happy with his own thoughts.

Dully Alex watched the scenery go by. Presently they came to the bend in the road where the track led off into the valley. Bleakly she remembered how it had all started at this spot; how Grant had stopped the bus here that day she had been leaving and whisked her away in his shooting brake to attend to Mike Stronowsky. How long ago it all seemed now!

With a vague trickle of hope her eyes swept searchingly along the track and around the road as they passed, but nothing moved in the sunny stillness. Only the dust leapt up at the truck's wheels and swirled and eddied down forlornly as they left it far behind.

Alex sat bumping along to the steady rhythm of the chugging engine and the falsetto whistling of the youthful driver until the store buildings and work sheds of Denver's Creek showed up ahead.

On the strip of ground fronting the railway track she gave her thanks for the lift, and accepted an obliging hand down, a little stiffly. With a grin the jean-clad driver swung into the job of unloading the crates.

Ben and Howell, the venerable brothers whose acquaintance she had made on her arrival here, were working as usual trundling sacks back and forth. Rangy, loose-limbed and slow-moving, they drifted towards the truck when they heard the businesslike clatter of the fruit crates.

His empty trolley rumbling along, Alex felt Ben stop beside her where she was standing waiting for the train. He obviously remembered the day he had driven her out with the mail to start a new life in Noongwalla. He stood and looked at her and her suitcase for a long time, then deliberated, giving her his penetrating squint, 'It didn't work out?'

'No,' Alex tried desperately to smile, 'it didn't work out.' She felt his faded blue eyes boring holes through her brave front. Touchingly, as he detected the tears behind it, he made a clumsy attempt at consolation by telling her, 'You don't need to get straight on the train. We got freight to load when she comes in.'

At the sound of the whistle shrieking in the distance, Alex persevered with her smile to reply, 'I think I'll get on anyway.'

Howell, who had been hovering in the background giving her his bland blue stare, sloped slowly off, back to his work. Both men were down stacking fruit crates when the train flew in, a hissing, snarling monster, all metal and speed, until the brakes brought it cringing and squealing to a stop.

Alex boarded and walked down the cars towards the front. The seats were filled with all kinds of people, none of whom she could bring herself to take any interest in. Halfway down the train she found herself an empty corner, where she could be alone, and sliding her suitcase in beside her she sat down to wait.

Amidst the impatient sighs and creaks of the wheels beneath her, she could hear the freight being loaded in the distance. Several times during the twenty minutes of faint shouts, clattering wheels and thumping boxes, she was tempted to look out; to take a last glance at a part of the world she would never see again. Only a slackness, which drained her physically and mentally of purpose of any kind, kept her from doing so.

At last she heard the final slamming of doors and the guards whistle. With a shudder the train slid into motion. At the last moment she turned and with an over-bright gaze, she watched Denver's Creek falling away behind her.

With a three-hour journey ahead of her she had plenty of time to work out what she was going to do when she got to Adelaide. She would have to collect the rest of her things from the Muellers, of course. She had written to them occasionally during her stay at the logging camp. It would come as a surprise to them to know she was leaving Australia. If she could, she would get a berth on a boat sailing tonight. It wasn't, she told herself with a lump in her throat, as though she had anywhere particular in mind.

Half-way through the journey, she walked back to the dining car for a meal. It would be as well to eat now, that way she would have more time to do what she had to do, when she got to town.

There was no hiding away for her in the restaurant car. Every table was full. Alex had to take the vacant seat beside a tot of about four. The mother on the other side, with a similar flaxen-haired toddler, reminded her a little of Ilka Strasser when she smiled.

She was soon learning that the family were travelling up from their home in Victoria to see the children's father who was working on some job in Adelaide. Over her aching heart, Alex forced a smile and listened to the woman's conversation, occasionally helping the ringleted little girl beside her with the food on her plate. Though she found them a charming group, it was nevertheless a relief, after the meal, to get back to her own quiet corner.

Towards the end of the journey she went off to fresh up. Serene and well groomed above the inner desolation, she came back to the hubbub of people rising and reaching for possessions, as the buildings of the city came into view.

She reached for her own suitcase, feeling the engine slacken speed, and gradually as the fixtures of the station swung into view, the train pulled up to a screeching stop. All was pandemonium at the doors. After being imprisoned for several hours, everyone wanted to get out at the same time. Alex slung her handbag over her arm and allowed herself to be sucked in with the flow.

She had a struggle getting her case down the high steps with no one paying any attention to her. On this Saturday night the city station was a noisy, clanging hive of activity and latecomers hurrying for other trains. Alone in the crowds, Alex stood on the platform and looked about her for a porter. It would be useless to try and manage her luggage in the crush at the barrier.

Her heavy heart lurched at the sight of a big man hurrying along to another train. Damp-eyed, she swung her gaze away from unfamiliar features and searched for a porter who wasn't busy.

All were occupied at the front of the train she had arrived on. The other direction towards the rear compartments might be better. The people were thinning out there and — chokingly she took her gaze on from the dark-haired man stepping down from the train. She was seeing Grant everywhere tonight. She searched amongst the sprinkling of people up that way for a uniformed figure. Then something that had lingered in her mind about the certain angle of those wide shoulders, the craggy line of a tanned profile, sent her gaze winging back to the dark-haired man standing beside a small week-end bag.

Her eyes swam with tears. It couldn't be! Grant here in Adelaide! She must be dreaming! How . . .? What . . .?

He stood there in his light grey summer suit looking down to where she swayed beside her suitcase. Was he too afraid that his own eyes were deceiving him? He took one step towards her as though he daren't trust himself to find out.

Without knowing it Alex took a step forward too. The platform was alive with passers-by. Yet she and Grant might have been the only two people in the world as they stood there yards apart, yet drawn together by an intangible force; the look perhaps in each other's eyes.

His pale face working in an odd way, Grant was striding along now. In a dream, her lashes glistening, Alex was walking slowly towards him. At least she thought she was walking slowly. She had no idea at all that her steps had quickened. And in those last few moments she had never intended to run.

All she knew as she came in was a feeling of drowning in Grant's darkened brown gaze, then her feet were carrying her across the dwindling space as though they had wings.

Rapidly narrowing the gap, Grant's arms caught her close against him. She lifted her face to his and there and then, amidst the noise and clamour around them, he dropped his mouth on hers.

For a long, long time, Alex travelled in a world where everything was rose-coloured and bluebirds sang sweet songs. It was a land she had never expected to reach, and now that it was here, she was unable to drink her fill of its wonders.

It was only when she realized just how deeply she was giving herself up to it that she drew away from Grant's lips at last and a slight colour creeping in beneath her radiance, she smoothed her hair to quaver up at him in embarrassment, 'I . . . I thought you were in Oaktown.'

Grant kept one arm around her to say with his slow ironic smile, 'With you married to Lloyd I couldn't see myself carrying on at the Noongwalla logging camp. I came up to put in for a transfer at head office, first thing Monday morning.'

Close to him, Alex told him with her soft grey gaze, 'I could never have married Lloyd.'

Grant gave her his grin and replied, 'Oaktown lost its appeal for me the day I drove you back from Mount Gambier after seeing Mike Stronowsky.'

They stood soaking up each other's nearness, musing disbelievingly on the fact that they had both been hurrying out of each other's lives on the same train, until the curious glances of the people passing prompted Grant to say, never taking his eyes off her, 'Let's go somewhere where we can talk.'

When he had retrieved his own bag he picked up her suitcase which was still standing where she had left it, and side by side they walked down the platform and out of the barrier. In the twinkling lights of early evening in Adelaide, Grant hailed a taxi and assisted Alex inside. Within minutes they were cruising towards the centre of the city.

They stopped beside the entrance to a park, lush with green lawns and blossoming trees and set amidst sky-scrapers. The taxi was paid off. Grant carried the bags along winding paths to a seat hidden away beneath flowering poinsettias and the shadows of a darkening sky.

There he dropped everything and drew Alex towards him. It was a long moment later when she slanted a starry look up at him to smile, 'We're a little old for kissing in the park, aren't we?'

'It's the only place I could think of where we could be alone,' he murmured against her, and brushing his lips along her cheek, 'If you knew how long I've wanted to do this!'

When the sky had deepened to violet, tinged with a deep rose, he led her to the seat. Sitting with his arm about her, her head resting on his shoulder, she asked, 'Did you catch the train at Denver's Creek?'

Grant nodded. 'Just made it. I had to leave everything okay at the camp, which took some time, after you'd gone. I left the car in the care of a young truck driver at Denver's and nipped on with only seconds to spare.'

Alex gazed at the stars with something of an amused light. 'People are going to wonder in Noongwalla. The nurse and the logging camp boss leaving at the same time.'

'I don't think so,' Grant shook his head. 'You left to make way for Mrs. MacTavish. I found Wes just before I left and told him I'd been called up to head office for a conference. It's understood that if I don't go back within the week he'll take a day off to drive my car and my gear up here.'

'Will you go back?' Alex raised herself to look at him.

'No.' The reply was emphatic. 'On the train journey up here, I was thinking in terms of another logging camp somewhere. Now things are different. I wouldn't want my wife to come within miles of one.' He drew her close, trailing his lips along her throat.

'But if it's your job,' Alex breathed against him.

'There are others,' he grinned. 'One with the company if I want it. They've always been stingy with the help at Noongwalla, because they've wanted me, for some time, to run their main sawmill down in Victoria.' He kissed the tip of her nose. 'I think I might finally give in to pressure.' Then he brought his lips down to brush hers. 'There's a house to go with the job. A little like the bungalow at the camp, only a permanent structure with plenty of rooms. It's been built for a man and his family.'

Alex met his gleam with one of her own. '*Plenty* of rooms sounds ominous,' she said with a smile.

A long time later she sighed on the silence. 'Poor Lloyd, I hated leaving him. He was so upset.'

'He'll be okay,' Grant said. 'My information in the company literature is that the settlement is going to get a small hospital in the near future. An Australian Sister has been selected to run it. She's about your age and unmarried. Lloyd probably has all the information on his desk somewhere.' Grant grinned. 'He'll soon get to know her.'

Alex thought about what she had been told. It would be nice if it worked out like that for Lloyd. Him and this Australian nurse. She liked to think it would. Perhaps when he was happily married he would realize, as she did now, that they had both been in danger of mistaking loneliness for something deeper.

She felt Grant stir slightly against her as he asked, 'Where were you planning to stay in Adelaide?'

'I wasn't.' Alex sat up. 'I was going to get the first boat out to anywhere.' Her eyes dilated at the thought as she looked at him. 'If you'd missed that train . . .'

'I'm a good swimmer,' he joked.

On the question of accommodation she replied, 'I've got

some friends who are looking after some luggage for me. Helen and Karl Mueller.'

'Can you stay with them until I get my job fixed up?' Grant asked.

'I should think so,' Alex nodded. 'It's a hostel.'

His arms about her, Grant queried, 'Seen much of Australia?'

'Only around Adelaide,' she told him.

'Got anywhere in mind for a honeymoon?'

At the white gleam of his grin, she laid her head back on his shoulder to dream. 'I saw some exotic photographs in a travel brochure once, of the coral islands off the coast of Queensland. I've always wanted to see them.'

'We'd better get booking that plane.' He rose after kissing her lingeringly. 'But first of all we'll get you fixed up with the Muellers.'

The white beach curved away around satin-smooth green water. The huge palms spread their inky black shadows at the foot of climbing tropical growth.

Alex, lying in white swim-suit in the shade, raised herself on one elbow and gazed soft-eyed towards the hotel in the distance. The big man in the cream shorts, coming down the steps, was her husband and they had been married three days, four hours, and twenty-six minutes.

She watched him walk towards her. smiled up at him as she tossed his towel down and glinted, 'Move over, Mrs. Mitchell.'

Alongside her, his warm lips brushing across hers, he gleamed, 'Reckon after a month of this, you'll be ready to set up house for a working man?'

'Just about.' Alex stretched luxuriously, knowing that this would be her ultimate happiness. To live her life with Grant under the blue skies of Australia.

16 GREAT RE-ISSUES

Here is a wonderful opportunity to read many of the Harlequin Romances you may have missed.

- [ ] 917 TIMBER MAN
      Joyce Dingwell
- [ ] 920 MAN AT MULERA
      Kathryn Blair
- [ ] 926 MOUNTAIN MAGIC
      Susan Barrie
- [ ] 944 WHISPER OF DOUBT
      Andrea Blake
- [ ] 973 TIME OF GRACE
      Sara Seale
- [ ] 976 FLAMINGOS ON THE LAKE
      Isobel Chace
- [ ] 980 A SONG BEGINS
      Mary Burchell
- [ ] 992 SNARE THE WILD HEART
      Elizabeth Hoy

- [ ] 996 PERCHANCE TO MARY
      Celine Conway
- [ ] 997 CASTLE THUNDERBIRD
      Susan Barrie
- [ ] 999 GREEN FINGERS FARM
      Joyce Dingwell
- [ ] 1014 HOUSE OF LORRAINE
      Rachel Lindsey
- [ ] 1027 THE LONELY SHORE
      Anne Weale
- [ ] 1223 THE GARDEN OF PERSEPHONE
      Nan Asquith
- [ ] 1245 THE BAY OF MOONLIGHT
      Rose Burghley
- [ ] 1319 BRITTLE BONDAGE
      Rosalind Brett

To: **HARLEQUIN READER SERVICE, Dept. N 401**
    M.P.O. Box 707, Niagara Falls, N.Y. 14302
    Canadian address: Stratford, Ont., Canada

- [ ] Please send me the free Harlequin Romance Catalogue.
- [ ] Please send me the titles checked.

I enclose $_____ (No C.O.D.'s), All books are 60c each. To help defray postage and handling cost, please add 25c.

Name _____

Address _____

City/Town _____

State/Prov. _____ Zip _____

INTRODUCTION

I t just isn't the same."

My dad sounded so sad. We stood on the walkway of a freeway overpass, looking out across a sea of new houses. Miles of houses, street after street.

"That line of trees out there is Sugar Creek." He waved an arm toward the hives of condos. "All this used to be farmland. When Paul Hutchens wrote those books about the Sugar Creek Gang, this is the area he wrote about. Right here."

I'm eleven, and, according to Dad, I'm older than most of the *homes* out here. "At least there's still a Sugar Creek," I said. "How far is it from our new place?"

"Couple miles. But the past—that was another world." He looked at me. "I'm sorry the fun is gone."

Dad walked down the slope to our car. I fell in behind him, wishing he didn't feel so sad.

When I was little, he read to me every night. And my favorite books to read were about a bunch of kids called the Sugar Creek Gang. They lived on farms near a creek and had a zillion adventures, mostly out in nature somewhere.

When Dad switched jobs, he found out we were going to move into the very area where

1

As I look back, I guess it all started when our grocery store over in the strip mall put fresh turkeys on sale for half price. If they hadn't done that, I wouldn't have made a major career decision. And the new Sugar Creek Gang would not have gotten tangled up in a wolf scare. Well, on second thought, maybe we would have anyway. We tend to do that—get mixed up in stuff, I mean.

There are five of us, as weirdly different as you could imagine. I, Les Walker, am redheaded and freckled and never tan. Burn, yes. Tan, no. Bits, who lives across the street (her name is really Elizabeth Ware), tans just fine. She has plain brown hair in a ponytail.

Mike Alvarado and Tiny (Clarence Wilson on his school records) live close to each other. Tiny is extra tall and extra thin for his age, and Mike is stocky like his dad and short for his age, which is ten, a year younger than the rest of us. Tiny's black skin doesn't mind sun a bit. Neither does Mike's brownish one. Mike claims he has some Yaqui blood in him, but his blood looks just like mine when he cuts himself.

And then there's Lynn Wing, with her Chinese dad and Japanese mom. Except, she insists, her parents really aren't Chinese and

Japanese. They're American, as their parents were before them. But the family way back was Asian. She is quiet and slight, and you don't notice her. But when you need bright ideas in a hurry, she has them.

The thing that ties us together is Sugar Creek. We all five enjoy the old Sugar Creek Gang adventure books. That's what brought us together in the first place. Best of all, we live within a couple miles of the real Sugar Creek, which is now in a county park. We go there all the time.

Anyway, let me tell you about the wolf scare. And that turkey.

* * *

There is shopping, and there is shopping. My mom takes me shopping mostly so I can carry stuff. My sisters, Catherine and Hannah, are older than I, and they love it. I am bored out of my skull five minutes into the trip—like before the car even gets to the mall.

Except when it's groceries we're shopping for. Now that's different. I enjoy shopping in the grocery store. Mom chooses practical stuff, reads labels, and shops for value. I tend to shop for shape. For example, asparagus and green beans are not a good shape. Potato chips and tortilla chips are.

We were in the meat section that fateful day. The huge, long cold cases displayed the packaged meats. Mom leans strongly toward chicken, and she does wonderful things with it. She doesn't buy parts. She buys the whole corpse and cuts it up herself.

And here, in one of those big bins that's shaped like a chest freezer, was the "Special." Fresh turkeys. My first thought was, *Why turkey? It's not Thanksgiving*. But then I got to thinking about the warm, happy taste of turkey, a delight that should not be limited to one day in three hundred sixty- five.

I called, "Hey, Mom? You love bargains. Look here."

Hannah, fourteen, sniffed. "Why turkey? It's not Thanksgiving." Hannah was very quick to point out that good ideas never *ever* come from little brothers.

Mom looked in the bin. "Good price." She shoved a few aside to look at others. "Les? Which would you pick as best?"

I know a trick question when I hear it. "Well, if these were chickens, I'd say pick the heaviest. A batch of chickens are all about the same age, and the heavier ones have more meat per bone. But I don't know if that applies to turkeys. Does it?"

She shrugged. "I have no idea. I was hoping you knew." But the way she smiled, I knew it had been a test and that I'd answered right.

Mom picked a big one with a lot of yellow in the skin. I bucked it up into her cart for her.

Pushing the cart, I followed her down the next aisle. "Mom? Do they ever make turkey l'orange like they do duck? How about turkey au vin? That kind of thing. All I've ever seen a turkey is roasted."

"Come to think of it—" she pursed her lips, "—I have many recipes for turkey, but they all start with cooked leftovers."

"There's gotta be more than roasting." I pondered this question as I mindlessly shoved the cart along behind her.

Next, I thought: *Most chefs are men. They don't just instantly become great chefs; they must spend years practicing. But some are fairly young. Therefore they were cooking at my age, probably— eleven or so. No time to start like the present.*

"Mom? Chefs make a lot of money, don't they?"

"The good ones do. Yes."

"If I were a chef, I'd be the best."

I tried to imagine how neat it would be to be able to just bomb around in the kitchen awhile and whip up some fantastic dish. "Mom? Can I cook the turkey? Please?"

She stared at nothing for a moment. "Sure."

Yee ha!

Catherine, the sister who's a year older than I, met us at midaisle with her load of cereal. We take turns picking out cereals, and this was her day. She dumped them in the basket. "Why turkey? It's not Thanksgiving."

Mom smiled. "It's for your brother to practice on. He's going to become a great chef."

2

As I walked in the door of the animal rescue shelter, tall, gangly Tiny yelled, "Man, Les, am I glad to see you! Gimme a hand here!"

You know, a greeting like that makes a body feel real good. It's almost always nice to know you're needed. I say *almost* because occasionally I'm needed to wash dishes. That's not so nice.

But Tiny really did need me today. Cages of various sizes lined one wall of the long, windowless reception room, and nearly all of them held injured wild animals. The food dishes hadn't been taken care of yet, the gurneys and examination tables were dirty and blood-streaked, the floor was a mess, and . . .

At the big exam table by the door, Tiny and a gray-haired woman in blue jeans tussled with a struggling fawn. The front of the lady's clothes were all smeared with blood—the fawn's blood, obviously. She must have carried it in the way you carry a small dog, pressed close to her.

Tiny had tied the little guy's legs together, but it still managed to throw itself around. The woman held it as best she could. Tiny fought to get a big, black cloth sack over the fawn's head. Once an animal can't see, it usually calms down.

Finally he got it over the top of the deer's head and ears. The little guy quit trying to kick.

9

With the head not flailing around so much, Tiny could wrap a towel around its eyes, a blindfold. Then he opened the black sack in such a way that the fawn's nose stuck out in the air. It was a slick arrangement, and Tiny really knew how to make it work.

He reached for the dressings on the lower shelf of the table. "Mrs. Dexter here found the fawn in her front yard this morning."

"Wow. What happened to it?"

"Dogs, I suppose," Mrs. Dexter said. She had a soft, pretty voice to go with her soft, pretty face. "I heard a commotion before dawn, but I didn't see this little fellow until I went out for the paper."

"You live on a farm?" I asked. I always wanted to live on a real farm. My dad grew up on a farm.

"Edge of town. Just a little place. But we like it."

Some of the fawn's rips and gashes were huge. I never would have thought dogs could do all that.

Tiny paused from bandaging big gashes in the fawn's rump. He pointed to the far corner. "Les, we're almost out of Ace bandages. See if you can find something in that cabinet."

"Ace bandages are those tan, stretchy things, right?"

He grunted something as I hurried over to paw through the cabinet. I wasn't the first person looking for something and leaving the shelves all messed up. In fact, it was such a jumble I just started dumping stuff out on the floor. I found a couple of boxed Ace bandages way in back.

I brought them to Tiny. "I think these are all."

"They won't be enough. There's bed sheets in the cupboard left of the sink. We can tear one of them into strips."

I knew who the "we" was going to be. I dug out a sheet, found scissors to start each tear with, and ripped sheet-long strips about the width of the Ace bandages. Three inches or so. I would much rather have been helping with the fawn, but this had to be done.

Half an hour later, we finally finished. The fawn was all trussed up and bandaged and tucked into a big floor cage. The woman complimented Tiny and left.

Tiny looked beat. He flopped into a chair and let his arms and legs sprawl.

"Mike usually helps you," I said. "Where is he?"

"Out working with his brothers. He says he's gonna get rich. He wants lots of money. I said, 'You ain't gonna get wealthy by weeding flower beds.' And he says, 'Not by giving my time away at the shelter, either.' So he hasn't been around for a few days."

I flopped in a chair, too. "But you aren't the only person who volunteers."

"No, but two of them are on vacation. Tiff sprained her ankle playing softball. Mrs. Forster had to go to a wedding. And that

Tammy somebody was here one day, saw the blood and guts, and decided not to do it."

I hopped back up, in no mood to goof off. "Well, those blood and guts are all over the place today. I'll start cleaning up. I'll do the tables first and then the floor."

Tiny lurched to his feet. "I'll get the food dishes filled. It's past feeding time."

So I spritzed all the gurneys and exam tables with disinfectant spray and cleaned them off. It took a while. Some of the blood smears and fur bits were dried on hard.

I called across the room, "How come so many animals are inside here? You usually put them in outdoor cages after you take care of them."

"Dr. Meyers hasn't seen them yet. She got called out to a farm. A pack of dogs or something ripped up a farmer's sheep."

Maybe living on a farm wasn't such a hot ticket after all.

Tiny crossed the long room with an armload of dog dishes from the dishwasher. "I'm sure glad you're here. How'd you know I needed you?"

"Well, it's this way—" I paused for dramatic effect "—I'm going to become a great chef. I suppose if I were cooking for four hundred people, I'd be busy most of the day. But cooking at home seems to be a once-in-a-while thing, so I had time on my hands."

"Then I can sure take some off your hands for you. We're behind with a lot of stuff around here."

We filled the food dishes and loaded them into the beat-up old coaster wagon. Then we went out to feed the animals in the outside cages. It's an old farm, this rescue shelter. The main part is in the Quonset hut sort of building, where we'd just been. But most animals and birds were housed in chicken wire cages out in the farmyard. Many, many cages, most on rickety two-by-four legs. Feeding all those animals is a kick; you give each one just enough of the exact kind of food it needs. It's an art.

I didn't tell Tiny that I had been bored spitless this morning and that coming out here to see him was an act of desperation. My big sister Hannah went to the mall with some other shopping freaks. Not-as-big-sister Catherine went up the street to a friend's house. I crossed the street to see if Bits wanted to play Monopoly, but she was all wrapped up in a computer game and didn't want to. Lynn wasn't home. And when I called Tiny's house, no one answered, so I figured he was out here.

But I enjoyed working and taking care of animals, especially in a sort of animal hospital like this. What really surprised me, though, was that so many of the cages outside were full. It looked like there'd been a Texas chain saw massacre without Texas or chain saws.

I watched a really mangled bunny nibble at carrot greens. "What happened to all these poor beasts?"

Tiny paused beside me, watching the rabbit. "Some say wolves."

3

I hungered for adventure. I hungered for the great outdoors. Actually, I hungered to goof off somewhere, because, if I stayed home, I'd end up mowing the lawn. I called Bits. She was busy. I called Lynn. She felt like going to Sugar Creek Park. So I rode my bike out there with her.

As we crossed Crestline, I yelled to her, "Dad says that out beyond town, Sugar Creek still has farms all along it, just like the old days."

"My father says it's big enough to be a river more than a creek," Lynn called back to me. "You haven't been here in the spring, yet. Wait till you see it during the spring melt, especially when it rains."

"Really howling, huh?" Someday, I decided, I would travel the length of Sugar Creek from its beginning to its end.

Today, though, we merely went to the park. Within the town, Sugar Creek County Park cut a broad swath of green trees and brush right through some of the nicest neighborhoods. The park was a couple miles long and maybe half a mile wide or a little less; that's quite a swath. A chain-link fence separated the park from the homes and lawns. Deep inside its cool, quiet woods, nature trails laced in and out along the creek. It's a peaceful place. Pleasant. And enough interesting animals live there that you never get bored.

We locked our bikes to the rack in the picnic area at the west park entrance. We hung our helmets on the handlebars, because who wants to tote a "brain basket" all over? Then we went for a nature stroll.

Did I say "peaceful"? About a quarter mile back along the main trail, we heard shouting up ahead. It sounded like a man and woman, not just kids messing around.

I broke into a run toward the noise, with Lynn right behind me. Who would be screaming like that? Beyond the Swamp Loop side trail, we came upon two grown-up hikers in shorts and lug sole shoes. The woman, with blonde hair cut short, sniffled, and I realized she was crying.

She stood staring down at her husband. He was kneeling. And in front of him lay a fawn. A bloody fawn. But it was still alive.

He wagged his head. "I don't know what we can do for it. It will die, I'm sure."

"Maybe not, sir." I stepped up to them. "A friend of ours volunteers at a wild animal rescue shelter. Yesterday we patched one up that was hurt as bad as this one. I called Tiny this morning, and it's still alive. We can take this one there."

He stood up, looking disgusted. "Well, you can waste time on it if you want, but I say it's not worth messing with. It's going to die."

"George!" the woman exploded, half furious and still half crying. "If there's a chance of saving it, we're going to try!"

It was sure obvious that George didn't think much of trying. But what could he do? He picked up the fawn, trying to keep it at arm's length but couldn't. It got blood all over him, and that seemed to *really* fry his eggs. Just as angry as the blonde woman, he stomped back on the trail toward the picnic area parking lot, as the fawn struggled weakly in his arms.

Lynn and I followed.

By the time he got to his car, his shirt and shorts were a mess. He was all sweaty, too. It's hard work carrying a deer, even one that small. "A fine walk this turned out to be!" Grump, grump, grump.

I thought about the woman who had brought the fawn in yesterday. She had gotten all smeared and dirty, too, but she never seemed to notice. The fawn had been the important thing to her. I liked her attitude better than this man's.

Lynn and I explained to them how to get to the rescue shelter. Since his clothes were a mess anyway, George was elected to hold the deer while his wife drove. They offered to take us along, but neither one of us was allowed to get in a car with strangers. So we just rode our bikes out there as fast as we could.

We got there only about five minutes after they did. I think they might have gotten a little lost.

George's day was definitely not going well.

The fawn had made a further mess on him. And when they got inside, he saw this kid less than twelve in charge of the whole place.

George blew up. He roared about incompetence. He threatened to call the police and the Humane Society and the Game and Fish Department. Nobody bothered to tell him the Game and Fish Department licensed the shelter to keep game birds and animals. Nobody explained to him that the place operated with the blessing of the Humane Society, or even that the police themselves often brought in injured animals.

We ignored him because we were all working on the fawn. Quickly and expertly, Tiny trussed it up and blindfolded it. He got the blonde lady to work with him. It was amazing. She changed instantly from a weeping, sorrowful woman to an eager helper. She really seemed to enjoy the work, messy and sad as it was.

Finally, we had done all we could. Tiny put the fawn in a plastic clothes basket in the corner under a table, because he was out of cages.

The woman wandered about the room, peering from cage to cage. "I never realized so many animals get hurt."

"It's not usually this busy. We have a sort of rush going on," Tiny said. "Dog-bite sort of injuries."

George frowned. "The wolves?"

Tiny and I looked at each other. I said, "A lady in here yesterday claims wolves attacked a deer."

Tiny added, "And the vet who takes care of our animals here was busy most of yesterday stitching a farmer's flock back together. The farmer said it was wolves."

George snorted. "Yeah! That's what we saw, all right! A pack of wolves. They couldn't be anything else. The leader was this big!" And he held his hand three feet off the floor.

"Wolves come in different colors, don't they?" the lady asked.

Tiny nodded. "I think light gray through black. But I'll have to look it up. I'm not sure."

"One of them was brown. Actually, more like tan. A baby. But it was definitely wolves."

Mrs. Ferguson, the afternoon and evening volunteer, showed up then. The adults all introduced themselves and started talking. In an instant they completely forgot about us kids. So the three of us went outside.

We sat down in the grass beside the bikes. Tiny looked just plain pooped.

Lynn frowned. "What's all this about wolves?"

I bobbed my head toward Tiny. "You're the naturalist with the binoculars around your neck half the time. You know all this stuff. It isn't wolves, is it?"

"Wolves?" Lynn asked.

Tiny wagged his head. "Don't see how it could be. It could be a coyote, though. A family of coyotes. They're around here, and there's getting to be more of them. Yeah, that's proba- bly it. Coyotes."

I grunted. "You off tomorrow?"

"At last. Been here all week."

"Know where we want to go tomorrow?"

"Yeah. For ice cream."

"Good idea. Also to the natural history museum. I bet they'll know if wolves are here."

Lynn repeated, "Wolves? Here?"

Tiny stared straight ahead a few moments, seeing nothing. He licked his lips. "Les? There's so many people around here. Families. Kids. What if it *is* wolves? Do you suppose they'd bite a child?"

4

Our family was eating breakfast the next morning (I with my favorite, a ham sandwich and an orange—but eaten separately, not at the same time—when Catherine asked, "So what are your plans today, Squirt?"

I don't suppose I even have to mention that "Squirt" is her most commonly used term of address to me.

"I," I announced grandly, "am going to explore the intriguing prospect that a pack of wolves has invaded the county. And maybe, this very moment, they are ravaging some innocent kitten." I said that because she loved cats.

"You're sick. You are very, very sick." She continued eating her ordinary breakfast of cereal and toast.

Dad cocked an eyebrow. "Wolves?"

I got serious with Dad, since he always wanted to know where I was going. "Tiny's shelter is running over with animals that have been all bitten up. And a couple people say they saw wolves. So Tiny and Lynn and I are going over to the natural history museum to ask the curator there about wolves."

"Good idea. Back by lunch?"

"Yes, sir."

You know, that wasn't a bad thing—Dad's

always knowing where I was. If something nasty ever happened, he'd know about where to start looking for me, and when. So when he asked, I didn't resent it, the way some kids do. He wasn't checking up; he was just keeping track.

Hannah was staring at me, wide-eyed. "There really are wolves? Do they really eat cats?"

"Tiny thinks it's coyotes. I'll let you know."

I finished my orange. The doorbell rang, so I tossed the peel into the trash, grabbed my helmet, and hit the road. Not literally. I try desperately *not* to hit any roads, especially when on roller blades.

Lynn was all smiles as she climbed aboard her bike. "I love going to the museum."

"Me too."

A girl's voice called to us. Bits stood on her porch, across the street. "Where you going?"

We pulled into her yard. I said, "Natural history museum. Tiny's coming, too. Come along, why don't you?"

"When you coming home?"

"Lunch." I glanced at Lynn. She nodded.

"Can I use your computer till then?"

I was about to say yes, but Lynn burst out with, "Oh, please, Bits! Your father chased you out of the house and said, 'Go do something outside on a nice day like this.' Right?"

"None of your business!"

"You and your computer games." Lynn wagged her head.

I suggested, "Come along. You can hole up

in the museum's computer room and play rain forest population games while we talk to people about wolves."

"Why wolves?"

"Why not wolves?" I tooled my bike out across the yard and bumped down off the curb. I practiced trying to do wheelies while she got her bike. Notice, I did not say *practiced doing wheelies*. I said *practiced trying*, because that's all the farther I could get.

Then Bits rolled out onto the street, and we were on our way.

The natural history museum is on the north side of Metro Park. When we got there, Tiny's and Mike's bikes were locked to the rack outside the museum's huge front doors. I was glad to see Mike's bike there. He spent an awful lot of his life working harder than many men, and he was the youngest kid in the Sugar Creek Gang. Maybe today he could relax and have some fun.

Bits headed straight as an arrow for the museum's kid section and its computers. Lynn, Tiny, Mike, and I walked back to the education director at the end of the hall, and she called the mammal curator for us.

Yes, he could talk to us a few minutes. She smiled and directed us up a flight of stairs, past the hall of mammals and the marine displays. Did you know a humpback whale suspended from the ceiling can fill the length of a very big hall? The four of us paused a moment to look straight up, gaping. Imagine being in a whale-boat a hundred years ago, harpooning one of those things, and away it goes. And you're hanging on to the end of a puny, little old rope attached to it.

The curator looked like how you think a professor ought to look. Slightly built and slim, he hid behind a really neat beard. A few gray hairs in the beard and around his ears were the only sign that he was probably older than Dad, and that's *old!*

"Dr. Owen Morgan." He introduced himself and offered his hand. Tiny shook hands and introduced himself, Lynn, Mike, and me. I felt curiously important and grown up.

Tiny explained his job. He told about the animals. Then he said something I didn't know until then. "The wolves—or whatever they are—are doing a lot of damage. Almost three-fourths of the animals that come to us end up dying."

Three-fourths! That really slapped me.

Dr. Morgan nodded. "Let's go out to the dioramas."

It had never occurred to me, but the curator probably knew every detail of every display lining the walls of the Mammal Hall. He led us directly to a scene showing Arctic tundra.

I love dioramas. Those are those displays behind glass with stuffed animals in natural poses and set up in their natural habitat. The plants all around in the foreground look real. A painting of the scenery, arcing around the background, makes it seem you're really there.

The tundra one had snow as the base, with

some rocks sticking out. Green and gray lichens on the rocks were the only plants. Wolves were attacking a circle of musk oxen. The display had only one mounted musk ox. The others were painted on the backdrop. But the five snarling, slinking wolves were all mounts.

"See how the running wolves are holding their tails?" Dr. Morgan asked.

"Straight out," Mike said. "They do that for real?"

"Yes. Now come down here to the desert scene." Dr. Morgan led the way. In the desert diorama, quail and a jackrabbit squatted behind a bush as a coyote trotted by. A snake, two peccaries (wild, piglike animals), and a mule deer watched it all.

Lynn pointed. "The coyote's tail droops."

Dr. Morgan smiled. "Exactly. When the animal is moving, if it holds its tail straight out, you're watching a wolf. If it holds its tail at a downward slope, it's a coyote."

I pointed, too. "But this coyote is a lot smaller than those wolves."

"True, but it's hard to judge size at a distance. From a hundred yards away, they'll seem nearly the same size, unless you see them together. And you won't. Coyotes and wolves don't run together."

"I read that coyotes are extending their range—spreading out into areas where they didn't used to be," Tiny said. "Are wolves?"

"No. Especially not here in the lower forty-eight." By that, I knew Dr. Morgan meant the states other than Alaska and Hawaii.

Tiny stared at the mounted coyote a few moments. "Do coyotes ever go after livestock? Farm animals?"

"Rarely. Usually, if you see them with a dead farm animal, it was dead when they found it. They'll scavenge domestic animals."

Mike asked, "Do they eat rabbits and squirrels?"

"Yes, indeed. Small mammals are their preferred food, but they'll eat just about anything humans eat—and a whole lot that's downright repulsive to humans. Carrion. Green nuts."

Mike started looking worried. "They ever attack . . . you know . . . kids? Little kids?" Mike is short for his age.

Dr. Morgan laughed. "Almost never. I can't think of a single instance of coyotes attacking a person. There are stories that wolves used to a hundred years ago, but not coyotes. You're safe."

And at that, Mike looked embarrassed.

"I doubt, though, that your problem is wolves." Dr. Morgan absent-mindedly scratched his beard. "I'd go more for feral dogs. They can actually be more dangerous than wolves or coyotes. They have no fear of humans."

Mike frowned. "What's 'feral'?"

"A domestic animal that has gone wild. For example, people don't want their dog anymore, so they dump it along a country road. It learns to live off the land, out in the wild. Pretty soon, it doesn't need people. That's feral."

Lynn added, "I've heard of feral house cats."

Dr. Morgan nodded. "Many of those, and they do terrible damage to wild birds."

Tiny asked some more questions, but I wasn't listening closely. Now that we knew how to tell coyotes and wolves apart, we were ready for the next step. The next step was to *see* the animals. But they seemed to be hitting all over the area—a farm here, a subdivision there, Sugar Creek Park—there didn't appear to be any pattern. Where would we go to find them?

And why in the world would anyone in his right mind deliberately go out looking to get face to face with a wolf?

5

Want to hear about one of the world's great coincidences? And I mean world-class, all the way. Now it's true, our downtown Metro Park was world-class, just as great as New York's Central Park, which I have visited. All it lacked is the zoo. And, like Central Park, it had a world-class natural history museum on one side and a big art museum on the other side. The coincidence was: Right next to our natural history museum was the world's greatest ice cream stand. Now is that planning or what?

The result of this coincidence: Less than ten minutes after we left Dr. Morgan, the five of us were sitting around a table under an umbrella in Metro Park, licking away at the world's greatest ice cream.

Bits scowled. "I would have won if I could have played that population program another twenty minutes. You guys shouldn't have pulled me away from it." But then she brightened noticeably as she dug into her maple nut sundae with extra whipped cream.

"No, you wouldn't." Tiny examined his raspberry hot fudge sundae from all four sides—figuring out how to tackle it, I guess. "It's rigged so you can't beat that one. All six species end up going extinct. I know. I tried all day on it once."

"You weren't doing it right, then." Bits started working on her ice cream in earnest. "Nobody invents a game you can't win."

Tiny shook his head. "That's the whole point of it, don't you see? Everything eventually goes extinct. The only thing you can do with that game is stretch out the species life a little longer."

"Wrong. You can beat it. I'm sure you can beat it."

Then it got real quiet as we all wallowed in the rich flavors of the world's finest treat.

I took a big slurp off my peanut butter chocolate chip cone. "I've decided I'm going to be a naturalist when I grow up. Like Dr. Morgan there. Can you imagine going to work every day in that museum? I mean, you walk past those dioramas, and when a stuffed bird or something falls out of its tree, you go in and put it back up. And you know everything in the whole museum."

With his tongue out as far as it could go, Mike trimmed the edge of his double-dip chocolate cone. "Tiny already does."

"Do not." Tiny dipped a big spoonful. "But someday I'm gonna."

Lynn paused to savor a spoonful of her French vanilla butterscotch sundae. Then, "I'm glad you got the day off, Mike."

"Didn't get the day off." Mike slurped his cone again. "I quit. My stingy brother don't pay me enough money doing that yard work."

Lynn smiled. "So you're going to go wolf hunting with us?"

"Nope. Got a real job."

Bits frowned. "You do not! Who'd hire a ten-year-old? It's not legal."

Mike looked smug as a cat with canary feathers in its whiskers. "Gonna help at a pet-grooming shop. Sweep up and stuff. Five dollars an hour!"

Bits growled, "Liar."

"Am not!"

Lynn wasn't smiling anymore. "That pet shop on Eleventh Street?"

Mike nodded. "They board animals, so I'll help out in the kennels and the salon both. Feed and clean. 'Zackly the same as I did at the rescue shelter for free, only I get paid. He hired me 'cause I'm experienced."

"Paid how?"

"Cash! Gonna be rolling in money real soon. I start Monday."

"Five dollars an hour." Lynn looked at her sundae as if counting the crushed peanuts on it, then began eating again.

It sounded like a fortune to me, but I knew Bits had a point. The only job a kid our age could legally hold was stuff like delivering newspapers or working on a farm. But if Mike said he was working, he was. He never lied about things.

"Oh, hey," I said. "Before I forget. You guys are all invited to my place tomorrow for Sunday dinner. Roast turkey and the trimmings."

"Why turkey?" Bits grabbed a paper napkin that was blowing. "It's not Thanksgiving."

"If you must know, it was on special. I'm going to be a great chef if I don't become a naturalist, and I'm fixing it."

Tiny grinned. *"You're* cooking? Quick! We all gotta think of some excuse to stay away!"

Bits scraped the sides of her plastic sundae bowl. "I'm busy. I'm gonna make sure I'm busy."

Lynn licked her spoon. "I have to wash my hair. Maybe two or three times. It's very dirty."

It was not.

"I have to sort my socks. Organize my sock drawer." Mike bit into his cone. "Black on the left and white on the right."

"Oh, come on, guys!"

Lynn laughed. "Relax, Les. Of course we'll come. We want to. We have to see if you have the makings of a great chef. If this is going to be anything like those cookies we tried to bake once, it will certainly be entertaining. You do have a fresh battery in the smoke alarm, don't you?"

Tiny snorted. "Entertaining, yeah, but we'll starve."

My friends are a whole herd of clowns. I brought the conversation back to the subject at hand. "So where are we going to find wolves?"

"I've been thinking about that." Lynn pointed up the street. "Let's get a county map at the drugstore. They sell them on a rack right by the checkout stand. And mark all the places someone saw the wolves. Or coyotes."

"Hey, yeah!" Tiny grinned. "If they have a home range, maybe we can figure it out."

So when we finished, we pooled our money. Ice cream treats sure make a big, big dent in funds. We didn't have enough for a postcard, let alone a map.

"No problem," said Lynn. "I'm sure that tourist information kiosk out by the freeway has them."

I would not in a million years have thought of that. But we biked out to the kiosk—staying on back streets as usual—and there they were. A whole rack of county maps. We took one map but didn't pick up any of the many brochures that tell visitors about the parks and restaurants and museums. Lynn even signed the guest register.

We called my mom. She was cooking pork chops for dinner, and, yes, there was enough for company. So then we stopped by Tiny's and Mike's houses and asked their moms if they could eat at my place. Yes, but be home by dark.

We rode on past my door to Lynn's. Her mom said OK. We were going to get permission for Bits, but she decided she wanted to eat at home and left us. Lynn wagged her head sadly as Bits put her bike away and went inside.

Dinner wasn't ready yet, so we could spread the map out on the kitchen table. I got out my colored markers.

We all leaned on the map on our elbows, staring at it and not knowing beans what we were looking at.

Lynn pointed. "This is the rescue shelter, here. Right?"

"Right!" Tiny took the black marker and made a little circle. "No wolves reported near us."

"If they *were* near there," Mike asked, "do you s'pose the smell of all the injured animals would lure them in close?"

"Probably, yeah. So they don't likely prowl around that area."

"Here's the park." I pointed. "We know they came there." It wasn't that tough a thing to find, considering that the parks were coded in green and there was this huge green block labeled *Sugar Creek County Park* west of Crest-line.

Tiny put a big red spot in it.

The woman who brought the fawn in had filled out a facility-use card. Tiny sort of remembered her address and made a big red mark there too. He also remembered where the farmer whose sheep were attacked lived. He marked there.

"Way cool!" Mike cooed. "Look at that!"

And he was right, it *was* cool. The red spots were clustered in a big loose circle, ragged-edged but obvious.

Tiny stood up straight and nodded. "There's their home range, then. There's where we go wolf hunting."

6

Someday the newspaper headline will read:

Les Walker, World's Greatest Chef, Visits City

And the newspaper would be the *Seattle Times* or maybe the *Post Intelligencer*, because I'm from Seattle originally. That's home. We had just moved halfway across the country to this house because Dad switched jobs to a new law firm. This house didn't feel completely like home yet.

I took the turkey out of the refrigerator and set it on the counter. (You know, don't you, that you always, *always* thaw frozen chickens and turkeys in the fridge and never out in the room. Poultry and poultry products such as eggs carry germs, *salmonella* bacteria specifically. I mean, they nearly all do. And if the bacteria count builds high enough, the way it can at room temperature, you can get food poisoning from it. Also, do you realize how hard it is to work *salmonella* into an ordinary conversation like this?)

While I fought that massive beast, I wondered if maybe, when I went back to Seattle someday for a visit, they'd have a parade for me. I couldn't remember right off if I ever heard of a great chef getting a "welcome home" parade. But then I couldn't think of any great naturalists getting a parade, either.

The turkey was heavy and cold. I groped around inside. The body cavity was *really* cold.

"Mom? I can't find any heart or gizzard or liver."

Mom was making potato soup for lunch. "In a store turkey, they're in a little bag where the craw was removed."

The craw. The craw. That was a sacklike place in birds' gullets—their throats—where they store food. I dug under the flap of skin up front, and wouldn't you know, there was the bag. "Do I stuff this hole too?"

"Sometimes. Usually not."

Hannah came in with a tray. She had just set the table for lunch out on the deck. "I think it's really interesting what God did in church this morning."

"What's that?" Mom asked.

"You know. Here's Les, all hot to catch wolves, and where does the pastor preach? Luke 10:3. I mean, there are only thirteen verses in the whole Bible that mention wolves, and bingo."

Aha! Obviously, she had just looked up *wolves* in a concordance and counted the verses where it occurred. Also obviously, she was very smug about knowing all this.

Well, aha right back. I was one up on her. "Ah, my sweet sister. Of those thirteen, the ones that are *wolves of evening* don't count, because that's how somebody translated the

Hebrew word for hyenas. Wolves of evening are really hyenas."

Mom raised an eyebrow. "Now where'd you learn that? I'm impressed."

"There's this great computer program that's like a concordance only better. Goes into a lot of detail with pictures and everything."

"Computer. I should have known."

"Hey, at least I don't play computer games all day. Lynn says she's starting to worry about Bits. Bits spends too much time on games, she says." You don't realize how many slices there are in a loaf of bread until you have to tear up every one of them into little pieces.

"Know what you are?" Hannah glared at me. "An intellectual snob." And she marched out with the tray of extra stuff—salt, pepper, butter, rolls. When she can't win on points, she calls her little brother names.

Mom chopped me an onion for the stuffing when she chopped one for the soup. She seemed to be in deep thought. "So Lynn has noticed it, too. I think Bits's father is getting worried about her. He blocked certain Web sites off-limits for her, but he's concerned anyway."

But my mind was working on other things. "Mom? I hate to admit it, but Hannah has a point. I mean, was God saying something to me when the pastor talked about wolves today? If it's a coincidence, it's sure a weird coincidence. I guess what I'm saying is, how do you know when God is telling you something and when it's something else?"

She smiled at me. "Do you realize what you are doing?"

"Yeah. I'm mixing the torn-up bread with the chopped onion and garlic and sage and savory and thyme, like you said. Shouldn't I?"

Mom laughed. "No, that's right. Keep going. I mean, you are asking a theological question people have asked since time began. Exactly how is God speaking to us, if at all, and what is He saying?"

"Yeah! That's it!" I added milk and chicken bouillon to the bowlful of dry stuff. Stirring got a lot harder instantly. "So? What's the answer?"

"I don't have one. Each person is different. So God speaks to each in a unique way. Do you understand what I'm saying?"

"Yeah." My arm was getting tired from trying to mix that glop.

"Good. Then give me an example to illustrate what I just said." My mother, the teacher.

"I just scoop a handful and shove it in, right?" I had seen Mom stuff a chicken many a time. I assumed stuffing the turkey was the same.

"Right."

I thought about an example as I worked.

And it *was* work. Raw stuffing just doesn't cooperate. The goo escaped being pushed in by squeezing out between my fingers. It globbed and pasted up all over my hand. And my arm. For a while there, I had more on me than I had in the turkey. "I don't have quite enough to fill the whole inside. Does that matter?"

"Nope."

"An example. Like, when God announced the birth of Jesus, a star was enough to tell the wise men with. But He had to hit the shepherds over the head with a choir of angels."

When Mom laughs, her whole body gets into the act. It's the neatest thing. The noise of laughter exploded out, her hands flew up, her back arched.

She finally got back to being serious. "Listen to what God would tell you, Les. But also listen for ways He might do it. And I'm proud of you that you care enough to want to hear Him."

Dad came in waving the Sunday paper. "Did you see this, Les?"

"No, I'm too busy cooking. I didn't even get to read the comics yet." I slipped the turkey into the oven. That doesn't sound hard. But remember that, when it was stuffed, that old bird weighed almost a fourth of what I weighed.

"Some newspaper reporter got wind of the wolf rumors. Big picture story here. They interviewed farmers about the ravaged sheep and deer. Lots of quotes."

"Wow! They mention Tiny? He knows more about it than anybody."

"No. Too bad, too. I don't know how much of this is hype, but it sounds like they're taking your wolves very seriously."

7

Dad and some friends went sailing a couple times when he was in college. He says that sailing is hours of boredom punctuated by a few moments of terror. Cooking is something like that, too. After I hurry–hurry–hurried to truss up the turkey and put it in the oven, there wasn't much left to do for five hours.

Then the phone rang, and my afternoon was instantly saved from boredom.

It was Tiny. "Hey, Les! Want to come along with Dr. Meyers and me? We're going out to a farm to take care of some animals."

"Yeah! Where do I meet you?"

"We'll pick you up at your house in ten minutes. Bring a raincoat. It's raining. And call Lynn and Bits."

I did that. Lynn was on my doorstep almost before her phone receiver went *click*.

Bits said she didn't have time. Her father yelled something in the background that I couldn't make out. She said, "Yeah, I'll come." So it sounded like her father was chasing her outdoors again. In the rain, yet.

Veterinarian Helen Meyers's van pulled up at our door, and the three of us piled in, all wrapped up in slickers. Tiny and Mike were in the front seat with Dr. Meyers.

Tiny twisted around in his seat belt shoulder harness. "Dr. Meyers asked me to give her a hand and asked if I knew anyone else who could help."

"Thanks for remembering us!" and I meant it, too!

And so Dr. Meyers showed up at this farm with five noble assistants. The Sugar Creek Gang.

The farmer, a big, blond, hefty guy, was waiting for us by his barn door. He seemed the kind of man who would be cheerful and always smiling, but he looked grim now.

His wife, in blue jeans and a T-shirt, stood beside him. Her eyes were all wet and red and puffy. She had been crying.

Dr. Meyers introduced us to them. Their names were Bob and Jan Bradhurst. But they weren't in a mood to be casual.

"This way." Mr. Bradhurst wheeled abruptly and led us to a nearby shed. It was obviously a poultry shed. It had a regular door for people, and on the side was a door for birds. A ramp led from that door down into a big, bare, fenced in yard.

What caught my attention was the size of that bird door—bigger by far than a chicken would need.

Mr. Bradhurst opened the people door. Bits was the first to step inside. I heard her cry out, "Oh, no!"

The farmer grimaced. "There's this mess, and there's the sheep and a couple calves."

Dr. Meyers glanced inside and nodded. "Les, you and Bits triage the turkey shed here with Jan. Tiny, you and Mike and Lynn come with me." As she hurried off, I heard her say, "Tiny, you and Mike will help Bob with the sheep. Lynn and I will see to the calves."

Triage. I knew what that meant. You have a lot of injuries in one place, so you sort them into minor, major, and horrible. But you tend to the major ones first, because the victims with the horrible injuries will almost certainly die anyway, so you spend your time where it's most likely to save the person. When Mom learned that, she said it sounded heartless, but I can see the sense of it.

Bits and Mrs. Bradhurst and I stood in the middle of this big turkey house, looking at disaster. The house was just one big room with perches all around the walls. Skylights made it very light, and a turbine vent whirred in the roof, keeping it fairly cool. It smelled bad—but then, you don't expect a turkey shed to be a bed of roses. I learned, though, that when turkeys are very upset, they do unspeakable things.

Most of the turkeys, dozens of them, were nothing but big piles of motionless feathers. Another couple dozen had been mauled badly. Their white feathers were dirty and all bloody. That left just a few that were still alive and unhurt.

Mrs. Bradhurst started to weep silently. "They're stupid birds, but they were so friendly. So—"

Bits was the first to snap out of it. "Let's throw all the dead ones over by the door, just for now. Mrs. Bradhurst, can we chase the ones that aren't hurt out into the yard?"

And that moment, Mrs. Bradhurst stuffed her sorrow aside somewhere that it didn't show. "Yes. Yes, of course. Not that one. Its wing is half bitten off. Not that one, either."

It took us awhile. We caught each turkey and looked it over, because some had blood on them even though they weren't hurt. It was just plain hard work. A big turkey can weigh over thirty pounds. That's OK if you're a sumo wrestler. It goes without saying that we weren't.

As soon as the healthy ones had been chased outside, we closed the poultry door. Then we dragged the dead ones over and piled them by the people door. Two of the injured ones died right in front of us.

"Chickens and turkeys stress easily," Mrs. Bradhurst explained. "If they're terribly upset or their environment is bad for too long, they just keel over."

"This is stress, all right." Bits was sweating.

The summer before this, back in Washington state, Mom enrolled me in a summer enrichment program at my school: first aid. We learned to dress cuts and bandage them, splint fractures, and perform mouth-to-mouth resuscitation.

And no, you better believe I did *not* do mouth-to-mouth on a turkey. But we splinted and bandaged them aplenty.

Mrs. Bradhurst brought a couple buckets of water. We sponged blood off, applied dressings and bandages, and taped popsicle-stick splints to broken wings and legs. It was absolutely the weirdest hour I ever spent in my whole life.

That was only the first aid. We knew that when Dr. Meyers got done with the sheep and calves, she would come here to administer *second* aid, you might say.

We hauled all the dozens of dead birds out the door. Then Mrs. Bradhurst drew a shade across the skylights. The big room turned dim. Darkness, she explained, would help them calm down.

We stepped outside, closing the door behind us. And I realized just then how much I had been missing fresh, odorless air. I just stood there awhile, breathing in and out. Mrs. Bradhurst ran off to help the others.

Bits stood beside me in the light rain, staring at the bedraggled mound of dead birds. The rain made those rumpled, ratty feathers even rattier. "You know what 'cold turkey' means, don't you?"

"Yeah." I couldn't keep my eyes off them either. "When you're addicted to something and you all at once quit whatever it is without any help. Or you don't taper off or anything."

"Well, here's a new meaning for it. Dead cold turkeys."

Along with the others, Bits and I followed Dr. Meyers around, helping where we could.

She gave injections to animals and to some of the turkeys. She quickly and gently tended injuries. She peered into eyes and mouths and ears and somehow guessed exactly what she needed to know about their health. Very mysterious.

I decided then that if being a famous chef didn't pan out, I might be a veterinarian. In fact, by the time we climbed into the van, being a vet had edged ahead of chef as a career choice.

We would get back to town around five, I figured. Just in time for the gang to troop into my house, clean up, and sit down to a turkey feast.

No, our afternoon didn't really dull my appetite for turkey, and that's strange to me. But you somehow don't associate those big, fluffy white birds with the roasted bird in front of you. They don't look enough alike, I guess, and the ones in feathers still have heads and feet.

Besides, this was going to be the feast of the century. Well, maybe the decade. Year? Last twelve hours, at least.

"This dinner better be good, Les," Bits said.

"Delicious!" I crowed. "I wrapped the bird in foil, and it's been stewing in its own juices ever since church."

"Your mom's keeping an eye on this, I hope."

"Nope," I said proudly, "she told me I'm on my own. She and the girls had to go to some kind of shower with the church women this afternoon. This is *my* creation, beginning to end. I did the potatoes and corn myself."

"Gravy?" Bits didn't look at all convinced.

I grinned, pretty sheepish. "Out of a can. Hey, I'm not a pro yet, OK?" At home, I hurried to the kitchen.

I had it all planned out. I would put the potatoes and creamed corn, both already partly cooked, in the oven. I'd unwrap the bird and brown it for another twenty minutes or so. Then it would all be ready to go on the table at once. Slick, huh?

I saw that Mom had gotten back. She was in the kitchen, looking bleak.

"Hi, Mom." I frowned. "Didn't your get-together this afternoon go all right?"

"It went fine. Uh, Les . . ."

I popped the oven door open. No heat rushed out.

Mom stepped up beside me at the stove. "The oven has two controls, Les. This one sets the temperature. And that other one turns it on. To bake something, you have to set them both. I'm sorry."

I had adjusted the temperature control just fine. But I hadn't touched that other dial.

The oven was still cold and always had been.

So was the turkey.

8

The Bradhurst farm disaster made the national news. They showed pictures of the dead livestock all tossed onto a huge heap in the rain. It looked so sad and dismal. They showed the bandaged calves, the splinted turkeys. In fact, they showed a closeup of a turkey that I, Les Walker, had personally treated (they didn't mention my name, of course). Then they ran footage of wolves from some nature show while they guessed about who could do all that damage.

It's not a nice way to get on the national news.

Monday morning, Lynn and I went out on our bikes into that circle our map had defined, looking for wolves. It probably won't surprise you to learn that we didn't see any. In the afternoon, we biked out to the rescue shelter to help Tiny feed the animals. The shelter director had managed to round up a few more volunteers, but feeding was still a humongous job. Every single cage had animals or birds in it.

I hope Lynn becomes an ambassador when she grows up, because she's already as tactful as all get out. For instance, all that long day, she never once mentioned the cold turkey. She never once commented on the bucket of fried chicken that Dad went out and got. Actually, it went with the potatoes and corn just fine.

In contrast, my sisters could not be diplomats if their lives depended on it. I bet it will be years before they quit teasing me. If ever.

Lynn and I had helped out at the shelter more than once. The minute we arrived, we hustled right in and filled food dishes because Tiny was still busy cleaning out pens.

Then Tiny and Lynn and I fed all the animals. That was the fun part. After that we bagged over a dozen dead animals and put them in the Dumpster. That part wasn't fun, but it had to be done, so we did it.

I think sadness is a part of death. I mean, for instance, here was Jesus coming to raise His friend Lazarus, right? You remember the story. He knew what was going to happen. In fact, He thanked His Father God in advance. But when He first joined the mourners with Mary and Martha, all of them so sad, He wept, too. He knew He was going to sit down to supper with Lazarus, but He cried anyway. See what I mean? It's a package, so to speak.

The sadness was part of those dead animals also. Live animals are cute or funny or dangerous or huge or whatever. Think about bunnies and Kodiak bears. But dead animals are never cute or funny, no matter how lifelike some taxidermist tries to make them look. I don't know how to say it except that once they lost life, they . . . well . . . lost alive-ness. That eerie difference between life and death never shows in movies or TV. Death doesn't seem real there, especially when you're old enough to know that the actor is going to get up and walk away as soon as the camera stops.

I'd never really thought about that until we disposed of those dead animals.

We helped Tiny close up for the night. It was an important job, and I felt very grown-up doing it. We followed a list of things to do that was posted on the back of the front door. Lock up the supply closet. Check the back door. Turn out the lights. It was a long list.

The whole thing took maybe twenty minutes, because Tiny made certain we didn't skip an item. I'm sure that was why he was allowed to be in charge; he never goofed off or got sloppy.

He slipped his bird-watching binoculars around his neck as always. We climbed on our bikes then, the three of us, and headed home, single file along the country roads.

The shelter is a ways outside of town. Except for a few subdivisions—clusters of houses all clumped together with fields and woods around them—you're pretty much out in the weeds. By now we knew three or four ways to get to the shelter from our neighborhoods by using one set of country roads instead of another. Lynn was leading this evening. I noticed she was taking one of the longer ways.

We passed a gang of farmhands making hay. I love the smell of fresh hay. These folks were using a baler that stuffs the hay together and shapes it into a rectangular bundle. Some balers make a huge cylinder-shaped bale you have to pick up with a forklift. I like the rectangles better because, if you're big enough and strong enough, you can handle them all by yourself with just a couple hay hooks. Someday I'll be big enough and strong enough.

Tiny said, "Hard day." He trailed behind. Usually, he led.

Lynn said, "Oh, but it's beautiful. Feel how nicely it's cooled off already this evening. I love this time of year."

I said, "Hey! Stop! Look out there!" I pulled aside into the grass and jumped off my bike.

"What?" Tiny braked and laid his bike down in the deep grass of the roadside ditch. "Where?"

"Animals moving—way out there beyond the wheat field. You see them?" I pointed east.

A wire fence topped by a strand of barbed wire closed the wheat field away from the road. The wheat had already been combined; only the golden-brown stubble was left. Brambles and bushes covered the fence at the far side of the field, so you couldn't see very well into the overgrown pasture beyond it.

But you could see some movement. Half a dozen something were out there, and they weren't deer. Deer are tan. They weren't cows. Cows come in various colors but not these colors. It looked as if these were shades of gray.

Tiny bounded up onto the fence, sticking

the toes of his athletic shoes through the wire squares. He balanced himself by pressing a leg against the red steel fence post.

He whipped his binoculars up to his eyes.

"What is it?" Lynn asked. She climbed up on the fence on the other side of the post, but she swayed some.

I climbed onto the fence beside the next post down and shaded my eyes. "Can you see them?"

"Yeah." Tiny stood there, taller than tall because he was two feet off the ground up on that fence, and just watched. And watched. He breathed a word in an amazed tone of voice, but I couldn't hear what it was.

And then the animals moved along the far fence to a place where we could see them better. I could make out five. One of them, dark gray, had to be almost pony-sized. Three others, a little smaller than the big one, looked light gray with lighter faces. The smallest was a dull sort of brown.

"They're out in the open!" Lynn pointed excitedly. Despite being so shaky, she had climbed another couple strands.

They turned then and headed away from us, out across that overgrown pasture. The weeds and sumac and clumps of thistles swallowed them up.

We watched and waited awhile, but they didn't show themselves again.

I asked Tiny, "Could you see with your glasses how they carry their tails?"

"Yeah. Wolves carry their tails straight out, right?"

"Right."

"And coyotes carry theirs sloping down, right?"

"Yes." Carefully, Lynn stepped back off her perch.

Tiny jumped to the ground. He sounded almost scared. "I could only see the biggest one well. The grass was too high. It looked a lot like a wolf. But it held its tail sloping *up!*"

9

Early the next morning, Tiny and Mike met Lynn and me at Sugar Creek Park. We had decided to go on a serious wolf hunt.

Tiny spread out the county map on a picnic table near the park's trailhead. When he leaned over to look, the binoculars around his neck clunked on the table. "Where were we yesterday?"

"Nolan Road." Lynn studied the map a few moments, then ran her finger along a thin black line. "Would you say here, about?"

I nodded. "We had just crossed that dirt road there, remember? Where they were putting up hay." To tell the truth, I wasn't all that eager to go out looking for wolves. Not after we saw those animals out there that looked a whole lot like wolves. But I'd rather chew tin foil than admit I was scared, so I didn't say anything.

Mike looked a little uncomfortable, too, come to think of it. "Tiny told me all about those things you saw yesterday. That's awesome."

Lynn looked up from the map. "Tiny, did you tell anyone else about them? I mean anyone official?"

"Didn't have to." Tiny scowled. "They—the officials—seem to know all about it. More than all. You wouldn't believe some of the screwy stuff they said on TV last evening. Lies, false 'facts' . . ."

"So it was on local TV too." I wondered if God was speaking to me through more than just the pastor. "The paper had that piece on it, but then they're always looking for stuff to put in the Sunday paper, Dad says, because it's thicker."

And then, surprise, surprise. Here came Bits. She rolled her bike up to us and dumped it casually in the grass. "Your dad said you were all out wolf hunting, Lynn."

Lynn frowned. "When did you talk to my father?"

"This morning."

"But it's so early."

"I saw you leave, and then he came out to get his paper, and I said hello. Neighbors. You know."

"Four doors away." Now Lynn scowled. "Bits, did you ask him to let you use my computer?"

"Not exactly. Besides, Miss Selfish, don't you want anyone touching your precious mouse?" Bits looked at Tiny. "I thought you were working today."

"I called them and told them I wouldn't be in."

She dipped her head toward Mike. "How come you're not somewhere making five bucks an hour?"

"They got scared. They was afraid they'd get caught and have to pay a fine. They decided not to let me work there." Mike shrugged. "So I'm out of a job again. But I'll find another one. A better one."

"So you become a big game hunter instead." I turned back to the map. "Where we going to go?"

"I suggest out to Nolan Road again." Lynn plopped her helmet on her head. "Maybe explore that dirt road near where we saw them."

Tiny strapped his helmet on. "Look for tracks. If they've crossed that road, we'll know it."

Now that was exciting! I'd almost rather see tracks than the whole wolf.

Off we went. I sort of remembered that the sky was clear when I left the house. By now, and it wasn't very late in the morning at all, the blue had turned milky, and our shadows lost their sharp edges.

Tiny must have noticed, too. He said, "Bet it might rain this afternoon," as we paraded single file out onto Nolan Road.

The farmhands were back out in that field as we passed, putting up their hay.

We waved as we went by, and they waved back.

"That's it!" Mike cranked his bike around into a tight U-turn and headed back the way we'd just come.

We stopped and looked at each other.

"What's it?" Bits asked.

We followed Mike back to the fence along the hayfield. He left his bike in the ditch and climbed over the fence. Wading through hay stubble, he strode across the field toward the haying crew.

"Now what's all this?" Tiny dumped his bike and climbed the fence.

I was as curious as anyone else. When I struggled up over the fence, I tore my shirt on the strand of barbed wire along the top. I looked back and noticed that the girls were coming, too.

I had to lift my feet high to walk in the cut-off stubble. Extremely stiff and about eight inches tall, it crunched under my feet. Every now and then, a stem would throw me off when I stepped on it. And all the stubble that I didn't step on tried to trip me.

Mike was talking to a man in blue jeans and ball cap who was probably in charge.

The fellow turned to look at me, Tiny, and the girls. "So you guys need work, huh?"

That was news to me.

The man whipped out a cell phone and punched in some numbers. "Harry? Bring the other baler over right now. We might get this in yet." He slammed it shut. "You guys are lucky that it looks like rain."

He walked away.

Mike glowed. "We got jobs! All of us. And it's legal. Kids are allowed to work on a farm!"

Lynn wagged her head. "I don't understand. What's going on?"

Mike stepped in front of her. "You know how they make hay?"

"Not exactly. They cut grass and bale it."

"This isn't grass; it's alfalfa. But, yeah. They cut it with a mower. It lies in the sun and dries, then they come along with a tedding machine. That's a machine that flips it over so it dries on the other side. And makes it into long rows. Then the baler scoops up the rows, like here, and makes it into bales. If they're little bales like these, you store them in a barn. If they're the big roundish things, you leave them in the field."

Lynn shrugged. "I still don't get it."

Tiny explained, "If the hay gets rained on before they put it in the barn, it gets all moldy inside the bale. Spoils. It's ruined. So they have to make hay while the sun shines, see?"

Now Mike was jumping up and down, he was so excited. "They're bringing in another baler, and we're going to help them get the rest of the field put away before it rains. They need us, and we need them. Instant money, *compadres!*"

It didn't take me long to figure that one out. We would work only a couple hours at most. Either it would rain or the job would be finished. We had nothing to lose, and the farmer had everything to gain. So the Sugar Creek Gang was about to become a hay-making gang. Not bad.

Who knows? Maybe from the top of the hay wagon we'd have a better viewpoint, and we'd see some wolves.

10

The five of us, the gang, were lined up and waiting when the farmer brought his second hay baler into the field. I don't know much about farm machinery, but I know *old* when I see it. This baler was rusty, and it creaked. The tractor pulling it looked really ancient. It was a dull, faded green with rust and mud for trim. I knew nearly all new tractors have a cab to protect the driver. This one didn't. Behind the baler rattled an aged flatbed trailer the color of dry, gray wood.

The fellow who brought in the second rig must have been the farm owner. He pulled alongside and stared at us. He did not look happy.

The fellow in the ball cap stepped up beside us.

The farmer scowled. "I thought you said you got more help!"

The fellow in the cap shrugged. "They want to work. Do you want your hay in or not?"

"Bah!" The farmer scowled darker. "You kids ever work a baler before? Did you kids ever *see* a baler before?"

Mike nodded. "I can tell 'em what to do. We do fine. We work good. You'll see!"

The farmer slid down off his tractor. "Joe,

you run this rig. I'll take the other. You and you—" he pointed to Lynn and Tiny "—come with me." He strode over to the other tractor and sent a man from that crew to help us. The man introduced himself as Cal.

So it looked as if Bits and Mike and I would be working on the old, rickety equipment. Really old or brand-new didn't make any difference to me. I didn't have the foggiest idea what to do on any of it.

Joe's face looked a little as if he was regretting this. "OK. Who knows how to drive a tractor?"

And then Mike surprised us all by saying, "I do!" He clambered up to the tractor seat, but he didn't sit in it. He sort of stood in front of it, his feet resting on the pedals.

Joe said, "I don't quite think—"

But Mike was on his way. He arched his back against the seat, shoved one of the big pedals down, and hauled on a long lever with both hands. The tractor lurched and began to rumble forward. Mike was too short to see over the hood; he sort of leaned to one side and craned his neck out to see around it.

Joe wagged his head, grinning, and pointed to the far corner of the field. He yelled, "We'll start at that end!" and the Sugar Creek Gang was in business. Hay business.

That, my dear friends, is the grimiest, itchiest, hottest, dirtiest, dustiest, hardest business in the world.

As Mike explained, the tractor drove along

a ridge of dried hay that was raked into place by the tedding machine. The ridge of hay, called a windrow, traveled up a chute into the big, boxy baling machine. Clumsy arms and wheels and things clunked and whirred. The hay got mashed together inside and was pushed out the back as a solid, rectangular bale. These bundles weighed from eighty to a hundred pounds, Joe told me.

A conveyor sticking out the back of the baler dumped the bale out onto the flatbed trailer. There someone would scoop it up and stack it at the back. When the trailer was full, the tractor would haul it off to the barn.

Except for that someone who scoops up bales, it sounds like an automatic process, right? Wrong. Cal, the other hired man, did most of the bale stacking at the rear of the trailer. I dragged the bales back to him from the front of the trailer bed where they dropped off the baler. That's right; I was dragging a hundred pounds across that trailer floor, over and over and over.

Using a pitchfork (which, I was told, was not a pitchfork—it was a hayfork, and apparently there's a difference), Lynn walked along behind to rescue any hay that the baler missed. She flicked the wads of missed hay over onto the next windrow. The old baler missed a lot of hay.

Joe spent all his time unclogging the baler when it jammed up or wedged a bale in cock-eyed. Usually he could keep things working while we rolled along. Sometimes, though, he'd yell to Mike to stop.

Then Mike would push on the brake pedal as hard as he could, and the tractor would jerk to a stop. Soon Joe would yell, and the tractor would lurch forward.

When the rig turned a corner, sometimes a bale would get pushed off the back, not onto the trailer but onto the ground. Joe would buck it back up on the trailer.

Hay is not soft. Especially not alfalfa. It's hard and scratchy. Alfalfa hay consists of stiff, dry stems with lots of dry little roundish leaves. The leaves and dust and hay bits swirl all around. They stick to your sweaty skin and work down behind your collar and inside your shirt. Your arms itch. All those dry, scratchy little pieces rub and burn.

I hate to admit this, but, more than anything else that day, I wanted a *bath*. I wanted to wash off the grit and dirt and hay that covered me. I got hot and cranky.

Bits and Tiny and even Lynn got grumpy. The only person who really loved what he was doing was Mike. He bounced around like a Labrador retriever playing fetch, always eager for more. Drove me nuts.

During a break while Joe hauled the filled trailer off to the barn, the farmer came over to us and said, "You kids are working out better than I thought you would. How about ten dollars instead of five?"

I thought, *How about a hundred dollars*

instead of ten? but I didn't say it. OK, so ten dollars wasn't much for all that work, but it was ten dollars more than we started out with that morning.

Toward the end, I noticed that, now and then, Mike would simply let the tractor drive itself and he'd climb down behind the seat to help Joe. So there the tractor would go in a straight line, nobody in the seat, no hand on the wheel. It would just keep chugging along at a little less than walking speed, all by itself. Amazing!

And then the accident happened. I don't know why I knew it was coming, but somehow I did.

As it turned the corner, the baler spit out a bale, and Joe walked over to get it. At the same time, the next bale in the conveyor wedged and stuck. Mike jumped down off the tractor right in front of the baler and darted to safety before the baler's wheels got to him.

I was going to yell at him, but, just that quick, he jumped up on the trailer tongue—the long wooden pole connecting the flatbed trailer to the back of the baler. The conveyor extended out directly over the tongue, so he grabbed onto the side of the conveyor, off balance.

"Mike, be careful!" was all I had time to shout.

Mike yelped. His arms flailed. His hands waved, trying desperately to find something to grab. His feet slipped. He was tipping off his perch! Falling!

The trailer wheels were sure to run right over him—flatten him. That trailer was half-loaded with tons of hay.

I couldn't think. All I could do was dive toward him, my arms stretched out straight forward. I grabbed.

I had his hair in one hand and his T-shirt in the other as I hit the deck of the trailer. Thumping down on my belly like that knocked most of the wind out of me. I couldn't move; I just hung on, with my chest on the deck and my arms hanging out in space. And I hung on. Hung on.

All Mike's weight was on my arms and chest. At the back of my mind, I knew he was still up off the ground, safe and away from the wheels.

The rig lurched to a stop.

Joe was yelling to me, but I couldn't let go. I was sobbing. I sort of realized that it was over, and Mike wasn't dead after all, but I couldn't let go of him. I don't know why. Joe and the farmer had to pry my fingers open.

And then I shifted from scared and relieved to embarrassed. Terribly embarrassed. Joe was saying something about a hero, but I sure wasn't one. Heroes don't cry when they do something heroic.

And I didn't have any way to blow my nose —no tissue or anything—and that was embarrassing, too.

Tiny was just plain furious. "We're outta here!" He grabbed Mike's arm. "No pay in the world is worth dying for, and Mike almost did just now. We're gone."

Mike started to protest, but he was crying, too. He didn't say anything. He stumbled a little and headed out across the hay stubble—the vast, clean, harvested field—toward the bikes.

A couple of big raindrops splattered against my arms.

The farmer came up then. "You kids saved my hay. We'll throw a tarp over this and take it in. Here. Here's a hundred. Split it up among you."

Lynn took it, solemnly agreeing that we would divide it evenly. We headed out across the long, empty field after Mike, as distant, rumbling thunder announced the rain.

11

Rain is cool. I mean, cool in all sorts of ways. We were really hot and sweaty and sticky, and the rain cooled us off as we rode along Nolan Road. It cooled us off emotionally too, I suppose. Tiny wasn't mad anymore, Mike wasn't crying, and I was back to normal—whatever normal is. And it was cool in the way it changed the whole mood of the world, gray and wet and yet hopeful. I don't know how to explain it.

We stopped at a little cowshed beside the road. It didn't smell like cows or manure anymore, and the grass around it grew long and green and tangled. Therefore, no cows. It surely had a door once, but not now. It yawned open, inviting us in.

So we rolled our bikes in to it to wait out the rain. Sitting in the shed doorway watching the rain made a welcome rest. A long, straight line of water running off the tin roof spattered by our feet. Big bubbles would appear along the row and then pop just that fast.

The hundred dollars that the farmer gave us was a fifty, a twenty, a ten, and four fives. It was probably everything he had in his wallet.

Lynn gave the twenty to Mike and the four fives to Tiny. "We'll have to break the fifty before we can divide the rest."

"It's way past lunch." I was really hungry. "Let's go back to town and eat at the Extra-burger."

Bits sniffed. "Not exactly way past. Twelve fifteen."

Lynn pulled the map out of her bike pack and opened it up. She pointed. "We're here. If we go north on this dirt road just ahead, we'll come out around Fifteenth, here. See?"

Tiny bobbed his head. "And there's an Extraburger at Fifteenth and Crestline."

So I wasn't the only one who was hungry.

The rain didn't last long. But since that little barn was comfortable and pleasant, we waited awhile for the leaves. When you're in a car, it doesn't matter. But when you're riding a bike, the trees that hang out over the roads are still dripping long after the rain quits. You might as well be in the rain. Finally the sky lightened, and we hit the trail again.

Tiny led the way onto that dirt road Lynn showed us. We passed a very old-fashioned-looking farm that had a two-story white house and a huge barn with two silos. All kinds of equipment stood about in the barnyard, and all of it was a lot newer than what we had spent the morning with.

I tried to imagine what it would be like to live on a farm like that and drive a tractor and milk cows and do all the stuff that goes along with it. My father grew up on a farm doing chores. He said I was missing a lot. Every time I had to mow the lawn, though, I didn't quite believe that.

And I imagined growing your own food. You raise a baby chicken or cow up to full-grown and then kill it and cook it. What a weird idea, until you think about it awhile.

According to the circle we drew on our map, we were pedaling right square up the middle of wolf country. Dr. Morgan at the museum had told us that wolves are usually nocturnal or crepuscular. *Crepuscular* is a fifty-dollar word meaning they get out and about in the very early morning or very late evening. Predawn and dusk. So we wouldn't expect to see wolves this time of day, midafternoon, even though the clouds made the day dark.

The next farm we passed was just the opposite of that big, prosperous one. This one had a tiny house that was probably all of two or three rooms. It needed painting. There were a couple of sheds and a chicken coop out back, also needing paint. A windmill that didn't turn stood in the side yard, and a rusty push mower had stalled out beside the white gravel driveway.

We were just about past the place when Lynn called, "Whoa!" She whipped around and pedaled back into that driveway. Of course we all followed her.

Beyond the house, a big blob of flowered-print cloth was squirming around at the base of the chicken shed. The shed's corners rested on blocks, putting it about a foot off the ground, and the fabric was mashed down against the gap.

Tiny wagged his head. "Now what?"

Lynn dumped her bike beside the chicken coop and anxiously asked the blob of fabric, "Ma'am, are you all right?"

A small, very old woman pulled her arm out from under the shed, rose to kneeling, and sat back on her heels. I'd never seen so many wrinkles in one place, but her face looked kind. "Now, who are you?" She wore a sunbonnet—a real, old-fashioned sunbonnet—made from the same cloth as her housedress.

"We were just passing by, and it looked like you were in trouble. Can we help?"

The lady studied us through scratched-up glasses. "Why, isn't that nice." She pointed under the coop. "I have to put up half a dozen chickens. I was going to have that chicken for dinner, but it got down under the coop, and I can't reach it."

Lynn dropped down to her knees. "Maybe I can. I'm smaller than you." She flopped down on her belly and stuck her face in the gap. "I see it. A white one?"

"Yes." The lady knelt down with one ear on the ground. She peered under. She sure was flexible for being so old.

Lynn squirmed and kicked and forced her body into the gap between the coop and the ground. When the gap had more than half swallowed her, she began to squirm back out.

Tiny and I grabbed her ankles and pulled. It speeded up the process a lot.

"Oh, my! Thank you, child!" the woman exclaimed. She sat back on her heels again.

Lynn reappeared, pretty grimy—but then we were all hay- and dirt-covered anyway. She was gripping a wad of bloodied white feathers. She gasped and threw it on the ground. "It doesn't have any head!"

The woman smiled. "No, dear, that's how you prepare a chicken to eat. You start by cutting off its head."

"But how . . ." Lynn looked again at that gap under the shed.

"Even after the head is gone, the body flops around awhile," the woman explained. "Didn't you ever hear 'running around like a chicken with its head cut off?'"

Lynn's eyes were hubcap size. "They actually *run* with no head?"

"All over. This one flopped under the coop."

So this old woman could start with a live chicken and come out with fried chicken or roast chicken or something. And then I got this brilliant flash of an idea. "Ma'am, you said you have to cut the heads off six of them and cook them?"

"Well, five of them I'll dress out and put in the freezer. Cook one."

"Ma'am, please, may I stay and help you and learn how to do it?" Boy, did that sound silly! So I tried to explain better. "You see, I'm going to be a great chef when I grow up, and I want to find out these things."

Bits giggled. "The first step is to turn on the oven, Les."

I shot her a dirty look.

The woman smiled. "So you're going to be a great chef." She got her feet under her and stood up. "Well, son, I'm not a great chef. I'm just an old widow who cooks plain food. But certainly you can stay and help, if you like."

"Thank you, ma'am! My name is Les Walker," and then I introduced everyone else.

Her name was Bertha Monroe, which tells you right there how old she was. How many people do *you* know named Bertha?

With the five of us following, she carried her headless chicken to a screened-in porch across the back of her house.

In a crate by the back door were her other five chickens, all with their heads on yet.

Tiny knelt beside it. "Miz Monroe, what happened to these chickens?"

"Dogs or something got into them. I heard a commotion, but I didn't see. These are the ones that got mauled. Best to butcher them right away before they start losing weight."

"Dogs." Tiny stood up, looking grim. "In the chicken yard?"

"Of course." The woman looked at him oddly.

"When?"

"Half an hour ago, I'd say." And then she reached into the crate for a chicken.

Tiny headed back out to the chicken yard, so I followed him.

"Think it's them?" I asked.

He studied the rain-wet dirt in the bare yard around the coop. "I know it's them." He pointed.

The damp soil was perfect for taking a footprint—not too dry and not too sloppy. Dog-like prints both huge and small mixed with chicken footprints all over the ground. Here and there you could see where a chicken's wing or tail had brushed briefly. If Mom were describing it, she'd say there'd been a melee—action all jumbled.

Tiny got down on his knees to stare at a nice set of tracks. "Look, Les. It's not just a couple wolves or coyotes or whatever. It's a family group. Big ones and little ones."

I could see it, too. I laid my hand, palm side down, on the largest print I saw. My hand didn't quite cover the print.

Tiny sat back on his heels and looked at me. "We had a sixty-pound dog once at the shelter, when the owner couldn't find a vet in town. He brought his dog out to us because Dr. Meyers was there. I thought that dog's feet were big."

"This one's bigger than sixty pounds? Is that what you're saying?"

"A lot bigger. This is getting ugly, Les."

12

I've never been able to figure out why I have the friends that I do. I mean this: You meet someone who is like you, and you two get along fine and do mostly the same stuff, but the friendship doesn't really click. And then you meet someone who's as different from you as horses from fleas, and that something clicks, and you're friends for life. Go figure.

Bertha Monroe was one of those friends-for-life people ten minutes after we met her. I can't explain why. She got along great with all five of us, in fact. She instantly became the whole Sugar Creek Gang's pal.

She was a real old-fashioned farm lady, too. She made jam and apple butter. She grew her own vegetables, canning some and freezing some. She raised chickens, a few beef cows, and a couple geese. She hung her washing out on long rope clotheslines propped up with poles. And, she said, once in a while she'd go down to a small pond at the back of her twenty acres and catch a few sunfish for dinner.

What a great life!

As Tiny and I went back to the house after looking at those tracks, Mrs. Monroe and Mike were dispatching yet another injured chicken. It didn't run without its head because the wolves had mangled its legs. But it flopped all over the ground awhile.

"Miz Monroe," Mike said, "when my mama kills a chicken, she hangs it upside down from the clothesline with its feet tied together. Then when she cuts its head off, it doesn't go anywhere." He reached into the crate for the last chicken, grabbing it expertly by a leg.

"So could I if my line was wire or plastic. But it's cotton rope, and the blood would soak into it. Then it would spot my clothes when I hung them." She picked up her hatchet. "You children had lunch?"

"Not yet, ma'am." Bits seemed fascinated by the dying chicken. "We were on our way to the Extraburger on Crestline."

"Afraid I can't make you the Super Deluxe Extraburger with curly fries, but I have fresh-baked bread and peanut butter and more strawberries than I can eat by myself. How about I hang these birds and then fix you a little something. We'll pluck them after lunch."

"Well, uh . . ." I hesitated.

So she showed us to the phone in her house, and we called our moms to get permission. Her phone was black and looked like something out of a 1950s movie. It had a dial. Dialing a phone is the slowest thing in the world. You turn the dial and wait for it to come back, and then you mess up the last number and have to start over.

And so we ate late lunch in the home of Bertha Monroe. I was right about the house.

Three rooms. It had a kitchen, a front room, and a bedroom. We gathered around a little kitchen table that only had three chairs, but Tiny sat on a box, and Mike simply stood there and seemed happy.

The homemade bread was even better than store-bought white bread, but I'd never tell my mom that. Mom thinks that if bread is pure white, it's lacking something.

Mrs. Monroe asked, "Lynn, are you feeling well? You've hardly touched your sandwich."

Lynn smiled, "And it's delicious, too. I guess I'm not very hungry."

Bits sniggered. "She's not used to blood and guts much. But if she hangs around us very long, she will be. Isn't that right, Tiny?"

And so Tiny explained about the rescue shelter where he volunteered. Mrs. Monroe asked all kinds of eager questions. Tiny did not mention the wolves or how crowded the shelter was because of them.

I noticed a set of dog dishes in the corner by the stove. So she had a dog. They were very heavy crockery; you don't find that much anymore. The name *TUFFY* was personalized on them. Was Tuffy the dog she had now, or did her present dog inherit those old dishes from some former dog? I didn't get a chance to ask because we were all talking about other stuff. And then I forgot to.

Lynn eventually did finish her lunch. I think it's because her parents taught her to eat what's served, not because she got her appetite back.

After lunch, we followed Mrs. Monroe out to her summer kitchen. This was a kind of shed separate from the house but attached to it with a sidewalk under a long roof. She called the walk "the breezeway." In the shed she kept canning jars, a big propane stove, and all sorts of giant tubs and pots.

"I make jam and can out here in summer," she said. "So that it doesn't heat the house up so bad."

She put a big pot of water on to boil, and we fetched in the chickens. They didn't move at all now, which suited me. We sat down around a big, round basket.

Mrs. Monroe dipped a chicken in the boiling water. To loosen the feathers, she said. Then she warned, "Let it cool a bit," and handed it to Mike. But he started right in, yanking out feathers by the handful.

We each got a dipped chicken. Man, was that fun! You grab a big wad of feathers and just pull them out. The wet feathers stick to your hands and arms so bad you can't let go of them. So here you are with these huge clumps of feathers at the ends of your arms. And then, naturally, your nose itches.

Tiny showed us how chickens (almost all birds, he said) are not covered all over with feathers. The feathers grow only in certain places, in patches, and the rest is bare. But the feathers in the patches fluff out to cover everything. Tiny even knew the correct words—*pterylae* for the feather areas and *apteria* for the bare spaces between. It's a poor day you don't learn something (but when I tried to tell Mom and Dad about it that night, I couldn't remember the words and had to look them up).

Mrs. Monroe took the last chicken for herself and still finished first. She grinned. "I've done a few of these."

I bet.

She turned on a gas burner and showed us how to singe the chickens. A lot of little pinfeathers, just tiny things, remain behind when you're done plucking a chicken. You burn them off carefully over an open flame.

She slit the chickens' bellies open with a sharp knife. She wouldn't let us do that. "Don't want your folks coming to me when you cut a finger off."

We all pulled the innards out of our chickens and separated out the heart, liver, and gizzard. She showed us how to cut the gizzard and turn it inside out to clean it.

And I'm proud to say that Lynn got up the nerve to do her own chicken. She didn't dive into the work nearly as eagerly as Mike did—or me—but she did it. And she finished it, even the gizzard part.

When we got done that afternoon, there were six dressed chickens just as if you'd bought them at the grocery store. Mrs. Monroe bagged up five of them for her freezer. She wrote the date on the bags.

"If you don't use in a year," she said, "out they go."

Bits asked, "Do you throw much away?"

"Very little." She smiled. "But now and then I have a pretty strange menu for awhile, trying to use something up."

I heard a dog whine at the back screen door. The first thing I thought was, *Oh no! Her dog tangled with the wolves and got hurt!*

I glanced at Tiny, and it was obvious that he was thinking the same thing.

But no. The dog was fine. Mrs. Monroe walked over and let him in. "Tuffy"—that answered that question—"these are friends from Sugar Creek."

I liked that.

"How cute!" Lynn cooed. "His face is so sweet."

I got to admit it wasn't a bad dog as small dogs go. It stood maybe fifteen inches high. Pale brown, it was shaped and upholstered more or less like a mop. And talk about friendly! It squirmed around, licking us and being petted, and just getting acquainted in general.

Mrs. Monroe huffed. "Look at you, Tuffy! You've been playing down in the pond again."

The little pooch was all muddy and wet.

Mrs. Monroe warned, "Shove him away. Don't let him get you all dirty."

But you will recall we were already filthy from that haying. A little more dirt off a dog wasn't going to make a bit of difference.

And, sure, I petted him, too. I often wished we owned a dog, but I'd want a bigger one than this. It was curious—Dad called big dogs, especially big dogs of no particular breed, "farm dogs." Here was a dog on a working farm, and it was terrier size.

The chicken dressing was done. But just before we left, Mrs. Monroe showed me how she cut up a bird, and how she dredged it in seasoned flour and egg and milk. So I got another step closer to the goal of being a great chef.

On the bike ride home that afternoon, I thought a lot about Mrs. Monroe. There she lived, working hard every day, with a little brown dog as her only companion. She obviously wasn't making much money.

And I had never seen a happier, more contented person.

13

You can't buy a live chicken in this town.

I came to that conclusion when I looked for one to try out my new chef skills with.

Somehow, buying a chicken in a bag at the supermarket just wasn't the same thing. Mom suggested that if I wanted to try the flour-and-egg recipe Mrs. Monroe had shown me, I could slice up and fry an eggplant. That is absolutely not the same thing. I couldn't tell if she was teasing me or not. Probably, she was.

All this talking took place at breakfast the morning after our adventures in hay and feathers. Mom said I could make supper that night. So I decided to buy a chicken and wow them all.

I called up Bits to see if she wanted to go grocery shopping and also get some ice cream. No, she said, she was busy. I know what she was busy at. Computer games.

I called up Lynn and got their answering machine.

I called up Tiny, but he was volunteering at the shelter.

I called up Mike. His mom said he was out helping his brothers. Apparently they'd promised him a raise.

It was starting to look like a long, long day.

Ice cream doesn't taste half so good when you eat it alone.

Since it would be hours and hours before I'd even think about starting to cook dinner, I killed some time by riding out to Nolan Road again. The ground was still a little damp from that rain yesterday. Maybe, I thought, I could find some more wolf tracks.

And now you're thinking, *Why not just buy a chicken from Mrs. Monroe?*

I thought of it. But then I remembered something she mentioned yesterday. Losing six hens was putting her short; she was afraid she would no longer get enough eggs. It seems she sold eggs to some regular customers—people who bought from her because they wanted eggs from free-range chickens. And now some of her best layers were lying naked in her freezer. She needed every hen. So I wasn't even going to ask.

The bank thermometer by Crestline Plaza said 83, but it felt a lot hotter than that. I guess that was because of the moisture in the air left over from yesterday's rain. The humidity. When it's humid, warm feels warmer.

I took 22d Street south. At Cedar, the pavement ended. It was still several miles to that dirt road that went past Mrs. Monroe's place.

And there, trotting along the roadside, came Tuffy!

I dropped my bike and sat down beside it. "Hey, Tuffy! Come here, old top! Come to me."

Tuffy didn't remember me at first. He growled and backed away, his white teeth bared.

"Oh, come on, Tuffy. It's me."

He thought about it, I guess, because after a moment or two he came trotting over and squirmed against me, licking. His wiggly little body felt very warm beneath that silky brown fur.

"You're not going away from your home, and you're not going toward it. What's the matter, fella? Lost?"

Squirm, squirm, squirm. Lick, lick, lick.

He wasn't wearing a collar. I suppose dogs that stay on the farm wouldn't need one. But if someone else found Tuffy, how would he or she know whose dog this was?

"Oh, wow!" One of his floppy little ears was torn, and the injury was fresh too. In fact, blood was drying into his coat in a couple places. "So you got into a fight. I don't think getting hit by a car would do this. Well, come on, Tuffy. Let's take you home."

Tuffy wasn't very heavy. Once I straddled my bike, I scooped him up and cradled him in my left arm. That kept the right hand free for steering, shifting gears, and braking. OK, so it wasn't the safest way to ride a bike, but it wasn't the most dangerous, either. And I didn't have a rope or leash or anything to walk him with.

Tuffy didn't like going anywhere that way. But I held him tight, and pretty soon he resigned himself to being hauled home.

When I got there, Mrs. Monroe was sitting on her front porch shelling peas. "Well, hello, Les! And *Tuffy*. Now what?" She was wearing a different housedress—this one had stripes instead of flowers. No sunbonnet, but, of course, she was under the porch roof.

"Hello, Mrs. Monroe. I found him out on the road and was afraid he was lost." I dumped my bike and carried the dog up onto the porch. "He tore an ear." I showed her.

She wagged her head. "That dog. His mother was the same way. Always getting into something." She gathered her little pooch into her lap to get a better look at the ear.

"Do you ever tie him up, ma'am?"

"Oh, no. Gracious, no. He doesn't go far. Just up to the corner of Lindsey."

"But I found him clear up by where the pavement starts."

"Oh my. Maybe he did get lost. Chasing a rabbit or something, forgot where he was." She smiled. "He never manages to catch anything. And he doesn't chase the chickens, or he'd be out of here in a flash."

A big brown delivery truck came rumbling down the gravel road. It managed to raise some dust in spite of the dampness. The driver, a blonde woman, stopped in front of Mrs. Monroe's house. She looked at one of those little computer boxes that you sign with an electronic stylus, and then at the numbers on Mrs. Monroe's mailbox. She frowned.

She disappeared into the back of her truck. Moments later, she came out with a big brown box sort of like a deep-dish pizza box. Little round holes ventilated all four sides.

And it peeped. I mean, the whole box peeped. In fact, it peeped very loudly, sort of one long, continuous chirp.

She stepped up to the porch. "Bertha Monroe?"

"I can't believe it. My chicks arrived already! I only phoned in the order yesterday afternoon." Mrs. Monroe set her bowls of shelled and unshelled peas aside and stood up.

"Mail order chickens?" I gaped. "Alive?"

"The world is happening much too fast these days, Les. It used to take a month to order and receive chickens."

The driver handed Mrs. Monroe the sign-in box and smiled. "My truck has been sounding like the inside of an aviary all morning. Those little 'leather lungs' make a lot of noise."

Mrs. Monroe signed for her loud parcel. "Les, I'm glad you came. I can use a little help setting up the brooder. I think it's up in the top of the barn."

And do you know what we did? Pretty much forgot about Tuffy, that's what we did.

I climbed up into the haymow of her little barn and handed a shallow sheet metal cone down to her. She also wanted some cartons full of metal brooder pieces. We put it all together on the floor of the chicken house.

What we had when we were done looked like something from a *Star Wars* movie. The shallow cone was a roof, which we suspended from the top rafter by a chain. The wide part down, it hung a foot or so off the floor. It had a light bulb up inside it so that the area under the cone was very brightly lighted. The bulb was more for heat than light, Mrs. Monroe explained.

We put up a little portable fence to keep the chicks confined to the area under the roof. We set up a long, narrow feed trough and a watering device. We scattered sawdust and chick feed. Then she turned her babies out into their new home.

"Half are barred Plymouth Rocks and half are buff Orpingtons." Mrs. Monroe put the emptied box aside. "I get chickens that lay brown eggs because the brown eggs sell better."

"They all look alike to me. Fluffy little yellow chicks."

"You'll be able to tell them apart once they start getting feathers."

So we were finished. "I really enjoyed this, Mrs. Monroe. Thank you for letting me help."

"Why, thank you for helping! Can you stay for lunch?"

"I better not. Thank you for asking me. I have things I gotta do at home."

One of them was cooking a chicken. But I didn't mention that. I headed back for my bike. Then I stopped. "Is Tuffy around?"

"Gone again." Mrs. Monroe shook her head. "Silly dog."

I didn't want to scare her. On the other hand, I had seen the full house at the rescue shelter. I knew what those wolves or whatever could do.

I licked my lips. "Uh, ma'am? I don't know if you heard, but coyotes or something have been causing trouble around here lately. Some say it's wolves. Whatever, Tuffy's awfully small. He could get hurt or killed if the pack finds him."

"Mm." She frowned. "I did hear something about it, but I didn't realize it was around here. You're probably right. I should keep him closer to home. I'd better keep his collar on him, too. It has my phone number on it."

"Yeah, that would be good. It was lucky I happened to know him. A stranger wouldn't have. Well, g'bye."

"Good-bye. And thank you again, Les."

I didn't say any more, but that comment about a collar sounded as if she was not going to keep him tied. Tuffy was her dog, not mine. It was none of my business whether she let him go out roaming. Still, I worried. He was so little.

As I got on my bike and started pedaling back toward town, I heard her say again, "Silly little dog."

14

Now in case you are wondering what happened to that cold turkey that was my first attempt as a chef, we managed to make room for it in the fridge. We roasted it the next day. But the Sugar Creek Gang wasn't there the next night to help eat it, so we had an awful lot of turkey left over.

Still do.

Probably always will. The thing is endless.

Mom showed me how to freeze meat—the turkey, specifically—to keep it fresh. Now over a week later, I went back into the freezer and labeled all the packages of frozen turkey with the date.

"That," I explained importantly to Mom, "is so we know to use it before it dries out or goes bad."

She wasn't as impressed as I thought she'd be.

She wasn't impressed when I cut up the whole fryer I bought, either. She and Mrs. Monroe didn't cut up a chicken in exactly the same way. When I suggested that Mrs. Monroe did it the "right" way, things got pretty cool in the kitchen. So I just shut up about Mrs. Monroe.

You'll recall that Mrs. Monroe did all the knife work when we helped at her house. Now I got to do my own cutting. It's not nearly as easy as it looks when someone else is doing it. Not nearly. Mom showed me how to break the joints backward so I wouldn't cut my fingers off.

For a few cents a pound more, you can get your chicken already cut up. Next time, I decided, I might consider that.

It took me a little longer to put the meal together than I intended, and we ended up eating past 7:30 that night. That didn't go over real well, either. The chicken was OK but not nearly as good as Mom's, the potatoes weren't quite done, and the peas turned out mushy. I don't know how that happened. I'd put salads together at four o'clock, so they looked a little wilted by the time we sat down.

To top it off, it was my week to do the dishes. I didn't realize how many pots and pans I'd used until I had to wash them.

I finished in the kitchen well after 9:00. I was pooped, discouraged, and confused. Other than that, I was just fine, thank you.

The overhead light was on in the garage, and loud noise came from there. So I went out to see what Dad was doing.

He was making something. Every now and then he'd get this urge to use the expensive woodworking tools Mom and his folks gave him from time to time. Tonight he was doing unspeakable things to a couple of pressure-treated one-by-fours.

I waited until the radial arm saw stopped. "What's all this gonna be?"

"Adirondack chairs."

"We don't live anywhere near the Adirondacks."

"You don't live anywhere near Paris, but you eat french fries."

Well, you can't beat that logic with a stick. I watched him cut some angled boards. It's a firm rule at our house: If someone is using power tools, no talking. No distraction. That even includes using the lawn mower.

When the saw stopped again, I asked, "Dad? Do you suppose God is telling me I'm probably not gonna be a great chef?"

"Maybe. Or maybe He's just telling you that you need practice."

So not only did you have to figure out where and how God was speaking to you, you had to figure out what He was saying too. This was getting very complicated.

Before I had time to think much about that new twist, Dad asked, "How long does it take your mom to make dinner?"

"Hour or so. Give or take."

"How long has she been doing it?"

I shrugged. "Forever. Since she got married. I dunno."

"We had hot dogs three times a week when we first married. And half raw chicken a few times. Skill comes with doing it awhile." He set his band saw table at a twenty-degree angle and locked the gate in place.

I remembered when my grandparents gave him that saw. It took him hours, with the instruction manual propped nearby, to figure out how to do things with it. Now he could make all sorts of weird shapes without even thinking about it.

He asked, "How long did it take you to learn to rollerblade?"

Now that was a touchy subject. I broke an arm rollerblading. "Not quite long enough."

He laughed. "Get my point?"

"Yes, sir. But I still don't know what God is saying or how He's saying it."

"You will, Son. Isn't it about bedtime?"

"Yeah, I guess. G'night."

"Good night."

So I headed back into the house, wondering about God speaking and also wondering what an Adirondack chair was. As I passed the family room I heard Catherine whining, "But, Mommy, it's summer vacation! Just a little while?" So I knew the girls were trying to renegotiate bedtime.

Not me. I was going to fall asleep so fast, I wouldn't even hear the pillow crumple. But I sure wasn't going to admit that to Mom or Dad.

I good-nighted everyone and dragged my weary body up the stairs. The phone rang when I was halfway up, but I'd let one of the negotiators answer it.

I was halfway through the bathroom door when Mom called, "Les? It's for you."

Me? At almost ten o'clock at night? I picked up the phone in Mom and Dad's bedroom. "Hello?"

Bits growled, "I sent you an e-mail. Why didn't you answer?"

"Huh?" Then my brain connected back up. "Well, two reasons. One is, I was busy and didn't pull my mail down today. The other is, I've adopted my father's policy about e-mail."

"What's that?" she snarled accusingly. "Ignore it?"

"A long time ago, he got mad when people would expect him to do something instantly just because they sent him an e-mail note. He said, 'Other people's mail does not instantly obligate me.' And you don't know how long it took me to learn to say all that fast. Anyway, his policy is, when you get to it, you get to it."

"Thank you for sharing that, but it's more than I wanted to know."

"You asked what his policy was. If you don't like the answer, don't ask the question."

OK, so I was being crabby with her. And I knew I shouldn't, even though she was crabby at me. But I was tired and not in a good mood. That's not an excuse, understand. But it's the reason.

She didn't sound any less cranky. "I don't know why I bother with you. But I need you tomorrow. Daddy has to be in court, and he's taking me with him. I'm not allowed to take anything but books or paper and crayons. I don't want to go alone. He said you could come."

"You mean spend the whole day in the court-house? I always said you were a bad customer, Bits, but I didn't think you were that bad."

"Hah, hah." But then her tone of voice changed from cranky to pleading. Even scared. "Come with me, will you, Les?"

"Sure." If I had to do something like that, I'd be scared, too—scared of being bored to death. "I'll come."

15

So the next morning, Bits's dad took us to the courthouse.

You don't know *boring* until you sit six hours in a courthouse. If we got to watch a murder trial, I bet it wouldn't be boring. But we had to stay in this little room near the room where people come to get selected for juries. We weren't supposed to talk to any of those people. No TV set. Not even a phone. Just Bits and me and a pad of paper and crayons.

We played hangman. That lasted about forty minutes. Five hours and twenty minutes to go. We drew pictures. Another half hour gone. Tick-tack-toe: ten minutes.

On a shelf I found a long telephone extension cord with a jack at each end. "Bits? Do you suppose your dad had the phone taken out?"

"Wouldn't put it past him." Her mood had not improved a millimeter.

I tied the ends together as best I could and set it up among my fingers for a cat's-cradle game. So for an hour or so we passed the cat's cradle back and forth. One time, we didn't lose it until the tenth pass. She showed me how to make Witch's Broom, and I showed her Magic Diamond. By then, our fingers were so tired from working that bulky phone cord that we quit.

She sprawled back in a chair that was too big for her and put her feet up on the table. "You're not near as much fun to be with as I thought."

"You're no vacation at the beach, either. Why's your dad doing this?"

"Because he hates me, and he's torturing me."

"Yeah, sure. You know, sometimes I make a lousy decision, but this one was one of the lousiest—agreeing to come along with you. He gets to torture both of us."

And from behind me came her dad's voice. "Ready for lunch, you two?"

I sure was. I jumped up.

Sergeant Ware looked really fine in his full police officer's uniform. He stood in the doorway a moment studying us oddly. He frowned at the tangled, kinked telephone cord on the table. "This isn't working, is it? Well, let's go eat."

We walked down to the Dog House on Le-Grande without saying much. I ordered two footlongs. Bits fussed over the overhead menu awhile and picked chicken nuggets. Her dad got a burger and fries. I snatched a couple napkins each (they were small), the catsup, straws, and relish. Bits went off to claim a table.

When we settled in with lunch, we still hadn't said much except for Bits. She dipped her nuggets in catsup while she complained because she hadn't ordered hot dogs.

We were nearly done when her dad said, "If

I drop you two off at Sugar Creek Park, will you stay there until I take you home later this afternoon?"

"Yes, sir!" I was ready for that.

"Daddy, can't you just take us home?" Bits whined.

I looked at her. "I thought you liked the park. That's where I first met you."

"Daa-deee?"

"It's the park or the courthouse, Bits. Either way, you stay where you're put." Her father sounded put out.

She didn't say anything, so I won the vote by her abstention.

Sergeant Ware drove us to the park and dropped us off in the picnic area parking lot. "I'll pick you up as soon as court lets out. Remember what I said: you two stay together." And away he went.

I gestured toward the trailhead. "Where do you want to go? Want to go see if the big painted turtle's hanging out? It's usually sunning this time of day."

"I don't care. I don't want to go anywhere." She kicked a loose stone out across the asphalt.

"Hey, look!" I pointed. "Here come Mike and Tiny!"

The two of them rolled up to us on their bikes. I walked over to the rack with them as they locked up.

Tiny asked, "Where's your bikes?"

"We buried them. What are you doing here?"

"Just thought we'd come see what's happening. Lynn's coming, too. Don't you read your e-mail?"

"He prefers to ignore it." Bits sounded really sarcastic.

"Let's wait till Lynn gets here and then find that big turtle." Tiny ambled over to the nearest picnic table, all elbows and long strides. He sat on it the way he usually did—sitting on the table part with his feet on the seat.

He grabbed the binoculars around his neck and whipped them up to peer at bushes. "Goldfinch."

I twisted around just in time to see a blur of black and lemon yellow flit from the grass into the brush.

Mike was bubbling, but then, Mike usually bubbled. "Hey, Les! I made ten dollars this morning!"

"That's great." He made ten dollars while I sat around all morning in the courthouse in a vacant room with a crabby girl. For that I got lunch.

Mike went on. "I helped out my brothers, and they gave me some money. And then Mrs. Muñoz across the street needed some trash hauled to the curb, so I did it, and she gave me a dollar. A dollar for five minutes of work! That's twelve dollars an hour!"

Bits scowled. "Mike, all you ever talk about is making more money. Money, money, money! You're obsessed with it."

"Am not!"

"Are too! Look at you! You were more than willing to break the law and work in a grooming parlor where you're not legally allowed to. You take big chances just to make a few bucks. I mean big—on that farm, you almost got yourself killed on machinery that's too big for you. You're obsessive, all right. You're nuts."

And Mike exploded. "Who you calling nuts? *You're* the one plays them computer games all day long. Don't even stop to breathe. You're the obsessed one!"

"Am not!"

"You're the one is addicted, girl!" Mike was yelling now. "Addicted like my uncle is to booze and my cousin Raphael is to gambling. You do it all day. Can't stop."

"I can quit anytime I want to!"

Mike laughed. "You mean anytime your papa makes you."

Tiny roared, "Cut it out, you two! Quit slashing at each other."

"Tell *him* to cut it out!" Bits barked.

"Hey, come on, Bits." I held my hands up. "He's right. Lynn's worried about you. She thinks you got a problem. And I know for a fact your dad thinks so. That's why he made you come with him today, right?"

Well, as soon as that came out of my mouth, I knew it was the wrong thing to say.

So I tried to patch it up. "I mean, you're both right, you know. And both wrong. Mike, you do have a money problem, and, Bits, you do have a game problem. Leave it at that. Just

94

quit fighting, both of you. You guys are supposed to be Sugar Creekers."

Mike and Bits blew up at me in unison, yelling and accusing me of being wrong and nasty.

Then here came Lynn on her bike. If anyone could calm the whole scene down, it was Lynn.

On the other hand, an awful lot of hurtful things were already flying around. I just hoped she wasn't too late.

16

Lynn pulled in beside us, and I know she didn't realize until just then that she was rolling into the middle of an argument. She looked confused. "What's going on?"

"'Blessed are the peacemakers,' Lynn," I said. "You're about to be blessed. At least, I hope you are."

Bits pointed hand and arm at Lynn. "You stay out of this, Little Miss Perfect!"

Lynn mouthed, *Perfect?* as she stood there. Then her mouth silently sagged open.

"Hey, come on, you guys . . ." I begged.

Tiny was a little more direct. "Quit this, all of you, or I'm leaving."

"You stay out of this, too!" Bits hollered at Tiny.

"What is this?" Lynn looked more confused.

I'm sure Mike sensed an ally, or maybe he remembered that I had just mentioned Lynn's fears about Bits. "Here, Lynn will tell you. You got a big problem, Bits. Lynn knows it. She said so."

"Oh, she did! Since when was it any of your business, Miss Perfect?"

"*What?* Now stop it, and please tell me what's going on." Lynn glanced from face to face. "I thought we were here to go look for the turtle."

"Mike's here to straighten out the whole world all except himself," Bits sneered.

"I am not!" Mike wailed.

Lynn still hadn't lost her calm. I don't know how she did it. "I'm sure it's something you can talk out. Why can't you—"

"Oh, stuff it!" Bits yelled.

"Stop it, you two!" Tiny raised a hand.

Then Mike started yelling at Lynn too, and that surprised me. "Just cause my pop ain't no zippy-do professor like your pop is, don't mean nothing! We ain't poor!"

Quietly Lynn purred, "Nobody said you were."

"Everybody says that! We're on so many charity lists, you don't believe how many. We got four turkeys last Thanksgiving. And three food baskets at Christmas with turkeys in them!"

"That's a lot of turkeys." I remembered how many leftovers we still had in our freezer from just one.

Mike was still rolling. "But when my pop got laid off and we couldn't pay the light bill unless we went hungry, where were all them fine charities? You charity people, you give stuff to poor people on holidays so you'll feel good. It don't have nothing to do with helping people who need help."

"But—"

"And I ain't never gonna be a charity case, understand? Never!" Mike was so revved up he had tears in his eyes.

Bits hadn't mellowed in the slightest. "You don't know the first thing about charity giving! Sometimes people give just 'cause they care. People who give help don't have to, you know. Besides, you don't have to blame us for what grown-ups do! And it doesn't change anything, anyway. You're still a money addict!"

Tiny leaped off the picnic table. "I get enough fighting at home. I don't need this." He marched toward his bike.

"Hey, come on! All of you!" I yelled, but no one listened to me.

Bits and Mike were arguing back and forth about who was the worse addict.

Lynn wagged her head. "I can't believe you two. Why can't you just—"

Mike turned on her. "Let's see you apply for food stamps, and then you can say what we ought to do!"

Lynn looked hurt.

Mike brushed past her and headed for his bike.

If Lynn broke into tears—and she looked ready to—none of us knew about it. Tiny was gone, Mike was going, and now she got on her bike and just rode away.

I'd promised Bits's dad I would stay with her all afternoon and that we'd both stay in the park.

It was going to be a long, long afternoon— longer even than the morning had been.

Forget about being a great chef. I'd make better money as a lawyer.

17

You could safely say the day was a fizzle. Make that two days. My less-than-stellar performance cooking chicken the day before still bummed me out. And then Mike and Bits blew up. And Lynn went home hurt and sad. And Tiny went home angry. And Bits and I sort of pouted together but apart all afternoon, our backs to each other most of the time. For hours, until her dad got there.

We climbed into his car without saying anything. He pulled into their driveway, I thanked him for lunch, got out, said good-bye, and walked across the street to my own house.

Hannah greeted me as only Hannah can: "Mommy wants you to take the garbage out. And a friend of Daddy's will be coming for dinner, so get a shower and wash your hair. You look like you were dragged through a swamp."

"I was not dragged through a swamp! I went through it voluntarily."

And I *had* gone voluntarily. Bits and I found that big painted turtle a couple hundred yards back in the swamp trail, where it usually basked. It was the only positive thing we did all day.

Dinner tasted good because this time Mom cooked it. Dad took his friend, a fellow he went to law school with, to the airport. I did the dishes.

I went upstairs to my room to read. But I couldn't concentrate, so I gave that up. I tried to work on my half-finished airplane model (an F-16 fighter, if you're wondering which one). Even that wasn't interesting.

I imagined what it would be like to live on a farm. Hard work. That part I could see. But it would be fun too, with a lot of open space to run around in. Maybe we'd have a farm pond like Mrs. Monroe's and stock it with catfish and crappies.

Mostly, though, I just sprawled out in my chair by my little dormer window. I was all jumbled up inside. Mike was as much of it as anything. Poor old Mike, so angry at the world.

It was getting dusk now. The light from Dad's headlights flowed across the barberry hedge. I heard the garage door grind open and shut. I went downstairs past the family room, where the TV was blaring, and into Dad's den.

He was just sitting down with the newspaper. "Isn't it about bedtime?"

"Yeah, about."

So I flopped down in the chair beside his and tried to tell him a little of how Mike felt. I didn't bother with the gang's blowup. That was too complicated to describe. I didn't get Mike's story across very well, either, I thought.

Or maybe I did, because Dad put aside his paper and sat back in his recliner with his eyes closed. Some might think he was falling asleep, but I knew better. He was thinking. He had just turned his full attention to the inside of his head.

A few minutes later he sat bolt upright and, reaching mightily, pulled his computer keyboard off the desk behind him. He settled it into his lap and hit a couple of keys without looking at the monitor.

I craned my neck to see over the back of my chair. The screen saver disappeared, and his writing program popped up.

"OK, Les, can you tell me verbatim what he said?"

"Word for word, you mean?"

He nodded. "As much as you can."

"I don't know. It's a stretch." So I sat back, too, and stared at the ceiling. I managed to dredge up most of the bits and pieces but not in the right order. Dad said the order didn't matter. He was copying down what I remembered, typing wildly.

When I'd about got it all, I asked, "What are you going to do with that? I don't want to embarrass Mike."

"I'm not sure what I'll do with it yet." Dad smiled. "But we won't embarrass him. I promise. Go to bed."

"OK. Good night." And I headed back upstairs.

I didn't go right to bed, though. I was still too churned up inside. I turned out my light and sat in the dark by the window to watch the moon come up. It was just past full, a wee bit lopsided but still very bright.

The window didn't have a screen—Dad said he was going to get to that one of these days—but I opened the window wide anyway, clear open. The fresh, cool air of night came floating in.

The sky was light gray from all the city lights. The rising moon washed it grayer and lighter. Now I could see the moon peeking out beyond the Herrons' rooftop. Then Herrons' old TV antenna, still attached to the chimney years after they went to cable, cut the moon in two with a long black line.

I didn't know what to do. Everything weighed so heavy. It wasn't *heavy* heavy, like someone getting very sick or dying. Just sort of heavy. An annoying heavy. You feel unbalanced. Unsettled. At loose ends. The world isn't quite right. Know what I mean?

Every night when I was a little kid, Mom would sit on the bed while I got down on my knees and said my prayers. I didn't really know who I was talking to then. I was just a little kid. So I said those prayers and ended them by blessing everything, including the cat we had at the time.

I was older now and on my own at prayer time. I was sure Mom and Dad expected me to be praying by myself. I hadn't been.

The moon rose above the chimney and nearly got blotted out by Herrons' maple. Just above the tree, the power lines waited, ready to cut it in half crossways.

Where do you start? Those prayers I rattled off when I was little didn't seem like the right stuff anymore, what with me going on twelve now.

Besides, I wasn't exactly on easy speaking terms with God and couldn't tell if I ever had been. That was discouraging in itself.

I didn't get on my knees. I didn't even close my eyes. I watched the world out there change, feeling its cool breath come in the open window.

Mom always said you begin with thanks and praise, whatever the prayer. She said God more than anyone else in the universe deserves it.

I thank You for thinking up the gift of Your Son Jesus. For letting Him pay for all the messing up I do. You didn't have to do that, and I'm thankful You did. Especially since I can't begin to pay for all these messes by myself.

I didn't know how to frame the next part in prayer language—you know, the fancy words preachers use sometimes when they really get wound up. Finally, I decided I probably didn't have to.

You know what I've been thinking, because You know all our thoughts. The Bible says so.

The gang just exploded. I don't know what to do or how to help it get back together. I don't know how to find out what Your will is. I want to, I really do. I just don't know how. Please help me. Help us.

The moon finally coasted clear of the maple, the wires, and the power transformer.

I didn't ask God for anything more. I'd already asked for plenty, I figured. I just kind of waited. It was the first time I'd prayed without quitting as soon as I'd listed what I wanted. I guess you could say I stopped to listen.

So here I sat in this chair, not on my knees

with my face mashed into the bedspread the way I used to. I was watching God's moon and the interesting things it did with its light. How black the shadows were. How silver the lighted areas. How different it was from the sun—or from stars, for that matter. How it pulled itself free of the antenna and tree and power lines and soared triumphant over everything.

The moon seemed to slow down and just hang there. It filled our yard with soft, gray light.

Did God speak to me then? I don't know. I heard no voice or anything. I didn't get this strong notion that I must go out and march around the city seven times blowing trumpets or something. Nothing like that.

But pretty soon, things didn't weigh so heavy anymore. That off balance feeling quietly went away. If God wanted me to do something, He'd let me know. He wouldn't ignore me. I could depend on that. Sure, I'd keep trying to think out His will, but He'd help. I just knew it.

I'd keep asking Him to give Mike and Bits comfort, and He would. The problems among the kids would work out. Maybe I'd have a hand, with God's help, in healing the split. Maybe. Maybe I'd even learn how to cook chicken.

I was talking to God, and He was talking to me, and no words were passing back and forth. Sure, God could do that—He can do anything! —but I never before knew that I could. It was the most amazing thing.

Whatever happened, the moon—God's moon—would rise tomorrow and the next night and the next. The sun would come up on schedule. I wasn't in control of any of that, but He was. I couldn't control anything at all. But He could.

The world was all right.

18

The next morning at breakfast, I was going to tell Mom and Dad about my prayer time last night, but I didn't know how to describe it. It was still amazing me, but it wasn't something solid you could talk about. I wasn't even sure I could describe it in words. Then Dad mentioned that the grass was getting pretty long again. Nothing kills a vague spiritual happening like a megadose of reality.

So after breakfast, Dad went to work, Mom went into the den to write, Hannah and Catherine went off to the neighbor's, and I headed for the shed.

The grass was green and juicy and still a little wet. It kept wadding up under the mower and choking the hole where it was supposed to blow into the catcher. What I'm saying is, it took me a long time to do a fairly short job. I did up the trees and flower bed edges with the trimmer.

And yes, I knew you never ever let the fishline in a trimmer touch tree bark. Never. Sooner or later, a fishline trimmer will chew all the way through the bark of most any tree. Then it cuts off the tree's tiny little pipes—the cambium—that the tree uses to draw water and food up from the roots. If the tree can't get water and nutrients anymore, it shrivels up, and there's nothing you can do to save it.

You're hearing the voice of experience. I accidentally girdled a couple trees in Seattle, and they died.

Mom said, "Les, you're a great chef. How about making lunch? I'm in the middle of things here."

All great chefs started at the bottom, I was sure, so I guessed I would, too. I got out some of that cooked and frozen turkey, the bread, lettuce, mayo, and all, and a can of soup.

The soup was an easy hit. I just followed the directions on the label. The label even said what size pan to use. Medium.

The turkey I thawed in the microwave. It was still cold, but no ice. It took me awhile to build the sandwiches. It's a slower process than you'd think.

I set out the dishes and flatware, poured iced tea, swiped the vase of flowers out of the living room and put it on the kitchen table, and found napkins. When I yelled, "Lunch is ready," the table looked pretty good.

Mom seemed surprised. She sat down and lifted her bread slice to peek under. "Why, Les, this is excellent!"

We said grace. No sooner was the "amen" spoken than the phone rang.

Mom sighed. "Mealtime. It never fails."

I picked up the phone on the kitchen counter. "Walker residence. Oh, hi, Dad. Here's Mom."

But he said, "It's you I'm calling, Les."

"Why me?"

"Remind your mom that the church board meeting is tonight. I'll pick you up as soon as I'm done here. We'll grab a burger and go to the meeting."

"We? You mean both of us?"

"Yes. You too."

I was about to turn down the invitation—I mean, how boring can you get?—but then I decided he must be doing this for some good reason. "OK."

"So tell your mom we won't need dinner tonight."

"Wouldn't you know it. Here I finally become a great chef, and you don't need me anymore. OK, I'll tell her."

So there I was seven hours later, sitting in a church board meeting. Dad was not a board member, but he gave them free legal advice as a gift to the church. He was in on nearly all the meetings. I felt very out of place among that bunch of business folk.

And I'm here to tell you it was every bit as boring as I feared. More, even.

Until they got to "new business."

Dad said, "I have some. A young friend revealed to Les here some of his thoughts about charity. They are things we as Christians must know." He brought a sheaf of papers out of his briefcase and handed them around to everyone. He even gave me a copy.

He looked at the secretary. "I request that this be entered into the minutes."

He had written down Mike's complaint pretty much word for word. I followed along as he read it out loud to the board. It reminded me all over again about Mike's frustration and anger.

The room was awfully quiet. Dad laid the paper aside. "This boy is absolutely right. We appear to give to the needy seasonally in order to feel good. His feelings are extremely intense. They should be. And now mine are as well."

I couldn't believe it! This was amazing.

Dad continued, "I will work out with you how you want the mission statement worded, but I will pester and push until we act on this. No more seasonal giving unless it is an extension of a program already in place. We are called to help people when they have need, not just when it feels good to us."

The pastor asked, "What are you suggesting? We already have a food basket program . . ."

"Perhaps have a closet full of nonperishable items—so people in need can come anytime, without being looked down upon. The church secretary could handle distribution to people who come during office hours. We can set up deals with local merchants, so the church can obtain at cost the things people in need might have to have. Simple things, often. Shoes. Personal necessities."

Boy, was I glad I came!

Dad ended with, "This boy has hit on the head the problem with the charity program in most churches. I'm not throwing rocks at us. Most churches. We never hear from the other side, so we think we're doing just fine. We have to do better than that. Jesus expected it."

What Dad did not mention was that our old church up in Seattle already did what he was talking about. They delivered bags of groceries to people who needed them, fed the church members who were poor—did their thing day by day. In fact, now that I thought about it, they didn't do anything extra on holidays except throw big "everybody come" feasts. At the holiday feeds, people with lots of money and people with none sat together around the tables.

The pastor frowned. "It will be hard to sell the congregation on a change. I'm sure most of them will say we're already fulfilling our obligation to the needy."

Dad sat back smiling. "Like I said, this is very important to me. We can surely get something going."

And I knew from the way he said it that, yes, they would get something going.

That night I sat down in my chair again and opened the window wide. Whether the gang's blowup got healed was important to me. Sure. But even if that never happened, Mike's part of it had led to great things to be done to help many people. That really impressed me. I thought for a while about how God turned those few minutes when Mike spilled out his anger into something good.

I went to bed before the moon came up, because, as you know, it rises later every night.

But still I spent a long time in the chair, just thanking God over and over. For Mike and what came of it and also for the cold turkey sandwiches turning out so well.

The world was really looking up.

19

The next morning, I was assigned cleanup duty. As if that wasn't bad enough, the place to be cleaned up was my room. I thought it was just perfect the way it was, but, of course, Mom had other ideas. My only comfort was that she leaned on the girls just as hard to clean *their* rooms.

It took me all morning. I kept wondering whether that little triumph with the cold turkey sandwiches was going to condemn me to making lunches forever.

But no. I had piled in the middle of the floor all the dirty clothes I found. As I was scooping them into a laundry bag, Mom appeared in the door.

"It could look better. Your shelves are messy. But it's good enough. What would you like for lunch?"

And I said, "A picnic."

So she packed me some stuff to take out to the park. I couldn't pull down e-mail because the computer was downloading some stuff Mom had looked up, but it didn't matter. I was going to let the gang alone awhile. I thought it would be best to just cool it and let the dust settle.

Besides, I hadn't visited the park by myself for awhile.

Sugar Creek County Park was a couple miles long and one-fourth to one-half mile wide. It took in only a small part of Sugar Creek, which went for miles and miles through farmland.

The park was another world. Lots of trees and brush muffled the sounds of traffic and sirens and barking dogs—all the noise that insists on reminding you that you live on a planet with billions of other people. Frogs, turtles, raccoons, and more insects than you can imagine called the park home. Very rarely, I'd spot a snake or a muskrat. When I walked along the trails, it felt as if I could be doing exactly this a hundred years ago.

Sometimes I'd leave the trail, especially on the swamp loop, and just sit on a log in the middle of the woods. For a while it would be only me alone. Then I'd start noticing insects—dragonflies, butterflies, beetles on the leaves. Flies. Ants. Lots of flies and ants. Then the birds would forget I was there and go about their business, sometimes pretty close.

I thought about doing all of those things this particular day and decided to do something different. I almost never went clear to the far end of the park. That's where I'd go this time.

I took off my bike helmet and hung it on the handlebars because I hate wearing it. Out in traffic or anywhere near traffic, it stays on. But today I would be riding two miles in granny gear—and nowhere near a paved road. I would be the only traffic.

I dropped my gears down to the lowest possible and pedaled back on the trail through the woods. I swung around the swamp loop just because I like it. The big turtle was not out today, but heaps of little turtles were crowded together along the top of a floating log, sunning. I stopped to count them. As I watched, one more turtle tried to climb up on the log. With a gentle swish, the log rolled over. The whole slew of turtles slid into the water, and I'll bet the ones that were snoozing woke up mighty surprised. When I left, a few were climbing clumsily back on the log.

The swamp loop crossed a little log bridge and rejoined the main trail. I helloed a man and woman who passed me, walking back toward the trailhead. And then I had gone about as far as I could go.

At this far end of the park, the woods opened up into a weedy meadow splashed with wildflowers and waist-high brush. Already, milkweed and clusters of thistle plants here and there across the meadow were spinning clumps of white silk. Summer couldn't be over this fast, could it?

Scratchy brown weeds tangled in my spokes and pedals, so I laid the bike down and walked out across the meadow. Now the scratchy brown weeds tangled in my shoelaces and stuck sharp little seeds in my socks.

If there were any deer around to see, they would come here to this meadow or along the brushy wood margin, where open grass met forest. A lonely, gnarled old oak tree squatted out in the middle of the meadow. Maybe if I just stood under that tree and watched and waited, I'd see one.

I hadn't gotten anywhere near the oak yet when a doe exploded out of the woods to the southeast. She bounded along at full speed, all four feet off the ground at once and her white tail flashing. Tiny once told me that whitetail deer signal each other with their tails that way.

What could spook her so badly?

She was a mama, because here came her baby, running full tilt also. The little guy was doing the best he could, but the weeds were taller than he was.

And then this huge spear of pure ice slashed down through me, chilling my heart and chest. I saw what was chasing the deer. They came barreling out onto the meadow close behind the fawn.

Wolves.

I didn't stop to think, and, believe me, I should have. I ran forward toward the fawn and the wolves, yelling and waving my arms.

The fawn was so scared he didn't pay much attention to me. He darted right past me, very close. He just kept running after mama as fast as he could. But the animals behind him faltered. They stopped and turned aside, snarling and snapping.

And they weren't wolves after all, although the leader might have had some wolf blood in him. He had to be over a hundred pounds; he was *big*. His blue eyes glinted. He had more than a little German shepherd or husky in him—probably both. He was grizzled gray like a shepherd, but German shepherds hold their tails down. Huskies curl their tails over their backs. His angled upward, half and half.

Two others, mixed breeds of some kind, might have been litter mates. They were gray, also. And the black chow-chow with them looked just plain nasty. His lips curled above his teeth. He wore a collar.

The smallest one wore a collar, too. *And I recognized him.*

I was no longer worried about Mrs. Monroe's Tuffy getting eaten by a wolf.

Tuffy *was* one of the wolves.

20

Long ago in a galaxy far away—that is, at my school in Seattle—every Friday was Safety Friday. We'd have an assembly in the afternoon, and an outsider would talk to us about safety. A firefighter would come in during Fire Prevention Month and teach us to drop and roll. A lifeguard would show slides of what not to do at the pool. That kind of thing.

One of those assemblies was about vicious dogs. An animal handler told us what to do if a dog challenged us. I could not remember a single solitary thing she'd said.

And right this moment, with five dogs snarling at me, I really, *really* wished I had paid better attention.

But Tuffy, little old Tuffy, wasn't a vicious dog, was he?

"Hey, Tuffy." I said the name again loudly. "*Tuffy!* We're friends, remember?"

Tuffy wasn't having any of it.

When Mrs. Monroe said her phone number was on his collar, I'd assumed she meant on a metal tag. No, it was written with a thick, black marking pen in huge numerals right on the nylon webbing of his collar, easy to read.

I made a quick mental note of the number.

It took me a moment to realize how stupid that was. Where was I going to get a phone?

I realized then why Tuffy had growled at me the day he tore his ear. He had just been out with his buddies, and he was still "wild."

The dogs were wild now.

I glanced toward the oak. It was too far. I could never outrun them that far. Then one of the dog handler's rules did come to mind: *Never run from a hostile dog.* Dogs are wired to chase things, the handler told us. If you run, they'll automatically chase you without even thinking about it, when maybe if you hadn't bolted, they wouldn't have.

There was nowhere else to go.

Oh, God, help me! Send someone! Do something!

Another rule came to mind. *Never stare at a hostile dog.* The dog takes it as a challenge. So I tried to keep a close eye on them without looking directly at any of them.

And dogs, I remembered then, like to attack from behind. *Don't let them get behind you.*

These dogs were hesitating for some reason. Maybe their training was getting in the way of attacking a human being. I bet they wouldn't have hesitated if I'd been a deer or a sheep. Or a toddler.

But then the lead dog moved in closer, snarling, and the two gray ones started circling to my left. The black chow began slinking around my right. I was guessing it was the chow who would go for my back or the backs of my legs.

I saw what was going to happen, but I didn't know how to stop it. Didn't know what to do.

Lord, help!

I couldn't outrun them. I couldn't outfight them. I couldn't climb anything. I couldn't even back up against something to protect the rear. If I had just gotten closer to that tree!

There was only one thing left to do. I was sure I would get bitten, but I'd have to chance it. I dropped forward, face down on the ground. I pulled my knees and elbows in under my belly. I knotted myself into as tight and smooth a wad as I could. With my legs under me and my elbows tucked in, I locked my fingers across the back of my neck, so that my arms protected my face and ears.

They could still chomp on me all they wanted, but they'd have to work at it, with nothing sticking out that fit easily into those horrible mouths. I could hear my own heart pounding. I waited, terrified, for that first ripping bite.

And waited . . .

Then I heard howling away off by the woods. Oh, no! These weren't the only dogs in the pack! Others were joining them!

The howling came closer.

But, no, it wasn't howling; it was yelling. People's voices yelling. Kids' voices yelling!

And I knew those voices!

I wanted to leap up and scream, "Run away! Run for your lives!" I should have done that, but I didn't. You know how people say they're petrified, when they mean they're scared? Stiff as stone? I really was petrified. I couldn't move. I just stayed in that tight curl while the world swirled and snarled somewhere out there.

The snarling and the yelling both got louder and louder. Then something grabbed my shoulder, and I was sure I was going to get eaten alive. The noise died down.

"Les?" Lynn's voice. "Les! It's OK. You're safe." Hands were pulling on me. Human hands. Not teeth.

"Les, did they get you?" Tiny's voice.

"No. You got here in time." I sat up and rocked back on my heels mostly because they were dragging me up. I felt weird. Dizzy.

"They're *dogs!*" Mike was turning inside out he was so excited. He still gripped a dead branch that was long enough to reach a star. "We got a good look at them. They're dogs! Did you see 'em good?"

"Yeah." I shuddered. "I even got their phone number."

It was over.

Not only did God send help when I asked, He sent the Sugar Creek Gang!

And then I started crying.

21

I certainly don't recommend getting attacked by wild dogs. In fact, I strongly recommend against it. But once in a very great while—a very, *very* great while—it pays off.

It paid off now when the gang sort of scooped me up out of that weedy meadow. I was still so shaky scared I had trouble keeping my bike on the path. We left the park and rode straight to the world's greatest ice cream stand by the museum. And the gang paid for my ice cream!

Even at the ice cream stand, sitting in a chair, I was shaking. My cone vibrated a little in my hand. "I don't get it, you guys. How did you show up there like that? And why? I thought you were all mad at each other."

"You see?" Bits flapped her hands. "I told you he doesn't read his e-mail."

"Where should we start?" Lynn was hard at work on a single dip of peanut-butter-chocolate. "It's a lot of different things that came together."

"I'll start with me." Bits had a double dip of marshmallow Neapolitan. "Night before last when we got back, Daddy could tell we'd been fighting. And when he asked about it, I kind of came apart. Really screamed and raved about how lousy all you guys were and how you were saying these terrible things about me. And when I finally stopped for breath, all he said was, 'I'm glad your friends love you enough to tell you the truth.'"

Tiny's eyebrows popped up. "He's smarter than I thought. He didn't yell back at you?"

Bits snorted. "If he had yelled at me, it would have been easier to stay mad. All he did was look real sad with those big brown eyes of his. Les, I apologize. I'm sorry."

Mike slurped the spoon from his vanilla hot fudge sundae. "I didn't dare do no yellin'. I'da got in trouble you wouldn't believe. But I was just as mad. So I sat on my bed that night and counted my money. I thought I was a dime short. And I was thinking, *Who stole my dime?* Then I thought, *Wait a minute, enchilada-head. Here you are accusing your own parents and brothers of stealing nothing. That's all a dime is. Nothing. And they all love you! What's the matter with you?* And I got thinking how maybe you were right, Bits. And you too, Les. I didn't like to believe you, but you were right."

Tiny chimed in. "So this morning, Mike came over to my place and said he wanted to apologize to you two, so we got on the e-mail and spread the word to meet at the park. It was easier than trying to find each other at home."

Mike nodded. "I already apologized to everyone else. I apologize to you, Les."

Lynn was nearly finished with her cone already. "I got to the picnic area after the others did because I came around the back way from O'Leary Avenue. And I saw these big gray dogs going over a stile into the park. I wondered if maybe those were the 'wolves.' Remember what Dr. Morgan said about feral dogs? When I got to the park I told the rest of them what I saw."

Bits pointed to Tiny. "And Daniel Boone here looks at some tracks on the ground and says, 'I bet that's Les's bike going back through the woods. Same kind of tires as ours.' So we followed your bike tracks and looked for the dogs at the same time."

Tiny grimaced. "Found 'em at the same time, too."

"Wow." I took another lick. That's all I could think of to say. So I said it again. "Wow."

"What do we do now?" Lynn asked.

"Call my dad and tell him," Bits suggested.

"Where's the nearest pay phone?" I asked. "I'm gonna call my dad, too."

Lynn pointed. "Museum lobby."

As soon as we were done nourishing the inner man, as Dad would put it, we headed up the big, wide museum steps. The phones were just inside the door in an alcove. Bits fished in her pocket for change.

Tiny handed her a couple quarters. "I'm going to go tell Dr. Morgan what we found. Or leave him a note if he's not there." He strode off across the shiny marble floor.

That was a good idea. I was thinking that if I washed out as a great chef, maybe Tiny and I could be great naturalists together.

While Bits jammed in the coins and punched her numbers, I wondered what I would say to Dad. "Hey, Dad, guess what. I almost got eaten alive." Nah. My folks would never let me leave the yard again. "You know those wolves? It's worse than wolves." Nah. Or maybe, "Oh, nothing much. Just the usual danger and mayhem. And how was *your* day?"

My attention snapped back to Bits. She had just said, "And they attacked Les!" A pause. "No, really! We saw him fall down on the ground, and we thought they ripped his throat out, but he was just protecting himself." Pause.

Just protecting myself?

"At the museum." Bits stared at the far wall a minute. "OK. We'll wait here." She hung up. "Daddy says he's coming over here. And you don't have to call your dad, Les. Daddy is going to call him and talk to him." She frowned. "Daddy sounded pretty upset."

"I don't blame him," said Lynn. "I think this is more serious than we realized. Like Tiny said, what if they went after a little child? I mean, Les is small enough. What if we'd waited for him at the picnic area and didn't go back there?"

I didn't want to think about it.

"Maybe your fathers will know what to do about the dogs." Mike polished off the last of his ice cream.

I nodded. "I'm glad they're both coming. I probably wasn't going to call mine anyway. I'm a dime short."

Mike reached into his pocket. "I got a dime here." He held it out to me. He looked sheepish. "I was wrong about somebody stealing from me. I found it in my bedcovers this morning."

22

It was 5:00 P.M. My mystery-novel-trained mind figured out what time it was from the clues. The clues were: (1) The museum chased everyone out and locked up. (2) They close at five.

So we sat in a line on the museum steps, like crows on a fence rail.

Someone in a white shirt and tie and black suit came out a side door. "You young people will have to move on. We don't allow loitering."

Bits replied, "We're waiting for our dads."

The man was going to say something else—probably chase us off—but Bits simply pointed toward the parking lot. Here came her father in full police uniform. Suddenly it was OK to loiter. The man said good-bye and went back inside.

My dad arrived right behind Sergeant Ware. They had plenty of parking slots to choose from—the lot was emptying quickly.

Sergeant Ware climbed the steps and sat down beside us. "So you got eaten alive, huh, Les?"

"I'm still too scared to make fun about it."

"I don't blame you. Good evening, Bill," he said to my dad.

"Evening, Jim." Dad looked at me. "Can you describe the dogs?"

I could. We all could. And we did. Then I told them about the phone number Mrs. Monroe marked on Tuffy's collar. I was surprised that I could remember it. The human brain is a weird thing.

The two men looked at each other.

Sergeant Ware started jotting notes rapidly. "Give me that number again."

I did.

He scribbled a minute and then asked, "Les, did Tuffy's collar have that number on it when you found him and took him back a couple days ago?"

"He wasn't wearing his collar then. First time I saw it was in the meadow this afternoon."

Both men nodded silently.

Dad asked, "The other dog with a collar—could you make out a name or read anything on the tags?"

"No, sir. I didn't want to get that close. In fact, I didn't want to get as close as I did."

Dad snickered, but he turned serious again instantly. "Jim, is the law what I think it is?"

Sergeant Ware nodded.

"Think we can do anything tonight yet?"

The officer nodded again as he stood up.

"Do what?" Bits looked from face to face. Her voice was getting that edge to it again.

"We'll start with Tuffy, then track down the other dogs and their owners. All five."

"But *then* what? Catch them?"

"If we can. Shoot them if we can't."

"Shoot *Tuffy*?"

"Kids, it's not nice, I know." Sergeant Ware included us all as he spoke. "But we have a solid identification, and when those dogs turned on Les they proved how dangerous they are. We're wrong if we don't do something. According to the law, this situation allows us to kill them. And as a public safety officer, I'm required to do something about the problem."

Bits looked furious. "I'm sorry I called you!"

"Are you sorry for all the animals they hurt and kill? Or for the little kid who's bound to get in their way one of these days?" He pulled the cell phone on his belt and punched in some numbers. He waited a few seconds and punched in some more—extension numbers, probably.

He held it to his ear. "Hi, Grace. No, I'm working a little late. Need a phone check." From his notebook he read off the number I had given him.

It didn't take Grace, whoever Grace was, long to find out who belonged to the number. Sergeant Ware repeated it. "M-O-N-R-O-E. Got it. Thanks, Grace." He clapped the phone shut and told Bits, "Grace says hi." So Grace and Bits knew each other.

I felt as sad as you can get. I could tell by the way they drooped that Tiny and Mike and Bits felt the same way. We started down the long, long bank of steps toward the parking lot.

"Wait. Where's Lynn?" I turned to look.

She was still sitting on the steps, silent, leaning forward with her face buried in her hands.

What could you do? Bits knew. She jogged right back up the steps, sat down beside Lynn, and wrapped her arms around her. Lynn sort of melted over against her, and they just sat like that, comforting each other. I could see Bits was crying, too.

Sergeant Ware said quietly, "Bill, we'd better get these kids home first. It's suppertime."

Dad nodded.

But Tiny said, "No. Please, Mr. Walker—Sergeant Ware. We been up against this wolf business since the beginning—all of us—since the first chewed-up rabbit got brought in with a leg missing. We came up against them today again. We want to see it through."

"Yes, but—" Dad started.

"I know. Kids ain't s'posed to be exposed to death and violence. I'm saying, sir, we already been exposed to it since the beginning of this. We already know what they do, and we understand what has to be done yet. Please let us stay with you."

The sergeant looked at Mike.

Mike nodded. "I want to go. Please."

I nodded, too.

Dad climbed the steps and crouched down in front of Lynn and Bits. He loaned them his handkerchief. All three of them muttered awhile. The girls nodded, and then nodded again.

When Dad stood up and turned, the girls stood up, too, and strode down the steps with him. You could see they'd been crying, but they looked just as determined and strong as everyone else. They were going to see it through, too.

We were a pretty gloomy bunch as we crawled into Dad's car and the sergeant's pick-up. We all knew that before this mess got any better, it was going to get a whole lot worse.

23

Tuffy was curled up asleep on his porch when our two vehicles pulled into Mrs. Monroe's driveway. He jumped up and barked dutifully. Mrs. Monroe opened her front door as we were getting out.

She stepped down off the porch and smiled. "I'm having chicken for dinner. I'm sorry I didn't fix enough for guests."

Sergeant Ware grimaced. I suppose he thought it was a smile. "Mrs. Monroe, is this your telephone number?" He showed her a notebook page.

She craned her head a bit. "Yes, it is."

Dad had let Tuffy sniff his hand, and now he was twisting Tuffy's collar around so that all could see the number on it. He didn't say anything. No one had to.

Mrs. Monroe looked at Dad, at the sergeant in his police officer's uniform, at us. "What's going on here?"

"Your little dog, Tuffy, was out with a pack of feral dogs this afternoon. They were chasing a deer when Les here interfered. They turned on him."

"You're mistaken. Tuffy doesn't do that." She listened to the silence a moment and apparently couldn't stand it. She raised her

131

voice a couple notches. "I assure you, Tuffy wouldn't do that! He knows Les." She stared at the girls, so I looked at them, too.

They were still all puffy eyed and wet nosed.

Dad stepped forward. "Mrs. Monroe, we haven't met, but I've heard very good things about you. I'm Les's father, Bill Walker." He extended his hand.

She took it cautiously, distrustfully. "I'm surprised Les thought Tuffy would do such a thing."

Dad crossed his arms. He looked very large. "Mrs. Monroe, dogs do what dogs do. I suspect you know that. When they get going in groups —in packs—they'll chase, given the chance. Chase and kill."

"Maybe huge, dangerous dogs. Certainly not my little Tuffy!"

Sergeant Ware said, "All dogs. It's their nature. They're fine when they're in the home, in a family situation. But running loose, they revert to wild ways. It's just their nature to do that."

Mrs. Monroe glared at me. "You got that phone number when you brought Tuffy home that day! Les, how could you!"

"No, ma'am. He wasn't wearing a collar then, remember?"

Then she stared angrily at Dad. "You're trying to pin something on my little dog! You need a scapegoat and so—"

And Dad exploded. "Those dogs attacked

my son!" He roared so ferociously that she stepped back a step.

She looked stunned for a long moment. Her voice dropped to almost a whisper. "Do I have to put Tuffy down?"

Lynn pressed her hand over her mouth, but she kept her cool.

Sergeant Ware said quietly, "The attack took place in Sugar Creek County Park. That is within my jurisdiction. I'm empowered to cite you and impound the dog, if necessary. I don't want it to be necessary. Can you keep Tuffy under physical control at all times? A tie rope? A fence?"

"But he's too used to roaming. It would be cruel to confine him!"

Tiny spoke up. "Miz Monroe, you ain't seen the rabbits and deer and sheep and turkeys—all the animals they hurt for the fun of it. Tying Tuffy up won't be half as cruel as what they're doing to other things."

She looked at Dad and Sergeant Ware. Then she said quietly, "I'll build a fence. I'll keep him tied until then."

Mike said, "Ma'am? My brothers and I, we've built fences before. You get the stuff—the wire and stuff—and the gang here, we'll help you build it. For free. Won't cost you much that way."

All of us Creekers jumped on that one, eagerly offering our services.

Bits's dad was nodding now and smiling. "Bill and I can lend a hand, too. Now we need your help. We have to contact the owners of the other dogs . . ."

"I know every family in this township and just about all their dogs. Describe them."

An hour later, the job was done. One of the owners wasn't nearly as nice as Mrs. Monroe. He wasn't going to cooperate the way she did until Sergeant Ware explained the county's shoot-on-sight law. Also, Dad threatened to take him to court. Dad used the words *initiate a civil action*, and that's why I don't plan to be a lawyer when I grow up. They don't speak English. But his threat worked. The man decided to keep his black chow fenced in.

That night when I opened up my window and sat down in my chair, I had plenty to be thankful to the Lord about. Sometimes when I would say thank You in a prayer, the only thing I'd thank Him for was for making me His child through Jesus. But this time, look at all He did for me—for all of us! I got saved from the dogs. We solved the wolf problem. The gang had healed.

And there was old Mike, the penny pincher. He was the first one to offer to help Mrs. Monroe. For *free*. It looked to me like God really did a work on him.

And I was finally on my way to becoming a great chef.